INDIVISIBLE

NEW SHORT FICTION BY WEST COAST GAY & LESBIAN WRITERS

Stressing the common concerns and goals of gay men and lesbians, *Indivisible* presents 24 new West Coast writers from various ethnic backgrounds who go beyond established literary boundaries.

"Murder Is My Business" by Lynette Prucha honors and satirizes Raymond Chandler with an L.A. private eye in a twisty lesbian mystery.

"Eternity" by Bernard Cooper takes a kid's view of California's health-obsessed culture and finds that immortality may have more to do with love than yogurt.

"Unprotected" by Gilbert Daniel Cuadros grittily describes sex between strangers—an act that evokes the war between lust and responsibility.

"She Who Keeps Laughing" by Jeane Jacobs spins a stunning tale of Native American friendship, feminism, and love.

Here is the next wave from the West Coast.

★

TERRY WOLVERTON is a writer and the teacher of gay and lesbian writing workshops in Los Angeles, where she discovered many of the contributors to *Indivisible*.

ROBERT DRAKE is a literary agent and writer.

EDITED BY
TERRY WOLVERTON
WITH ROBERT DRAKE

INDIVISIBLE

New Short Fiction
by Gay and Lesbian
West Coast Writers

★

A PLUME BOOK

PLUME

Published by the Penguin Group
Penguin Books USA Inc., 375 Hudson Street, New York, New York 10014, U.S.A.
Penguin Books Ltd, 27 Wrights Lane, London W8 5TZ, England
Penguin Books Australia Ltd, Ringwood, Victoria, Australia
Penguin Books Canada Ltd, 10 Alcorn Avenue, Toronto, Ontario, Canada M4V 3B2
Penguin Books (N.Z.) Ltd, 182–190 Wairau Road, Auckland 10, New Zealand

Penguin Books Ltd, Registered Offices: Harmondsworth, Middlesex, England

First published by Plume, an imprint of New American Library,
a division of Penguin Books USA Inc.

First Printing, September, 1991
10 9 8 7 6 5 4 3 2 1

Grateful acknowledgment is made to the authors for permission to reprint previously published
material:
"Now, I Have to Tell This Story" by Ayofemi Folayan. First published in Gay Community
News, Vol. 17, No. 17, 1989.
"Skyfires" by Michael Lassell. First published as "Skyfire" in Male Review, Vol. 1, No. 3,
1984.
"Study for Darkness: Two Views from Vertical Cliffs" by Eric Latzky. First published in Tribe,
an American Gay Journal, Vol. 1, No. 2, 1990.
"Dignity/Uniforms/Dignity" by Robin Podolsky. First published in Lucky, No. 2, 1989.
"Murder Is My Business" by Lynette Prucha. First published in The Womansleuth Anthology,
Irene Zahava, editor (The Crossing Press, 1990).
"My Face in the Faces of Others" by Aleida Rodriguez. First published in Calyx, Vol. 8, No.
2, 1984.
"Förster & Rosenthal Reevaluated: An Investigative Report" by Rick Sandford. First published as
"Mann and Thalberg Reevaluated: An Investigative Report" in Revolt, 1980.

Ⓟ REGISTERED TRADEMARK—MARCA REGISTRADA

LIBRARY OF CONGRESS CATALOGING IN PUBLICATON DATA:

Indivisible : new short fiction / by west coast gay and lesbian
    writers ; edited by Terry Wolverton, with Robert Drake.
        p.   cm.
    ISBN 0-452-26676-9
    1. Gay men—Fiction.   2. Lesbians—Fiction.   3. Short stories,
American—West Coast (U.S.)   4. Gays' writings, American—West Coast
(U.S.)   5. Lesbians' writings, American—West Coast (U.S.)   6. West
Coast (U.S.)—Fiction.   I. Wolverton, Terry.   II. Drake, Robert.
PS648.H57I54   1991
813'.01083520664—dc20

                                                              91-7804
                                                              CIP

Printed in the United States of America
Set in Perpetua

Designed by Steven N. Stathakis

PUBLISHER'S NOTE

to Gene Wirth and "Bucka"

Contents

Acknowledgments

The editors would like to acknowledge the support of Ann Bradley and James Carroll Pickett, of A Different Light Bookstore, Los Angeles; the California Arts Council, a state agency; the literary agency of Sandra Watt Associates; and for their ongoing support Susan Silton and Christopher Schelling.

... ONE NATION, INDIVISIBLE ...

INDIVISIBLE: CREATING AN ANTHOLOGY OF LESBIAN AND GAY FICTION

Indivisible, we say, despite evidence to the contrary.

We never set out to make a political statement with this book. We set out instead to provide editors with what they have been asking the agent for a number of years: "We feel sure the brave new writing is out there in California, we just don't know how to get to it."

As we embarked on this anthology with a commitment to include literary fiction by both lesbian and gay writers, we were amazed to discover that it hadn't been done before. While there has been *Men on Men* and *Lesbian Fiction*, this is a book that asserts a sensibility of "one people, one volume" (please).

Indivisible, we say although we remember a recent past in which this claim would have been laughable. At its very birth in 1969 the gay liberation movement was already torn in two, as lesbians responded to the urgent call of the feminist movement. Radicalized by their oppression as women, many lesbians looked to gay men and found in them not "brothers" but the same male privilege lesbians had committed themselves to struggle against.

Although some lesbians did remain active in the gay movement, large numbers embraced a degree of separatism. They perceived that only by working on their situation as women would their lives as

lesbians be improved. Among the numerous consequences of this decision is the thriving network of lesbian and feminist publishers that has
built and nurtured a generation of lesbian writers and readers.

For the most part gay men seemed content to let the lesbians
go their own way. Bright with the flush of newly gained freedom, gay
men in the seventies were creating and exploring a new world. Both
the terrain of the senses and the arena of political power were
uncharted territories for a community used to the dark confines of
the closet, and the need to locate and then push the boundaries was
uppermost. Gay men too have created an ample literature and a bur-
geoning market for this work, through the founding of alternative
presses but also, increasingly, with mainstream publishing.

All this changed in the eighties, when the entire culture of the
country seemed to shift. As the movement toward liberation slowed
and the values that had guided the sixties and seventies were over-
turned, it began to seem more necessary to seek allies wherever they
could be found, including across lines of race and class and gender.

For the gay and lesbian community, this necessity is heightened
by the AIDS crisis. Some women, jolted by the loss or threat of loss
of so many gay men, were moved for personal reasons to reinvest
energy in those men. Other women began to see a change in men
who were coping with the health crisis in their communities: these
men were becoming vulnerable, they were nurturing, grieving, and
engaging in introspection. Still others came to realign themselves with
gay men because of the political threat they mutually feared.

And men have seen women rally to meet this crisis—with money,
with leadership, with commitments of time and labor, with words.
And in the midst of all the loss and grief, there is a healing going on,
a healing between lesbians and gay men, a recognition of what is
shared as well as what divides.

This is not to suggest that all is forgotten. There is still unequal
access to money and power. Mistrust still lingers on both sides. If the
community is to truly unite, there will be much work that has to be
done. But whether a momentary truce or the beginning of rapproche-
ment, it is the first time since Stonewall that gay men and lesbians
have felt so much common ground.

It is this historical moment, this perhaps temporary cease-fire in the gender wars, that makes this collection possible. To bring together some of the finest literary fiction by gay *and* lesbian writers, to seek out a readership of both men and women, to locate commonalities and to highlight differences in such a way that suggests that we might yet learn from one another: no less than this is the task of this collection.

—TERRY WOLVERTON AND ROBERT DRAKE
Los Angeles, 1990

BERNARD COOPER

ETERNITY

FOR HIS FORTY-THIRD BIRTHDAY, my mother gave my father just what he'd been hinting for: a subscription to *The Cryogenic Science Newsletter*. When the first issue fell through our mail slot, Mother read it over and over. She had the stories memorized by the time my father came home from work. As soon as he stepped through the back door, she held the newsletter up and blurted, "Frozen Rodent Resuscitated." My father dropped his briefcase, sat astonished on the kitchen stool, its vinyl exhaling under his weight. He scanned the article then and there, brown eyes darting back and forth. Mother leaned against the sink, gazed through the window at the darkness outside, her arms folded as though she were cold.

My parents dreamed of living forever. The newsletter's logo could have been them—a man and woman in a block of ice. They believed that cryogenics would be perfected soon. If not in their lifetimes, then in mine.

"The average life expectancy," Father said that night at dinner, "has increased dramatically since I was young and, given leaps in technology, I'm certain our lives will continue to grow. Grow *better* as well as longer."

"In the meantime," added Mother, "it's our duty to stay fit."

A meal of raw cabbage and whole carrots, tops included, graced our plates and assured our longevity. "Remember," said Father, waving a carrot in my direction, "slicing vegetables breaks down their cellular structure and ruins their nutritional value." On weeknights he ate in his suit and tie; everything he said seemed true.

"What about when you chew them?" I asked.

"Chewing," said Mother, "is another matter." She patted a strand of stray hair and proposed a toast to Vigor. We lifted our cups in unison, sipping her concoction of papaya tea, bonemeal, and brewer's yeast, our faces moist with steam. After my cup was drained, heat radiated through my ribs; I leaned back in my chair, certain I'd tasted eternity, time made edible, aromatic.

My indoctrination into the world of health food was gentle but constant; no meal was complete without a discussion of its physiological benefits, both long and short term, proven and hypothetical. Some claims were so overblown, I believed I would one day walk away from our dinette set able to see in the dark, to hear sounds from across town, my senses perfectly nourished. Once, I ate a one-pound bag of sunflower seeds after my mother casually referred to them as "brain food." In our kitchen—a corridor of green Formica, bits of glitter embedded in the ceiling—the blender, juicer, and steamer were used to coax the nourishment from all five food groups. By the time I entered the seventh grade, I could use *monosodium glutamate* in a sentence and identify those preservatives suspected of causing tumors in laboratory animals. I knew the ingredients for recipes like sesame stew and soybean cutlets. I lifted from my lunch bag not the typical, limp baloney sandwich tainted with nitrates, not corn chips coated with iodized salt, but a Tupperware container filled with sprouts that were doused with yogurt and sprinkled with wheat germ. My schoolmates reacted to my eating habits with disdain, glancing my way and rolling their eyes, or huddling together to whisper and point. I admit their taunting bothered me, but I knew the price one paid for a diet of bleached flour, animal fat, and processed sugar—arthritis, said Mother;

ulcers, said Father—and I smiled back with a twinge of pity. Under the shade of the pergola, tether balls twirling in the distance, I was certain I'd be rewarded with nothing less than perpetual life.

As if to confirm my belief in things everlasting, Mrs. Robinson, my geometry teacher, showed us a model of a Möbius strip, a seamless loop of paper. She spent almost half an hour talking about it, the carnation in her buttonhole heaving, her eyebrows dancing up and down. "Endless," she sighed. "See for yourselves." We passed the strip from desk to desk and ran our fingers along its surface. My friend, Bobby Keegan, was so mesmerized by its twisted impossibility, Mrs. Robinson had to snap her fingers and remind him that he wasn't the only kid in class. For a finale, she drew on the blackboard the symbol for infinity, shaped like a fallen figure eight.

Bobby and I understood that, although the infinite was hard to grasp, it was something you could aim for in conversation. "I thought Robinson would go on forever," he said after school. We had to walk home in the same direction.

"Yeah," I said. "It takes her a million years to get to the point."

"A trillion," said Bobby, blowing his nose.

Bobby was allergic to just about every substance known to man. He droned the list like a robot: pollen, crabgrass, dust, wool, cats, and macadamia nuts. Red-nosed and rheumy-eyed, Bobby was a boy who wheezed through the world, squinting to focus on his locker combination, balls of Kleenex falling from his pockets. My mother had taken it upon herself to "fix that poor boy's constitution." On the days he came over after school, she plied him with vitamins. At first he'd been unwilling to swallow the pills my mother thrust into his hand. "No," he'd moan from behind a tissue. But she ooh-ed and aah-ed over every tablet as though it were a precious jewel, explaining the marvelous effects he could expect once they entered his bloodstream. Zinc, she promised, would ward off germs like a suit of armor. The B's would stop his urge to sneeze, the A's dry up his mucous membranes. But it was an E capsule that finally brought him around; he rolled it between his fingers, held it up to the light; he stared at my mother through that gold translucent bead and finally believed she might be right.

I was torn about the state of Bobby's health. On one hand, I wanted to join my mother in her mission to change him. We would sculpt a new and better boy from the soft clay of sickliness. We would rescue him from a dismal future of doctors' bills and decongestants. Bobby was my ward as well as my mother's, and we reported to one another any sign of his improvement—fewer sniffles, a rash that had vanished—shaking hands and sighing with pride. My father expressed concern as well; he'd ask, "How's the Keegan case coming?"

On the other hand, I found Bobby's extreme sensitivity thrilling, and secretly hoped he would always be weak. Bobby trembled at the thought of the irritating particles carried on the air; when he was wary and delicate, I felt calm and strong. His sneezing fits were fascinating; he looked the way a wet dog looks, suddenly starved and baffled and sad, and I couldn't take my eyes away. After his attacks were over, he would glance up at me, red from exertion and embarrassment, and I could barely fight the impulse to stroke his shoulder or rumple his hair. Instead, I pretended to wipe his snot off my clothes, watching his eyes grow wide with horror. "Sorry," he'd gasp. "Did I get some on you?" It made me laugh like a maniac. Once, I told him that my basketball was the biggest chunk of pollen on earth; I chased Bobby through the rooms of our apartment, dribbling him into a corner. When he flailed his arms and begged me to stop, my need to tease him boiled up like lava.

Even at school, when Bobby would begin to sneeze in class, I'd stick my fingers in my ears and wince like everyone else, as if bombarded by sonic booms. Mrs. Robinson would wait for the sneezing to stop; she'd twist her ring and tap her foot, lips crimped in a grin. As long as Bobby was a figure of fun, I believed I'd be spared from ridicule, left to eat my sprouts in peace.

At least I continued to call him by his name; the other kids in our class had branded him with the nickname "Dodus." On our way home from school, he turned to me for reassurance.

"But Martin," he whined, "what does it mean?"

"Jeez, Bobby. I don't know. Sounds like the name of a foreign sports car."

He smiled faintly, chewed the last of a Three Musketeers. "Yeah. Wow. The Dodus X-11."

But it was instantly clear that this was wrong, and the name, we both knew, described a boy who was clumsy and hunched, a boy who didn't fit in his body, a boy who never would. We were walking up Westerly Avenue past dozens of clapboard bungalows, their wide roofs spread like wings. A canopy of branches rustled above us, the street and sidewalk mottled with light. Bobby was quiet, contemplating cracks in the pavement. How slender his neck appeared, barely able, I thought, to hold up that head of oily black hair. His long eyelashes made him seem demure; he blinked like someone who had just woken up—groggy, uncertain, a little surprised. He swung his skinny arms when he walked, or they swung him, back and forth from his short sleeves like clappers ringing in bells.

Half a block away from his house, we could smell the eggs Mrs. Keegan was frying for Bobby's after-school snack. I, at least, could smell them. Bobby's deviated septum prevented him from sensing the odor of food, no matter how pungent or close to his nose. If anyone were to blame for Bobby's life-sentence as a bumbler, a weakling, and outcast, it was, as far as I was concerned, Betty Keegan. Not only had she compromised her son's health and appearance by allowing his poor diet, but her own arteries were clogged from a steady intake of eggs— fried and deviled and poached. Night and day she claimed to be cold: bad circulation. She always wore a fur coat, even when she cooked. After meeting Mrs. Keegan for the first time at a party, my mother said to me, "It was boiling, right, and Bobby's mother was wearing a mink that was splotched, I swear, with dried egg!"

"Bur-r-r," said Mrs. Keegan when we walked into the kitchen. She buttoned her mink, warmed her hands above the skillet. "Some cold snap we're having, huh?"

"Ma," said Bobby. "You could have fried those eggs on the sidewalk."

"You're quite the comedian," she said. She scraped the eggs from a pool of burned butter and slapped them on a plastic plate. She signaled for Bobby and me to take our seats. The kitchen table was covered with paper place mats that were stained in the middle and shredded at the edges. The biggest difference between the Keegans' kitchen and our own was that everything here seemed crooked—dish towels, spice rack, the dusty porcelain horn of plenty that hung above the stove. Mrs. Keegan asked, "And what may I get for you, Martin? Perhaps a glass of celery juice?" She threw back her head and brayed, a gold tooth glinting in the light. When she saw that Bobby and I weren't laughing, she blushed and cleared her throat. "I amuse myself. What can I say."

I asked for an apple and, once Mrs. Keegan had gone, held it under the tap until I was sure the insecticides were washed away. When I came back to the table, Bobby was drawing an infinity symbol with yolk. We could see Mrs. Keegan sitting in the living room, smoking a Kool, sunk in a plush floral chair and shrouded in a menthol cloud. She talked to herself and caught us watching. "You boys want something, just let me know." Bobby asked if he could come over to my house for dinner. Mrs. Keegan flapped her hand at the smoke. "Why not?" she said when the smoke cleared. "Anyway, we're out of eggs."

The sunset was brilliant by the time we reached my neighborhood, an avenue of apartment houses, their names emblazoned on stucco walls: The Sherri-Lee, the Trop-O-Cal, the Starland Arms. Buildings, cars—everything was tinted orange, including Bobby and me. I wondered if we looked alike to passersby—brothers maybe, maybe twins—a pair of orange and awkward boys. Until that moment, I believed that my friendship with Bobby was safe beyond the bounds of school, that we could meet and solve geometry problems or play Parcheesi in secret, and now it occurred to me that strangers who saw us talking together might assume that we were two of a kind. Here I was, walking down Prospect Boulevard, my street, my own street, but I thought I might suddenly stop being me and start becoming Bobby. I had once seen a movie called *Devil Doctor* about a surgeon who had to inject himself with radioactive isotopes every day or else he'd become a heap of raw flesh, and that awful monster reared up in my mind, and I wondered if my mother's papaya tea, with its bonemeal and brewers yeast, kept me from a pitiful fate of wilting posture, a running nose, and worse, the scorn of the whole world. What hideous transformation would occur if I didn't drink it every night? Bobby was rambling on about Mrs. Robinson's Möbius strip and I was gripped by the fear that we'd walk around the block for eternity, saying the same things over and over, never reaching home (and my mother's tea), always in plain view of the cars whose drivers I now scrutinized to see if they were staring at us, smirking and shaking their heads. I started to sweat and there it was: the asphalt path at the side of my building, two cement steps, the kitchen door.

I couldn't bring myself to speak to Bobby or even stand near him once we were inside, which was fine because my mother was all over him, crooning about the three pounds he'd gained since she last saw him, clucking at his dandruff and rummaging through the cabinets for a bottle of balsam conditioner he could take home with him. She mixed beets and yogurt in the blender, invited him up on the kitchen stool to watch the lavender whirlpool. She let him press apples into the juicer, saying "perfect" after each slice. She handed him a glass of purified water and after he gulped his vitamins, she smiled and brushed the hair from his forehead. During all this fussing and doting, I worried that, instead of me turning into Bobby, Bobby might somehow turn into me; he fit right into our glittering kitchen, happy to be pampered, anxious to please. Or he might, with enough of Mother's nutritional supplements coursing through his veins, become someone better and stronger than me, an Adonis in one of the muscle magazines coach Willis read while we ran laps. My heart was pounding as it had on the track. My neck tightened. The room went black.

"Guess who," said my father, pressing his hands against my eyes. I tried to pull them away. Bobby and my mother were squealing names: J. Edgar Hoover, Jack the Ripper, a man from Mars . . .

"Dad," I pleaded.

"Right," he said. But his hands stayed clamped in front of my eyes. "There's something else you have to guess. A surprise for you and Bobby."

Mother was chanting, "I know what it i-is."

I felt the heat of my father behind me, his tie grazing the nape of my neck. The blender roared in the background. Dots glowed in the dark.

★   ★   ★

Five days later, Bobby arrived at our front door with an overnight bag. Sticking out from the pocket of his seersucker shirt was a sheet of typewriter paper covered with Betty Keegan's cramped handwriting. "My goodness," said my mother, skimming the note, "she's awfully grateful we're taking you along. I'll have to read the rest on the road." She gave the note back to Bobby. He was quiet and amazed, as if my parents were angels who'd drifted down to earth. He just stood there, gazing up from under his long eyelashes while they double-checked the windows and made sure the faucets and lights were off. He was expert, I noticed, at dodging my parents as they raced through the room, like he'd practiced staying out of the way. His ordinarily nervous expression had vanished. In its place was expectation. His skin was flushed. The part in his hair was straight for a change. He looked okay. Almost pretty.

I felt carsick as soon as we got into the car. My mother rummaged through the Styrofoam cooler she'd stuffed beneath the dashboard, and fed me a lemon enzyme lozenge. "Martin," she whispered, squeezing my knee, "get in the back with Bobby."

I turned to face Bobby. He sat alone in the backseat, feeling the upholstery, rubbing the plush with both hands. Bobby was too interested in the velour to notice he was being avoided; this was further demonstration of his ineptitude, his lack of attention, and it made me more determined to avoid him. "I'm sitting up front," I announced to my mother. I looked out the windshield, feigning interest in the scenery though the Pontiac hadn't left the curb. My father locked the kitchen door and almost tripped coming down the steps. He was happy to be leaving town.

Mr. Ludlow, my father's boss at the printing shop, had given him a vacation in Desert Hot Springs for his birthday. A color brochure from the Coral Sands Spa and the receipt for a two-bedroom suite were enclosed in a card. Mr. Ludlow had drawn it himself with a Magic Marker on cover stock. It read "For Your Forty-Third" beneath a shaggy palm tree.

It was Mother's idea that Bobby be included. "After all," she said, "the rooms are free, and no one needs sunlight more than Bobby;

it'll get rid of his eczema, fast." When it became clear to her that I was reluctant (I'd never spent the weekend with Bobby, never wanted to or imagined I would), she held me by the shoulders and told me what life was all about: getting well and spreading it around. Don't, she urged me, be selfish with health. I caught a whiff of Yolanda's Organic Garden perfume. Her voice was deep with conviction. Highlights burned in her hazel eyes.

The Coral Sands brochure boasted a wide variety of exotic treatments available in their private spa, from Swedish massage to the invigorating Roman-Celtic brush treatment with herbal soaps and lotions. On the night before we left, my parents sat side by side on the couch and tantalized each other by reading the descriptions aloud. The costly treatments weren't included in the price of the rooms, and my parents had to be selective, deciding which ones they couldn't go without. This led to mild debates about the virtues of relaxation versus rehydration, or lymphatic versus muscular massage. I could overhear them from my room; I was sprawled on my bed, plotting isosceles triangles. Would my mother, I wondered, be kneaded by a man, my father by a woman? Or suppose they stood naked before their own sex, would either be embarrassed? Hearing my parents' talk about being touched by a stranger was made all the more bewildering by words like *shiatsu* and *exfoliation*.

I was startled by a sudden motion. At first, I thought the Pontiac was standing still and our stucco apartment, with its rows of shallow balconies, was floating down the street. Then I realized the motor was humming, the trip underway. We'd barely reached the end of Prospect Boulevard before my father was telling Bobby the story about his leg, which made me bristle because he reserved that story for people he liked, whose understanding he hoped to win.

"So I found myself facing the crisis of my life: either lose the leg because some doctor, some know-nothing kid fresh out of medical school says, 'Sorry, pal, the leg has to go,' or find a way to save it myself. So you know what I did, Robert?

Seconds of silence. Buildings and phone poles rushing past.

"I read, that's what I did. Everything I could get my hands on. I read books and pamphlets and mimeographs. You'd be amazed how much material there is out there about phlebitis, curing it the natural way. I read tracts by nutritionists, psychic healers, and one by some swami whose name I can't remember. And do you know who furnished me with all this reading material, searched it out in libraries, at bookstores, on the bulletin boards at health food stores? Do you know who snuck it up to my room and hid it so the nurses couldn't see?"

Mother smiled, examined her hands.

"None other than my wife, who was Miss Aldeen way back then."

"What I knew about nutrition could've fit in a thimble," said my mother. "I was waitressing at the Happy Steak on Vine. Happy Steak, can you imagine. Think of the hormones, the antibiotics. I swear, in those days I thought a square meal was a slab of ribs. Anyway, I learned a lot by getting those books for Allen. And I had to learn fast or his leg would be lost. A holistic approach was the last resort."

"It was time for the great escape," said my father. "I'd had enough of that doctor and his dire predictions. I was so distraught, he wanted to sedate me. And, Robert, can you guess who was waiting to rescue me the night before the operation?"

Silence again, the swoosh of traffic.

"You guessed it. In her daddy's wood-paneled station wagon, idling right outside the gift shop. It was just like eloping, except I was wearing a hospital gown and my leg was throbbing to beat the band."

I figured Bobby was listening because my father would glance in the rearview mirror and seem inspired to keep talking. At a red light, he lifted his right leg high enough for Bobby to see that it was real. He wiggled it too, in case there was doubt. He said, "Pretty limber for a man of forty-three."

The car sped onto the freeway. We glided through downtown Los Angeles. The silhouette of City Hall loomed above restaurants and department stores. Banks of ivy lined the roadside, dotted with litter and a few squat palms. The farther we traveled from the city, the stranger the buildings became, their shapes and functions like something from a dream: a brewery constructed from rusty tin, nothing inside but vast shadows; a stockyard where parts of billboards were kept, a giant wedge of chocolate cake facing the oncoming lanes of commuters. Still farther outside the city, large structures gave way to farms and vineyards and strip-mined hills. Signs for food and gas and lodging pointed their arrows into the distance. Mother yawned and rummaged through the cooler. "Anyone for a nice cold carrot?"

"No thanks," Bobby called from the back.

Thin clouds drifted overhead, the landscape dimming every few minutes. We passed a bar called the Play Pen and a shack with faded words above the door: Madam Caroompas-Your Future Foretold.

"The future," said Father. "Now that's a broad topic."

I fiddled with the radio. It broadcast torrents of static.

"Robert," my father asked, "have you ever heard of cryogenics?"

"Push-ups and jumping jacks?"

My parents laughed. So I did, too.

"Not calisthenics," he continued. "I'm talking about a new science, a science that might allow us to live longer than we ever expected." Bobby leaned against the front seat. I could feel his breath against my neck. My father told him about how people could be frozen in cryostats that were filled with liquid hydrogen, their bodies defrosted far in the future. Bobby struggled to understand. "You mean," he kept saying into my ear, "like some kind of sleep?"

I finally lost patience. "Bobby," I said, "remember in *Refugees from Island Earth*, how it starts off and all the people on the space station are laying in metal tubes with windows so you can see their faces and there's frost on the windows and they stay in suspended animation till the computer wakes them up at a pre-programmed time?"

"Yeah," said Bobby. "I remember."

I said to my father, "Go ahead."

"Well," said my father, "some insurance companies are so excited about advances in cryogenic science, they're thinking of writing policies that would guarantee the monthly replenishment of a cryostat's liquid nitrogen into perpetuity."

"Perpetuity?" Bobby and I said it together.

"Enough," said Mother, nudging me. "I need some room. My foot's asleep."

I climbed into the backseat and sat next to the window, hugging my knees to my chest. Bobby's overnight bag was rattling between us. "What's in there?" I asked. "Stuff," he said. We were dropping below sea level, the landscape flat, studded with scrub brush and broken rock, eddies of dust twisting in the wind. The air became hotter, but the sun was hidden behind the clouds and the heat seemed to have no source. My parents rolled down their windows. The air was percussive, pouring in, rippling our shirts and thrashing at our hair. The floor of the desert wavered before us. Tumbleweeds spun past the car. "Moon River" blared from the radio, and my mother, unable to hear herself above the rushing air, sang along, completely off key: "I'm comin' round the bend, my Huckleberry friend." Bobby faced me, smiling broadly, his black hair flying in every direction, stripes writhing on his seersucker shirt.

It was evening when we drove into the parking lot of the Coral Sands. Gravel crackled beneath the tires. My father parked the car in front of a boulder with Guests Only stenciled on its side. We jumped out the moment the car had stopped. Lit from beneath by colored lights, the fronds of palms and ocotillo were rocked by currents of balmy air. In the distance, windchimes clinked. Dozens of small cottages were connected by a meandering stone pathway. Canvas lounge chairs glowed in the moonlight. My father looked around and sighed, "Thank you, Mr. Ludlow."

We carried our luggage into a small hexagonal building, which my father guessed was the office. It was dark and still inside. A cone of incense smoked in an ashtray. The instant my father cleared his throat, a door opened behind the desk, sending a slice of light through the room. "Hi," said a woman, extending her hand. Her skin was weathered. She wore a caftan. "I'm Lois, the owner. First time here?" Her voice was hushed, as if our stay was top secret. Then I noticed an old man asleep on a couch in the back room. His mouth was open but no sound came out, not even the hiss and gurgle of breath. My parents talked in whispers too, trying not to wake him. "There's plenty of time to soak," said Lois. "The mineral pool is open till midnight." She peered down her nose at Bobby and me. "It's delicious," she murmured. "You'll cook like dumplings."

We followed Lois single-file to our cottage, passing a few people in bathrobes and bathing suits on their way to the mineral pool. "Voilà," she said, stopping in front of number fourteen. She dangled the key in the air before her. "When you boys grow up, I'll be waiting." Lois winked at Bobby and me. She tossed the key to my parents, turned and walked away.

"Wow," said Bobby when we closed the door to our bedroom. "Is she some kinda psycho?" He walked like Lois, dragging his feet on the carpet, thrusting his hips from right to left. It made me laugh; I inhaled the musty odor of the room. Encouraged, Bobby minced between the twin beds. He looked at me and batted his eyes. "I'll be waiting when you grow up."

"Bobby," I snarled. I felt like a bone had lodged in my throat. "You're such a . . ."

"What?" he whined. "What did I do?"

I unpacked my clothes while Bobby sat on his bed, staring into space, clutching his overnight bag as though it were a doll. Running nose. Dejected expression. The impulse to console him welled up in me, but inwardly I shouted it down. I moved from bureau to closet and back, hoping that motion would keep me from thinking.

I shot from the cottage after I unpacked. I took the stone pathway toward a stand of trees. "Don't be long," my mother called out. Her voice was overwhelmed by wind rumbling over the desert floor.

The path branched off in different directions, and I wasn't sure where I was headed or why I took one fork instead of another. I walked past a Coke machine standing alone on a slab of cement. The bulbs behind its buttons flickered. Further on, I passed an arbor with a stone love seat in its center. Finally, I found myself overlooking the mineral pool. It was set in a small dale, surrounded by foliage, lit from within by blue lights, clouds of steam curling from its surface. Rivulets of hot water poured down slopes of glossy rock. A hand-painted sign warned patrons not to drink alcohol while in the pool. Enjoy, it read, at your own risk.

A gray-haired woman was bobbing on her back in the shallow end, her eyes closed, mouth slack. Another elderly woman in a bathing cap sat in the water near her, reading a paperback book. Lois was helping an old man into the pool, the man who had been asleep on the couch. She held onto a wooden handrail with one arm, and with the other supported the old man's waist. His skin was loose, untouched by sun. "That's good, Pop," she repeated. "That's the stuff." He lurched unsteadily into the pool. He eyed the water suspiciously, as though he couldn't be sure what it was. Half submerged, her father leaned over an inner tube and floated away like a leaf. Lois busied herself by picking up the towels that people had left by the side of the pool. Her caftan filled with wind and billowed. She waved at my parents who sauntered toward her in identical robes and rubber sandals. They shucked off their robes and stood by the edge of the pool. They dipped their toes in, tentative. They glanced at one another and started down the steps, my father doing a little dance that meant his tender feet were scalded. Mother's cheeks puffed out when she was in past her ankles, and even from far away I could hear the moan that escaped her, the pitch of pleasure mixed with pain. Lit from beneath and tinted blue, their every sag was accentuated—cheeks, chests, bellies, hips. Their bodies seemed uneven, ancient. The shadows they cast on the rocks behind them were huge and stooped. I watched, swallowed, barely breathed; I'd never seen them look like that, pulled and paled by time. My parents went under, inch by inch. They joined the aged in steaming water.

Heading back to the bungalow, I walked slowly, watching stars blink in the sky. The desert moon hovered overhead, as strange and full as my own heart. I wondered what I would say when I saw Bobby, how I could explain to him, to myself, this need to take flight again and again, even though I liked to be with him.

Bobby had his back to me when I entered the room. He was still sitting on his bed, clutching his overnight bag. Both of the bedside lamps were on.

"You should see the mineral pool," I said. "It's really something." I pried off my tennis shoes without untying them. I flopped on my bed. The bedspread smelled like a century of dust.

"Hua wheah," muttered Bobby.

"What?"

Bobby coughed. I heard the crinkling of cellophane. "I wheah," he said. An audible swallow.

I sat up. "What's wrong?" I asked.

"Nothing," he said. His head was bent. He was stuffing something into the bag.

When I stood up to look, Bobby shouted, "No." He tried to zip the bag shut before I could see, but he tugged too hard and the insides flew out. There, scattered on his lap, on the bed, on the threadbare carpet of our bungalow bedroom, were Bit-O-Honeys, U-Know Bars, Milk Duds, Raisinettes, Hershey's Kisses. Ropes of red licorice festooned the bed's dust ruffle. In the folds of the blanket were miniature wax Coke bottles, some filled with slugs of cherry Kool-Aid, others with their tops bitten off, only a faint red residue left. Half a Krazy Kake had landed near the bedside table, still in its wrapper, the white squiggle of frosting smeared. A broken Pixie Stick spilled purple granules down Bobby's pant leg and into his cuff. Chiclets covered the bed like confetti.

In the midst of this sweet bounty was a Baggie filled with hardboiled eggs, compliments of Mrs. Keegan. There must have been half a dozen. Most had cracked from their fall to the floor. When Bobby saw me staring at them, he lifted one of the eggs. It was perfectly white, smooth, unharmed. He just held it between us for a minute, as if it were the evidence of some theory he was about to prove. I waited for him to say something; his lip quivered as though he might speak. But our stunned silence dragged on and on. Into perpetuity, I thought. It was crazy, but that egg seemed to shine at the center of the room, both of us glaring at it, everything else growing indistinct: the big lamps that flanked the beds, the palm trees rocking outside the window, the shapes and colors of scattered candy. And then Bobby began to sob.

"My mother made it," he said. His cheeks were wet. A thread of spittle hung from his lips. He tucked the egg back in the Baggie.

"I know," I said. I sat next to him.

"Don't tell your—"

"I won't," I said.

"I like candy." He announced this calmly, as though it had just occurred to him. Then his face went taut. "I'll never be healthy. Your Mom says candy causes diabetes."

"It doesn't matter, Bobby." I put my arm around his shoulder.

"But my life expectancy," he said. "Don't you believe that stuff about refined sugar? Organic produce? Cryo-what's-it?"

I went into the bathroom to get Bobby a Kleenex. When I returned, he was gnawing on the licorice rope, sniffling and coughing. I turned out the lights. I put my arm around him again and we leaned back against the headboard, quiet for a long time. My travel clock glowed in the dark.

"Do you?" asked Bobby. His breath smelled like licorice.

"Do I what?"

"Believe that stuff?"

At that instant, I believed only in things I could touch, things I could see: the oval of a hard-boiled egg, the glowing face of the travel clock, Bobby's back against my arm, hard beneath his seersucker shirt. Bobby offered me a strand of licorice. I ate it cautiously at first, then greedily, wracked with guilt, stunned by its flavor—raspberry rubber. I scooped the Krazy Kake from the floor and bit into its cocoa dome, whipped cream seeping through my teeth. The Bit-O-Honeys, hard as rock, threatened to wrench the fillings from my mouth. My tongue stung from so many flavors. An ache chafed deep in my stomach. I felt as though I'd start to shake. And still I ate, scavenging the bedspread for food, plundering the overnight bag. Bobby showed me how the tart stuff from a Pixie Stick clings to a wet finger, so we licked our fingers and dabbed it up, out of his cuff, off his pant leg, our lips and hands turning purple. When we reached his belt, I tugged his shirt above his stomach and ran my chin across the skin; it smelled like sweat and Ivory soap. The muscles in his stomach jumped. Bobby let his head fall back.

Amid the litter of candy wrappers, side by side on the bed with Bobby, I pretended I was drunk from sugar, the glucose blotting reason from my brain, making me reel, willing and pliant. I pressed away the space between us, arching into Bobby's kiss, kissing Bobby back. We parted slowly, unable to look at one another. "We'd better not," I muttered. But I found myself holding him tight again.

Hangers chimed in the next room. My parents were back, dressing for dinner. Words vibrated through the wall—maybe they plotted how to live longer—but I couldn't understand what they said. Their voices sounded far away. Miles away. Years.

★

ROBIN PODOLSKY

DIGNITY/ UNIFORMS/ DIGNITY

PART 1

LIKE THIS: SHE HAD pink waxy cheeks, a plump neck, and a stiff hedge of hair, which bleach and Lady Clairol had rendered a uniform solar yellow. She wore a black leather jacket, thick and waxy as her skin, with many zippers. Her jeans were dark and crisp. Her boots were square and hard. Her jaw was set and her eyes were wary as she walked. Still, she didn't see them until one slapped her shoulder. She started to turn, but two of them grabbed her arms. By then they were all over her. She booted one in the knee and he went down but two others got her leg and then she was on her back, bellowing, her face lobster red.

The young men were clean, beaming with vigor and relaxed. A few leaned back on their heels, sucking cigarettes and grinning loosely as they watched. A couple of them turned and addressed the people on the street who either watched from a distance with closed faces

19

or scurried away. The boys' voices rose and fell, hollow and rhythmic as church bells. They were cleaning up the city, they said. They were Modern Youth, they said. They would save the dignity of the white race, they said.

They had her jacket off and were working on her boots and pants. One of them, a chunky boy with a faint corona of hair, as yellow as hers, around his square pink skull put two solid kicks into her ribs. He had "Positive Attitude" stenciled neatly in white on the back of his khaki jacket.

By the time her long pink breast flopped out of her shirt and disappeared under their hands, her screams had fallen to moist stifled wails. In no hurry, the boy who held her jacket folded it neatly. He put it into a canvas knapsack that hung from the immobile shoulders of an older Modern, more man than boy, who watched the rape with no expression. Over the pocket of his khaki jacket, the older Modern wore a brass nameplate with "Unit Commander" neatly etched onto the front.

PART 2

Like this: She had never seen anyone beaten to death before. Determined to live and ashamed of it, she held still and kept her face empty. For months, she had worn only dresses. Her makeup was blue and pink. Black around the eyes made a woman look too hard.

"Cocksucker. Mexican faggot." The blond boy's voice was friendly, almost tender. He nudged the black-haired man with a hard square boot. The young black-haired man with a long mustache had stopped moving. Syrupy blood seeped from his ears.

Ten minutes earlier, the black-haired man and a friend had been sitting across from each other at a small round table, having coffee in the sun. They had laughed all afternoon, because the tiny table wobbled on the uneven concrete patio and coffee kept sloshing over the rims of their cups, and because they were giddy in each other's company. When the slim young man with the long mustache looked over his companion's shoulder and saw the squad of Modern Youth moving up the street, he stopped laughing.

As if it had been planned between them, one of the Moderns gave the young man a sunny smile and lifted him out of his chair by the armpits. Others grabbed his torso and, hand to hand, they passed him over the low iron rail that separated the patio from the street. He jerked in their hands, bellowing, his face brick red. He clipped one on the kneecap with the edge of a brown loafer. That one went down, but two others got his leg and then four of them held him upright while a fifth sank a fist deep into his belly and twisted it. That Modern, a chunky boy with a corona of yellow hair around his square pink skull, had "I ♡ White People" neatly stenciled onto the back of his khaki jacket.

The young man's friend had vaulted over the rail. He grabbed the graceful little chair on which he'd been sitting, a wrought-iron fantasy of roses and vines, and swung it against the wall of khaki backs and bristled heads. Laughing, the boys took his chair and threw it away. Turning from the older man, they continued to kick and spit at his friend whose hoarse screams spasmed out and choked off in helpless response. Several times, the bearded man rushed the Youths, but good-naturedly, they pushed him away.

Two Moderns turned and addressed the people on the street who watched from a distance, like she did, with empty faces. They were Modern Youth, the speakers said. They were cleaning up the city, they would clean up the world, they said. They were fighting for manhood and decency, the values of the white race, they said.

The young man's friend ran to a huge brown man in a T-shirt and Sears jeans. The big man was in a crew that had been doing something to the sidewalk with a pickax and jackhammer. The big man watched the beating with a closed face and would not look at the man with a neat curly beard who cried in front of him, begging in Spanish for help.

The crying man and the big man were very close to her. She was afraid that the crying man would turn to her next and she trembled with resentment at the thought.

The young man with the long mustache had become quite still

under the boots that thumped his ribs. She watched and tried to think of what she'd do if they came after her, but nobody looked at her at all. She was a young white woman, properly dressed, and she had her dignity.

PART 3

Or, like this: She was sitting with a friend at a small round table, having coffee in the sun. When she looked over her companion's shoulder and saw the squad of Modern Youth moving up the street, she wanted to cry. Her pulse slammed through her throat. She tasted acid and blood.

All afternoon, she and her friend had argued. She hated the café. She didn't want to be seen there. She didn't want to be seen in public with just another woman. She didn't want to be seen with a woman whose stiff hedge of hair was bleached white and who wore a thick jacket of black leather, punctuated with plastic animals and chrome studs. She herself was properly dressed in a sweater and skirt. Her makeup was discreet, but flattering. Her friend had insisted that if she didn't start facing things she wouldn't have a life anymore and she couldn't hide in her apartment forever. She didn't see why she couldn't do just that, except that the headaches and nightmares were driving her crazy and she had to do something.

The boys in clean khaki had moved close enough for her to see their bright eager smiles. She held very still, her face empty. She hated her friend.

The street was quiet. The crew who had been doing something to the sidewalk with a pickax and jackhammer had stopped. One of them, a huge brown man in Sears jeans and a T-shirt, still held his ax. Without expression, he watched the Moderns move up the sidewalk across the street from where he stood.

She felt the scream as a jolt along her vibrating spine. Her body contracted and shook. The noise went on. It came from a man with a neat curly beard who cried and struggled in the arms of his friends while he raged in Spanish at the Modern Youth. The bearded man had run out of a square gray building that was still a bar but, now, had no sign to mark its entrance. The Youths turned and waved at the crying man. A few blew kisses. An older Modern, more man than boy, turned his back and kept walking. The others followed the older Modern who wore a small brass nameplate with "Unit Commander" etched onto it pinned over his front pocket.

The Unit Commander led his squad to a brick building with a wide glass door. Over the door, a hand-painted sign read "Clinica de la Familia." A chunky blond Modern with the American and Confederate flags neatly painted onto the back of his khaki jacket kicked in a pane of glass before he shouldered through the unlocked door. Most of the Youths followed him.

She heard screams and breakage. She and her friend had climbed over the low iron rail that separated the patio where they'd been sitting from the sidewalk. Half a block away, the Youths began to push people out of the clinic and onto the street. A short woman with a seamed red face and gray streaks through her thick black braid was bleeding at the mouth. Two reed-thin men with sparse blond beards held each other. Children shrilled.

Two of the Moderns addressed the people on the street. They were Modern Youth, they said. They were cleaning up the city. They would clean up the world. One of the thickly muscled boys had begun a barking tirade against wetbacks who wanted to live off the taxes of white men with jobs when the bearded man sank a fistful of keys into his belly and twisted them. Another man from the bar stabbed the second speaker's freckled face with a slim shiny pen. The boy screamed. Without haste, the big man with the pickax crossed the street. He swung the ax in a wide clean arc. Whimpering, the Unit Commander watched parts of himself spill onto his clean jacket and then to the dusty street. He had lost his dignity.

A growl in her throat blossomed into a full bellow. She grabbed the graceful little chair of wrought iron on which she'd been sitting. She ran forward, her girlfriend behind her. Roaring, they smashed chairs into bristled skulls.

Later, a former friend called to tell her that she and her girlfriend had sunk to their level. On the news, the Chief of Police called the

people who had defended the clinic "animals without human dignity."
She didn't agree with her former friend or the Chief of Police, because
the headaches and nightmares had stopped, because she no longer
hated herself and everybody else and because the people in her neighborhood talked to each other a lot more often and, for the time being,
had coffee in the sun whenever they wanted to.

★

GIL
CUADROS

~~~~~~

UNPROTECTED

I CANNOT GET THIS smell of hand lotion off of me. I've washed three times today, covered myself in cologne, sat in the steam room so that I could sweat it all out; but it's still there. It is faint in my beard. It is underneath my nails and I can smell it when I bring food to my mouth. It is here in my bed. It smells of cock and ass. It smells unnatural. It smells unsafe.

I knew I was too drunk, six bars already that afternoon, and on the Sunday that I promised my parents I would visit them. They wanted to have dinner with me, watch some TV. They worried about my ARC diagnosis, but they would never ask about it. They wondered when was I going to look like those men they had seen on the news, men who were dying of AIDS. They wanted to know when was I going to be sorry for the things that I did to become this way.

AIDS had already become an issue when I came out in '83. I was twenty-one. So along with the usual guilt trips to stop me from coming out: "What will your father say?" "What will your brothers say?" "Where did I go wrong?" my mother asked, "Aren't you afraid?"

"But, Mom, I'm in love." He was ten years older, wiser, blond hair, blue eyes, a furry chest. I loved the way he'd grab my ass, tell me, "Come on, baby, let me fuck you."

It wasn't a tragedy to move out, but I could hear my father crying, hitting the drywall that separated his room from mine. My mother sat at the dining room table, with its lion claw feet tearing into her slippers. She just stared into the china cabinet and wept.

John had met me at his door. He told me I could live with him forever. I lived with him for more than four years, then he died. I don't know why he ever went out with me. I couldn't even imagine going out with a kid of twenty-one. I tested soon after his death. A friend had said, "Not even cold in the grave yet." I found out that my T-cells were only thirty-five, my platelet count was critical, and my white cells said I needed a transfusion. Since then, I've stabilized, I have no symptoms except low T counts. I rarely think about being sick when I take my AZT capsules.

On this day, I took my four o'clock pills with a swig of beer and headed for a new bar. My friend Nick drove. We'd been friends for more than ten years, and we've known each other since elementary school. It was this last bar that did me in. It was called The Brick. It had a rougher edge than the rest of the west-end bars. Today it proudly proclaimed it was "Hawaiian Daze," stenciled in black marker over a cheap Tom of Finland poster. It showed two sailors; one had his hand down the other's pants.

Nick and I were feeling great; our feet dragged in the white sand that was thrown on the hardwood floor. A cut-out hula dancer was pinned at her nipples to a cork bulletin board, and the moose head was strangled by a thin red lei. As we walked further into the bar, two men in leather jackets, faces uncut by razors, hair cropped to the skin, sporting grass skirts and fishnet stockings, lay on the pool table. They waved under the blow-up shark that was spinning like a record. Everyone was flashing back to disco, The Village People and their hits, "YMCA," "Macho Macho Man." On the video monitor they showed one of the singers, a telephone lineman, working the pole, his jeans ripped just below the crotch. Everyone was screaming and I was full of their energy. I was ready to explode. I needed to do something, make something happen, and like a cat, I pawed at the great white shark, suspended by the smallest test line. It made the bar stir, its waters already in a frenzy.

Nick and I played pool in the back room, smoking cigarettes and drinking vodka tonics. I was losing badly, knocking his striped balls into a pocket, making the cue jump in the air and land a few inches away. Missing shot after shot, I gave up. I put my head down on the table, in line of Nick's victory shot and told him, "Shoot the fucking ball, I'm ready." That's when I saw him.

His handlebars caught in my eyes, making me turn my face. Nick was still at the table trying some impossible trick. I bounced the rubber tip of the pole between my legs, grinning. This guy looked straight at me. I didn't really expect him to sit down next to me, on my stack of beer crates. I didn't think I was attractive enough, especially now with the virus. His confidence was apparent, like an open, madras shirt. His rib cage was strong and voluminous. There was a serpentine chain around his throat. It clung tightly and moved when he said, "Do you want to go to my place?"

John had always said it was that easy. Go up to a guy and ask him point blank. I had thought it was a bit sleazy. I imagined it should be more like a wild, bird ritual, with ruffled feathers, heavy squawking, and beaks intermingled. I really had no experience cruising, it seemed to have become some lost art form. I thought about it, saying, "Well, maybe. What's your name?" The music was too loud and I just winged it, catching his question again, "Do you want to go to my place?" Nick was setting up another game. I told him, tugging on a loop on his jeans, "I'll see you later." I staggered out of the bar, following a man whose name I didn't hear.

We stopped at Rocky's liquor on the way to his place. I asked for a Pepsi. He came back with Coronas and a pot of spider mums. Driving up to the hills, he told me they were for a friend who was sick in the hospital. He started talking about his condo, saying it was real nice. He then told me he had brought someone up there once and was ripped off. He talked of Louise Hay, philosophically. He told me of his gay brother who lived across the street, pointing out the top floor of a refurbished hotel. It had a history. Hollywood's best actresses had all lived there at one time. He started reciting the prices of other condos around his. I put my hand on his lap.

Inside the garage, we walked side by side. His steps were hard, businesslike shoes on wet cement. The puddles reflected the bars of fluorescent light. They shook nervously as we went by, while the chrome doors of the elevator opened for us. He held the door open for me with his arm. When I stepped in, he pressed the stop button. I thought that maybe he wanted to kiss me or something. Instead he looked at me, as if he wanted me to stare down. I did, embarrassed at what I was doing. He asked if I was a hustler. I said no. He didn't seem convinced.

He wasn't going to touch me, even after I crossed the threshold. Without much grandeur, he showed each of his rooms. The place was beautiful. There were beveled glass tables and shelves, a leather sectional. Each room was immaculate, unlike my place. There were dishes in my sink that I would sooner throw out than wash. He led me to his balcony. Comfortable chairs of azure were accented by a pale blue rattan table, on which thick green candles absent of burning wicks rested. He unbuckled his pants, then sat down, rubbing his cock, thumbing the shaft. He then pulled out his balls, letting them rest over the teeth of his zipper.

Other apartments crowded in on us, like a cubist painting. Their large black windows were opaque because of the screens that were made not to be seen through. There was no space here either, no breathing room. I thought that other people could see us out here with his fly open. I undid my belt and pulled on my button jeans. I told him I liked the sound of Levi's opening.

He got up to get us a drink. He said from the kitchen, "Did you notice I have no curtains." Coming back out on the balcony he said, "I have nothing to hide." I looked around: there were no curtains, no blinds, "just doors," I thought.

I had to hide everything. Like the gold wedding band that is on a chain my parents had given me. The chain had a cross on it too. I had promised my parents that I'd wear the cross all the time. They didn't know I wore it with John's ring. To them it would seem immoral; John was the reason I was sick. Clothes can hide these defects, like the blue-red pinpoints on my veins, a sign of bimonthly blood workups and the virus. I wondered if he could tell, if that's why his smile was a bit wicked. I thought at this point I should be responsible and make sure we play safe. I didn't want to get too carried away.

He started walking toward me, to the bedroom that was behind me. I stopped him, "I'm feeling a little uncomfortable, maybe we should talk first."

He said gently and reassuringly, "Don't worry, I won't hurt you." The words fell out of him like a whisper. I did begin to worry. First he tells me about getting ripped off by some previous trick, he asked me if I was a hustler, now he tells me don't worry I won't hurt you.

I said, "I should tell you something first." I hesitated, afraid of rejection, as his face changed to annoyance. I went on, "I'm positive." I felt like a child confessing his sins, kneeling in a dark room. I felt or thought that maybe he was positive too. He talked about his sick friend, the Hay group, it seemed probable that he had the virus.

His face registered nothing. "I tested negative to HIV." It hit me like a broom. I saw him in my imagination, in the tearooms getting blown by the porcelain bowls, cruising parks under lattice-covered walkways, walking around in a wet white towel at a bathhouse late at night. I knew I was being unfair to him, thinking that he was some seedy person who escaped the curse. I saw him do these things, in my mind, things that are considered unsafe, almost sinful now. I couldn't help but feel cheated, I had done none of these things. I didn't deserve this disease.

He sat back in his chair, lighting a cigarette. "Do you feel comfortable with this?"

I said, "I feel a little weird."

"Like how?"

"Like I'm infectious material." He winced at this remark. I saw myself being transported in an orange-red garbage bag, getting tossed out by sallow-colored gloves.

Recomposed, he said rather smugly, almost challenging me, "Well, if you don't feel right about this, it's fine with me. I accept myself for what I am." I thought it must be easy when you're negative.

With a softer voice he said, "We can just beat off." I took a drink from my beer. Cold liquid went inside of me, shutting down parts of me like a machine. He closed his argument. "That's all we have to do." He pulled off his shirt and hung it over the rail. I began to undress in the doorway of his bedroom.

He uncovered his bed neatly, folding the spread in half, then quarter. His room was spotless. Lights came from behind the head-board. The cream-colored wood twisted like a Bernini pulpit. The shadows bent around the corners of the room. The ceiling sparkled with glitter. One wall was all closet doors. He opened one, placing the comforter on the center shelf. I expected him to pull out a plain percale to protect his Southwestern sheets. Sheets like that need to stay clean and sex was dirty. He just pulled down his pants. I took my lead from his, tossing my shirt to the floor, lacking his grace for folding it away.

We got on the bed slowly, our knees pressing into the soft mattress. He reached for my left nipple and I withdrew. His hands were cold as the air coming through the open door. He stuck his fingers into my mouth to warm them. I felt their tips on my jagged back teeth. My tongue tasted the saline skin pulling out, over my lips, then slipping back in again. I was like a scavenger, hands tearing the hair that grew over his shoulders, tugging at his prick, pointed upright and bent. I was gentle with his foreskin, letting it peel back on its own; but he asked for more, "Pull harder, grip it tighter, twist it around." He reached behind me for the nightstand and brought out a bottle of hand lotion. He poured it on the both of us. The cool, motherly scent filled the room and oppressed me. I couldn't get hard now. When he made me hold out my hand, I couldn't help but think of my mother using this every day. She would put it on, spreading it evenly over her arms and white hands. She would remove her wedding ring that clutched a diamond. I also remembered mornings where John would pour it on his shoulders and ask me to rub it in. He would fall on the bed and wait for me. After I finished, I would cuddle into his side, trying to stay warm, drifting back into dreams.

I kept on shrinking, becoming smaller and smaller. I thought of how I hated hand cream as a lubricant. I said, disappointed, "Go ahead and finish, I can't."

He stopped stroking his cock and looked at mine, limp and unexcited. He asked me, "Why don't you spend the night?" Then without any response from me, he pulled me under his covers, wrapping his legs over my body. His thighs became binding material. I could hear him mumble something. I started trying to fall asleep, glad because of all the alcohol that was inside me, it was making the room spin. His hard dick was still touching me, coming up inside the crack of my ass. He wasn't sleeping. His mouth was at the back of my neck, warm air blowing on my nape. I stared out the open glass door that led to the balcony, where this whole thing started. I thought that maybe I shouldn't have said anything about being positive, that if I could get his leg off me, I could get up and put my clothes back on and leave.

He was so near, he whispered, "Why don't you lie on your back?" He got to his knees and I could see the shadowy outline of him against the stars of the ceiling. Shadows were thrown onto every wall and corner, lewd shapes of worms, snakes and mushrooms. His chest billowed like a sail. I became his cabin boy, learning the ropes. My ankles began to sweat. My wrists were held down by the weight of his hands and body. He sat on my chest and I could smell his cock a few inches from my face, taunting me. He told me, "Suck that dick," and I did. I didn't even hesitate. I swallowed him like meat. It made me choke. "You like that big dick, don't you?" I nodded. It seem enormous, really too big. I began to split in half.

One side of me was screaming, "This is wrong. This is unsafe. What are you doing?"

The other side said, "Shut up, you're going to die anyways. Enjoy this because this is going to be your last time."

It was easy to take him in. My mouth stretched as wide as it could. My chin would rub against his balls, regulating his speed. The hair on my face would mix with the hair on his nuts, and they would pull on each other. He began to pump hard and I gagged. Later, his hands were between my legs, his fingers touching my ass. I knew I let him fuck me, there wasn't even an afterthought. I couldn't sleep

in the unfamiliar room, quiet now as a church. At five in the morning
I picked up my things, the damp shirt, my wrinkled jeans, my unlaced
shoes. I ran to catch the bus and it waited for me. It was filled with
Mexicanos, some from South America. The men all looked at me as
I entered, and I took my seat quickly. I was afraid they could smell
the shit that was in my beard, see the sticky shine of cum over my
body, and know what I had done that night. Each one of those short,
stocky men with their black hair and Indian profiles would know. The
seat next to me was empty until a young Mexican man sat down. He
spread his legs open till they touched mine. The bus tore down the
street, hitting a pothole. It jarred the riders and made my neighbor
rub his leg against mine. He smiled at me. I pulled my legs together,
closing them tight. I fell asleep against the window that was cracked
open, my hands acting as a pillow, breathing in the exhaust from
outside and the lotion that was over my hands, heavy as spring air.

★

JANE THURMOND

EXOSKELETONS

I KEEP CAREFUL NOTES. There are times when, hunched over my row of jars, I must write over and over "no visible change." And then, there are nights like this. When specimens inside their casings erupt into clicking, whirring jewels. I should be celebrating. Instead I sit at my window, staring out over the yard simply counting the flashes of fireflies. Because only hours ago, I saw a side of my father I had not seen before.

Now he rumbles down the hallway. This time he's in from Alaska. Next week he's off to Yemen. He whisks in and out between consulting trips for Delta Oil. We see each other at dinner when Celia, our housekeeper, presents us with steaming plates of biscuits, chicken-fried steak smothered in creamed gravy, fried okra, and greens. Celia's cooking is what Dad misses most about home. And time to stretch out on the lawn chair where he shuffles through stacks of mail, or stares up into the sky.

Years ago, when Mother drove off with Ray Freed, she left her Waterford displayed in the china cabinet, her piano in the living room, and her bridal portrait hanging in the hallway. I still pass the portrait on my way to the bathroom. Sometimes I consider removing it, but I feel that's up to Dad. I once heard him say that Mother had a poker face, which she must have been wearing for that pose. Out of all the times I've stopped and searched, I've never understood what's behind her smile.

I should explain that I'm a scientist, and through research and observation I make sense of the world. The arthropods teach me. Take the word *family* as we use it to classify these wasps: the Pompilidae family, the Sphecidae family, the Vespidae family. The members of these families know little of each other—like us, the Wiggins. And like us, they are spread, unacquainted, throughout the world. Surely, by instinct, they know they are related when they pass. Perhaps a familiar sound or mark jars them. Perhaps my yellow jackets—the Vespidaes—see their mother's bright bands buzz past, turn and, at the very least, find the rhythm of her wings familiar.

Outside under the streetlight I count the Gillespie family, the Reynolds family, the DeLeon family. When a man leaves one of those houses in the morning he returns at night, kisses his wife, plays catch in the yard with his children. When he leaves for weeks he takes his family with him. I earn cash in summers and on holidays. I collect their mail, and feed and walk their dogs, and always I water their roses.

A decade ago, when we were the only house on the block, there were no cultivated roses. Our yard was leveled to bare soil, but the wild neighboring lots were full of foliage. Spring displayed its every color on the other side of our fence, and in March after I turned ten, Mother left. Two months dragged by before Dad wrote the ad that hired Celia. "Live-in needed for motherless 10 year old. Cooking, housekeeping, companionship. No yardwork." At first, Celia tapped daily on my bedroom door to offer fried pies or cobbler or biscuits and honey. Gradually, she coaxed me until, one night, I ventured outside with her to see the magenta sky. We sat in our shorts, our thin thighs against the cool soil. Celia's lips were red, the ice was clinking in our tea glasses, and mayflies drifted up from the marsh in a purple cloud. I could smell new mortar and timber.

Celia leaned back on her bony hands and told stories about when she was a girl on the edge of Lake Superior. One summer night, she said, the mayflies swarmed up from the lake and into her neighborhood. They surrounded streetlights in their confusion. Unable to find their way back to the water, they died in town, causing roads to be slippery as ice. Unsuspecting motorists skidded and crashed. In response, the mayor ordered the lights dimmed on nights the mayflies mated.

My insect encyclopedia describes the mayfly nymphs, living in lakes sometimes for years. One day without warning, they rise up at once in a humming cloud, spreading their new adult wings for their last few hours of life. The females drop their eggs into the water, then die. You can see mayflies the day after, dead and floating on glassy surfaces of water. The eggs give way to new nymphs—children left alone to fend for themselves in the dark bottoms of lakes.

Since Celia came to live with us she has busied herself with projects, puttering around the garage with new tools or plopped in the middle of the living room clipping pictures from magazines to paste in loose-leaf folders. Her knit shirts reveal muscle stretched over a wiry frame—features as distinct as head, thorax, abdomen. She and I haven't always been close but things happen. Suddenly you learn something about someone that touches you. Like the things I began to learn about Celia soon after I finished high school.

One steamy day I found her standing in the driveway with a neighbor's rose to her nose. Stems reached for her through the chain-link fence. Leaves fell against her face. Her eyes were as green as scarabs. "Judy Ann," she said, "there's something happening in our yard."

The noon sun was hot on my head. I perused every inch of area meant for a lawn where, years ago, Dad had covered the soil with white quartz chips. The only sign of life was water dripping from a hose. Even birds avoided us.

Celia rattled the fence. "When was the last time you saw a bee fly over here from the Reynolds' bushes? Developers are sealing over the earth with cement." She shook her graying head. "You think I'm complaining again about our lack of grass. That's not it. Meet me at sunset and bring a white sheet."

Celia sheds her housekeeping uniform whenever Dad is away. I looked past the buckles on her overalls, over the back fence where bulldozers had removed the last stand of trees for new lots. There were a few young hedges that hugged fences and several neighbors had seeded their lawns. The Gillespie boys were bounding around their new pool, over soft green shoots, like fuzz on the ground. Compared to that, our yard was quiet. I looked up at Celia. Her eyes were slits against the sun.

She smiled down at the yellow petals. "The world is slipping away and we're going to save it."

Later that day I was hiking to the Snackin' Shack, taking a shortcut through fields not yet leveled. The air was soupy and warm. White cattle egrets swooped and disappeared into the green salt grass. All I wanted was a lemon-lime to beat the heat, so I didn't notice the bulging vines beside me until I heard the rustle of leaves. "Why aren't you in class?" came Celia's familiar voice.

Even now almost everyone still thinks I go to school, but I don't. It started years ago during one of Dad's trips home when I told him I enrolled in junior college, but I didn't really.

Celia peered out through vines of ivy. I shifted my backpack full of library books. "Can I trust you?" I said.

"You can come in here and discuss it if you promise me something. You never show up uninvited and you don't mention this place to anyone."

Through a small opening, I crawled through overgrowth shaped like an enormous inverted bowl. My knees hit moss, soft as carpet. The walls and ceiling were formed by a canopy of the low, dense foliage of a live oak woven with ivy. Squat candles with charred wicks were lined up on wooden boxes where the delicate dried bodies of insects were stuck with pins through to the crate wood. Feathers were woven in and out of palmetto. Strewn about were a magnifying glass, thermometer, a clutter of bottles, and corks and tubes. I picked up a stack of pencil sketches. "So this is where you disappear to," I said, shifting them in the dappled light. "So this is what you do."

One by one she removed her pencils from a rusty soup can, laid them end to end along the ground. Quietly, she returned them to the can. "What do you think of them?"

I held up a study of a rhinoceros beetle with a horn the size of my thumb. "The detail . . . ," I said, shuffling through the rest, "they look alive."

Celia pulled at the loose skin on her neck. "There ought to be a specialist on everything."

I looked her right in the eye then, and confessed. "I don't take English. I don't take history or math. I haven't finished a course since my high school graduation."

"Do you think I don't know that? What do you take me for?" she said. "Come outside. I want to show you something."

Her hideaway was perched on a rise that overlooked our entire neighborhood, Silver Prairie—its grid of black streets, its vacant yards, its similar colonial houses with chimneys jutting up from all the same spots. The upstairs windows gazed blankly back like rows of eyes. From the path we could read the sign above the main gate with its flapping row of pink flags. "Phase III. Homes for the Elegant Lifestyle."

"Down there the earth feels embarrassed," she said. "See how pale it is, stripped down to its shorts. But up here"—she curled her arm and bowed—"up here it's still proud."

I brushed honeysuckle with my foot. A red trail of ants zigzagged toward the marsh where frogs croaked from the other side. The Snackin' Shack was a blue dot down the highway. It was then I vowed, urgently, to help save what was left.

"You won't tell Dad about college, will you?" I had given it a try from a front-row seat. The professor had droned. The students on either side were snoozing. I just couldn't stay. "I'm still learning." I patted my backpack of books.

I point to that afternoon, almost three years ago, because the purpose of my life began to show itself.

Tonight muffled laughter from the TV floats down the hallway, past my mother's portrait and under the crack beneath my bedroom door. It sounds as if Dad is dragging belongings and scooping them into boxes. He plods from room to room. The front door clicks open. Clattering garbage cans clang in the dark down the driveway. I keep watching for fireflies and for Celia. And still, like any other night, I gather data.

As the development spreads, the number of fireflies decreases. Looking back at our first year's notes, on this particular night we averaged thirty-three per quarter hour. Last year they dwindled to seventeen. Tonight, sadly, I enter eight. Celia's fears are coming true. She is also right about this: insects are emeralds. The photos in my books are lacquered jewels.

But photos can't substitute for a good collection. These first mounted specimens are nearly three years old, gathered on a night that still brimmed with fireflies. This was the night three years ago that I met Celia in the yard with a bright white sheet.

From the clothesline we stretched its flapping ends and secured its bottom edge to chairs to form a V, a path into a wide-mouthed gallon jar. Behind the sheet she set a blazing electric bulb. She said, "Because of our white yard we get extra reflection. There *is* something good about not having grass. It's a beacon brighter than a streetlight!"

Against the blue-black sky, light reflected on flapping wings. Insects buzzed and hawed. Celia huddled with me in the middle of the driveway as they bobbed and thumped against the sheet, funneled down and batted their wings against the sides of the jar. Shadows cast by the jagged quartz chips turned the yard to salt and pepper, filling in the space between the circular driveway and the street. Stars dimmed on the other side of our dome of light.

I felt her breath against my shoulder. She placed her palms against my cheeks and pushed my head down. "Look at them," she said into my ear.

Watching their bodies bang and churn, my lips curled back. "What good will come from killing bugs?"

"There's more to collecting insects than arranging them for show. We won't begin to understand their habits until we learn to identify them, first in our collection and, then, in the wild. Until we learn to identify, how can we help them?"

She clamped her fingers around my arm and led me to the jar

where insects were several inches deep. Moths batted their wings against each other. June bugs scraped their legs against the slippery glass. Exoskeletons ticked and bumped.

"Look," she said, "each of them is unique. In time they will become as familiar as the people you know."

There's a small grove of laurel just north of here where Celia and I drive up for fresh leaves. We've been doing this weekly since that first collection. We crush the leaves and place them in the bottoms of our killing-bottles. Sometimes we use chemicals. Ethyl acetate, carbon tetrachloride, ammonia, chloroform. But laurel is our favorite. Insects that die from laurel stay flexible, as if they are alive. I don't kill without reason. I have one each of some four hundred mounted insects, and I can name and recognize them all. Now wherever I meet them, I notice how their habits have become familiar.

I have come to understand the importance of our work. Even the smallest insect, as much as any living thing, is Divine.

A few weeks after mounting our first specimens, Celia woke me by tapping on the edge of my bed. "Come with me," she said. "It's starting." She pushed my flip-flops between my toes and pulled me up and outside where the moon hung as slim as a mayfly's tail.

Her room above the garage was pastel green, not unlike her leafy hideaway with insects bristling from the walls. Photographs of birds covered the ceiling above the bed. Scrawled notes were strewn about on yellowed paper. Sleepily, I plopped into the chair at her table.

"I sensed something," she said, setting a cup of coffee on the pink tabletop, "so I got up out of bed to take a look around. And look what had emerged from its pupal case." Steam curled from the cup against her chin. She picked up a box made of wire screen where green wings tapered and curved against the mesh. "A luna moth." She smiled, showing the gaps between her teeth. "I found its cocoon under the DeLeons' hickory a few weeks ago, the same day you discovered the hideaway."

Slowly the luna's wings unfolded and revealed, first, purple trim, then markings that resembled eyes, until the wingspan reached the size of the upturned palm of my hand.

"While she's still weak we'll tie her up." And before I could form words, Celia lifted the moth out, gently slipped a thread around the thorax, and let the luna dangle over the kitchen table. When it started to flap about she carried it outside, letting it sway, its wings opalescent in the porch light. "She releases sex pheromones. The males can't resist. They'll sense her and fly for miles." She tied the thread to the tip of a fishing pole and protected the bobbing luna with an inverted bushel basket nailed high to the wall. "Now all we do is wait."

Since that night we've raised and mated skippers, buckeyes, coppers, and blues. So far, it's impossible to tell that their populations have increased. Years from now, when the new lawns are thick and the hedges have filled in, we hope to see moths and butterflies lighting on the patio furniture in all the neighbors' yards.

I explained to Dad that this could take decades. He questioned the significance of our study with a sullen gaze. Although he has been home for an entire week, he and I have hardly spoken. Then just after dinner tonight I was in the den, sprawled out before the big TV. Through the hallway I could see him in the dim dining room light, sitting at the rolltop desk flipping through the ledger, glasses low on his nose. His pink scalp shone under the chandelier. Since his last visit home I see his hair has thinned. Celia sat stiffly in her white uniform sporadically clicking the calculator. On the TV, "Candid Camera" tricked a waitress with a toaster that kept spewing out bread that she hadn't put in.

Dad's voice rose, "My heavens. Oh, Celia, oh, Lord."

"What is it?" Celia said. "Mr. Wiggins?"

This was not a voice I had ever heard from Dad. It was panicky and shrill and drowned out the laughter from the TV. I rushed into the hallway as he jumped up and faced the mantel, his elbows up like wings. Each of his hands was fastened to his head with fingerfuls of hair. He let go one arm and pointed over the mantel. "The green one. The green one is moving his legs. Lord, Judy Ann, you didn't kill it."

I saw the dung beetle I had pinned the day before, between the ox and the six-spotted tiger. Its legs scraped against Styrofoam, a sound like the dull tear of paper. It even spread its wings in a feeble attempt to fly. And with that faint flapping my legs froze.

"Judy Ann, do something," he said, flitting from side to side. "Put it out of its misery. Pull the pin out. Help it."

Celia ran to the kitchen. The light flipped on. I heard her clanging through bottles stashed under the sink.

Dad leaned toward the beetle. "Judy Ann!"

Shaking a can of bug spray, Celia leaped into the room.

"Don't use that," I said. "It will ruin the whole display."

Celia raised her arm and aimed.

Dad jumped back into the hallway where I covered my eyes. I heard the pssst and peeked between my fingers. "Is it dead yet?" I said from the doorway.

Dad bunched up his shoulders and turned to face me. "Is it dead yet? What do you care? Take some responsibility, Judy Ann. Can't you see you're torturing these creatures? Senselessly torturing."

"Mr. Wiggins, your daughter is a scientist," Celia said, trying to be cheerful. "Wow, this thing is hardy. He just won't give up." She gave another squirt and waved the fumes from her face.

"Years ago I was pleased." His face grew pink. Veins bulged from his neck. "Your studies were within reason. But look at this place now. Bugs pinned to the ceiling. Strange chemicals in the kitchen cabinets. Cages stacked so high against the windows I can't get a view outside."

Celia ran to the sliding glass door and snapped it open. Clean air rushed in. "Rest assured," she said, "deader than a doornail." She examined the collection, holding the spray can high like a trophy.

Dad stormed behind her. "I have been more than patient," he said. "In the past year I have pretended to ignore it. But this"—he picked up a box with a wild rabbit Celia had sacrificed that morning to collect and study parasites—"but this is beyond the scope of amateur curiosity. Celia, for God's sake, what are you doing to my daughter?" His fist fell so hard against the dining room table where we'd set up the microlab, the microscope shook and sent newly mounted slides skidding over the parquet floor.

"What am I doing?" Celia heaved the can through the doorway and it clanked across the driveway. "Taking an interest in her, that's what. How dare you come back here a few times a year and accuse *me* of not caring." The back door slammed and she faded out of the porch light. "I'm all the family she has," she hollered over her shoulder.

Dad studied the palm of his hand as if it were a mirror. Wrinkles deepened around his eyes. His lips barely moved as he mumbled to himself, "This doesn't feel like my home anymore." He stumbled into the hallway, bumping my mother's portrait, and disappeared behind his bedroom door. Lepidoptera I had pinned to her picture frame shook loose and tumbled down, their dry wings sifting into the shaggy carpet.

After an hour of my waiting motionless in the hall, Celia still didn't reappear from the dark outside. I crawled over on my knees to pick through powdery pieces of wings lodged in the carpet and imagined them working inside their cocoons. And sure enough, when I pushed open my bedroom door, I found the whole world had cracked open.

Inside its cage a buckeye had laid her green eggs along the leaves of potted snapdragons and its bright wings brushed the yellow blossoms. Striders skated back and forth on the surface of the aquarium water and sent beady black whirligigs spinning. A cicada's eyes bulged from its newly split skin. Transparent as opals, a hundred spiders spread across my desk. Their webs, fine as baby hair, draped from the lip of their nursery jar where their egg sack floated on the glassy floor like a wisp of cotton. Crickets chirped from the closet. June bugs flipped and burst against the screen.

From my window I found Celia's small smudge of light glowing from a rise in the brush. She would have candles burning on the fruit crate and surely moths, spiraling from the night into her hideaway, confused by light that was not sun or moon, but fire.

★

ARTHUR
REKER

DO YOU WANNA
DANCE?

SCOTT HAD TROUBLE GETTING out of bed all day. Every time he tried, the guy would pull him back and they would be into it all over again. It was before eleven in the morning the first time Scott had made it as far as the bathroom. Even then, there was the guy behind Scott, hands on skin, playing with him until he finished whizzing. And before Scott had a chance to dry himself off, they guy turned him around and there in the bathroom took him in his mouth again. The next time Scott remembered, it was past three in the afternoon and they had spent all night and half the day making it every way Scott could imagine. On top of the covers, under the covers, beside the bed, against the brass headboard, in the shower, sideways, frontways, standing up, kneeling, leaning, rocking, gently, hard.

What was his name?

"I've really got to get up," Scott said and raised himself from the damp sheets and the guy's warm, damp, hairy muscular arms.

"I love you," the guy said, his wet mouth moving down to Scott's stomach and beyond.

Scott knew the guy's name the night before. He even looked

familiar. They had met and talked and danced and smoked. He knew his name.

"I love you," the guy said again.

The night before at the bar, mirrors and colored lights reflecting on his strong-featured face, he had whispered the same to Scott's ear. They were weaving, close and ragged and high, maybe too high, on the transparent flashing dance floor, barred from much in the way of free movement by the crush of amyled dancing bodies crowded around them.

Scott had been sitting at the bar, tip-tapping his off-balance barstool back and forth and peeling the label off his beer bottle when they first looked at each other. It was ten o'clock or so, early for the bar, even early for Scott, usually the hour when dwarfish closet sales-men came on with motel and marijuana offers. This face was familiar though, remembered from some party, or the bar, or the bookstore. Or work. Scott was a teller and saw hundreds of faces and bank balances. Being a teller made him good at names and good at faces. He pulled out a cigarette and began to smoke. When next he looked down the bar, the guy was smiling at him. Scott signaled the bartender and sent a drink to the smiler, who held it up in a toast and walked around the bar, walking like a tall and good-looking young man should, growing extremely handsome as he emerged from the dimness of the near-empty bar.

What was his name?

"Do you talk?" He smiled and asked loudly over the disco beat, his hand coming to rest near the crook of Scott's arm.

"Sure, anything," Scott said, and using his feet to push and turn around on the barstool, pulled his arm away to shake hands. "I'm Scott."

"Thanks for this." He held up the drink.

"What is it?" Scott asked.

"Gin tonic," he said. "I've seen you here before, but you were always with someone. I didn't want to bother you, you know." He looked to the floor and laughed, sipped his drink, and then looked, all green eyes and big lips, at Scott. "So," he breathed. "What brings you out tonight?"

"You're cute." Scott smiled. He was. Scott judged him to be over six feet, way over. Long brown hair, gorgeous full lips, generous green eyes, soccer-striped cotton T-shirt over tight chest and flat stomach and fading, frayed jeans covering strong legs.

"You'll do," he said, waited, and, seeing Scott's eyes narrow and forehead wrinkle together, he laughed and wrapped both hands around Scott's neck.

By ten-thirty they were kissing and laughing loudly. By eleven they were dancing. Eleven-thirty they smoked a joint in Scott's car. At midnight they were drunk, clutching, dancing to a thumping, chanting song endlessly repeating Mandalay, hey, hey, Mandalay, and he whispered into Scott's ear, "I love you."

Scott leaned back smiling, tried to focus. "What?" he said, weaving and shaking his head.

He put his hand into Scott's hair and pulled him closer, "I love you, that's all."

"That's good." Scott giggled. "I'm glad."

"Yeah," he said and stumbled into Scott. "You're hot. I love ya."

"Well, that's good," Scott repeated. "That's real good. I like hearing that. Thank you. That's good. But we're only dancing."

"You're a good dancer, too," he said. "I still love you."

"You say that to all the guys." Scott laughed.

"No, no," the guy said, his face suddenly serious. "I love you."

"Okay." Scott nodded his head. "That's something you're gonna have to prove."

"Prove? How?" he said. "Anything. I love you."

"Okay, okay, that's good, I can deal with this," Scott said, knees weakening as he pressed into the guy's hips and tried to focus on the shimmering ceiling. "Tell me something you don't want me to know."

His name? The guy's name? Did the guy say his name?

The guy said a lot of other things in bed, but nothing that Scott didn't want to know. The guy moved them around into different positions while they made it. He went on and on with smiles and talk about how beautiful Scott was, touching and remarking about specific areas of Scott's body, even comparing himself to Scott. For Scott there was no comparison. Small, compact, Scott had taken good care of himself, jogged regularly, played volleyball occasionally, so he had a strong, lithe body. The guy's, though, was built for a magazine fantasy. His chest was big and strong and hairy, while Scott's was strong, but not exactly massive. The guy's legs were long, his feet big, his arms muscled. Scott could stretch out face to face over the bigness of the guy, his feet rubbing the guy's shins, his hands chock full of the guy's chest, his stomach rolling across the guy's hips, all without touching the bed.

But his name. Did the guy ever say his name?

Then it was half a day later with the mid-afternoon bird songs of the last day of October pouring sun through the open window and across the bed. Scott was hungry, spent, weak. He had a party starting in a few hours that he had to get ready for and the guy was down on him again.

Jesus, I don't know if I can do this, Scott thought. The guy looked up at him and smiled, then pressed himself, swiveling hard and full into Scott's legs, squirming down and between, lifting legs up over his shoulders. Scott's brass bed squeaked, creaked, rolled, rocked against the wall, ringing out in a quick and steady rhythm the bang, bang, clang of a brutal blacksmith hammering away ozone demons, pounding white-hot metal and a bell with alternating fury. Scott arched electrified, his head burrowed back into the pillow, fists grabbed sheets, toes outstretched, his breath gasping involuntary fast bursts, eyes squeezing out cosmic, stinging tears of good, good, good.

★

DAVID VERNON

NEGATIVES FROM MR. TOBIAS'S VACATION

MR. TOBIAS AND JACQUES have broken up. Split. They are history. I am deeply saddened by this as I had real hope for them. The *Weekly Globe* recently reported that only one out of every seven relationships lasts. I thought this one had a chance. Also I guess I feel that I had a vested interest in this relationship because I was there in the beginning.

It started on a Monday. A Monday in January. If I check my desk calendar I could probably find the exact date. The morning started out the same as always. I arrived at the office at eight, Mr. Tobias came in at eight-thirty. I gave him his phone list, the paper, and a cup of herbal tea. He is usually a bit frantic on Monday mornings, but I remember thinking that day that Mr. Tobias seemed a bit anxious as if he were expecting something to happen. His mind wasn't really on the office. Usually while I'm placing his calls Mr. Tobias sits in his office and reads the paper, from top to bottom or from headline to obituary as my late husband Rodney used to say. But that Monday Mr. Tobias just sat in his office and gazed out his window. After I placed the calls Mr. Tobias seemed fidgety and left to take a walk down the hall. While he was gone there was a call.

"Mr. Tobias's office."

On the other end there was this small, nervous voice.

"Could I please talk to Mr. Tobias?"

"May I tell Mr. Tobias who is calling?"

I screen all of Mr. Tobias's calls because people phone just to badger him into making donations to this charity or that fund-raiser. Mr. Tobias would give money to all these people too, he's such a pushover. When these donation people call I get all the information from them and put them on hold as if I was passing the information on to Mr. Tobias. When I get back on the line I inform them that Mr. Tobias wishes to commend their commitment to such a worthy cause and to wish them the best of luck; in other words, beat it. Anyhow Mr. Tobias gives every year to The City of Hope and to Jerry's Kids. I've seen it on his taxes.

"Would you tell him that Jacques Finney is calling?"

"He's not here. Can you spell that for me?"

"Yeah, that's Finney, F-I-N-N-E-Y."

Now I know all of Mr. Tobias's friends, many of them middle-aged bachelors like himself. There is Mr. Denfeld, a CPA, and there is a friend of his from Stanford, Mr. Sacks. I get along well with all of his acquaintances. But until that morning I had never heard of any Jacques.

"Will he know what this is regarding?"

At this point Jacques began stuttering a bit.

"Well, let's see, you might tell him that, or remind him that we met last night over at the Avery's and he asked me to call him."

"I see."

"He can reach me at home today, if he wants. Let me leave you my number, it's 555-1876."

"I see. I will mention this to him when I see him, Mr. Finnish."

I do that on purpose, mispronounce names. When Mr. Tobias is socializing with someone that I do not approve of, I always let him know in this subtle way. He was seeing this woman two years ago, a real social climber. She knew of Mr. Tobias's peculiarities, but I guess she just liked being seen with him. Her name was Renata. I wouldn't ever get that poor woman's name right—oh dear, let's see, I called her Renaldo, Reunite, Rowena, Roldolfo, and once I even called her Bennito but I admit perhaps Bennito was pushing it.

Mr. Tobias would say to me, "Mildred, for the life of me sometimes I think you mispronounce Miss Garibaldi's name on purpose."

He knew. He also stopped seeing her shortly after that.

That Monday morning when Mr. Tobias returned from his walk, I gave him his messages. When he saw the one from Jacques his eyes lit up like a nickel slot machine in Reno. He had JACKPOT, JACKPOT, JACKPOT written on his face. I decided to let him know how I felt about it.

"That Mr. Finnish said that he had met you at the Avery's last night. Do you want me to pass the call on to one of the clerks?"

"No thank you, Mildred. I'll take care of it myself."

After he left that evening I was cleaning out his wastepaper basket before the janitors got there and I found a crumpled sheet of paper completely covered with Jacques Finney's name written over and over again, at least fifty times in all different types of handwriting. As I said, I was there in the beginning.

I told Mrs. Lewis, another widow who lives in my apartment, about Mr. Tobias's odd behavior. Of course whenever I tell Mrs. Lewis about Mr. Tobias I always substitute women in the place of men. Mrs. Lewis wouldn't understand and besides it's none of her business anyway. She said that I should leave poor Mr. Tobias alone and let him live his life. What Mrs. Lewis couldn't possibly understand is that in many ways I feel responsible for Mr. Tobias.

I'll be working for Mr. Tobias nine years next November. Before that I had worked for Mr. Jaska in Accounting for a year. My husband Rodney was ill and I was having trouble keeping my mind on my work. Mr. Jaska kept finding all these accounting errors I had made, bills weren't getting paid and it seemed like I couldn't do anything to please him. I overheard Mr. Jaska telling someone from Personnel that he was going to fire me. All of a sudden a few days after I overheard this I came into the office and Mr. Jaska wasn't there. It got late and he still didn't come in. Dorothy from Personnel called me up to her office and told me that Mr. Jaska had died in a car accident on the freeway that morning. Exactly eight days later my husband Rodney passed on. Of course I was out of my head with grief, but I wanted to get back to work right away to get my mind off of all this death. But it seemed that Mr. Jaska's replacement had heard stories about me. Turns out I had a bit of a reputation. Mr. Jaska had been telling everyone that I was incompetent and senile and frustrated and some other things that I'd rather not repeat if you don't mind. Nobody in the office wanted me working for them. And you know it's tough for us old gals to find a job. Now God knows that I don't wish harm on anyone, but this Mr. Jaska I do not miss.

Mr. Tobias started working for the company around that time, and I had seen him in the lunchroom and chatted with him in the elevator. He was always polite, meticulously dressed, and very funny in a quiet sort of way. He attended Rodney's funeral. He was the only one from the office who did besides a couple of girls from the front office. At the reception he asked me to work for him and I've been with him ever since.

I've seen Mr. Tobias succeed and move up in the company. He's had three promotions and he's not through yet. And he's much younger than most of the other executives; he'll be thirty-six in July.

Mr. Tobias and I have a wonderful relationship. I take his calls, make his appointments, make certain that he gets to where he's going on time. He trusts me. We never talk about it but I know about his life. We never talk about it but he trusts me to watch over him and shield him from those who want to take advantage of him. Mr. Tobias and I keep a very low profile. We get our work done and stay away from the rest of the office. We never talk about it but I take care of Mr. Tobias.

What Mrs. Lewis couldn't possibly understand is that Mr. Tobias is basically lonely like the rest of us. Even if he is peculiar in that way he deserves to be happy, too. Not to mention my livelihood is at stake. Suppose Mr. Tobias was to get real depressed about being alone and threw himself out the window or down the stairs, God forbid, then where would both of us be? I try and make him feel like he's not so alone.

I met Jacques a week later. He had stopped into the office without notice, which Mr. Tobias never appreciates.

"Do you have an appointment?"

He looked dumbfounded, as if the concept of an appointment never entered his mind.

"No, not really, just thought I'd stop by."

"I see. Well, we're on a schedule and cannot usually afford to be that spontaneous, but if you'll have a seat I'll let him know that you're here."

Jacques took a seat. I was quite confused by him. He was tall and thin and had a head full of black curly hair. His clothes were baggy but tastefully wrinkled. Now I've always said that an ironed suit is an attractive suit, but I must admit that the harried look suited him.

"Mr. Tobias, I am sorry to disturb you but that Mr. Finland decided to stop by without an appointment."

"Tell him I'll be right out, Mildred."

Jacques sat on the couch and nervously flipped through the magazines on the waiting table. I stopped what I was doing and took a cigarette break. I turned my chair around and just stared at him while he was reading, which only made him more self-conscious. He was wearing a strong cologne that I couldn't place. It filled the room. I coughed a bit to let him know that he was wearing too much. And every time he came to the office after that he wore a bit less.

Mr. Tobias came out of his office and greeted Jacques.

"I was around the block so I thought I'd find out what you're doing for lunch."

"Nothing, I'm free."

"Excuse me, Mr. Tobias, but you have a one-thirty lunch with Mr. Benjamin."

"Well, he always cancels out on me, Mildred. Everyone cancels out on me. Now it's my turn. Just call him and tell him I'm sorry but something came up. We have to learn to be a little flexible in life."

Then they left for a three-hour lunch. Imagine.

I called Mr. Benjamin and apologized, but I also sent over a bottle of wine 'cause that's the way to do it.

So Jacques started calling every day and Mr. Tobias would always take his call no matter who he was talking to. Once Mr. Tobias even put Derwood Mendelson, the company's vice-president, on hold so that he and Jacques could decide on which restaurant they were going to meet at.

One time I overheard Mr. Tobias tell Jacques, "Sometimes I forget what my life was like before I met you."

Another time I heard him say, "It frightens me that I find myself missing you the way I do."

Then Jacques started sending cards every few days or so. Now I open all of Mr. Tobias's mail except for anything marked Personal and Confidential. All of Jacques' letters came marked Personal and Confidential. He used different names each time in the upper left corner like Sammy Davis, Jr., or John Wilkes Booth, but I always recognized his handwriting. He has very distinct handwriting, very neat but the letters tremble a little bit and it puts the whole word off kilter. Mr. Tobias never threw any of Jacques' cards in the wastepaper basket so they must have been sweet.

What Mr. Tobias said that day about being a little flexible in life stayed in my mind. Perhaps it was time to loosen up a bit and let someone like Jacques into our lives. I began to accept Jacques and to be happy for both of them. I even noticed changes in Mr. Tobias as a direct result of this relationship. He seemed calmer and more at ease around the office. Now Mr. Tobias is very sweet, but he has always been a bit of a fanatic about certain things. He likes everything just so and he washes his hands a hundred times a day. He keeps a bottle of Lysol in his bottom left-hand drawer and scrubs his desk and phone receiver when he gets in every morning and right before he leaves. I noticed though that he had stopped worrying so much about germs and the centering of his nameplate on his desk. He was even late to the office a few times, but I think perhaps that was going a bit too far.

Mr. Tobias also started going out and doing more. He would tell me about ball games and concerts that he would go to with friends, but I always knew that he went to those events with Jacques. One time Mr. Tobias told me about a revival of *Camelot* he had just seen. A few days later when Jacques was in the waiting room he was humming that love song from *Camelot*. I'm familiar with the music 'cause Rodney and I saw the play years ago when Robert Goulet was in it.

The first time they said "I love you" must have been sometime between the first and second week in May. That is when I noticed that Mr. Tobias ended all his phone conversations with Jacques by saying, "Me too." It was really quite sweet. When I would hear Mr. Tobias say "Me too," it would send me shivers. Mrs. Lewis says that shivers can be caused by a lot of things, most of them curable. What does she know.

Even when Rodney was pretty far gone he would call me at work and say, "I love you." Of course I wasn't hiding anything like Mr. Tobias is so I'd say, "Rodney, hon, I love you too." And I did.

Sometimes in bed after the eleven o'clock news and when the apartment would get settled and the only sound you would hear would be of a whole apartment tucked into bed for the night, I would think about Mr. Tobias and Jacques. I'd imagine them lying on the flowered sofa in Mr. Tobias's living room. Jacques would be watching "The Animal Kingdom" on television and Mr. Tobias would be struggling to finish the *Herald*'s crossword puzzle. I'd imagine Jacques bringing Mr. Tobias his medication with a glass of cool tap water, which Mr. Tobias would take without looking up. Jacques would then rub the back of Mr. Tobias's neck with his two thumbs pressing upward. Mr. Tobias would never have to look behind to see who was there. It was Jacques behind him and it always would be. I would think of this while I was in bed. Real love. The stuff that people like Mrs. Lewis only read about.

Mr. Tobias and Jacques took a trip together in June to Hawaii. I know because I made Mr. Tobias's airline and hotel reservations. He told me that he was traveling alone but when I called to confirm the flight, I asked the reservations lady to confirm one for Jacques Finney as well. Sure enough, after a few minutes of checking, the lady told me that Jacques was on the flight and had a seat request right next to Mr. Tobias.

The office was quiet without Mr. Tobias. He said that he wasn't planning on calling in so I took a few days off to take care of my friend from down the block, Mrs. Glickenhouse, another widow. She had tripped and fallen down a flight of stairs a few days earlier. Mrs. Glickenhouse was a mass of bruises and oozing wounds. Her legs had swelled up with fluid. It hurt her to move in even the slightest way. She was also a bit down in the dumps because neither of her children who both lived on the other coast were planning on visiting her.

"If it's going to take something more serious than this for them to come see me, then I don't know what," she would say.

She was also a bit worried, because after I went back to work she would have to have a live-in maid to take care of her. Although we never talked about it we had both heard horror stories about these live-in people who trained at the Heinrich Himmler school of compassion.

I told Mrs. Glickenhouse what I always tell my friends when they get depressed.

"Don't focus on the bad, just think of everything else you have to look forward to."

Of course most of the time I didn't mean it. What most of these women had to look forward to was a studio apartment at Forest Lawn.

Mr. Tobias returned from Hawaii with a fantastic tan. I was dying to hear all about his trip, but naturally he gave me only the sketchiest of details.

Jacques came in a few days later with an even more impressive tan. While he was waiting on the couch I saw them in his hands. A white envelope from the one-hour photo lab. Pictures from their vacation. I was tempted to ask Jacques about the pictures. I wanted to tell him that I knew. I knew about the trip and I knew about him and Mr. Tobias. I wanted to tell Jacques that I didn't care and moreover, that I was happy for them. I really wanted to see those pictures.

I was hoping that Jacques would go to the restroom and leave the pictures on his chair.

"You're looking quite dapper today, Mr. Finney."

"Why thank you, Mildred, you're looking pretty snazzy yourself today. Do you have a date or something?"

"Oh, no, Mr. Finney, no date. I'm going after work to visit a friend of mine in a nursing home. Mrs. Wakefield, another widow."

Then I looked at Jacques. I stared at a place on his cheek where he was peeling a bit. He noticed me staring at him in that funny way. I pretended to catch myself staring and looked back down at a letter I was proofreading, then made certain that Jacques saw me sneaking glances at his face. I thought that if I made him self-conscious enough he would excuse himself to take a look in the bathroom mirror, and maybe he would leave the photographs behind. It would have worked too, but Mr. Tobias came out of his office and invited Jacques inside.

After they left I checked Mr. Tobias's office. They had taken the pictures but left the envelope with the negatives behind.

It's hard to tell with negatives. There was a lot of copper and a lot of green. I flipped through the negatives, careful not to get fingerprints on any of them and conscious of all the sounds of typing and people moving about outside Mr. Tobias's office. Their faces were bronzed and heroic. It was difficult to tell them apart. Their hair was silver except that Jacques's hair was wild and windblown and Mr. Tobias's was short and stayed put. There was a negative of Mr. Tobias by a giant rock three times his height. There was another negative of Jacques wearing what looked like a rubber snake around his neck. And there was a negative of Mr. Tobias and Jacques together, arms around each other's shoulders.

Seeing them together in Hawaii was sweet and heartening, but the negatives also looked a bit sinister. In all the negatives streams of light glared through their ears, eyes, and mouths. All of this light and distortion made even the happiest-looking image seem harsh and unsettling. I put them back in the white envelope just as I found them and took a long lunch.

A few weeks later it happened. Mrs. Lewis said that it wouldn't last. Mr. Tobias didn't come into the office for a few days. He was very short with me on the phone and told me that he had the flu that had been going around. I started telling about when my friend, Mrs. Lieberman, had the flu and how she was in bed for weeks. Mr.

Tobias usually enjoys hearing about my friends. But that day he just said, "Really, Mildred, I just can't talk to you right now."

I could tell from his voice that he and Jacques were having a fight. I can always tell, and I'm usually right about these things.

A letter came to Mr. Tobias in the mail from Jacques the same day that Mr. Tobias returned to work. A full letter. It felt like maybe three or four pages long. Jacques' full name was printed on the return corner this time.

When Mr. Tobias came into the office he was in a terrible mood. He left the paper and the other mail and took Jacques' letter into his office, shutting the door.

I turned off my typewriter and unplugged the phone. I heard him reading the letter, concentrating, turning the page. I listened to him reading it and found myself holding my breath. It didn't seem like such a good letter. Silence. Then I heard the sound of paper ripping, Mr. Tobias tearing this letter apart. I could hear the pieces of paper float into the wastepaper basket, hitting the sides as they fell. I could see them falling. Mr. Tobias left the office.

"Cancel my day, Mildred."

He didn't even look at me as he left. I heard him walk down the hall. I heard the elevator door open then shut. Mr. Tobias was gone.

I plugged the phone back in and saw my hand shaking a bit, my stomach was in knots. Something terrible had happened. What could Jacques have said to Mr. Tobias in that letter?

I snuck into Mr. Tobias's office and saw the tiny pieces of paper under his desk. Some had made the wastepaper basket and some had not. I took a handful and poured the pieces on his desk in a small mound and tried to make some sense of it. Letters. There were lots of letters. There were pieces of words. My hand was still shaking as I tried to put it all together.

I found a few *sorry*'s. I found a phrase, *miss it all*. The word *lover* at least twice. The word *coconut*, which confused me.

It was all laid out in front of me in hundreds of shreds of paper. I saw the word *caring* more than once. But the big picture still eluded me.

I dropped to the floor and looked on the carpet. There must be more. I scooped up a smaller handful and poured them on the table. A word, *never*. A bigger piece of paper. A big phrase. I felt as if I had uncovered an archaeological find. It was a sentence, *so sorry I lied to you about HIV*. And I found the piece of paper where it was signed, *Yours forever, Jacques*.

Well, I had to open a window in Mr. Tobias's office. I was stunned. The story was all laid out in front of me and made sense. Jacques had lied. He had lied to me and he had lied to Mr. Tobias. He had practiced deception. We had trusted him, allowed him into our office, offered him coffee, given of ourselves. We made him feel welcome. I was nauseous and repulsed. Then I thought of Mr. Tobias wandering the streets by himself, both of us hurting over the same lie. It all made sense. Jacques had had an affair with some man named HIV. I looked back through the scraps of paper and saw his name mentioned a few other times, always in capital letters. Jacques had been unfaithful. It felt like such a slap in the face to us.

Mr. Tobias returned to the office a few days later. We did our work. There was no humming from his office. He didn't come out and comment on my hair or my outfit. He just sat in his office and did his work.

I overheard bits of conversations Mr. Tobias had with a few of his friends about Jacques.

He told his friend Mr. Shankle, "The damage may have been done but it's the lie that I'll never forgive him for." Mr. Tobias told another friend on the phone, "He'll never hear from me again."

Mr. Tobias's friend Mr. Denton came to visit him in the office one afternoon.

I heard Mr. Denton tell him, "At a time like this you'll need to be together."

Mr. Tobias told his friend, "But I don't love him anymore, not a bit".

I too had anger toward Jacques. And I also felt responsible. I tried to protect Mr. Tobias from people, people who would be cruel to him. He put himself in my hands. I trusted Jacques and I accepted him. I had failed Mr. Tobias and I hated myself for it.

One night after work I was halfway home when I realized that I left my checkbook in my office. I went back only to find Mr. Tobias still there. He was in his office with his bottle of Lysol out on his desk. He was scrubbing down everything in his office. He was wringing out a thick red rag that reeked of ammonia. The top button of his shirt was undone and his tie dangled loosely around his neck. He didn't see me as I picked up my checkbook from my desk. Mr. Tobias was scrubbing his pens and pencils as I left for home.

A few weeks later I was sitting in the hospital cafeteria after visiting Mrs. Crenshaw, also a widow. She had hurt her hip while getting off a bus. I was in the cafeteria alone and looked around me. I saw brightness; the chrome in that cafeteria sparkled, the white of the medical uniforms. At these neighboring tables I saw people with failing health. These people were sick and dying. I saw a woman in a a wheelchair, so frail that a gust of wind would have taken her away. She was smiling and holding onto another woman's hand. I felt surrounded and overwhelmed with forgiveness. These people forgave doctors for being unable to restore their health, their youth. They forgave God for permitting them to suffer. They forgave their children for visits that never occurred. And in this cafeteria I too found forgiveness. I forgave Jacques. I let it go. I let it go right there in the cafeteria.

Jacques and Mr. Tobias have split. They're finished. It's difficult for me because I came to care for both of them as a couple. Did I mention the story in the *Globe* about one out of every seven couples? Perhaps I did.

Jacques does call from time to time, although not lately. Mr. Tobias never takes his calls. And it is hard for me to refuse Jacques, to not put his call through to Mr. Tobias, to lie to him, to be cold like we had never shared everything we had shared.

Mr. Tobias still does his work but he doesn't seem quite as focused as he used to. And he's not so careful about his appearance lately. From time to time I see him gazing outside his full-length window that overlooks the freeway. I want to walk into his office and tell him that life goes on. I want to tell him that to be healed, one must forgive. What I really want to tell him strangely enough is my usual comment to the women I visit.

"Don't focus on the bad. Let the bad go. Just think of everything you have to look forward to."

But in Mr. Tobias's case I really mean it. And if it can work for the ladies about to be shipped off to Forest Lawn it could work for him, too.

Jacques and Mr. Tobias have split. Broken apart. I was there in the beginning, you know. I still can't get over it.

★

BIA
LOWE

I ALWAYS WRITE
ABOUT MY MOTHER
WHEN I START
TO WRITE

WHEN I WAS FOUR I shared a bathroom with my mother and father. And one late fall afternoon, as my room was darkening, I sat at my tiny desk and watched my mother in the bathroom as she dressed for a dinner party. I loved to watch her stand over the sink. The sheen of her slip in the bathroom light slid over the curves of her body like my finger in a bowl of frosting. I loved my mother's body—her wide toenails, her skin smelling like tomato soup, the space between her breasts brown with sun and close to the sound of her heart.

She was in every way my female deity. Now every woman in the act of love resembles her—as I, looking up into a cherished face, reach through time to relive the only miracle I ever knew: I once lived weightless, in trust, without language.

But at that moment, as I watched her reel in a flurry of smells and powders, I must have felt myself to be quite separate from her, because I was suddenly seized with a desire to court her. To bear gifts as if riding on horseback from some faraway kingdom. I wanted to lay them, breathtaking, at her feet, and by doing so bind her heart to mine, ever after to be buoyed up like a life raft on a calmed ocean.

Alas, my kingdom at four was too small, and consisted only of treasures borrowed from her: my tiny green pegboard desk, my cup of cocoa, my pencils, my lamp, my bed, my coloring books. Even the shoes on my feet she bought me. Nevertheless, I was determined to have her see me as her suitor. I began to think of ways to transform the contents of my room into things which, by becoming personalized by me, would become extraordinary to her.

For example, a pencil could be sharpened at both ends. No longer that simple stick spilling color in one downward direction, the pencil was now a baton, risen up in such a vivid display of symmetry, it nearly spun into flight on its own.

And what of three of those former pencils—red, green, and purple—fixed together with a rubber band? Three wands, three wishes granted; not, no not, mere childish fragments scrambled together from my pegboard desk.

And then, my best idea came to me as I looked at my cup of cocoa. Like the prince trapped inside the body of the frog, that humble white cup, so maligned by the everyday, so misrepresented as a mere vessel, was a work of art waiting to occur.

I quickly snapped a rubber band around the cup, unveiling its true nature, and with my other gifts, presented it to my mother. I love you, I told her, as if those were the passwords to the gate, and my gifts the tickets to prove it. And I waited for the gate to open.

My mother told me, in the kindest way possible, that she knew I loved her, that she acknowledged my eagerness, but that my gifts were hastily constructed, showed no real consideration of her, and did not, of themselves, express anything in particular.

"You really have to think about what you give people," she told me.

I returned to my room, which was by now very dark except for a ring of light around the lamp. It seemed to me to be a shabby light, too tiny, too yellow, and beyond its uncanny fringes the room loomed and echoed. And there in its plain and singular warmth were the vulnerable and common objects I knew so well, but could not transform. And as I stood looking toward that small circle of lamplight, I felt for the first time an inexpressible loneliness.

Now every act of writing resembles this, because I must think very hard about what I give people. I want to offer a cup with a rubber band around it and say, this is more than just a cup, take it and we will float up together like that moment in dreams, or that moment I reach for, looking up into the faces of the women I love, from some faraway kingdom, bearing the inexpressible.

★

DAVID WATMOUGH

THANK YOU SIEGFRIED SASSOON

PAIN GROPED ABOUT THE atramentous corridors of my gut. There on the ferry my contorted face offered no echo to the smiling tourists sprawled about the sundeck as the *Haida Queen* hooted her way through sail-dotted Active Pass en route to Victoria. I lay tense under the thrall of uncertainty. Was it a heart attack? Had cancer won an obscene victory under the smooth skin of my belly? Dumb questions! I had no clue to my agony.

There was *one* certainty. I loathed my jolly fellow voyagers. I yearned for the dark of a cave where I could sob unseen. Things which normally delighted, the numerous pairs of bald eagles disturbed by the ship's horn, degenerated into irksome distractions. Their soaring appeal atrophied under my pain.

Less than an hour later all was to change. My lover turned human again and no longer just a remote sounding board for my whimpers as he deftly sped the miles from harbor to hospital.

In the cool of that red brick building, soothed by the hum of high tech, the dreadful gnawing finally subsided. I was left only a containable ache as memento of the brutal eruption aboard the *Haida Queen*.

Self-pity stole as anodyne over a fifty-year-old hulk, wrinkled and

65

worn with excess. A Davey Bryant made nervous from the torrents of medical propaganda prodding all middle-aged America at the brink of a grosser reality about to envelop our gay community.

Would the hurt come back? That was the persistent nag as I lay prostrate before the therapy of strangers. Even those anxieties dimmed as I was wheeled down the interminable corridors of the building's basement and into the confines of an elevator where my stretcher competed for space with the muscular orderly propelling me and a Filipino nurse, who softly but persistently pestered me with questions for her open pad.

"Davey Bryant ... Aged fifty ... Home ... Vancouver ... Height: 'Have a guess' ... Weight: 'Don't remember' ... on and on, ending with the Anglican religion and a bachelor status.

Then I was out of the elevator, trundled down a polished hallway to a small ward that was seemingly empty. I lay on my back with my left arm nursing a needle leading upward via a series of plastically hinged capillaries to an intravenous drip.

A nurse with a resolute smile gave instructions over preserving my urine even when vacating my bowels, took temperature and pulse, and asked if I was allergic to anything.

"The sight of blood, Nurse."

"How are we feeling now?"

"Rather frail, Nurse."

She left me in the company of three empty beds, billowing drapes, and the sound of Victoria's brisk breezes playing in the screen over the lower portions of the window. Ken was coming to see me before his dinner, which meant two hours later.

I thought I would doze awhile. I really did feel as frail as I'd told her: drained and drowsy from the pain's roughing. But sleep wouldn't come. At first it was just the persistent words of the bearded young doctor who'd loomed over me in Emergency.

"We think you might have a kidney stone which is trying to pass. It's a very painful business, so we think you should be admitted."

Those crumbs of information provided a relief—however much hedged with scientific caution. I finally grew tired of imagining that sharp-edged *stone* describing the contours of my innards as it headed for the narrow confines of the urethra. Not only grew tired but restless with apprehension.

I forced my mind elsewhere—back to adolescence, when as a flu-struck student confined to bed I learned by heart a poem of Siegfried Sassoon.

> Night, with a gust of wind, was in the ward
> Blowing the curtain to a glimmering curve.

I spoke the words aloud. Somehow they helped shape my current experience and thus regulate it. I still felt tired but I also felt better.

In the end, though, I grew fretful—resenting the disruption of our weekend plans. I wondered whether at that moment Ken was sitting having drinks with Tom and Simon, with whom we had been scheduled to stay for two nights. Old friends both of them. Tom a librarian at the University of Victoria, his lover an assistant deputy minister with the provincial government.

I pondered *their* lives for a moment. Two healthy incomes, an agreeable Oak Bay home near the gentle coastline and sun-sparkling sea. That line of thought led to a fleeting anxiety over whether my current hospitalization would be adequately covered by my provincial medical plan.

My bed was cranked up to allow a sitting position, but what was about me didn't make for much viewing interest. I wouldn't look at my arm and the IV stemming from it. The contraption made me queasy. I recalled more lines from the Sassoon poem:

> He stirred, shifting his body;
> then the pain
> Leapt like a prowling beast,
> and gripped and tore
> His groping dreams with grinding
> claws and fangs.

Suddenly a blanket moved on a chair adjacent to the opposite bed. I felt my skin prick with alarm. I was mistaken. It wasn't a blanket but a tartan throw rug. The detail rapidly disintegrated in the emergence of an extravagant mop of red hair crowning an acne'd face.

The bed curtains were pulled close enough to effectively screen me from the vacant bed to my right as well as the one opposite. I'd drawn them to the degree the gap between them neatly framed the head I could now see.

Never had I felt more committed to the instinct of writer as covert observer clandestinely absorbing every aspect of the victim's unguarded moment.

As my fellow patient sat up I saw it was definitely a male. I also registered that he was young and appallingly crippled. Every straining gesture he made was an affront.

It wasn't only compassion that shaped my reaction. As I watched his quadriplegic contortions [which at one point brought his face upside down to the floor so that the red hair swept like a grotesque broom] I grew progressively upset.

Why did I have to witness such indignity? The intimidation of that onslaught of pain aboard the ferry and the subsequent apprehension was sufficient without this bonus obscenity! I longed to close the drapes, eliminate that offending peephole.

But I was afraid, fearful he'd take the action as a slight to those spindly legs folded monkey-like about his wheelchair. I didn't want my demeaning prudery recorded. . . .

Events soon proved that any discretion on my part was unwarranted. The "monkey-boy" didn't want communion with the likes of me. I'm sure his sharp glance across the polished floor noted my presence—but not by the slightest gesture did he acknowledge it.

The only thing betraying his awareness was the peculiar positions he proceeded to place himself in as he described mini-acrobatics in his chair.

His woolly hair brushing the ward floor was only the beginning of his performance. Parts of his body seemed infinitely stronger than others. His hands. And the backs of his knees, from which he appeared able to support his whole frame.

I decided his display of simian antics was a sly way of showing off. The reflection was interrupted by the arrival of a nurse. For the first time I heard his voice—and that was as disturbing as everything else.

From between the lips on the upside-down face came the plangent tones of a light tenor, the epitome not only of normality but of confidence, grace, and charm.

Listening to that voice in a radio play, say, I would have sworn it belonged to a handsome hero in the invisible studio. I thought it beautiful.

"What on earth are you doing, Philip?" the young woman asked primly.

"My *exercises*, dum-dum! Always after I wake up. I'm not really awake until I've done this."

"You'll break your neck if you aren't careful! And I can't talk to you properly while you're upside-down. Will you please stop acting like a sloth and behave normally?"

His voice didn't lose its modulation. It just dropped a whole octave. "You ask the *hardest* things, Patricia."

I couldn't see her properly, but I received her sudden silence and guessed at her cheek color.

"Philip, you can't be doing yourself any good. Now sit up properly in your chair. I want to talk to you."

"Ball me out more like!" said the upside-down mouth above the eyes, above the wiry Afro hairdo. "OK, angel face. Here we go."

I inclined my head as the apparition returned to a sitting position but peeked again just as Philip crossed his matchstick legs on the seat of the invalid chair. Thin arms attached to huge hands crisscrossed his chest. Fingers with incongruously long nails clutched the empty sleeves of his pajama top. He stretched out an arm in the direction of the locker under the window sill. From there he withdrew an odd-looking brush. He started to halfheartedly tackle his mop of red hair. As far as I could make out it had no effect.

"How does that look?" he asked. And before the nurse could answer—"Stupid, eh? It's meant for blacks—not redheads like me."

"Well, I can hardly see your face. You haven't shaved since you came in this time, have you, Philip?"

"Don't tell me you *care*, Patricia! You've never mentioned it before."

"Your beard's never been that long before."

His voice turned bitter. "I've got all these pimples. I'll only bleed if I try."

I again blanked out his looks. Just ached in sympathy for his teenaged self. But she wasn't to be swayed by adolescent preoccupations.

"Nonsense!" she said briskly. "Jim offered to help you. I heard him. You just enjoy looking a mess. I think it's some craziness in you."

He grew more sullen. "What the hell would you know? You're not a man. And you're not me."

She was remorseless. "Quite right. I'm your *nurse*—and I want your pulse, your temperature, and to change your tampon."

I observed her suiting actions to words as she bent her broad back toward him, grasping the emaciated wrist and inserting a thermometer into his mouth. The tampon business I could only surmise. I guessed it was something to do with his incontinence and his sad reliance on people like her.

The thermometer, plus the tampon change, kept him quiet for a while. When he spoke again it was with direct reference to the latter.

"I hate these goddamned things," he muttered. "I don't wear 'em at home—why do I have to in here?"

"Ask Dr. Hassid. Your temperature's down nicely, though. I have a hunch you'll soon be leaving us again."

"This evening? Like before supper?"

"No, Philip. It's just a guess on my part. I shouldn't have mentioned it. It's entirely up to Dr. Hassid, you know that. I will tell you one thing, though."

"What's that, angel face?"

"Stop your nonsense! You stayed up all hours last night, didn't you? That's why you've been sleeping all day. Did you go down to the women's ward again? That's just the kind of thing, young man, which'll keep you in here longer than you want. You get over-excited—then over-tired. It's *that* which brings on your attacks."

"You sound like my bloody mother."

"Thank you, but I doubt whether we're quite the same age."

"She's been dead for five years, so it doesn't matter. When you keep bitching at me, though, you turn into a battle-ax. You can't be much older than me. How old are you, sexy Patricia?"

The innuendo wasn't wasted on her. "*Nurse*, please. And my age for the likes of a minor like you, Philip McDairmaid, is a state secret."

"I bet you're younger than my sister," he continued unabashedly. "She's twenty-four. On the other hand, you're better developed."

This time she made no response. Instead she swung suddenly around to face eavesdropping me. I lay motionless.

"Supper will be along soon," she said, turning once more and collecting some bits and pieces from his bed before starting to leave.

"Aren't you going to help me get onto the bed?" Philip asked.

She didn't slow her step, let alone look around. "You're quite capable on your own. I've watched you *dozens* of times. Supper soon, remember."

When she'd gone he sat there staring in her wake. "Cunt," he said softly. Then heaved himself after a couple of botched efforts onto the bed from his chair.

Night with a gust of wind was in the ward . . .

I woke abruptly. It was now night and the drapes were being blown in my direction in:

. . . a Glimmering Curve . . .

I peeped between the slit of my bed curtains at my neighbor. He was sitting up, a knitted shawl about him, covering all save the pimply face and unruly red hair. The main ward lights had been turned off and we were illuminated only by the bulbs behind our beds. I looked at my watch. It was eleven o'clock. Supper seemed ages ago. I wasn't feeling hungry. I wished Ken were lying by my side.

My pain was now a dull thing—reduced really to discomfort. It was incessant, though. And I wanted to pee again. I reached down and brought the flask up from the floor to put between my legs. I tried to make no noise because I didn't want to attract Philip. But when I carefully placed the now warmed bottle back on the floor, I felt his eyes raking me, even if his head didn't move.

It wasn't just the absence of bright light that brought a new atmosphere to the ward. The moaning wind through the screens had something to do with it. So did the shadows and silence. I thought my nose detected something more than the persistent odor of my own urine. As I gave my olfactory imagination rein I was convinced I could detect the smell of feces from his bedside. That made me stir.

I wanted no more thoughts of things like the stench of blood or the purpose of Philip's grotesque tampons. I strove for fairer notions.

With persistence I managed to stretch recollection back to great gray whales migrating off Chesterman's Cove and how sunny the world had seemed that brisk May day. But the cameo proved fragile, impermanent: floated into segments, drifting finally into chaos as fresh configurations of wind-curved sails in Active Pass and the balm of the Gulf Island scenery conflicted with memories of my belly turning to fire.

I tensed there in bed—uncertain whether I was reliving the afternoon's journey on the ferry or suffering a new assault on my insides.

External events resolved all that. A new presence—the night nurse for C4—had entered the ward. It was to me she came first.

"Davey?"

I almost stopped breathing.

"Mr. Bryant? Are you awake?" It was a tough, no-nonsense voice which I immediately hated. "I have to check your statistics. Wrist please. And keep this under your tongue."

I reluctantly slithered my arm to the edge of the coverlet for her to take my pulse, and opened my mouth again for the intrusion of the thermometer. I looked at her through the fronds of eyelashes. I tried to rationalize my hostility—told myself I was feeling too wan to resist her bossiness as it savaged my vulnerable bed-self.

I was quite astonished when, to retrieve the thermometer, she leaned closer to my face and addressed me in a warmer voice.

"Not to worry! We'll soon have you on your feet and out of here! He's not been bothering you from across there, has he? Trouble is, he's a night owl and sleeps most of the day. That's why we try each time to fix him up with a ward to himself, poor kid. Can't often do it, of course. Like tonight."

I listened to her voice as much as her words. It now seemed more husky than gruff. I wondered if she were a dyke.

"He's no bother to me," I whispered dishonestly. "Thanks for asking, though."

She gave my arm a squeeze before she turned to her other patient. I noticed in the flare from the curtains slit that she was tall and slim. I'd already observed she was quite devoid of makeup when her face had confronted mine. I had subsequently to memorize her facial expressions, for it was too dim to make out much as she busied herself over Philip.

That didn't interfere with the sound track. I just strained my ears harder in comprehension. While young Philip continued to speak in mellifluous tones, his speech was louder than before—as if he and his helper were alone in the ward. It was also clear their conversation had been honed over many such nocturnal sessions.

"That bitch didn't do as I asked."

"You've no right to call her that. Or any other woman, for that matter! So don't be uncouth with me. I'm your friend, remember?"

"I hope you're going to cooperate, Enid."

"You know very well that depends."

"Yeah, well, *depends* is what it's all about with me, isn't it? I *depend*. I *depend* on bitches like that Pat, who refused to help me onto the bed. I *depend* on that fink Hassid, who treats me like a kid who should go bye-byes when it suits his fuckin' hospital routine. I'm sick and tired of it all. Now, will you *please* come over here, Nurse Bicknell, and brush my hair. My hand's tired."

"Do you need a change of things, Philip? If so, I'll call Jim."

"I don't want Jim. I want *you*."

That didn't earn an instant reply.

"Your hair looks all right to me."

"It needs brushing back there where it knots."

"I've seen you manage that perfectly well."

"I told you—my hand needs a rest."

"So let it rest."

"I didn't say it was tired from brushing my hair, Enid."

I stirred in my pool of darkness, hotly embarrassed for her. Now I wanted to repudiate all writerly instincts over playing the spy. I wondered how she was registering his insinuations. I also wondered just how far he dared go. Stupid me! I was soon answered on both counts. These were hospital *professionals* I was overhearing.

"I didn't think it was. You don't sit there brushing your hair in the middle of the night—not even you!"

"Come a bit closer, there's a gal," he wheedled. "You don't have to be so standoffish—like that asshole Patricia."

"What's the matter, Philip? Something bothering you?"

Her voice was softer again. More like when she'd addressed me.

"Jesus! You know what's bothering me!" He paused. "What have I got to live for like this? Answer me that!"

"You've got plenty, Philip. You've got more guts than the rest of them put together. Everyone on the staff admires you and what you've done with your life since you first came in. How many times do I have to tell you that?"

"I don't care about the staff. I don't care about all that other shit either. What I want to know about is *this*. Here! Take a look! What the hell am I going to do all my life with this useless object? That's the only male thing I've got left since the paralysis. And it's literally fucking useless!"

I winced as much for the sob in his voice as the bleakness of his expression. I saw her white uniform, framed against the window as she sat down beside him on the bed. Her voice underwent further transformation. It was soft to the point of crooning. I could think only of a mother and an unhappy child.

"There," she soothed, cradling his fuzzy mop of hair. "It's all right. Let me help. There . . . there . . ."

I could take no more. My trespass swamped me in shame—forced me to bury ears and eyes between my two pillows.

> *. . . night. He was blind; he could not see the*
> *stars, glinting among the wraiths of wandering cloud;*
> *queer blots of color, purple, scarlet, green,*
> *Flickered and faded in his drowning eyes.*

Under-the-eyelid sights, familiar since childhood, set me free from the complications of hospitals. Into my head came the sound of Sassoon's rain—or was it the noise of the sea we can always summon by sticking fingers into ears?

> *. . . rain he could hear it rustling through*
> *the dark; Fragrance and passionless music woven as*
> *one Warm rain on drooping roses; pattering showers that*
> *Soak the woods; not the harsh rain that sweeps Behind*
> *the thunder, but a trickling peace, Gently and slowly*
> *washing life away.*

The dreams from blind eyes and deaf ears were old friends. I didn't need the British poet for the wind in the waving fronds of tamarisk in a Vancouver garden, the dying mackerel skies over the northwest Pacific, or a glint of stars above yellow broom on the crumbling cliffs of Point Grey.

When I'd recouped my strength and poise, removed my head from those ostrich pillows, and craned my neck to stare once more across the ward, it was to find the nurse had gone. The contorted contours of Philip were barely detectable amid the heap of bed clothes. I raised myself on my elbows and peered harder.

I'd been mistaken. There *was* no Philip. Nor was there a wheelchair. Only the rumpled sheets and blanket piled in one corner of the bed—like a lonely desert dune. I didn't linger over the image. I returned to the safer familiarity of the close of gay Siegfried's poem about a dying soldier.

> *So he went, And there was silence in the*
> *summer night; Silence and safety; and the veils of*
> *sleep.*

The absence of both his body and doomed self was an immense weight lifted. But for middle-aged me—dimly aware of uncharted gay shadows—there was silence but no true safety, no veiled sleep. In a vain attempt to dispel a gathering apprehension I spoke aloud the poem's final ominous line.

Then, far away, the thudding of the guns.

But, of course, the guns came closer and finally decimated us. . . .

★

JEANE JACOBS

SHE WHO KEEPS LAUGHING

IT WAS THE SUMMER the Whites called 1875, an old Comanche woman saw the buffalo disappear into the ground near the Black Hills.

She Who Keeps Laughing would soon be thirty and had become the only woman hunter among the Crazy Dog Kiowas. She had heard stories of other Kiowa bands that had one or two women among them who were proficient at hunting. This encouraged She to continue to hunt long after her woman parts began to appear.

When She was twenty-one, her Brother, Horse With No Heart, arranged the marriage between She and Thunders Loud Voice. Thunders agreed to the arrangement because Horse had promised him the earsplitting rifle made by the Whites.

Thunders Loud Voice was an important man and already had four wives. Since he had to satisfy his other women he only came to She very few times. This was a good thing because She hated it when he crawled under her buffalo robe poking his huge man part into her.

She and Thunders had been married for eight winters and She had grown very close to his second wife, Rain Falls. During the winter they put their buffalo robes together and slept against each other to stay warm. She Who Keeps Laughing took pleasure in the way Rain Falls' breast fit in between her own as they wrapped their arms around each other's bodies.

Thunders Loud Voice seemed to spend most of his time with Brown Bear Cub, his third wife. Brown Bear Cub always had open legs when Thunders was anywhere nearby. On occasions when Thunders would be sitting by his fire after the evening meal, Brown Bear Cub would lift her buckskin skirt and wave her backside in his face. Thunders would smile and walk slowly into Brown Bear Cub's tipi.

She Who Keeps Laughing and Rain Falls would give each other a grin because even though many winters had passed they still enjoyed sleeping with their bodies touching each other, with their hands and mouths searching and satisfying long into the night.

Now it had been many moons since Thunders Loud Voice entered their tipi. She and Rain Falls kept up their share of the work, so the other wives had no complaints about them. She also brought in plenty of good meat from her hunting trips. Rain Falls had borne two sons for Thunders, but She Who Keeps Laughing was considered a no good wife because she was barren.

During the winter Thunders and She sometimes hunted together. He appreciated her skills and they shared a mutual respect for one another.

The sun was beginning to fade and the air became cool. She Who Keeps Laughing walked slowly into the camp. As she neared the circle of tipis belonging to Thunders Loud Voice, Rain Falls came out to meet her.

"Are you hungry?" Rain Falls asked as she gently stroked the dark thick braids of She Who Keeps Laughing. "I have prepared deer rib."

The two women walked through the Kiowa camp laughing and talking, stopping occasionally to speak to the other women who were busy preparing the evening meal.

Rain Falls was a small, fragile woman with refined features. Her dark eyes danced as she chattered on to She Who Keeps Laughing about the day's gossip. "There has been much whispering over the

Apache men who visited here yesterday. The council may decide that it would be a good thing for us to join them."

"It would be a good thing." She Who Keeps Laughing had given this matter a great deal of thought. "Before the Whites the buffalo were plenty and they disappeared into the ground when those pale creatures arrived. Their magic is no good and we should join with the Apache and Comanche to rid the earth of such beasts. The Kiowas thrive because of the buffalo. With them gone what will become of our people?"

"One of the Apaches said that if we could kill the Whites the buffalo would come back. What do you think, She?" Rain Falls asked as they approached the front of their tipi.

"That could be true." She Who Keeps Laughing sat on the ground near the fire and waited for Rain Falls to return with her food.

Thunders Loud Voice came out of Brown Bear Cub's tipi when he heard She talking to Rain Falls. "Woman, I have decided that you will go with me." He sat facing She on the ground pulling the back of his breechcloth under him.

"Go with you, where is it we will be going?" She asked as Rain Falls handed her a generous helping of deer.

"Thunders, would you care for a deer rib?" Rain Falls filled another bowl and held it in front of him.

Thunders took the bowl and turned to She Who Keeps Laughing. "The council has given their word that we will join the Comanches and Apaches in a battle against the Whites. You will go with me."

His narrow eyes grew serious as he spoke of the importance of the battle. "You will keep my weapons ready and attend my horses." Thunders tossed his thick black hair behind his shoulders and stared into the dark eyes of She Who Keeps Laughing. "I have found you to be a no good wife, but you are a great hunter and know the importance of well-maintained weapons." He took a large bite of meat.

The fact that he respected her gave She a soft heart toward Thunders Loud Voice. "I would be glad to go with you. I believe the White man is the reason the buffalo have gone away."

"I also believe that," Thunders slurred with a mouthful of meat. "This is good." He tossed a bare bone into the fire.

"I have heard stories that the Whites have put many of our people inside horse fences. It has been said that it is so crowded that many great warriors have to sleep standing up." She turned her face toward the tipi to keep Thunders from noticing that her eyes had filled with tears.

"I have also heard that." Thunders lay back and raised one leg to let his food digest. "Many children and old people have died inside those fences."

After he had rested awhile, Thunders jumped to his feet and walked back to Brown Bear Cub's tipi. "We will be leaving at sunrise."

She Who Keeps Laughing stirred the fire and sat alone with her thoughts until the stars were thick in the sky, then slipped quietly into her tipi and removed her clothes, lowering her firm body next to the warm nakedness of Rain Falls. The soft smell of Rain Falls' hair against She's face was the last thing She remembered before sleep fell upon her.

She Who Keeps Laughing had chosen her tan pony with the black mane and tail because it was swift in turning. The blood raced hard through her chest while she rode behind Thunders Loud Voice, who was leading the Crazy Dog Kiowa's War Party.

She rode bareback but wore a piece of leather between her legs to protect herself from friction burns caused by long hours of riding. She coated her thighs with wet earth and spread a thin layer of mud over the horse's back to soak up the sweat.

The War Party was divided into three groups of more than one hundred men each. The older warriors each brought along a woman to take care of their weapons. This was a custom; these men held high positions and could spare a wife in the event that they were killed. The younger men had not had enough time to accumulate more than one wife, therefore they were assisted by the horse-keeping people.

The Kiowas had not been in a wartime situation in a long while. They were excited when they reached the gray hills. It was a strange place, no trees, only small bushes and gray sand boulders. There was a watering hole, however.

She Who Keeps Laughing and a few of the other women took

the horses to drink. She carried her bow across her back with the string through the center of her breast. One woman at the pond noticed She.

"You are the one they speak of that hunts as good as any man. Why do you want to do that?" The woman whispered, because they were not allowed to talk.

She Who Keeps Laughing did not answer but only smiled. Any other time She would have freely told the woman how much pleasure she got out of hunting. She got almost as much gratification from hunting as she did from the touch of Rain Falls.

She respected the rules of the War Party and this was not the time to be discussing such delightful things. She had hoped that her smile was a satisfying answer to the woman's question.

When the moon rose into the sky, before the earth had completely covered up the sun, the drums sounded. Kiowa, Apache, and Comanche singers slowly began to chant their war cries, to awaken the spirits of past warriors.

The women of the War Party numbered about seventy or so, their faces painted and their hair covered. They danced slowly in line with the oldest going first to the youngest last. She Who Keeps Laughing was near the middle. Each stepped with her right foot forward and dragged her left on the downbeat of the drum.

The line of women formed a circle inside the clearing. They kept their steps as they stood beside each other. The horse-keeping people led the horses behind the women to form a protective circle.

The drummers and singers formed a small hub at the center of the spacious circumference created by the women. Their drumming grew louder and stronger after the horses were in position. The singers were forceful, their words cried out in the darkness.

"Ho you, enemy. The wolves will feast on your remains. I will not stop until the last one of you is wasted into the dirt. Ho you, enemy."

There were four small fires within the circle to mark the directions and light the way for the spirit warriors. The male dancers entered the circle with painted bodies. They danced in pairs, acting out a fight situation, with high kicks and jabbing spears and victory cries.

It was believed that to win a battle you must first act it out as if you had already won. To claim your victory and celebrate before the encounter was as important as the battle itself.

She Who Keeps Laughing had tears caking the red-and-yellow paint on her face. She let the anger in her belly whoop out into the dark sky as the drums sounded. The songs and dances went on until the first sign of the sun. Then the warriors rested a full day and night, but did not eat or bathe.

When the crescent moon was beginning its journey down the other side of the earth, the warriors mounted their ponies. They rode in silence to the bluff overlooking the camp of the Whites. The warriors spread out, encircling the wooden huts. They sat upon their horses and waited for the sun to rise.

In the first flicker of daylight She Who Keeps Laughing could see the entire circle of seven hundred or so warriors.

She had never seen such a magnificent display. Their bodies were painted blue, red, black, and white. Some wore long feather bonnets. Some wore bone breast plates, others wore plates made of pressed silver. Many wore silver arm bands and flattened silver strips tied in their hair. When the sun reflected off of the warriors it would blind the enemy.

Many carried rifles from the trading place. Some carried bows with packs of arrows on the horses' sides. Some carried spears and tomahawks strapped to their ponies. Most held tin or leather shields. They had all prepared well.

The Chief of the Silent Fighters raised his feathered war shaft straight into the air then motioned it forward. Fifty or so warriors rode quietly to the edge of the Whites' camp. They dismounted their horses and slipped over the fences, releasing the ponies belonging to the Whites. The horse-keeping people gathered them up and led them to a place behind the weapon stations.

The second Chief of the Silent Fighters raised his shaft and the remaining quiet warriors moved into position. They slipped into the huts, taking the lives of the enemy before they were even awake.

As the Silent Fighters were retreating to clean or replace their weapons, a Comanche Chief raised his long rifle and more than one hundred Rush-In Warriors rode furiously into the smoke created by the Whites' powder guns.

The warriors had forced their way into the wooden huts and killed many Whites, but a lot of their horses were coming back alone. Some warriors left standing would help the wounded onto the backs of their ponies and bring them to the edge of the reloading place.

The screams and cries could be heard over the deafening blast from the rifles. She Who Keeps Laughing was pacing back and forth in front of her lean-to. The thought of pulling her bow back and letting her arrows race through the air, landing in the chest of the white-eyes, excited her.

She strained her neck, trying to see where Thunders Loud Voice was in the middle of all the smoke and dust. Finally, she spotted his red pony racing toward her.

Thunders Loud Voice yelled, "Get my other rifle and reload this one. Pay attention, woman. The Whites are fighting with powerful weapons." Thunders was out of breath, but he made a brilliant glow in his silver armor. The brightness blinded even She Who Keeps Laughing.

Thunders bragged, "I like to see death in the eyes of my enemy while I'm plunging my knife into his heart. It excites me even more to know that life has not left his body before I rip the skin from his head."

That made She Who Keeps Laughing even more anxious to try her hand in battle. She knew it was the Whites who had caused the buffalo to disappear and the Whites who had taken the land and continued to force her people to the edge of the earth. There had never been hatred in her heart until she heard how white men killed the buffalo for no good reason. They left the dead carcasses to rot. The Kiowas killed only what they needed for food. She Who Keeps Laughing believed if there were no more white people the buffalo would come back. She wanted an opportunity to help rid the earth of such horrible creatures.

She Who Keeps Laughing laid Thunders's weapons open for him to choose the ones he would take into the next encounter. He mounted his gray-and-white pony and joined the others. The Crazy Dogs led the charge into the enemy camp, and the sound of guns roared as the dust rose from the horses' feet.

The sun shone directly above She Who Keeps Laughing when

Thunders's pony returned empty. An angry noise rose out of her belly and the taste of vomit filled her mouth. She spat on the ground and ripped off her buckskin dress, leaving her body bare except for the breechcloth she wore between her legs.

She covered one side of her body with black paint and the other side with red. She adorned her arms and legs with silver bands. She tied silver strands in her hair. She slapped a blue handprint on the right hip of her tan pony.

She Who Keeps Laughing gathered her own weapons as well as a few of Thunders's remaining things—a tomahawk, a long blade knife, and a rifle. She mounted her pony and rode fiercely into the bloody battleground.

Her heart was pounding furiously as she shot arrows directly into the chest of the enemy. Her mind kept hearing the way Thunders described the close contact fighting. Her throat felt dry and her eyes danced as she suddenly found herself on the ground face to face with a short, stocky man with hair covering his chin.

She Who Keeps Laughing forced the long blade knife into his heart and all the way through. Then she pushed her weight forward dropping him to the ground. His eyes stared at her firm breast as she placed her foot on his stomach and pulled the blade out slowly. Her dark eyes pierced his as she took her small knife and peeled a large handful of his red hair away from his skull.

She jumped back on her tan pony and yelled a loud victory cry. She quickly searched the warriors for Thunders Loud Voice. Her brother, Horse With No Heart, was lying on the ground nearby with blood streaming from his side. He reached for her hand. She pulled him over her pony in front of her and rode swiftly to the weapon stations. Two of the horse-keeping people helped Horse With No Heart to the medicine circle. She Who Keeps Laughing rode back to the battleground. There was no sign of Thunders Loud Voice.

Another one of She's brothers waved his rifle in the air when he saw her, then aimed it quickly at a burly white man who was about to fire his gun at She Who Keeps Laughing. The white man fell forward as the shot blasted a hole clear through his chest and blood rushed out his back.

She Who Keeps Laughing smiled at her brother and rode her pony near where many Whites were hiding behind their wagons. She leaped from her pony, plunging the long blade knife again and again into the enemy. She moved swiftly, surprising her opponents with the surge of blood escaping their chests.

By the time the sun was crawling behind the gray hills the War Party left behind dead white bodies to rot, just as the Whites had done the buffalo.

"Ho you, enemy. The wolves will feast on your remains. Ho you, enemy," She Who Keeps Laughing sang as she slowly rode her tan pony across the battleground.

She Who Keeps Laughing saw Thunders Loud Voice. He held his silver rifle in the air and She rode up next to him.

"I thought you were dead." She laughed as she swung her leg over the pony's back and dismounted. Thunders had lost a large amount of blood from a wound on his right thigh. She helped him onto her pony and led it to the place for the wounded near the water hole.

Two medicine women helped Thunders from the horse and took care of him. "You have done a brave thing," he said as She led her pony to the horse-keeping area.

A Comanche warrior came up to She Who Keeps Laughing and gave her an albino stallion. "You are a great warrior woman. This pony will serve you well."

The Kiowa, Apache, and Comanche War Party celebrated their victory long into the night. They honored She Who Keeps Laughing. She rode her albino stallion bare breasted with a feathered bonnet flowing across the horse's back. Her laughter rang out over the drums and the singers' voices. The warriors stood with their spears and rifles toward the sky in her honor. Even her wounded brother, Horse With No Heart, managed to pull himself to his feet long enough to wave to her as she rode by.

★

SCOTT W. PETERSON

GODS

WHEN THE NEW GOD came to Londinium, the first I noticed of it was that Basilus the cutler had become quite busy. I was a boy then, a long time ago. It was the year that the Christians call three hundred and three.

I knew Basilus because the course of my business took me to his shop, where I bought scrapers for the baths of my patron. These baths were my domain and I cared for them well; the patron, in turn, cared for me. His name was Aurelius and he was handsome as Jupiter. But I will admit that I did not love him.

I loved my mother. She was Elenais, a daughter of Krykos the Greek. She had been wealthy in her early days, and beautiful too. Though the passing of years caused her wealth to diminish, I will always remember how the beauty remained, like a summer bloom on her cheeks. It was there even when her troubles started and the cheeks began to be lined with care. Had she lived to become old it would no doubt have stayed forever.

But we killed her, Aurelius and I. And no god old or new can make it different.

★   ★   ★

I had come to the service of the Consul Aurelius at fifteen, handsome in the way of a young Celt with Greek blood, ambitious in the way of all boys. My childhood was spent with my mother and the shrine of my dead father in a brick house below Riverside Wall; it was near enough the docks to watch laborers toiling and get a lesson in how I did not want to live. When my uncle Leopidas saw a chance to present me to better prospects, he moved quickly and I did not complain. Mother fussed and cried and dressed me in white linen, better than we could afford, and Leopodis took me to see the Consul's steward. There I was given a bracelet of service, a gold stater with a portrait of our Emperor Diocletian, and a list of my duties. I was also given advice.

"Grow gracefully," the steward said. "When you have time to yourself, use it to improve your mind. You can read? Do so. Learn to speak well and of substance." He held my chin to turn my head one way and another. "Do not neglect your grooming. Rise early and visit the public bath before coming to the master's. Take time to curl your hair. No cosmetics; he cannot bear them, even on women."

There was much more. It seemed quite a lot for a servant who would only keep the inventory of the bath and hand the flasks of oil to guests. It was not even my task to tend the furnace; there were black Egyptians for that, who were thought better to withstand the heat. But I was not in service long before I learned what Aurelius thought Celtic boys better for.

He was never unpleasant about it or crude. I was the son of a soldier, of a free house, and he showed that he knew it. By way of courting he let me meet young men of his service who had been boys themselves once, and had done very well for good grooming. One such was Quintus the librarian, whose scrolls I busied myself with when I could; Quintus must have been a handsome youth, for he was a good-looking man, and he seemed very content. I fixed my eyes on a place such as his, and did my best to make my patron happy.

This did not require me to neglect my mother. I visited the brick house twice a week, and as my possessions began to reflect the Consul's satisfaction I shared with her happily. I shared with Leopidas too, though perhaps less happily since he seemed more to expect it; he was anxious to gain a place with the government, and impatient for me to produce something.

"Have you asked again?" he demanded one afternoon, detaining me in the courtyard beneath my mother's window.

"I gave your suit at the Feast of Venus, as we agreed. One does not badger a Consul of Rome."

"One may back a suit with a whisper or two. When one has such opportunities." His voice trickled some scorn on this. I never knew if he liked boys himself. I rather doubt that he liked anything at all.

"There will be a list of offices posted in a month. Only watch for it." I pulled away from him, brushing his finger marks from my tunic. I was dressed better than he these days, and didn't mind if he noticed. "Good day to you, Leopidas."

"A month you say?" he called after. "You have time to speak again. Think of Elenais. Her money is low, she only has us to support her. It's your duty!"

I was past the gate as he spoke, hurrying down the Via Classicianus. I knew my duties well enough, and needed to find hot irons for my hair before nightfall.

Though the offices were given out with much ceremony—a new governor from Rome had lately arrived, and took it on himself to present them—Leopidas did not find his name on the list. I don't know what he thought of me for this, because the governor's Roman officers were great bathers and I was kept very busy. During this time the Consul himself saw me less often; his new superiors had arrived with new policies to be implemented, and the luxurious steam rooms of his villa were not the only comforts he had no time for. I had become fond of my life and might have worried at this turn, but in truth I welcomed the hint that my tenure as a boy might be done. I was becoming impatient to advance to manhood and an office of my own, and to begin to make some real money. The gifts that came by way of the Consul's affection, generous as they might be, were baubles and trinkets compared to what a career could pay.

This concern with money came from Leopidas's remarks and

from what I knew on my own. My mother had gone through nearly all her fortune and had no more coming in. Already she no longer appeared at the Temple of Mithra, being too poor to manage the votives of that congregation; soon she would have trouble keeping her house. On one visit I found that the pewter service I had eaten from as a child was gone. It pained me to hear her praise wood as more sturdy.

I sought advice from Quintus, the well-off librarian. He looked at me in surprise. "But surely you've asked that she be cared for," he said. "Aurelius is not tight-fisted. My own parents live still on the gifts he made them."

I was embarrassed to admit that I hadn't thought of it. I had been raised to regard the women of the house as one's own responsibility. But surely it made sense; if I could ask an office for Leopidas, why not a pension for his sister?

"When you are with him next," urged Quintus, "let him know. You are well liked—I hear of such matters—and have no need to be timid." I took this advice to heart and left encouraged. As it turned out the chance was not long in arriving; Aurelius indeed still liked me, and within the week bid me to join him in an intimate dinner. I dressed with care, taking extra time for grooming.

We dined alone, on roe deer in fennel sauce, with quince and cherries. I shared his couch through the meat and the wine and was in the crook of his arm by dessert. Though I felt well-fed, warm, and comfortable, I remembered now and then to look distressed. He soon noticed. "My dear Krikos. These sad eyes would bring grief to temple stones. Am I such poor company?" He spoke kindly, as he had always done with me.

"I'm sorry, Consul. I will try to be of more spirit." I gave a great sigh and brought out a smile that looked worked-for.

"No, that will hardly do. I have no use for spirits not felt. Not another word to me but of your troubles." He put his hands on my shoulders. "Tell."

I told; I made sure to bring in the name of my father, who had served the Sixth Legion and died in Gaul, and of my grandfather, who had been a financier much used by the state. "Now the daughter of

Krykos leaves no bread for the starlings so she can have enough for
her table; and she must neglect her gifts to the gods, which can only
mean they will forsake her more."

He touched a finger to my face to brush the tears, which had
begun to fall honestly. "There, now. You should only have mentioned
it sooner. The good mother Elenais ought not to suffer." He kissed
my brow. "Leave your wishes with the gods, and with me."

Afterward, in his chamber, it seemed less likely than ever that
my station would soon change. But it also seemed less to matter. I
slept well, with Aurelius's breath in my ear.

It was around this time that I visited the shop of Basilus near the
Westgate and found there an odd change taken place. I was accus-
tomed to being well treated by craftsmen; the trade of the Consul was
lucrative and could make a reputation. In the usual course of matters
I would send a note ahead and then arrive to have the cutler's undi-
vided attention. But on this occasion I found the knife-master distracted, the rooms of the shop milling with people. They did not seem
much interested in his wares.

With difficulty I got Basilus to attend to me. He seemed startled.

"Krikos, is it? Indeed, of course. How wonderful to see you
among us." He was a large bearded man with wide eyes, which he
shone at me with pleasure. "I had not looked for it, to be sure . . .
given your place. But all are welcome."

He might as well have spoken the language of Picts for all I
understood him. "I gave you to expect me," I said, "as I always do.
Have you my order?"

"Ah? What? Ah, ah. For the bath. You are here for the bath." His
eyes suddenly shone less, and he mumbled in his beard. He gestured to
an assistant. "The order for the Consul," he said curtly. "The boy is
here for it."

The assistant bowed his head and ducked away. I stood mystified
while Basilus avoided looking at me. Momentarily the wrapped parcel
was placed in my hands. "I trust all is as I requested," I said, looking
with disapproval at the package. It was unseemly to have wrapped it
without my inspection.

"Of course, of course, naturally."

No one but the cutler spoke; the people grouped about the room seemed anxious for me to go. I nodded with all the dignity I could manage, in so strange a scene, and made my way through the door. The curtains closed behind me, seeming to seal a secret. I shook my head and walked back up the river road.

I reported this oddity to Quintus when next we talked, to see if he would understand it. He did, and was careful to check the hall outside his rooms before he spoke. Then he came back to my couch and raised his brows.

"Does the Consul know you trade with Basilus of Westgate?" he asked.

"I would suppose so; or not, I don't know. The trade was begun by the bath-keeper before me."

"Assume he does not. And Krikos, find another source for your goods. The Westgate, if you had not noticed, is becoming a hotbed of Christians."

I had not noticed. Londinium supported a score and a hundred cults, a god for every street corner. My Celtic father had taught me a dozen deities to pray to, my Greek mother a dozen more; if I wished to call myself a Roman there was yet another cast of mighty names to choose from, plus dead emperors. Since coming to Aurelius I had mostly made reverence to Juno, because it was what the Consul did. I tended to believe that all of it was partly real, none of it greatly serious.

"So what of Christians?" I wondered aloud. "Aurelius supports tolerance. He says so often."

"Aurelius does, because he is an administrator and knows good policy. Tolerance in religion has been the genius of the empire. But it has its limits and its rules. The public order must not be disturbed; thus the old Druids were stamped out because they sacrificed men. Another rule is this: the gods of Rome should not be mocked. These Christian believers push at the rules."

"I've heard their tales at market," I recalled. "All about the prophet of . . . I don't remember. Somewhere in Arabia. But I did not hear that they like to sacrifice anyone."

"You didn't listen to the second rule. The gods of Rome. Increasingly the Christian sect is exclusive, do you know what that is? That there must be no other god. In Rome they are becoming numerous enough to be a threat. And Diocletian has spoken: they are to be discouraged. Strongly discouraged."

I thought about it. "There are knife shops too on the Walbrook. Perhaps I should view their goods."

"Perhaps you should," agreed Quintus. "We have a new governor, he is reported to be stern. I would not care to be much in the Westgate over the next months."

I thanked him for his advice, which was good as always, and rose. But I remembered about my mother. "Do you know," I said happily, "that I asked the Consul as you told me, and he has promised to look out for Elenais?"

The librarian smiled. "I knew he would. He is a good patron, Krikos. All the more reason to take care of his errands in a safer place. You would not want to embarrass him."

When I returned to the baths and my duties, caring for my good patron's Roman guests, I unwrapped the new scrapers and found them oddly marked. The Christian symbol was etched on each one, just above the blade. I looked about the hot-room, which was becoming crowded with evening, and saw several of the governor's men; hurriedly I put the new scrapers behind an urn. The guests made do with old, and no one seemed to notice.

Aurelius sent for me the next day.

He was in his office, where I had seldom been before. The new governor sat beside him, tapping the ring of Rome on a chair arm. I knelt and made my respects nervously, keeping my head down. Then the Consul spoke.

"Up, Krikos. And smile. I have good news for you."

"Consul?"

"I have not forgotten our talk of the other night. And though you may have supposed it, I have not forgotten your requests at the Feast of Venus. It seems now that the two answer one another."

Leopidas would be pleased. But I was still nervous, and wondered why the governor was there. I waited for more. The governor, a terrible-looking old man named Contius, turned his beady glance on me. "This uncle of yours, boy," he demanded, "is he a reliable man?"

To his own interests, I thought, though I could hardly say so. "Yes, Governor."

"And quiet? Discreet? Does he know how to be slippery?"

He was asking, it seemed, if Leopidas could be a spy. "I suppose he could be all of these things," I ventured, "if the Empire required it. I know that he wants a commission very much."

The governor eyed me for a minute, then gave the Consul a faint nod. Aurelius said, "I think we may have one for him. It will pay a hundred staters for the six-month." He smiled at my widened eyes. "Quite enough to put Elenais's starlings back in bread crumbs. But secrecy is all. I will give you his duties and you will pass them along. I will not see him."

"Yes, Consul."

"You have heard of the Emperor's intention," continued my patron, "that the troublesome cult of Christ Jesus is to be suppressed. To do so we need information; names in particular, with places and times. Leopidas, then, is to become a Christian. He must work to be accepted and learn as much as he can. Each fortnight he will give you a report, written and sealed. You will pass that along as well."

My discomfort must have been evident on my face. "Consul, I'm sure Leopidas would try to find any talent asked of him. But he has little to do with religion, and nothing to do with Christians."

"Does he not?" interrupted the governor softly. "Then, as your Consul says, he shall have to work at it." He rose and went to the door. "I consider the matter done." The curtains parted and he was gone.

Aurelius relaxed slightly. "Well, Krikos," he said, "did I not promise you? One sees that the gods are not deaf to our prayers."

"Is it true of all gods, Consul?"

"Of course it is; whatever do you mean?"

"No doubt the Christians believe it too."

He looked at me. "You have a handsome face, Krikos, and a

good simple spirit. The combination has attracted me and served you well. Heed me now: keep both. Do not complicate yourself."

I made another bow and accepted his kiss; as I left he gave me a present of an opal on a silver string. With this, and with a spirit complicating by the moment, I went to instruct Leopidas in his fortune.

Through the next half year I became more and more uncomfortable with my role. It seemed the cult was larger than any had suspected; when Leopidas passed his reports to me, the leather-wrapped scrolls were thicker each time. Rumors told that the governor planned to be ruthless, and soon a large barracks of Imperial troops was planted near the Westgate. Tension in the city began to grow.

I had other cause to be unhappy. Leopidas's pay was delivered generously and on time, yet he seemed to do nothing for my mother. When his commission was nearly done I sought him out and challenged him on it. "She lives more poorly than before," I protested, "and still is not seen at the Temple. Surely your bounty can spare her the price of some incense and a pair of doves."

Leopidas looked evasive. "I offered her money," he said. "She refuses it."

"Your attitude must make it offensive. Open your hand more easily, Uncle! If we have to make a living as persecutors of fools, let us at least see some good of it."

"Good?" He looked at me as though the word were foreign. "What needs opening, Krikos, is your eyes. Have you ever stopped to wonder why the brother of Elenais was picked for this task?"

"I told them you were sly."

"Did you?" He stepped away from me. His eyes were cold and empty behind the fine new curls of his hair. "You haven't grasped the meaning of the word. Look to your patron for that."

"What are you saying?"

"Krikos the innocent," he mocked. "Who is the fool here? Your lover is too good to you." Leopidas turned on his heel and walked away.

Innocence or idiocy, it was some hours before I put his words together. It came to me as I prepared the bath oils for evening; I left them to sit when the thunderbolt struck me, and ran down the Via Classicianus to the brick house near the docks.

I surprised her in the inner room, knelt in prayer. The Christ altar was revealed beneath a lifted curtain. There was the *Chi-Rho* etched in red chalk on the plaster, and a cross of simple wood. I had sat next to it a dozen times unknowing.

"Why, Mother?" It was all I could think to say.

She finished her devotion, replaced the curtain, and looked at me peacefully. "Krikos, my love, I have been a long time alone. I am no longer."

"When I was a child you taught me to love Mithra. Do you abandon him now?"

"It is not a question of what I abandon, but what I embrace. The One God is all gods and more."

"The Empire requires that all gods be themselves and *not* more. It's for this that your worship is denied."

"Not even an Emperor can deny the truth."

"Then have truth, have all the truth you can find. It's nothing to me. But Leopidas—"

"Gave them my name long ago. My brother has always been ambitious. When Contius learned of it, and of you, his ambition was rewarded."

At least I saw why she had not taken the money. "You must warn your cult. Or when the end comes they will think you faithless too."

"The thoughts of ambitious men are clear on their faces. Leopidas's purpose is no secret among us. We give him our love."

"And he gives the governor your names. You will all be jailed or worse."

"Our Master was nailed to a cross."

I could say nothing to disturb the quiet in her face. "I tell you, anything that seems good to you must be to me. Only be sensible, Mother! You can love whatever you wish, here in your room, alone in your heart. The Empire will not pursue it so deeply. It's just that you meet, you gather and conspire, you make yourselves too public. Believe what you will, only cease to flaunt it."

"And would that not put the Emperor's bars on my heart? Can I be other than who I am?"

"You throw your life away, then. You abandon me."

"Dear son . . ." She took my hand, but I was choked with tears and turned away. At some point we cried together and held each other. She spoke a long time of things I cannot recall; though her soft words could not give me to understand, I pretended that they did. In the small hours of the night there was nothing more to say. I took her blessing, and gave her mine, and I left.

I never saw her again. At week's end the governor's soldiers moved against the Westgate in force. Many died in the burning of Basilus's knife shop; others simply disappeared. The slave ships left full for weeks. Leopidas left too, with a profitable army commission to Crete. He did not bid me good-bye.

But Aurelius did. One can at least credit the Consul with enough face to ask my forgiveness. "I did not know at first," he told me, "and when I did it was too late. In the end I am no more than a servant myself. I know that you loved her, Krikos. But like many others she was blind to her own good. Should I have let it ruin you too? You have more sense, whether you know it or not. It was better this way."

I said nothing. I think he knew from my silence that he would not kiss me again. Shortly afterward I was appointed to a position as Quintus's assistant in the library; it paid very well. Not much later, I heard that the Consul was seen dining a handsome young boy of the governor's household.

Youth was over. Life went on.

Nowadays when I recall this business I do so privately, and take care not to show it among my neighbors. Fifty years have passed since the worship of Christ became the religion of Rome. The few who cling to Mithra or Diana do so at peril of their lives; quite a lot of shoes have changed feet since Diocletian gave way to Constantine.

The past autumn I buried Quintus on Ludgate Hill. We stayed together all our lives, for as he taught me his love of learning we learned a love of each other. Neither of us married, so one must suppose we made it a happy thing. He embraced the Christ worship himself before his end, and I took care that all the rites were seen to.

For myself I have never become sure. What so many once suffered for believing, others now suffer for denying; even I suffered, who neither believed nor denied, but only stood dumb and unprepared while the lash swung to and fro. In my guilt I am left to wonder what gods must think of us, when they look down and see their mighty awe turned to fear and division, their sacred truths reduced to shackles by which men bind one another. I am certain that Elenais would never have loved the burning of temples and the stoning of unbelievers. She would have remembered that once the greatest wish of Christians was that men be left free in their hearts.

The Egyptians say the world has stood for ten thousand years; it seems likely to go on for as many more. Perhaps with so much time men will learn to do better by their gods. In my inner room, in my inner thoughts, I pray for it daily. I do not know to whom.

★

TRUDY RILEY

HIGHWAY FIVE

AS I SIT AT my desk doing the hospital report I feel my mind going numb. My boss loves this report but, for me, counting patient admissions, discharges, and lengths of stay leaves me feeling I have lost the capacity for abstract thought. I put down my pen and stare out the window. My mood is not helped by the fact that it has been raining for four days in Palo Alto.

The phone rings. I hope whoever is on the other end of the line has some complex problem that will allow me to escape for a while. I pick up the phone on the second ring.

"Hello, Ms. Thomas speaking," I say in my best professional manner.

"Oh, Jenny, I'm so glad I reached you!"

"Gail, what's wrong?" I grasp the phone tighter, wondering what could make my usually calm Los Angeles friend sound like she's being strangled.

"I hate to tell you this but Julia's had a heart attack! She's in the hospital in Fontana!" She stops to catch her breath.

"Oh, my God, how bad is it?"

"I'm not sure. Her lover, Carol, just called. She was so upset she couldn't give any details."

I peer out the window as though I can see all the way to Fontana. This can't be happening, I think, not to Julia. She was the strong one. Then the horror of the fact that she might be dying grips me. "I'm coming down. If I start driving now I can be there in seven hours."

"Why don't you fly? It's faster."

Gail is recovering, getting back to her super-practical self.

"No, I'd rather drive."

"But, Jenny, you could be in Fontana in two hours. I'm sure you could get a flight out of San Francisco immediately. They leave every—"

"Gail, you don't understand," I interrupt, "I can't deal with the airport right now. It's just too complicated."

After I hang up I rush out of my office to find my boss. He is in a meeting. I interrupt and blurt sentences with "urgent" and "emergency" in them. He says, "Yes, take a week if you need to, but keep me posted."

I nod, forgiving him for the hospital report.

As I leave the building I notice the puddles in the parking lot are rapidly turning to lakes. It's a lousy day to drive four hundred and fifty miles.

In forty minutes I'm at the base of the Pacheco Pass. It's the narrow road that joins the Peninsula with Highway Five. An endless line of trucks lumbers around its curves. This road has always frightened me, but today I drive it like a demented Mario Andretti.

When I reach the summit the road widens and I feel the first tears coming. I hold them back until I see the large green sign that reads "Sacramento North, Los Angeles South." Then I let the tears roll unchecked. Completing the gradual sweep of the onramp, I get my first misty look at the long, straight road that bisects California.

I am comforted by the fact that nothing has changed. No one has tried to make it pretty. It is as flat as it has always been, and the fields on either side are deserted. An odor of fertilizer hangs in the air. I'm thankful for the sameness of this highway. It's the perfect antidote to the turmoil I feel. Taking a couple of deep breaths, I put the car on cruise control and let myself remember.

I met Julia in 1972 at a retirement party given by the hospital where I work. It was one of those affairs where no one cared much about the person retiring, but we all showed up out of a vague sense of duty.

After saying some obligatory "hellos" I found myself standing in the corner of the room thinking, here I am thirty-five years old and surrounded by aging bureaucrats. My hair's getting gray, my skin is wrinkling, and my libido has vacated the premises.

I wandered over and congratulated the woman who was retiring. We talked about hobbies and leisure-time activities. I stared at her blue crepe dress and elaborate corsage. If there was fear in her eyes I didn't want to see it.

I had made a contract with myself to leave the party in fifteen minutes when a woman, wearing a T-shirt with the name of the hospital bowling league on it, walked up, handed me a beer, and asked, "Bored?"

Just what I need, I thought, standing around drinking beer with a woman who enjoys a tacky sport. I decided to have one of those conversations where I only use half my mind, so I asked her about bowling.

What a mistake that turned out to be! She faced me head on. She had the most fervent blue eyes I've ever seen, shiny red hair, and one of those complexions that made me feel I had spent too much of my life indoors. She vibrated with energy as she talked about "her team." In detail she described the joys of the sport: the release of tension, the power she felt when she made a strike.

Her enthusiasm was contagious because before long I was telling her all about my failed attempts at athletics. The sad, embarrassing falls, the missed catches, and the frightening awkwardness I felt whenever I was asked to compete.

The party was getting noisier, more drunken. We found a place to sit in one of the quieter rooms. She asked me what I enjoyed doing. I searched my mind for an answer and finally said, "Travel, I enjoy traveling."

"Where do you go?"

I felt cornered. I wanted to make up something, but decided to give in and tell her. "Well, the really big trip this year was to the San Bernardino Mountains with a Unitarian church group. If you can contain your excitement, I'll tell you all about it."

"Was it a camping trip?"

"Are you kidding?"

"No, camping's great," and she was off again, gesturing as she talked. I pictured her putting up tents and hiking mountain trails. She was doing all those things that had always sent me back to the tent with the impulse to bury myself in a sleeping bag.

After the second beer I told her all about the gray hairs, the dead libido, and my semi-delinquent children. "They're miserable teenagers. They snarl at me at least once a day. They stole my Visa and charged clothes on it. Once I went on a trip and they took my car and went all over town in it. I want to paint my bedroom and fix it up so I can lock myself in there and not ever have to talk to those kids."

"Paint the bedroom?" Julia asked, looking like she had lost track of the conversation.

"Yes, it's where I go to escape the chaos. It's *my* place and I want to make it pretty."

"Oh, I get it."

"It means so much to me I asked this guy I was having an affair with to help me out and do you know what he said? Domestic stuff like that made him feel trapped. Can you believe it? I mean, I was sleeping with him."

Julia stood up, put her hands on her hips, and said, "I hope you dropped that man like a turd from a tall horse."

"What a great way of putting it," I said, feeling like I had just stepped into a country music song. A place where I get to hate everyone who had ever wronged me. "I'm really having a good time."

"Me too, and I don't usually like straight parties."

"Straight parties?"

"Yeah, as opposed to gay parties. I'm gay, you know."

"Oh," I moaned. "I wish you had told me sooner."

"What difference would it have made?"

"I don't know"—I struggled to say something that wouldn't hurt her feelings—"I probably wouldn't have gone on and on about my kids. That couldn't have fascinated you."

"What are you talking about? I lived with a lover who had a set of twins. Helped raise them from the time they were babies to when they started school. I did everything for those little girls. Put together a whole playground. Got it from Sears and assembled it in the back-yard." She stopped talking suddenly. "You sure look troubled."

"I guess I don't understand about lesbianism. I mean how—"

Julia interrupted, a mischievous smile on her face. "Given the chance, I'll teach you everything you need to know."

Something unhinged in the middle of my body. I felt a mixture of excitement and dread. I smiled at her. She winked. I winked back. She told me my wink resembled a facial tic and offered to teach me how to do that too.

The party was ending. Julia went with me to find my coat. As I was putting it on she said, "Okay, Jenny, let's get serious. What color do you plan to paint that bedroom retreat of yours?"

"If I ever get around to it I'll paint it off-white. That way I won't have to match anything to it." I noticed that there was a lilt in my voice that I reserved for times when I wanted to be attractive.

"I'm a good painter."

"Oh?"

"Why don't you give me your address. I'll come over and take a look."

I printed my full name, address, apartment number, home and work phone clearly on the card she handed me.

Driving home I wondered if I would hear from her. Out loud in the darkened car, I said, "Oh, no, I think I'm attracted to her." I said it again. It was not quite as shocking the second time.

My attention snaps back to the highway. The rain has turned to mist and my windshield wipers make a complaining sound as they scrape the drying glass. In the distance I see a square of blue sky. I read it as a good omen. It means it will be warm in Fontana and Julia will be healing. I want to believe that only good things happen in the sunshine.

I increase my speed to seventy, reset it, and remember what it was like the week after I met Julia.

I looked for her in the corridors and regretted not asking her where she worked in the hospital. There were days I started work sure I would find her and ask her to lunch. Later the same day I would convince myself that such an idea was madness.

One night I had a dream that I was nuzzling and kissing the throat of a red-haired woman. I awoke in a sweat and scolded myself. "Stop all this crap. You're not going to have an affair with Julia and that's that."

On my lunch hour the following day I put on dark glasses, went to Sisterhood Bookstore, and bought a book called *Sappho Is a Right-On Woman*. I finished it that night, basking in fantasies of lesbianism. Then I yelled, "Oh, shit," and threw the book across the room.

By Saturday morning I was exhausted. Barely awake I went into the living room and picked my way through my children's droppings: clothes, musical instruments, and a floor sprinkled with potato chips. I sat in a corner feeling overwhelmed and lonely. It seemed I would spend this day as I had spent so many weekend days lately, in bed drinking coffee, reading the newspaper, and staring at the wall.

I went outside to get the paper and there was Julia unloading cans of paint from a Datsun station wagon. I stood in the doorway acutely aware of my uncombed hair and my granny gown turned gray with age.

When Julia saw me she put her hands on her hips and asked, "Where's the bedroom?"

"Do you really mean it?"

"No, I always visit people in the morning with a carful of paint."

I felt my feet starting to run, granny gown flapping. I reached Julia, threw my arms around her, and hung on.

I need gas so I exit the highway and pull into the first station I see. As I stand filling the tank, a chill wind whips my clothing and makes my hands feel cold and stiff. I am back in the car and on the highway in record time. I turn on the heater and feel comforted by the warmth. This highway always seems too hot or too cold. I recall a time when Julia and I traveled it on the hottest day of the year.

It was so hot we decided to travel from L.A. to San Francisco at night. All the car windows were open. I was feeling wonderful. I loved the heat. Julia hated it. I felt more alive, she felt claustrophobic. She was driving and I was talking.

"Feel that hot wind, Julia; aren't hot nights lovely? I feel so great, there's just no feeling like it. It must be over one-hundred degrees." I paused mid-monologue and looked over at Julia. She was driving with one hand and taking off her T-shirt with the other. I said, "What in God's name are you doing?"

"Appreciating those hot naked summer nights you've been raving about for the past hour."

At first I felt so embarrassed and giddy I covered my face with my hands. Then I sneaked a look at her through my fingers. Her profile seemed intense and determined as she concentrated on her driving. Her hair was blown back from her face. The contours of her arms, shoulders, breasts looked soft and round illuminated by the passing headlights. She was quite beautiful. I stopped talking about the heat.

As I approach the Fresno turnoff the weather clears. The rain-washed Golden Arches, Chevron insignia, and pink walls of Motel 6 glisten in the sunlight. I consider stopping for coffee but realize all I want to do is drive and reminisce. So far the memories have been pleasant. I search my mind for the first time I felt some hint of trouble.

Julia and I were fixing dinner. We had decided to be creative, try something new, make it up as we went along. I was peeling potatoes and talking.

"Do you know what happened to me on the way over, Julia? I was driving along and stopped at a light and this really contented feeling came over me. I had the feeling that my life was settled. Do you know what I mean? That everything is happening just the way it's supposed to. As though there's some kind of predestination. Right there at that light I knew one thing for sure: we would be together for the rest of my life."

Julia looked skeptical. I plunged ahead. "That's real different from the way I felt the first time we met. I used to worry that it was neurotic, the way you came into my life and took care of everything—me, my sex life, my apartment, and even my appearance. Now I know that's how it is with women." Pride creeping into my voice, I continued, "We are all things to each other—sister, mother, friend, child, and lover. Isn't that wonderful?"

Julia stopped chopping carrots. "You betcha," she said and leered.

"C'mon, I pour my soul out to you and the best you can do is 'you betcha'?"

"You betcha."

"Jesus, Julia, you're being about as sensitive as Archie Bunker."

"What do you want from me?" she asked, putting the paring knife down and turning toward me. "Things either work or they don't. It doesn't help to go on and on about it."

Silence. I huddled over the sink. The potato in my hand blurred. As I started to cry Julia came up behind me and began to smooth the hair back from my ear. She did this until there were only a few strands left. Then she took them one by one and tucked them away with painstaking care. When there were none left she bent and whispered, "I'm so sorry." For a long time I stood quietly feeling the warmth of her breath lingering in the caverns of my ear.

The roar of a passing truck takes my attention back to the highway. I see it through tears. Groping for the box of Kleenex I realize that driving and crying is a familiar experience. On the final trip I took with Julia, I cried for the last hundred miles, from Santa Barbara to Los Angeles. Those tears were prompted by the sure knowledge that we were separating.

Between sobs I told her I wanted my old life back. "Loving you takes too much of me. It's so different from the way I felt about men. When things go wrong between us I go out of my mind. I just can't do it anymore."

She reached to comfort me. I pulled away. "You're so afraid of being really close," she said.

"What are you talking about? I never felt this close to anyone."

"No, Jenny, you talk a good game but to you I'm just some kind of experiment."

"No, you aren't!"

"The hell I'm not! If you were really serious you wouldn't keep me such a big secret from your kids and your friends. You just wanted to play around for a while, but now you're ready to pick up your toys and go home."

I didn't know if she was right.

When I arrived home I grabbed the kids. We stayed in a long embrace and closed our life against her.

Years later she would tell me she wanted to yank us apart, to get my attention. I did not see her again for three years. It would be five before we would begin to talk to each other again.

It is getting dark. My back hurts and my body feels stiff. I see the lights of the San Fernando Valley. If I want to get to Fontana in one piece I must stop the flow of memories. It will take all my attention to manage L.A. traffic and the complex freeway interchanges that will take me to Julia.

When I arrive the visitor's parking lot is emptying and one of those arid Santa Ana winds is gusting. I enter the hospital and give Julia's name to a stern-looking woman at the information desk. She consults her computer. "Miss Keyes has just been moved from intensive care to the cardiac recovery unit, but visiting hours in that area are over."

"Oh, no! I'm her sister," I lie, "and I've just driven all the way from northern California. I'll only stay a minute. I promise."

I walk through the corridor, trying to look like I know where I'm going. Official-looking faces pass, but no one stops me. I find Julia surrounded by TV screens silently showing peaks, lines, and numbers. She also has a monitor resting over her heart, which buzzes, changing pitch and frequency as she breathes.

I say, "Julia," softly. She stirs, the buzz gets louder and she begins to open one eye. All the courage that has gotten me past those stern faces now vanishes. I stand looking down at her, my throat tightening. I'm not ready for this, I think. Too late. Recognition is dawning in that opening eye.

She mumbles something and the buzzer grows louder. I lean down to hear. She whispers, very faintly, "When was the last time you combed your hair, Jenny, it looks like hell." The eye closes. The nurse appears, and I leave swiftly.

I'm not much on beauty salons but the next morning I'm sitting in Fontana's finest, listening with sympathy to my beautician. She tells me her steelworker husband has been laid off and she is trying to support the family on her hairdresser's pay.

"It's real hard to make ends meet. The worst part is he's getting so discouraged." I study this woman in the salon mirror. Her face looks drawn under her elaborate hairstyle. She wears a frayed tank top and there are bruises on her arms. I close my eyes so I don't have to see the bruises.

She says, "That's it, honey, you just take a little nap. In a little while you're going to look like a million bucks." When she is finished she proudly places a mirror in my hand. I survey my hair, back and front. I act pleased and grateful. I now look like a steelworker's wife.

By mid-morning I'm sitting next to Julia's bed listening to her monitor's low reassuring buzz. She is asleep. Her round peaceful face is slightly flushed. Her hair is damp and matted. It sticks to her forehead. I sit quietly, not moving my head, trying carefully to preserve my curls for her to see.

She wakes suddenly and I am startled to see her looking at me.

For several moments I can't find any words. I take her hand. It's so warm that I worry. I find my voice.

"When Gail called me I was so anxious. I couldn't get here fast enough. I'm so glad—" I stop. I know I'm about to say I'm so glad that she's alive. I can't do that, so I pause and start again.

"I'm so glad you're looking pretty good. I'm sure you're going to be better real soon." I smile. I know it's a phony smile, the kind that only my mouth does while my eyes look like I have just seen a catastrophe. I decide to ask a question. Perhaps I can collect myself while she is answering.

"How did the attack happen, Julia?"

She shifts position, her buzzer grows louder, and she answers, laboring over her words, "I was chopping wood and this pain started in my chest. I rested thinking it would go away. When it didn't I called Carol in from outside. She drove me down the hill to Emergency. That's all I remember."

"Oh God, Julia, you must have been terrified. And then to have to drive all the way down from Crestline, it sounds so scary." I pause, finally hearing what Julia has just said to me. "What were you doing chopping wood in the first place?"

She looks at me with infinite patience and says, "Jenny, that's what you do if you live in the mountains."

"Not everyone," I reply. "Most people pay someone to do that stuff for them. You're not Superwoman, you know. You need help up there. I really don't know why you decided to live up there anyway. I think you should have kept the house in Reseda."

Julia looks like she has just smelled something bad. I continue undaunted.

"Now I find out that Carol is up there with you. I'll bet she doesn't have a job. So there you are chopping wood, working full time, remodeling the cabin, and supporting her. It's just too strenuous." I am about to continue but her monitor is making disquieting sounds.

Julia asks, "Jenny, what are you doing to my hand?"

In my agitation I have been pulling and twisting her fingers as I talk. I drop her hand. Suddenly I feel so tired. Leaning forward in my chair I rest my head on the edge of the bed.

I say into the mattress in a voice that sounds like a small child, "I got my hair done, too."

I feel her hand gently patting and smoothing my curls. After a long while she says, "Don't worry, Jenny. I'm going to be all right." Her monitor sounds low and steady, her breathing is regular, and her hand is still. We rest there, quiet and peaceful. Then I notice my breathing matches Julia's. Unconsciously I have been trying to help her breathe.

I sigh and whisper to her quiet form. "So much for letting go."
I get up, kiss her gently on her too-warm forehead, and leave.

I start down the corridor and then double back to the nurses
station. Three nurses are writing and watching screens. I say sharply,
"Nurse!" They look up. "I really think you should adjust the temperature in Room C-236. I work in a hospital and that room is far too
warm." One of the nurses starts to object but gets up instead and
heads toward Julia's room.

Outside I see Carol walking toward me from the parking lot.
Her head is down and strands of her long, brown hair are blowing
across her face. Her white blouse is open at the collar, showing a pale
section of throat. She has the same shy convent-girl look I remember
from the first time I met her. That was in the days when it felt like
every lesbian in L.A. showed up for the weekly pot luck in the Valley.
We had stood laughing over the fact that we had both brought the
same dish.

She sees me and we hug. I murmur words of comfort. She tells
me she is grateful I've come down from Palo Alto. "It will mean so
much to Julia. I hate hospitals," she continues, "I had to get away so
I went back up the mountain to get some of her things." She looks
up as though she is seeing me for the first time. "Jenny, what in the
hell did you do to your hair?"

"Oh, nothing," I murmur, hoping that the Santa Anas are blowing
out every last curl.

★

MICHAEL LASSELL

SKYFIRES
For Icarus, still a boy,
and a fledgling poet, now a man

1. DAWN

(ON THE PUBLICATION OF HIS FIRST BOOK OF POEMS)

The thing that hath been, it is that which shall be; and that which is done is that which shall be done: and there shall be no new thing under the sun.

—ECCLESIASTES 1:9

ON THE BACK OF the book is a photo of the poet (all lips and eyelids, shoulders, forearms). I could quote him in the sighing of a thigh, a hand hovering over a waist and never lighting, like a thrush or mockingbird. His eyes sink into me, into the muscle and bone. I loved him once ten years and am furious he has seen fit to live so fully and so long without me on his breath. His words tear into my chest like his lovemaking teeth into the hearts of other men than me. His face has aged and styles have changed over the years, but the eyes still have it; they conceal still whether his life is sin or blessing, a metaphor of unimagined depravity or a simile of unquenchable spirit. He looks into the center of things; what drops into him spills out in a dozen words arranged on paper—or in the arch of an eyebrow, shadow dimple, ironic glance in a mirror, or the lens of an antique camera he bought at auction in Singapore.

I stare into the photo and Gavin is in my eyes again as he has been, all these years, wrapped tightly in my heart and mind.

111

2. SUNRISE

(THE FIRST INKLING)

More worship the rising than the setting sun.

—PLUTARCH, *Lives*
(Pompey to Sulla)

Icarus woke earlier than his father. Incarceration had taught him that
... wake up earlier or fall asleep later, it was the only way to have
any privacy, any time alone. It was his father's fault, after all. Icarus
had had nothing to do with it, really. He had just carried his father's
message to the king's daughter (Ariadne, in love with the Athenian
traitor, Theseus). How was Icarus to know the old man and the
princess were in league to fashion the foreigner's escape from the
labyrinth his father had designed, had designed so cleverly that even
the inventor could no longer contrive to escape it without a ruse? But
Daedalus, always the thinker, had of course come up with a solution
and given it to his son pressed into a tablet of flattened red wax.

Daedalus had warned Icarus to keep the tablet out of the heat
of the sun until after Ariadne had decoded it, then they would let the
wax melt, the plan run, the message lost for all time with the evidence.
It was a perfect scheme, at least for the lustful Ariadne and her suitor
Theseus. For Daedalus and Icarus, however, the result was catastrophic.

Ariadne—vain, pampered, and shallow as she was most of the
time—could be a tigress when she got her mind set on something she
wanted; she had carried out his father's plan with the fortitude of a
warrior. Theseus had escaped and abducted the self-centered princess
along with, rumor had it, her younger and far more agreeable sisters
as well. As for Theseus's crime, the slaying of the bull/man Minotaur,
well, King Minos was so furious about the death, the escape, *and* the
abduction, that there was little hope either Icarus or Daedalus would
ever be freed. They were the only ones left in Crete who had had
anything to do with it. Ariadne's handmaidens, it was said, had been
sold into slavery in Thrace, just to assuage the king's humiliation.

And so, morning after morning, Icarus sat in the crude opening that served as their only window and stared out at the sky and the sea, going over it all again and again, blaming his father, ancient Daedalus, who sat up night after night until nearly dawn racking his brain for a means of escape, an escape Icarus knew would never come. The stone tower was too high to jump from; they were never given enough of anything to construct a ladder; there were armed guards encamped all around the base of the tower; and the tower itself was set on a minute island miles from land, boats being absolutely forbidden to dock except under the most stringent security conditions. But, futile as it seemed, the old man poured over his papers and perused his books and ruminated night after lonely night in the shadow of the moon and stars or the stingy supply of candles their captors allowed.

Icarus woke each morning just after his father nodded off on his pallet for a few hours of fitful sleep. He stood each morning at the window at dawn going over it in his unforgiving mind. His body had just begun to mature, and something he did not understand was growing inside him, swelling, demanding to explode from his body as urgently, as violently as he longed to break from his confinement, to be free to walk and run, to engage the boys of his childhood in contests and sports, to lay naked by a cool stream in an olive grove, to listen to the sweet panpipes of a precocious shepherd. The pressures of his body were enormous, and the discovery of temporary physical release, which his father absolutely forbade (on the premise that the habit sapped intellectual curiosity), only made him long for freedom more actively.

Morning after morning he would stand in the large window and feel the sea breeze on his face—a handsome face, his father had said. "Yes, you have a handsome and a pleasing face," he said, "but a handsome and a pleasing face is nothing compared to a quick and agile mind." Well, Icarus thought, everyone in Greece knew where a quick and agile mind had gotten Daedalus, and Icarus along with him.

Morning after morning he would stand in the window, his hands on his thin bare hips, and watch the soldiers below pouring urns of seawater over one another. The shock of the icy water in the cold dawn cascaded over the tanned backs and flanks of two dozen hard men, soldiers who were sworn to the death to maintain his imprisonment. All those men for one old man and a boy, he thought contemptuously as he watched them in their exercise and horseplay, as they sharpened spears, polished armor, slept together in their dark blankets, coarse as unshaved faces, their heads on leather shields, swords always ready.

He aped their exercises with the resources at hand. He would push against the floor and the walls, stand on his hands, lift his father's heaviest books again and again over his head, until his adolescent body began to show signs of muscle. "Yes, you have a good and a strong body," his father had conceded when Icarus asked him (often more than once each day), "but a good and a strong body is of value only when it is the temple of a quick and agile mind." Daedalus had tried to shape and hone that mind as the soldiers did their weapons, but Icarus, as well-proportioned as any youngster he'd ever seen, was easily bored by his lessons, constantly distracted by the sounds of the raucous men below, by the patterns of the clouds above them, by the great expanse of sea around them, and by the birds that swooped within inches of his son's outstretched, imploring arms.

And so Icarus stood at the window in the dawn before Daedalus woke and gave his body the only respite he could manage from his long aching to be free. And he gathered the feathers the birds dropped on the window ledge and drew them across his face and chest to feel their flight on his skin. He sat in the window and soaked in the sun that came through the opening and felt the warmth of it penetrate his flesh, felt the warmth as it turned to sweat that wet him, the cool breeze that chilled his skin as the prickly perspiration turned into air, cool sea air, leaving hard human salt on his unblemished limbs. "Old Minos may control the land and sea," his father would say as Icarus stood idly by the window, "but he will never control the sky . . . that is Apollo's realm."

And Icarus would sigh, knowing that he would now be called from his musings for yet another tutorial in the complex lexicon of his father's gods. If they were so powerful, Icarus thought, why did they not carry him off to freedom? Why did no ravishing swan or eagle descend to carry him off to liberation?

And one hot morning in the third year of their imprisonment, on a day that Daedalus had said was to be the fourteenth anniversary of his youngest son's birth, Icarus stood in the dawn window and waited for the sun to come up over the horizon. He thought, with an ironic smirk in his eye, of the charioteer god, Apollo, whose horses were hitched to the sun ... Apollo, the sun god, the god of music and the lyre, his father's personal favorite because of the god's particular affinity for a quick and agile mind. And as he stared into the sun that morning, he had to rub his eyes, then again. He looked down at the soldiers still sleeping at the base of the tower, their night fires nothing more now than cinders. Because as Icarus looked to the horizon that morning, he thought he could make out a team of blazing horses, a fiery chariot of burnished gold, and a charioteer of such magnificent face and form that Icarus held his breath. He looked at his father, slumped as usual over his workbench, his scrolls undone before him. And then he looked back into the sun and into the smiling face of a man unlike any he had ever seen, a man whose perfection dazzled young Icarus, a man who held his chariot team in check with one bulging forearm, and who held the other forward in an invitation, it seemed, for Icarus to take hold of it.

3. MORNING

(ON THE ARRIVAL OF A YOUNG MAN IN ACADEMY)

"The greater the love, the more false to its object,
Not to be born is the best for man;
After the kiss comes the impulse to throttle,
Break the embraces, dance while you can."
                    —W. H. AUDEN
           "O Who Can Ever Gaze His Fill?"

By the time Gavin woke up, the desert sun was already blazing down on his second-floor dorm room and in through the wide, open windows. His body was covered with perspiration. He kicked back the sheet and pulled his long, brown hair from underneath him and laid it on the pillow to his right. He ran a hand down his flat chest and stomach and wrapped his fingers around his erect penis. He closed his eyes against the sunshine and could see red through his eyelids, translucent as papyrus. He thought of Julian and came almost immediately, the semen puddling in his navel like a belly-dancer's jewel. He noticed that he came in greater quantity later in the day than in the morning and wondered why that was. Something about tension, he guessed.

It was too hot and too early for much, but it was too late for his first class.

He rubbed the cum around his stomach and squeezed the last of it out of his balls, and then got out of the bottom bunk and stood wet and naked in the middle of the room. Now that his roommate had dropped out of school, he would have the room to himself for the rest of the semester. He looked around for a hint of what to do next. The clock gave him a clue. It read 10:31. That meant his nine o'clock was over, his ten o'clock already begun, and getting to eleven would mean going without breakfast. He would be free until poetry at two.

Gavin walked into the bathroom and stepped into the shower, letting the tepid water gush over him while it heated up. He soaped away the sweat, the semen, the fatigue of the night, let the refreshing water drain through his yard-long hair, rubbed the blue soap bar over his body, drawing it hard across the tight pucker of his ass, which made him arch his back and sigh.

Downstairs in the graduate wing, Marshall looked around the dark room and wondered why he felt like a failure. He looked at Eric's bed and wondered where he'd been keeping himself. Eric hadn't been around the dorm for weeks, although he showed up in class now and then, never telling anyone where he was sleeping. Marshall wondered if he had done something to drive Eric away and let his eyes wander over the photographs he had pasted all over the cinderblock walls in Eric's absence. Almost every inch was covered with them, black and white mostly, these images he had cut out of magazines and library books—at great peril to his immortal soul, of course, but it was that important for him to possess these strangers and to surround himself with long shadows in which to live. He had painted the room first, a mute dark green, the color of a leather-bound photo album he had once prized and long ago lost. The pictures were taped neatly behind, showing no evidence of attachment and were meticulously arranged by size, shape, and content, fanning out from several thematic centers: here a writers' cluster, there a dancers' wall easing into movie stars and great stage personages of the last century.

Finding a new and wonderful photograph of, say, Emile Zola, could mean hours of rearranging. He had spent whole days, from morning to night, standing on ladders of beds and chairs, making the juxtapositions perfect—lining up Paul Robeson's eyes with those of Hedy Lamarr, Charles Laughton with Gertrude Stein—evaluating the infinite number of possible relationships between subjects, dimensions, and shadings of emotion before affixing each picture to its new place in the pantheon of his idols. "If the three Nureyevs from *La dame aux camélias* go on the top," he might say out loud, "then Maria Tallchief will have to move a row to the left because her attitude is the same as the Antoinette Sibley, in which case the Tony Dowell and Judith Jamison, so symmetrical, can go where Fred and Ginger were, and they can go over here to the movie stars...." He could go on for days immersed in his thousand faces, his celebrities and unknown, monumental nudes—mostly male.

He was restless this morning, but no one in his garden of faces needed tending. He hadn't finished his paper on the origins of the Chinese theater and hadn't learned all the *Julius Caesar* monologue, but he didn't feel like studying. Maybe he would type out a poem from his handwritten version to read in class this afternoon.

He took out a sheet of blank paper and rolled it into his portable Olympic. He typed from his chicken scrawl:

> Silence always silence:
> What makes it all so dread?
> So cold/so frightened/so all alone—
> when the silence moon and stars
> are animate in the heavens ...?

★   ★   ★

Upstairs, Gavin could hear in the hot, desert silence the faint clutter of keys hitting Marshall's typewriter platen. He could hear some music somewhere, too, and tried to figure out if it was recorded or just some music students in rehearsal. Naked and wet, he looked around the room, fixing his eyes on the desk. He took it as a sign, and sat down in front of it. He drew a fine-toothed comb through his heavily conditioned, fragrant hair and looked at a piece of paper on which he had written nine words the night before.

He stared at them for a moment, the comb in one hand, an old-fashioned fountain pen in the other. He put down the comb and added a second stanza of six words to the nine that comprised the first. He smiled. It was perfect. Then he wrote his name and the date on the paper and slipped on his white muslin drawstring pants.

Marshall was typing when the door cracked open. He never locked it, but most people knocked.

"Yeah?" he said.

Gavin opened the door. "Hi," he said.

"Hi." Marshall was noncommittal, but Gavin was used to it.

"What are you doing?"

"Typing a poem. You?"

"I just finished one."

"Sit down," Marshall said, and Gavin looked around the dark room, its thick green curtains still drawn against the sun, the air conditioner purring above their heads. He sat on Eric's bed under Leonard Bernstein and Anna Magnani, their faces and arms contorted in identical attitudes of hysteria. Marshall stayed behind his desk, Tennessee Williams grinning from a large wicker chair just behind his shoulder.

"Hot," Gavin said.

"Yeah." Marshall looked into Gavin's eyes and wondered how anyone could allow such unguarded access to the inner depths.

"You wanna hear my poem?" Gavin asked. "It's short."

"Sure." Marshall decided Gavin's unchecked vulnerability was in fact safe enough, since what the eyes allowed access to was so mysterious they revealed nothing at all.

And Gavin read the poem while Marshall paid no attention. He was too intent on the smooth curves of Gavin's torso, his legs behind thin muslin, his beautiful bare feet.

"I like it better than the last one," he said when Gavin's voice finished reading.

Gavin looked at him as he sat behind his desk and wondered why Marshall seemed to hide behind everything—clothes, the dark, his desk and books, words, the feelings he wrote about that Gavin, barely out of high school, felt but did not yet understand, his dark beard and suntan, his wavy hair and the eyeglasses he always wore: clear plastic frames and pink plastic lenses.

When Marshall looked at Gavin he thought of sunny days on a Greek beach, Mykonos, perhaps, riding nude and barebacked on a black Arabian, Gavin's smooth white-boy's ass pushing into Marshall's groin.

Gavin stared at Marshall for a while and wondered why he never made a move to touch him. It was obvious Marshall was crazy about him. Gavin had no idea why, and couldn't figure it out. Men seemed to go for him, older men in particular, but Marshall wasn't that much older . . . five or six years maybe. Marshall was saying nothing. He just stared.

"You want to read me your poem?" Gavin asked.

"Um, no, I'll read it in class later if I get it done. It's pretty long."

"Oh," Gavin said, not having anything else to say. "Well, I guess I'll go get something to eat. You want something?"

"No, thanks," Marshall answered too quickly, "I've got some food here."

And Gavin left, without an invitation having been tendered, closing the door softly behind him. And Marshall sat at his desk watching the door close on beauty and the white muslin draped across Gavin's perfect boy's ass, and he wished he had asked for something, anything, just so he could have eaten out of Gavin's hand.

Downstairs, Gavin pushed fully open the already partly open door of Julian, the Chinese puppeteer.

He wasn't there.

"Where's Julian?" Gavin asked.

"Not here," answered Miguel, roommate, actor, and dollmaker.

Gavin stood in the middle of the room. Miguel tried his best to ignore him. He was crocheting a flamingo to appliqué onto a teddy bear's bolero jacket.

Gavin sat on Julian's bed, a kind of harem couch covered with pillows and hung with hand-dyed Indian fabrics. He could smell the cloves in oranges Julian kept as natural scent. Apples with faces cut into them were drying on strings. He picked up one of the puppets.

"Julian doesn't like people touching the puppets," Miguel said without looking up.

Gavin continued playing with it, one hand up the princess's feathered dress to her head, the other manipulating the two sticks that carried her expressive hands. Gavin put on a princess's voice and said: "So tell me, Mig, how come you don't like Gavin?"

"I'm really kind of busy right now," Miguel replied, but Gavin tossed his waist-long, dark chestnut hair, whipped the princess's miniature carved hands up to her face, and persisted:

"Please, Migsy-wigsy, please tell me why you don't like Gavin."

Miguel continued crocheting his flamingo.

"Pretty please with sugar on it . . . ?"

"Because . . . ," Miguel managed after Gavin had already decided he wasn't going to answer.

"Because . . . ?" The princess prompted.

Miguel dropped his hands into his lap and exposed his sweet moon face to Gavin's eyes. "Because you can always get what you want."

Gavin put the puppet down and dropped the princess voice. "And what do I want?" he asked. He didn't have the slightest idea what Miguel's answer might be, or what his own answer might be to the same question.

Miguel's chin started to quiver. Then he looked into Hurricane Gavin's eyes and said, "Julian. . . . And Marshall." Then he picked up the black thread and angrily bit a length of it off with his teeth.

"And what does Gavin get?" Gavin asked, amused and saddened at the same time.

"Julian . . . ," Miguel said, threading a tiny needle without apparent effort.

There was a silence while Miguel tied a knot in the end of the thread. "And Marshall . . . ," he continued, concentrating on his work.

"And what do you want, Mig?" Gavin asked, genuinely curious.

Miguel was sewing a minuscule black jet of an eye onto the flamingo's head. He put in a stitch and looked up. "Same as you, Gavin, only you get it because you're beautiful, and I'm not."

"You think I'm beautiful?" Gavin asked. He had no idea what beauty was, and no sense of his own beauty except the reactions of others.

"Everyone thinks you're beautiful, Gavin."

"Julian?"

"Julian does not sleep with people he doesn't think are beautiful."

"Marshall?"

"Him most of all."

"You think Marshall wants to sleep with me because I'm beautiful?"

"Christ, Gavin! Yes, yes, I do. Can't you tell? I can tell. He *told* Julian."

"Marshall's slept with you," Gavin said.

"Once. It took ten minutes, and there was somebody else in the room."

"Don't you think he finds you beautiful?"

"No, I don't."

"The first time I had sex with Julian was in the back of a van."

"I know. I was there. I kept watching Marshall watching you and wanting you because you're so fucking beautiful."

"Marshall thinks everything is beautiful," Gavin said.

Miguel stared at him.

"Except himself," Gavin corrected.

Then he got up and walked toward the door.

"Oh," Gavin said before he closed the door on Miguel's dollmaking, "I never get what I want. Because I don't want anything. Nothing. I don't care."

Miguel didn't know what to make of Gavin.

"And, Mig," Gavin said, "I've never slept with Marshall."

And Gavin closed the door and tossed his mane of hair and wondered what everyone was always so upset about.

4. NOON

(ON WAKING, THE FATHER FINDS HIS HEIR ENGAGED IN
IMMORAL CONGRESS WITH THE SUN)

*"And the scene on my helmet tells the true story: a chariot, eight
naked boys, winged ones,
and the wine, the mirror, the parasol——my triumph
inherits me. He holds my sword. He is what I see,
that is why you see him: the naked boy without wings."*
                                        —RICHARD HOWARD
                                        "The Giant on Giant-Killing"

It was noon on the fifteenth anniversary of his son's birth, in the fourth year of their captivity, when Daedalus opened his feebling eyes and saw the child of his old age standing stark naked in the window of their tower prison.

"What in the name of the gods are you doing?" old Daedalus grumbled as he unhinged himself from a sleeping position.

"Looking for Apollo," the boy said. "He's right overhead, and I can't see him unless I stand like this."

"Well, be careful," the old man warned, "I don't want you falling out the window." But the fact of the matter is that the old man was proud of the boy, and quite surprised that the little one had taken up his ancestors' religion so earnestly. He had shown no such predilection as a child.

The boy's hair was long now, long and golden, as his mother's had been in her youth. Daedalus thought of his dead wife and was grateful that she had not lived to see the ignominy of his incarceration. How proud she had been of the honors heaped upon her ancient husband when he laid the last brick of the labyrinth, King Minos's crowning glory and deadly lair of the bull/man Minotaur. And how sensitive she was; she could not even watch the spring ceremony when seven Athenian youths and seven Athenian maidens were tossed to the Minotaur for sacrifice ... but that was how it all began, and Daedalus could not bear going over it again.

How he hated this stupid little room in its ridiculous tower, its dangerously gaping window nearly daring them to plunge from it to their own destruction. Daedalus sat at his table and looked at the books he knew now by heart. They had not suggested any way of escape. Nor had they suggested a convenient path to greater patience or acceptance. He did not want to rot here watching this fine young strip of a son growing old and useless before his eyes, his all-too-rapidly diminishing eyes. Daedalus scraped the candle wax off an old tome of Egyptian alchemy and rolled it into a ball. He tossed the ball onto the floor. It rolled into the corner where Icarus kept his pile of feathers. Well, it was a harmless enough occupation, Daedalus thought, collecting feathers. Daedalus passed on to the boy what he knew of each species' habits, and the boy listened with rapt attention, constantly wanting to know the patterns of flight—did they soar or glide, take off from a standstill or a run, land on ground or water? Yes, thanks be to the gods, the boy was finally showing an admirably agile mind, about some things, in any event, though he seemed a bit touched in the head sometimes, too.

Daedalus looked up and saw his naked son standing spread eagle in the window, the sun blazing white on his long yellow curls, burnished copper on the shoulders the child had built up lifting books over his head. Daedalus was sorry to have mixed his son up in his own hubristic plot to outwit Minos, but the king was notoriously unjust, even for a barbarian, which he surely was, and would probably have destroyed both of them on the spot if the boy had not been so patently innocent and Daedalus himself so well-known and so highly respected. The aged architect stood slowly and shuffled nearer to the window, a bit off to the side of the boy, where he could see quite clearly that Icarus, head back, basking in the sun, was fully adult and fully erect, his manly rod jutting straight out from a shock of golden hair.

"Come down off there like that," Daedalus croaked, but Icarus just rolled his head back and forth behind him, trailing his long woman's hair down his tan muscled back. "The soldiers will be having a fine time looking at you like that," Daedalus nagged, but Icarus stood there holding the window frame until his knees began to sag and his arms began to contract, and the hot fluid of his sex spurted like lava out the window toward the ground. Daedalus was amazed at the volume of it, and that the boy could carry it off without even touching himself, but he was more than a little annoyed when he heard the cheers of the guards below.

Daedalus strode to the window, grabbed the boy around the waist, and, surprisingly strong when he needed to be, dropped his son to the floor. Then he leaned out the window and glared down at the soldiers below. A small knot of them was standing under the window licking the boy's liquid off each other, manipulating their own and each other's organs. Daedalus was furious. "Get away from there," he sputtered, but the soldiers just laughed at him and pointed. He shook his fist, but they laughed the heartier. Beside himself, Daedalus lifted up his robe, pulled out his own ancient, sagging member, and let loose a jet of piss. The soldiers howled curses at him and scattered like birds from a stone hurled into their midst.

Daedalus pulled himself back into the room, where Icarus was sitting in the corner braiding feathers into his hair, singing under his breath. The sun glistened off the moisture of his new mustache. He was a beauty, no doubt about it.

Perhaps, Daedalus thought, we could lure one of the guards up here on a sexual premise—Hemner seemed to favor the boy—then knock him senseless and get out of the tower. That this was considerably dangerous did not cross the old man's mind. What did was that being on the ground among the other soldiers would put them no closer to freedom. It might, however, turn them both into the whores of the camp. The prospect was too odious for the risk. He would never turn his son over to apprentice for a soldier. No, a strong and healthy body such as Icarus quite clearly boasted was important only as the temple of a quick and agile mind, a tenuous quality in his son, though Daedalus was not going to give up nourishing it without a fight.

It had been the diligent father's plan, before the catastrophe, to present the boy to a statesman, a philosopher, a teacher, or mathematician. These men were gentler with their young lovers and taught them disciplines that would serve the boys all their lives—not battle skills, but the skills of the mind—those smiled on by Apollo. And now there was no one but himself to teach the boy, and so his education would, of necessity, be incomplete—incest being out of the question, at least in Daedalus's mind.

The old ponderer sat again at his books and watched Icarus, who was at the moment sitting cross-legged, exposing the souls of his dirty feet, moving a cormorant feather back and forth in the air with one delicate hand and wiggling the long, tapered finger of the other.

"What are you doing?" Daedalus asked.

"Playing the lyre," Icarus answered.

"What lyre is that?" Daedalus asked.

"Yes," Icarus sighed, "he said you wouldn't be able to see it. Only those he has chosen can see it."

Well, Daedalus thought, it was inevitable. If he himself had been imprisoned at the boy's age, he would be somewhat out of his head, too. But, being a doting parent old enough to be his son's grandfather, he gave in to the caprice: "*Who* said?"

"Apollo," Icarus replied, as if the answer were the most obvious in the world, as if the name were the most precious in the world.

"Apollo speaks to you?" Daedalus asked. This was bad.

"Of course he speaks. He sings, he teaches me to play the lyre. The strings are made of his hair, you know ... that's why I have to use a feather. They're so delicate even a virgin's fingers would snap them. He says only the chosen may play the lyre of Apollo."

Daedalus was becoming concerned. "And what else does he say?"

"That I am the most beautiful of all mortal boys. That Ganymede has jealously raged against my beauty to all the gods of Olympus. That Zeus and Hera have fought openly ... about me. But that Apollo has claimed the right to be my ... protector."

He certainly is a coy child, Daedalus thought. "Icarus——" he began.

"He says he has never before seen such beauty as mine—eyes that pour my soul into his like rain into the holy vessels of Delphi. He says my neck to him is the perfection of his temple. When he puts his mouth on my neck, I can feel the wind of the south on his breath. When his mouth is on my nipples, I shiver as though the wind of the north has slid down my back through my hair. And when he puts his mouth on my sex, I feel the center of a vortex in my heart, and my love for him pours out of me. And the warmth of him dries me as he pauses just at noon above the tower. He can't stay, but he watches over his shoulder at me as he drives his chariot away. He calls me sacred and says my flesh is softer than a god's, my fluid in his mouth sweet as nectar. I love to feel the thistle of his beard between my legs and his tongue . . . his tongue. . . . He is so gentle, Father, like no man I have ever seen."

"Er, yes . . . ," Daedalus managed to say, staring for a moment into the open sky-blue eyes of his youngest son. "Very . . . poetic."

Icarus smiled and continued to play his invisible instrument.

Daedalus went back to his workbench and remembered his teacher, Akmanadoros, who had taken him from his own father many years before. And suddenly Akmanadoros came to him in a small gust of warm wind and played with the old man's cheek the way he had done when Daedalus was merely a curious and not altogether conscientious schoolboy.

And Daedalus watched as Icarus in his corner began to work several owl feathers into the ball of candle wax he had found. Daedalus watched as his enterprising son flattened the wax in the palm of his hand and began to layer feather upon feather into the wax, weaving strands of his hair between the stems like golden thread.

"What are you making, my son?" Daedalus asked cautiously.

"A fan," Icarus answered. "A gift for my lover to cool his face as he races the course of the sun. . . . A fan in the shape of a bird's wing—because my lover's freedom is his flight."

Daedalus looked at the small wing Icarus had fashioned from wax, feathers, and hair. Then he stood and went to the window and watched the sea birds soar and glide and dive down over the shore. And Daedalus remembered his own voice saying: "Minos may control the sea and land, but the sky is free. . . ."

And Daedalus had an idea.

5. DAY

(AFTER POETRY ... PASSION OR THE APOCALYPSE)

"The beauty I saw in him was a cross between Marilyn Monroe and shade."

——DENNIS COOPER
"Boys I've Wanted"

Marshall stood in his window watching the red glow and black smoke of the hill fires that had been raging for weeks. They looked like news films he had seen from hills overlooking the Vietnamese terrain, blazing with war and hatred, napalm, ignorance, futility.

The school was out of danger for now, which is to say it was not in danger *yet*, but everyone had been instructed to pack one *small* suitcase in case the college had to be evacuated on sudden notice. Marshall had packed the pictures. All of them. The room looked like a tenement deserted before demolition. Hunks of tape hung from the wall, some with corners of pictures still clinging to them. In some places patches of the green paint had come off on the tape and left scars on the wall where white showed through. Well, he thought, if this dump doesn't burn down, I'm going to have a hell of a time cleaning up.

The red sky in the middle of the day gave an eerie look of sunset to the scrub-covered landscape. The black smoke from the fire and the white steam from the water pumped onto it from helicopters and airplanes swirled together in the sky, forming a bank of gray clouds over the mountains that included every shade from snow to coal. He wondered if a nuclear holocaust would be similar or different.

Gavin had been breathtaking in class. His own poem had been

only modestly received, if immodestly delivered, he was that sure of himself. Addison said he thought it was "outstanding," that was true, but Addison was a jerk. Gavin had nodded sagely and, without saying a thing, let it be known that he approved. But Dr. Paulson thought it . . . overlong and perhaps a bit repetitious, even though the repetitions had been intentional, a way of invoking the incantatory quality of Paulson's own poetry, of his wildly rhythmic *Bacchae* translation. One woman couldn't understand why his poetry was so sad and so intense all the time. "No one's life could be *that* bad," she snorted through an enormous nose, as if in twenty years she had never encountered pain. "Mine is," Gavin had said as simple as the Last Judgment, offering no further explication or assurance.

Dr. Paulson loved Gavin's new poem, the one Marshall had not been able to hear either in his own room or in class because he could not keep his mind and eyes off the poet. It was a poem he did not understand really. If he were being honest about it, which he would not be, at least not aloud, he thought the poem had too little in it to be much of anything, too few words that spoke to the soul. What was it Paulson had said—? Oh, yes: "Simplicity speaks to the soul." But Marshall had no soul, at least none that he could identify, and so he envied Gavin's words that sank into his thorax like barbed weapons even when they made no sense to his mind.

Marshall looked at the fire blazing over the hills, looked at the parched desert landscape, and rubbed a hand across his forehead, drawing a fine layer of silt across his furrows. He looked at the blank space near his desk where the picture of Picasso had hung and announced to its ghost: "I'm going for a walk."

There wasn't much place to walk, at least not on campus. There wasn't much place to do anything. If he strolled the perimeter of the college, all the paths and every hall, stopping at the cafeteria and the main gallery, it might take an hour. Just beyond the schoolgrounds was the freeway, cutting through the gap in the mountains like an escape chute, providing access to automobiles and automobile exhaust, city smog, and, all too possibly, a monstrous fire raging out of control just behind the southern ridge. If the evacuation order came, the exodus would be toward the cool green hills of the north.

All over the country hot cinders borne on desert winds had set off satellite fires, and the pessimistic evaluation was that millions of acres and several billion dollars' worth of real estate could be gone within hours if there were not some break in the weather—hot, dry, windy. The glow over the mountain seemed to heat the valley by degrees.

When Marshall turned his back on the impending conflagration, he saw Gavin, sitting on the roof outside his window. He was naked except for minuscule shorts and his voluminous hair. Marshall looked up and felt envy and lust, realizing he probably managed to commit all seven of the deadly sins on a daily basis. Gavin waved and shouted.

As they sat on the roof, watching the glow of fire, Marshall could not keep his eyes off Gavin's lap, where his balls had slipped out of the loose legs of his nylon shorts.

"How old are you?" he asked Gavin.

"Seventeen. Why?"

"Just wondering."

Seven years, Marshall thought. Seven years. Could Gavin possibly be as immune to life seven years from now as Marshall already felt himself to be, so bitter, so entrenched and lonely? And what would they each be like in seven more years? Would there even be seven more years?

Gavin turned his eyes on Marshall, and Marshall sensed a rush of Gavin crawling up the hair of his thighs, could feel himself engorging under scrutiny.

"I liked your poem in class," Marshall said.

"I liked yours, too," Gavin responded and shook his hair like a horse in good temper. Some of the long hairs stuck to his hot wet chest and curled around a dark nipple. In a small gust a good strand of it blew into his mouth. He spit it out, then pulled off the hairs that remained stuck to his face with saliva. He'd done it before. With his eyes closed.

"What are you going to do when you get out of school?" Marshall asked, embarrassed by his own banality and not caring at all what was going to happen any further into the future than the next hour. After all, hadn't he already decided he had reached the point of no more meaningful experience? From now on all the rest was decline and speculation, reflection and reinvention. Isn't that what he had decided one night in contemplation of his human menagerie?

"I don't know," Gavin said. "Go to San Francisco."

"What'll you do?"

Gavin shrugged silently. "Live off some old broad. That's what I did last summer." He turned back and dropped his eyes into Marshall's eyes. "Or maybe some old guy."

"It's hot," Marshall said.

"We could go in and cool off."

They climbed back through the window. Gavin slid the glass window shut, drew the curtains closed, and turned on the air conditioner. The room was immediately cooler. And more isolated. Gavin smiled into his dimples and nodded. Then he walked to a mirror, sat down, and took a brush to his hair.

"Let me do that," Marshall said. And he took the long, silky hair with the sun-red highlights and brushed it.

"Should I do it a hundred times?" he asked, not seriously.

"Do it as much as you want," Gavin said. "It feels great."

By the time they were both tired of the brushing, Marshall was hard in his jeans. Gavin stood and walked to the bed.

"I think I'll lie down for a while," he said looking at Marshall.

Marshall walked closer, then looked as deep as he could into the ambiguous vacuum of Gavin's black eyes. He waited for some sign; none came that he could decipher. He put his hand up to Gavin's face and touched a cheek, touched his hair.

"So beautiful," he said.

Gavin leaned his head into the hand, then tossed his hair once and turned his back.

Marshall put his hand on the crown of Gavin's head and drew it down the length of his hair to its ends, letting it settle in a friendly way on the black nylon of Gavin's narrow hips. He leaned in toward the perfect boy poet of his imagination and kissed him chastely on the shoulder. He smelled skin.

"I think I'll go lie down, too," Marshall said.

Gavin never forced anyone to do anything they didn't want to do. He was not yet clear about the mechanics of secret desire—not only because he wanted nothing himself, but because it was only beginning to dawn on him that other people did not do exactly as they pleased.

"Oh. Okay. 'Bye," he said.

Marshall knew the decisive moment had come, and he hated himself for letting it pass, when the slightest gesture would have meant fulfillment. It was one thing to fall for someone who couldn't love you back; he was an old hand at unrequited love and lust. It was another not to reach out and take what was so clearly offered. It meant his loneliness was more important to him than love, or at least more necessary. Was it better, somehow, was it even *noble*, to abstain from sex where the bruised heart was so confused it could not tell infatuation from appetite or romance? And what was suddenly so wrong with sex for its own sake? He'd had sex with a dozen men without any agony at all—beautiful, muscled men: dancers, gymnasts— men whose bodies could have validated his own desirability as easily as Gavin's willing embrace, if he had given them as much power, if their lack of interest could have crushed him as completely as Gavin's rejecting him would have. Why was everything so complicated, so difficult for him? And what did any of it matter?

"See you later," he said, and turned his back on all the possibilities of his mind.

Gavin pushed fully open the already partly open door of Julian, the Chinese puppeteer. The room was dark. There was incense burning in a small bronze burner shaped like a heron. In front of the window was an enormous packed suitcase with Julian's puppets in it, but the room was empty. Gavin turned to go as Julian stepped into the room from his bathroom with a small red towel around his middle. His indigo hair was a mass of curls that relaxed almost as far down his back as Gavin's straighter, lighter mane.

"Hi," Julian said, his face lighting up like a Renaissance wood-block sun.

"Hi," Gavin said.

Julian unwrapped the red towel and stood naked. He walked up to Gavin, close enough to feel the heat, inclined his head slightly to one side, and kissed him. He was already hard as he took Gavin's hand gently and walked toward the bed. Julian sat down and looked through obsidian eyes into the perplexed expression on the face of his occasional lover. He pulled the thin black nylon shorts off Gavin's hips and put his mouth around his cock.

Gavin sighed and stepped out of the shorts. Julian sank back into his dozen pillows and pulled his right knee to the side as an invitation. Gavin took a long look at Julian, beautiful by any standard, and felt his desire drain out of him. He wanted Marshall, and no substitute, even one as lovely as Julian, could ease that thought from his mind.

"Um . . . I guess I'm not in the mood," he said.

Julian sat up and leaned forward to take Gavin's hand, a look of panicked failure filling his eyes.

"I can't right now," Gavin said. "That's all. I'm sorry, okay?"

Marshall closed the drapes, turned on the cold air, and looked at the empty damaged walls where his pictures had hung so neatly and wondered where Eric was these days. Then he stripped off his clothes and stretched out on the cool green cover of his narrow bed.

He closed his eyes and tried to picture himself holding Gavin naked in his arms, as he had pictured them together so many times before. He could see himself taking that face with those equine eyes into his hands and holding the face still and leaning into it and putting his mouth on Gavin's mouth, could feel his tongue touch the slight opening between the two fleshy lips of the younger poet, could feel the jawbones of the poet press into his palms. And he could feel his hands sliding down the smooth chest and sculpted torso of this North Carolina teenager and slipping them under the waistband of the thin white muslin drawstring pants—

There was a loud knock on the door that echoed in Marshall's solar plexus. Was it the evacuation order? He held his breath, but didn't answer.

"Marshall, it's Miguel. Are you in there?"

He didn't answer.

"Shit," he heard from the other side of the door. Then silence.

He closed his eyes again and tried to pick up his fantasy where it had been interrupted but found he had to start again from the beginning: the face in his hands, the hands sliding down over the skin, smooth as chamois. . . . .

But the third dimension had gone out of it. No longer a wish to be fulfilled, it read to his own mind like a mediocre script he had read once before without liking it much the first time.

He grabbed his cock and jerked off fast and hard, thinking of the soft pained question of Gavin's face when he left him standing alone in his room. Marshall hated himself for his cowardice, hated his body and his desire and those who desired him, and he came in gushing spurts, the cum hitting him in the face, in his hair and eyes. There had never been so much of it.

In the accumulating silence he could hear the hum of the air conditioner. Then a door slammed somewhere, a voice was raised, and another door hit its frame too hard. Then he dozed off and dreamed of nothing he could remember.

When he woke up, it was raining.

6. AFTERNOON

("AND YET FOR ALL HIS WINGS THE FOWL WAS DROWNED.")

"Give me the splendid silent sun with all his beams full-dazzling."
—WALT WHITMAN
Leaves of Grass

It was the summer of the fifth year of our captivity, and I was bored with the project my father had been working on for nearly a year. It was in the afternoon, I remember, and old Daedalus was saying we might make our flight that very day if I would condescend to help him. I had helped him, all right—for months!—but right that minute I was restless, *preoccupied* I guess the word should be. I stepped up into the window ledge and let the hot breath of the air surround me. My hair was past my waist now, golden yellow and twined with all the smaller feathers we had gathered, the ones Daedalus said were too small for his use. I had fashioned a necklace of falcon feathers and a wristlet of raven. My beard had grown in gold and red. Father trimmed it with a sharpened stone. I was tanned darker than Hemner's horse, and I could tell from the way he looked up at me that Hemner would have loved the chance to ride me the way he rode that stallion he was so proud of. And I might have let him, were I not faithful to Apollo, and enjoyed it, too.

I was standing in the window, I remember, my hands above my head, feet together, one knee bent. I felt as if I might dive upward into the sky. I dropped my arms slowly, as gracefully as I remembered the bull dancers doing in the years before our captivity. I wondered what my cousin Perdix might be doing at home. Learning masonry in all likelihood. It's what he always wanted, to build and make things, like my father. I never had much aptitude for the sort of thing he reveled in. Daedalus always liked him, although I think my father might have been a little embarrassed to have such a bright child around, one who outshone me, that's for certain, particularly in those areas that meant so much to the old man, for Perdix has a quick and agile mind. But Perdix is not beautiful. Perdix was not chosen by Apollo, cannot sing as I can sing, play as my lover has taught me to play, write the lyrics and the odes I compose nearly extempore.

Poetry drives my father mad. He calls it immoral, artificial, deceitful, wasteful, a *caprice*—as if a labyrinth so complex no one can find his way out of it was not capricious.

I smile and say, "Of course—that's just the point."

He sputters and glowers and dives back into his wing-making. Oh, yes, Daedalus is making wings for us both. He got the idea from me, he says, though I can't think how, and he's convinced, based on his endless calculations, that he can construct wings strong enough to carry us out of this foul place, though where we'd go I have no idea. Certainly not back to Crete, where Minos would have us shot down like so many terns for his supper.

I told him I'd fly if he did. After all, if the wings work, we'll be free. If they don't . . . well, Hemner will catch me. I know he will.

It's taken ten months nearly to the day to get as far as we've gotten—Father's kept a record of our time here, which, of course, he will have to leave behind. He's finished three of the wings already, made them out of feathers, candle wax, strands of my hair and his beard, and threads from carefully unweaving my garments. I never need them anymore. Apollo prefers me naked. Just as I prefer him. Of his own cloak, Father has made strips of cloth with which he intends to fasten the wings to our shoulders and arms. It could work. After all, he was reputed to be a genius in his day. It's hard to see what Mother saw in him, though she told me once he was ravishingly beautiful and that she envied Akmanadoros my father's youth. It seems odd that my father's lover was a mere mortal when mine is a god. Just as it seems odd he would leave his lover for a woman, even one as even-tempered as my mother was. I would miss her terribly if it weren't for Apollo and his daily visits—and the way he bows down and worships me.

"Icarus!"

"Yes, Father?"

"You're preening like a peacock. Come down from there. The proud are often brought low. Do not forget . . . moderation in all things."

"Oh, Father, moderation is for mortals."

"And you are not mortal then?"

"Yes, for now. But Apollo promises me immortality, which means I shall someday be a god, doesn't it? I will be very happy to be a god and live eternally. I've even asked to retain my youth. He agreed."

"Exactly what did Apollo say?"

"He said that in generations to come—in eons to come, thousands and thousands of years from now—I will be known as the youth who found immortality in the love of Apollo."

"Well, your Apollo is certainly a fine wordsmith."

"I thought you didn't believe in Apollo."

"Of course I believe in Apollo. I just do not believe that you are his lover, pretty as you may be, or that he comes to you every day in the beams of the sun and all of that, or that he's taught you all you know."

"How else have I learned it then, Father?"

"You always were a dreamer. Perhaps it's inborn. Your mother always said that an artistic temperament was an inborn thing. But be careful, my son. The words of the gods are not always what they seem."

"Are you nearly finished?"

"Yes, come here and let me tie these on you."

Daedalus turned to look at his son for the last time. "Remember," he said, "you must fly directly *away* from the setting sun. Do not fly too near the water or the wax will become too hard and the feathers will fall out. Do not fly too high or the heat of the sun will melt the wax and the feathers will fall out. Do you have the courage?"

"Of course," Icarus replied. And Daedalus embraced his son for the last time, placed one kiss on each cheek, stepped up to the window and dove out into the air, plummeting nearly to the ground before he caught the first updraft.

"Come, Icarus, follow me," he heard his father shout, and outside on the ground there was chaos as the soldiers ran in all directions at once at the sight of the old captive soaring above them on the giant wings of an albatross.

Icarus stood in his window and watched his father glide. He was so absorbed in Daedalus's comical attempt to master flight, he almost did not hear the door of the cell open. Just as he turned to face the scraping sound, Hemner stormed into the room naked and aroused.

"Do not go, Icarus," Hemner said. "I am your slave. I must have you."

I smiled as gently as I could, for I actually had quite an affection for Hemner and that hard body of his encased in coiled black hair. And although we'd never even touched, the sight of him in high blood convinced me I couldn't have held out much longer. After all, I was only human.

"Hemner," I said, "I am the lover of another, of Apollo, the sun."

I could hear my father calling me from outside, over and over again. My name in his throat sounded like the cackling of crows. I stared deep into Hemner's eyes, which were, I had never before noticed, as green as the sea in summer and deep in pain knowing he would never hold me in his arms. I might have dawdled a bit longer, but Hemner made a lunge for me, quite understandable given his long-unsated lust, and I had to jump just to get out of the way.

The feeling was miraculous. It was as liberating as the pony races Perdix and I had along the shore as boys, the cool ocean breeze whipping our boyish hair. The strain on my arms was wonderful as I managed to float on air currents over the sea. The cool wind on my face was as welcome as the warmth of morning. The sensation of absolute power in my loins made my head light as spent passion.

"Not too high and not too low," my father caw-cawed at me from over the waves. "Follow me!"

I watched him for a moment, ever the dutiful son, and traced the arc of a graceful erne over the breakers. I watched him and the astonished affection in his prunish face. Then I shouted, "Farewell, my good father, and may the gods of your enterprise speed you to safety. Apollo waits!"

And I turned and set my sights on the muscled back of my lover as his sun chariot raced high across the sky. "Come, Icarus," I longed for him to say. "Come and find eternal youth in my embrace."

I heard nothing. But my heart smiled because of the love I felt for him and the surge I felt in my loins. I started upward after him.

I heard him calling my name, but I pretended not to. I found his insolence more than a little overbearing. When I finally turned around to get a look at him, he was flapping his absurd little wings like a lunatic. He had the most pathetic look of determination on his face, which was dripping with sweat, his hair sticking to it and to his neck and chest, shoulders and back. In fact, his wet hair was clinging all over him. He looked like Aphrodite rising from the foam. He was dripping feathers, too, which reeked and came unwound from the many plaits he had woven into what I must say myself was quite an ingenious design.

Well, it was near the end of the day, and I thought no one would notice if I just stopped and hovered over the horizon for a moment before sinking into the night. When he finally reached me, he slowed to a near stop, using his wings like the fins of a fish to hold him steady.

"Didn't you hear me?" he demanded. He might have tried a humbler approach, at least for openers.

"Yes," I said, "I heard you."

"Then why didn't you come to me?"

"My dear young friend," I said, every inch the indignant master, "it is for you to come to me. When have you ever heard it said that the sun reversed itself in its course to accommodate a pigeon?"

He looked hurt. I had succeeded.

Oh, he was a beauty, all right. One of the prettiest little men in Greece. Of course, he was much prettier two years ago, when I first noticed him standing in that window shaking his tight hips at me, luring me with the twin knobs of his pelvis and that sparse soft hair just beginning to sprout like moss. That was before he started all the nonsense with the chicken feathers. Yes, he was, in his day, the prettiest boy in southern Crete. But, he was not the first, and I had no intention of his being the last. There were others even during the time I was visiting him. He was special, it's true, and perhaps I did lead him mercilessly on, but none of the others took it so seriously. And I went out of my way to tell him that Hemner would make a fine lover in my stead.

It flattered me that Icarus wanted to be faithful. But I knew it was because he had not seen enough mortal men to make a reasoned comparison. He should have gone with Hemner and forgotten about me. After all, I am a god. He wanted to be immortal, they all do, but only Zeus can do that. When I suggested it, my father nearly roared the pillars of heaven down. "Just what I need," the old man cried. "What do you think my life with Ganymede would be like with another adorable adolescent traipsing around for the rest of time, not to mention Hera with that temper of hers."

Yes, Icarus had chosen badly by choosing me. Like Zeus, I have an eye for young men. And for women, too, as far as that goes. He should have flown off to Sicily with his father. Italians are obsessed with feathers.

"Well," he said petulantly, "you could at least have waited." The gentle thunder in the distance was Zeus laughing and warning at the same time.

"My dear Icarus," I said, "gods do not wait for small boys with feathers glued to their arms."

The look on his face told me he had just learned a lesson all mortals learn sooner or later, a lesson so fundamental they try to protect one another from it.

"You said I would be immortal."

"Well," I said, "strictly speaking, I said your reputation would last forever."

"And that I would stay young forever."

"Yes," I said as gently as I could without, I hoped, giving in to sentiment. "Those who die in youth shall remain forever young."

"But I *love* you," he said as sadly as I'd ever heard it said before— or since, for that matter.

I was going to suggest he turn tail and flap off to his father— or at least to Hemner—when a look of coy serenity came over his face.

"What is it?" I asked, thinking he was up to something.

"Nothing," he said. "Nothing at all."

And then he gracefully reached both arms over his head, letting his feet dangle before him. The position displayed him at his fullest length, his skin pulled tight across his trunk, his belly hollowed between his ribs and hips, his organ filling with blood. Oh, it was an appealing attitude, make no mistake. And I was sorely tempted. But then he looked into my eyes with those gorgeous orbs of his like lacquered robins' eggs, and he smiled. I was stiffening rapidly myself, he looked so extremely vulnerable and at the same time voluptuous beyond endurance. He looked like he could dive upward to Olympus on his own power.

I heard a louder groan of thunder, which undoubtedly meant Zeus was calling for some paramour to relieve his excitement.

"Don't you want me anymore?" Icarus asked.

I was by now in a state of great agitation, and I did want him— more than I had ever wanted him or any mortal before him.

"Yes," I said, "I do want you."

Then he bent his knees ever so slightly and rotated them outward just enough so that I could see the sack under his hard sex tighten with his own pleasure.

"Then come to me," he said.

I knew I shouldn't, but I could not help myself. A louder roar of thunder was Zeus's anger or pleasure—I could not tell one from the other. I tied the reins to the chariot and dropped my tunic, standing naked before him in all my glory. He arched his back, rolling his shoulders and pushing his hips slightly forward. I stepped from the chariot to approach him as he broke into a broad, childish grin. I reached out to grab him around the tender middle when he slipped out of his wings and, laughing giddily, dropped like a pelican into the ocean, never to be seen again.

I knew the sky-splitting thunder was Zeus's wrath at having lost the boy to his brother, the sea. And although both Zeus and I begged Poseidon for his return, the King of the Ocean was adamant. And quite, quite sated, I am sure.

Daedalus watched with horror as his son flew higher and higher toward the sun to disaster, the disaster that was certain to follow so foolish a prank. What was the boy thinking of? Had he not warned him again and again of the danger of melting wax? And he watched until he could no longer see his son in the glare of the sun.

He could see Hemner onshore. The handsome captain held a hand over his eyes to shield them, staring into the sun. Suddenly Hemner let out a moaning cry, and Daedalus looked up to see the boy plummeting into the liquid arms of the sea.

And Daedalus knew that Icarus was drowned by his own device

and had met his fate because they had both been guilty of striving beyond mortal propriety.

And Daedalus wept, as he flew alone toward Sicily, but in his weeping the order of the gods was confirmed in his mind.

7. SUNSET

(ON RETURNING TO LOS ANGELES AFTER THREE YEARS OF
POST-NONCOITAL DEPRESSION)

"Looking back I think he must have been an angel."
—DAVID TRINIDAD
Pavane

Yes, there is Gavin dancing at Studio One, all the hair off his head and all the magic drained out of him except for the pomegranate mouth and wellspring eyes—still as dark, as rich with their inscrutable vulnerability—that pained look of never knowing what will hurt, or who, or for how long.

He smiles and waves and looks at me after all these years as if we shared lunch just yesterday, not seven years ago in another world and time. He waves as if he is glad to see me, his gestures the stage directions for an unwritten play.

He dances in Levi's, shirtless, like a hundred or so others, identical. All the muscle must have come from so much flying so close to the sun. Dark hair sprouts between the mounds of his hard and handsome premeditated flesh.

I watch him from behind a beer. I think: And here is Gavin again like the moon through barbed wire.

He waves again, bent at the middle, dancing to the floor, his partner his double.

It was the year a planeload of undocumented farm workers slammed into a mountain in Mexico and set the valley on fire. It was the year the December sunsets over Santa Monica were so extraordinary from the towers of Century City. I had already been back in town, what, four years after a three-year absence?

And here is Gavin again, as he had been in San Francisco when I walked down the street and saw his pictures on a porn-house wall. And went into the dark and musty place and watched with longing as Gavin engaged in a series of encounters that paled beside my own past fantasies. I watched the engorging of organs, tongues in mouths, sweat sliding between tumescent nipples, and thought of his white-boy back and loose geisha hair and bareback ponies on the Aegean shore, my hand floating over the concave curve of his boy back, hovering.

I sat in the mildewed darkness with my hand through the open fly of my jeans and watched a black man on the screen put his cock up Gavin's lubricated ass. I clutched my own cock and felt the heat rising in my ears. I turned my head in the dark and saw the yearning eyes of a boy who had moved closer to me twice. I buttoned one button of my jeans and walked past him, nearly rubbing my crotch in his face as I went by.

I stood in the lobby and watched as he came out of the auditorium. He was older than I had been in the early Gavin days, older than I thought in the dark, and was wearing a red sweater. Our eyes locked and the boy/man walked into the ladies' room, the only bathroom that had not been boarded by the management. I followed. There were two men combing their hair at each other in a large, smudged mirror. The kid—I wanted and needed him to be a *kid*—was just disappearing into the last stall. I followed, stood outside the booth, its door partly open, then pushed it open all the way.

He was sitting on the porcelain stool with his red sweater pulled off and his pants down at his ankles. He held his dick in his hand. I turned and looked at the two men in the mirror. They brought their glances around to mine and started walking in my direction. I stepped inside the stall with my heart pounding the way it was when I almost touched Gavin. I slid the small chrome bolt into its caddy and moved between the kid's knees. He looked up through long eyelashes and, without saying a word, pulled my belt open. He pulled my jeans down off my hips and let out a flattering sigh at the sight of my stiff prick and the thick blond hair of my thighs. He took me in his mouth and massaged my ass while I pinched his right nipple with the tongue-moistened fingers of my right hand and held a handful of his hair in my left.

And I felt the warm wet abyss of this gray-eyed no-name close on my cock, and I pushed my hips into and out of his kindly stranger's face, shutting my eyes and thinking of the perfection of Gavin and his pony hair, his unshy mouth and lubricated ass filled with a stranger's cock. And I pulled the boy/man to his feet and turned him around and bent him over the bowl so his hands were flat against the cold white tile of the back wall. Then I slipped my saliva-slickened cock into his smooth hot ass without effort and thought about my hand hovering above the warmth of Gavin's waist, afraid to touch him.

And I walked my fingers up the knobs of the nameless red sweater's spine and grabbed his hips and thrust a little harder and deeper and faster than I might have, because I no longer saw beauty as unattainable. I no longer saw beauty at all. And I came so hard and so far into this small stranger, who no longer wore a red sweater, or anything at all, that I could feel the muscles of his abdomen clench, could feel the muscles of his asshole holding onto me for dear life, the same as my heart muscle clenched as I walked from Gavin's dorm room so many years ago without having tasted his body and its boy-sweet fluids.

And now here is Gavin again, dancing. Gavin like the moon through the barbed wire of Dachau, Gavin seeming to be glad to see me while he dances for the floor.

What year was it, exactly?

The year of the electrical storms and lightning, the fireballs ravaging Kansas, the solar eclipse that lasted three days, sinking the world into a pink miasma of fear. It was the year of the explosions in Pennsylvania, the Canadian meteor showers, Indiana mine disasters, the sub-Saharan drought, the chemical fires that raged four days in Texas, gas fires in Missouri, oil fires in the hulls of ships at sea, the volcanic eruption in Colombia, the burning of Atlanta and Hanoi, the bombing of Cambodia, the annihilation of Nagasaki, and the drowning of Atlantis, lost continent of philosophers' dreams.

Because all those years were all of him: so far, so much an eyeful, so willingly available had I but known, so much a Gavin in an eye like a hollow. How much I could have loved him, poet and alone.

★

LYNETTE PRUCHA

MURDER IS MY BUSINESS

MARRIAGE, LIKE DEATH, WAS big business in downtown Los Angeles. The storefronts along Broadway's Latino thoroughfare proved it. Behind the large window of Bridal City, lace-tiaraed mannequins wearing dusty peach, petal rose, or mint green gowns lined up like snow cones in seasonal shades of popularity.

Sticking out in the midst of all this tacky pomp and circumstance was the Bradbury Building. In that historic edifice, built in 1893 and recently made earthquake-proof, for the bargain price of fifteen hundred dollars a month in rent, was my one-woman detective agency, MARINO INC.

The INC was stenciled by mistake, but I never bothered to have it removed. It gave the business more authenticity. Business wasn't exactly booming, but I managed to cover my overhead, pay rent on a one-bedroom condo in West Hollywood, eat at City restaurant at least twice a month, and work out with a trainer at a prissy health club on Robertson. Not bad.

My office was done up in what I'd call minimalist chic. Not too much furniture and a view of an adjacent building with a fifty-foot mural of Hidalgo Rodriguez, patron saint of the streets. Actually he was the first capitalist to turn a peso into a million bucks. His image was all the art I needed.

It was a Thursday evening, somewhere between five and six. My part-time intern had gone home for the Christmas holidays, and for two weeks I was winging it on my own. I had reservations for dinner at Engine Company 28 and I was just finishing some paperwork on my last case, when the door to the outer reception area slammed shut.

A meek little voice managed to make itself heard, and I replied by shouting, "In here."

Heels clicked along the tiled floor and I had barely glanced up from an overdue account when my eyes did a ring-around-the-rosy at the looker standing no more than three feet in front of me.

She was younger than thirty, but old enough to know what she was doing. The two-piece lamb's wool suit smelled new and expensive. The glasnost hat had a faux cluster of jewels appliquéd on it. The entire outfit was black, including the silk seamed stockings and the patent leather bag she clutched in her gloved hands.

"Ms. Marino?" she inquired as I pointed for her to have a seat.

"Angie." I pulled out a pack of cigarettes from my top drawer, offered her one, but she declined. I had just inhaled my first puff of the day when she dropped the next line on me.

"My husband murdered me."

I stopped chomping on my cigarette long enough to watch the flicker of melodrama dance in her sea green eyes. For a minute I almost drowned in the turbulence of that ocean.

"You mean tried to murder you?"

"No."

I took another drag of the cigarette to help clear my head. Then I laid the burning stick in a clean ashtray, pushed up the sleeves of my camel jacket, the one I'd purchased in Neiman Marcus two months ago, the one I still owed $314 on. I figured by now I probably owned both sleeves. The rest of the jacket, along with the pockets and snazzy buttons, had a way to go.

She removed her gloves and laid them on my desk. "Let me explain. I don't have much time." She pulled out a handkerchief and clutched the embroidered talisman in her smooth hand. "My husband has been having this affair for three months. I was hoping it would peter out, that Roger would get tired and come back home and behave. We've been married nearly five years. Men are apt to stray sometimes." Her smile contained the thinest veneer of sarcasm as she crossed her legs and waited for my response.

"Before you go any further, it might help if I knew your name and you understood my fees."

She replied with hesitation. "Ramona Millicent Hunnicut and I'm sure your fees are reasonable."

"Hunnicut Textiles?"

"Yes. I gather you realize I value discretion above all else. If word gets out, it would be quite embarrassing."

"Of course." I was attracted to Ramona Millicent Hunnicut more than I cared to admit. My therapist said I'd moved beyond my damsel-in-distress syndrome. Thank you. No recriminations. Just a healthy dose of curiosity and simple animal attraction operating here. I ground out the tasteless cigarette, thought about my liaison later this evening, and wondered what Mrs. Hunnicut was wearing under the widow's weeds.

"A week ago I did something quite shameful."

I raised an eyebrow and hung on every word. I gestured for her to resume her tale.

"I hired someone to follow Roger. The detective took these pictures." She opened her purse and pulled out two photos. "I have more, but they are in my safe at home."

Roger was a handsome man, tall, with a soft fleece of hair on his muscular chest. The lady-in-waiting kneeling in front of Roger had divine curvature and curly brunette hair that fell on her naked shoulders in frenzied tendrils. The other photo was a little more of the same, only this time, Roger was the supplicant.

"Why did you come to me, Mrs. Hunnicut? Why not Thachter

& Associates? I understand they were involved in the Hunnicut investigation about three years ago." I'd suddenly remembered the rumors that had gone around town. Old-monied Hunnicut had been blackmailed by a drug cartel. It appeared Hunnicut refused to use his cargo as a front for laundered dough. The Colombians didn't appreciate his resistance.

Mrs. Hunnicut shifted uncomfortably in her chair. Her lips were creamy smooth, the jaw strong, the nose proud enough.

"My father hired Thachter & Associates. He's dead. I'm in charge now."

"Fine, then why not the dick you hired to take the photos?"

"Mr. Fletcher? I didn't like him. He was beginning to get too familiar."

I started to raise my eyebrow again, but it felt like old hat. I wondered if she meant Ned Fletcher, an operative I'd run into more than once.

"How familiar?" The words spilled out of my mouth.

Mrs. Hunnicut unbuttoned the top of her jacket. "He was a handsome man who tried to take advantage of my shame."

She gave me enough details to convince me she'd done the right thing. I'd had my suspicions about Fletcher, but I never thought he'd go this far. Lousy son of a bitch. He probably figured he'd capitalize on this delicate situation. It had been done before.

"Besides, a friend of mine recommended I work with a woman. At least I know where they stand."

Mrs. Hunnicut leveled a look at me that made my toes curl.

"That's why I came to you. I simply checked the phone book. Before my father died, he tried to buy this building. I saw your name listed, with the Bradbury Building as an address, and I called. Sorry I can't say you came highly recommended, but in my rush to find someone I didn't have the time to make extensive inquiries."

I nodded, waiting for more, but she didn't give it. Her perfume appeared to travel off her body first class and infiltrate my train of thought. I conjured a spring bouquet, the delicacy of thistles blowing in the wind, and a Brazilian rain forest.

"I have no one to turn to. My husband rigged my murder, never suspecting I knew about his infidelities. He had no idea I had gotten into the habit of . . . spying on him."

Nothing like a healthy dose of back-stabbing to spark a marriage, I thought. "That still doesn't explain the fact that you claim to have been murdered. The dead don't often get a chance to talk about it afterwards." Somewhere along the line, diplomacy had jumped overboard. Mrs. Hunnicut could be just another nut case looking for attention or drama in her life. But then again she could be telling the truth.

"Let me explain. The day before yesterday, I went sailing with my husband. I gave Roger *Siren's Kiss* as a wedding present. It's a fifty-foot, full-powered Trimaran. Anyway, that night he was in a very good mood. We'd just made love and he was preparing supper for me. Roger's an excellent cook. He insisted I go up on deck and make myself comfortable in this makeshift divan he'd built for my convenience. I often spend hours reading and sunbathing there."

Mrs. Hunnicut's pale face didn't look as though she'd spent too much time exposing herself to the harmful rays of the sun. I could picture her in a 1940s one-piece white bathing suit, though.

"We had been out sailing all day, so I'd imagine we were about two hours from shore. The sky was black and there didn't appear to be a ship in sight."

I opened my desk drawer, stared at the bottle of Rémy, thought better of it, and pulled out a pad instead. "Go ahead," I said, scratching a few notes on the yellow paper.

"Anyway, I felt for the first time in months that perhaps Roger *did* love me, that this affair was just a meaningless diversion. Even on the open sea, I could smell the delicious aroma of the fresh lobster fettucine he was preparing. We both love garlic and herbs."

My stomach did a flip-flop at the mention of food. I had promised myself I wouldn't order an appetizer at dinner, but mentally blew off my good intentions.

"I'd had several glasses of champagne—he'd seen to that. But it must have been something more than champagne because I started to feel as if I was slipping away, like I was becoming one with the sea. The ocean was a bit choppy and I felt the spray of sea salt on my face. I was preparing to get up off the divan when I heard a clicking noise. I opened my eyes and stared into the darkness, but no one was there. Then I heard music coming from down below and Roger's deep baritone voice as he attempted an aria from *Rigoletto*. I was just about to close my eyes again, I suddenly felt so weary, when something snapped underneath me—like a spring—and before I knew it the divan flipped over starboard. I felt my body slap the ice cold ocean." Mrs. Hunnicut shuddered and clutched her handkerchief in her hand.

I urged her to continue. She measured her breathing carefully before commencing.

"I screamed and flailed my arms—I'm a poor swimmer and I was absolutely paralyzed with fear. Fear and an almost crippling relief that it would soon be over."

Her eyes narrowed in pain. Mrs. Hunnicut's voice was chilled with the terror of her recollection. I wasn't quite sure I should believe her story, but something in her straightforward manner told me I'd already bought it.

"I caught sight of the ship receding. I felt myself giving up on it all, Ms. Marino—Angie—and then I succumbed." Mrs. Hunnicut paused, dropped the photos in her bag, and then continued.

"When I came to, I was shivering, my teeth were chattering. In fact the gentlemen who found me thought I was having a seizure. It took several minutes for me to realize I wasn't dead, that I had miraculously been rescued. I had been fished out of the water by two men who were on their way back to shore in a small power boat. They saved my life."

Here Mrs. Hunnicut's voice cracked and she put her handkerchief to her eyes to dab at the tears. Then she coughed.

"What were these men doing out so late at night?"

Mrs. Hunnicut nodded her head. "Needless to say, I really didn't care, but once I had sufficiently calmed down, I was able to observe that they'd gone fishing and probably had a bit too much to eat and drink. I daresay, they didn't expect to fish me out of the Pacific. If it wasn't for the light they had attached to the side of the boat, I wouldn't be here to tell you this story."

I knew a little about boats, enough to know that a floodlight off side would illuminate the dark sea. "Are you sure your husband tried to kill you?"

"Positive. Once Roger returned to the dock, he took his time and thoroughly cleaned down the boat—it's an obsession of his. I borrowed my rescuer's binoculars and watched him from their boat. I could see that he was whistling as he left the dock." Her voice contained an undertone of acidity. She winced slightly and continued. "Then he walked over to his car and drove away."

"But surely the power boat didn't dock at the same time your husband's boat did?"

"No. We made it about a half an hour later. Both boats were motorized, but I'm sure Roger was traveling at a much faster speed."

"He didn't contact the coast guard? No one? Just pretended you disappeared into thin air."

"Yes." Her voice cracked.

Mrs. Hunnicut pulled out a cigarette, tapped it on the desk, and waited for me to light it. I did. I looked at the clock and figured I still had a good forty-five minutes before my dinner engagement. I urged her to go on with her most remarkable tale. "But what about your rescuers? Weren't they suspicious? What did you tell them?"

"Of course they were quite alarmed. I think they thought I was rather mad—you know, off my rocker. I was incoherent for quite some time. They gave me a change of clothes so I'd keep warm and I asked to borrow a hat, so I wouldn't be recognized when I got to shore, just in case. You see, I still didn't know what I was prepared to do."

I leaned back in my chair and listened to the growing stillness outside the window. The process of detailing this confession had a soothing effect on Mrs. Hunnicut. A dead calm.

"You may think this rather strange, but for the past few months Roger's solicitations have been growing in proportion to his infidelity. He'd always been attentive, but lately there didn't seem to be enough he could do for me. Now that he was . . . misbehaving."

Misbehaving? Mrs. Hunnicut had a way with words. I almost expected to hear she'd pulled down his pants and given him a good spanking.

"I think I hate him more for that ... the false solicitations, the simulated display of his affection, than for what he did to me. He'd stop at nothing to get what he wanted."

"And what *did* he want, Mrs. Hunnicut?" She didn't flutter an eyelash. It never failed to amaze me, this business of murder. How nearly thirty-five percent of all homicides are caused by family members, a lover, or children. Someone close. Someone trustworthy. Domestic violence is fast becoming the number one crime in the good old U.S. of A.

She looked at me, surprised. "My money of course." Then she took a deep breath. "Before this nightmare happened, I had decided to spend a few days visiting a college friend to clear my mind."

I smiled without knowing it.

"Did I say something funny?"

"No, of course not, Mrs. Hunnicut. Excuse me. But I just got this flash."

"A flash?"

"I know a little about your family, in fact a great deal. You see, it just so happens that we both grew up in northern California and while I didn't go to Stanford, as you did, I attended my fair share of wild sorority parties in my days. I have this hunch that you were one of the Delta Chi's? Class of '80. Am I right?"

Mrs. Hunnicut looked relieved. A blush brushed her face with a tinge of rouge. She smiled broadly and nodded her head. "Please don't remind me of any war stories. I was quite a wild young lady."

There was a twinkle in her eyes, but I couldn't tell if she was laughing with me, or at me. "Please continue, Mrs. Hunnicut."

"Well, I'd only been away for a day when Roger called me. He was telephoning from a phone booth because as he said, he'd been walking down the street, realized that he missed me immensely, and called—just like that—to tell me he loved me. Needless to say, I was delighted, especially when he said he was sending me a surprise. In less than half an hour, a chauffeured limo pulled up in front of my friend's house and I was whisked away. Mary was off at a conference all day so I left her a note and said I'd call and explain everything later."

"So the limo dropped you off at the Marina?"

"Precisely."

"Any witnesses?"

"No. Just the driver."

"Did you get the name of the limo service or the license plate number?"

"Of course not." She dashed out her half-smoked cigarette in the ashtray. "I hardly suspected foul play."

Mrs. Hunnicut got up from her seat and walked to the dusty window. I knew I shouldn't have fired the cleaning crew until I found a suitable replacement. Having a woman like Mrs. Hunnicut in my office suddenly made me realize how drab and undramatic my work space was. I made a mental note to do something about it. Trade in minimalism for a little Italian avant-garde. I fought off the urge to light up another cigarette, my quota being one a day, as I examined Mrs. Hunnicut's long legs. A low whistle involuntarily escaped my lips. She whipped around and looked me in the eye.

"But I was wrong. My husband murdered me. And now I need your help." She moved back over to the desk and leaned as close as decency would allow.

Help her? The entire story smelled as rotten as a bonito left out in the sun. "Why didn't you go to the police?" I asked, pulling away from her. I got up out of my seat.

Mrs. Hunnicut found hers and sat down.

"It seems to me you have a pretty good case," I continued. "Even if it was an accident, your husband never reported you missing. You had the two fishermen as witnesses. And some pretty incriminating proof to support his motive. Why didn't you go to the hospital or your physician if you thought he slipped you a Mickey? We could have used this as evidence in our investigation."

"I don't care to have him arrested." Her lips tightened and puckered slightly. "I want revenge."

I caught a glimpse of myself in the mirror. I didn't look as bad as I should have after twelve hours of work. Pushing back a few stray hairs that had fallen into my wide-opened eyes, I examined Mrs. Hunnicut's determined face. I wasn't in the line of business to avenge murderers. I just helped to put them behind bars, the old-fashioned way. But I was curious, it comes with the territory, and Mrs. Hunnicut looked desperate. The calling of my trade whispered in my ears, you should know better. But the warning was drowned out by a suggestive bellowing in my head: go ahead, take that occasional walk on the wild side.

"I'll help you," I said. Sure she had a pretty face and a nice pocketbook to match, but I was a sucker for a woman in distress. And more than that, I was intrigued.

Mrs. Hunnicut looked relieved. She smiled. The whites of her perfectly shaped teeth glistened. She wet her lips with her tongue and then smoothed back her hair.

So I hadn't worked out all the kinks in therapy, and when I did, I somehow suspected I might be six feet under.

The restaurant was half-filled. Downtown on a Thursday night was like a ghost town. The Bunker Hill yuppies headed to Beverly Hills and Westwood for their recreation. That's why I liked it here. I was chasing down my double espresso with a Rémy Martin at this rather pricey eaterie, when Katherine leaned across the table.

"You've been preoccupied all evening. Is it another case?"

Katherine knew me too well. I'd managed to focus on how beautiful she looked in that cobalt Lanvin dress. The string of pearls around her neck were the ones I'd given her nearly a year ago. When I'd handed her a black velour box she was surprised. It wasn't her birthday, Christmas, or Valentine's Day.

"These," I had said softly, clasping the expensive trinket around her lovely neck, "are for taking my breath away every time I see or think of you."

"Hey you," Katherine teased, waving her hand across my face.

I returned from my reverie, looked into her warm playful eyes, and smiled. I knew I shouldn't have ordered the lobster fettucine. Not only was it too rich for my troubled stomach, it kept reminding me of what could have been Mrs. Hunnicut's last supper. I downed the double espresso and took a deep breath. "I can't get this woman out of my mind."

Katherine sat at attention. "Oh?!" she probed, drawing out the exclamation. "Is she pretty?"

Leave it to Katherine to worry about "pretty" in my line of work. "No." I sipped a glass of ice water with a sliver of lemon floating on the surface.

Katherine looked relieved.

"She's beautiful."

Katherine's face dropped slightly and she rallied her defenses. "Suppose you start from the beginning, darling. We've got all night."

"No, we don't. I've got to get an early start tomorrow."

A cloud darkened Katherine's lovely face.

"Sorry, angel. But there's nothing to worry about. I wouldn't trade you in for anyone in the world."

"You'd be a fool to do so, my dear. I was just worried about you. Last time you were rather mysterious with me, I ended up racing down to Cedars Sinai in the middle of the night. You were so doped up with painkillers you called me 'Mommy.' "

I couldn't help but smile. The Camerino case. Pretty nasty stuff. A kiddy porn shop on Western and Sunset. A mother had hired me to find her four-year-old kid. The old man skipped out with his daughter. He was pimping the poor baby to feed his habit. Nice times. "Don't you think I can take care of myself?"

"Only too well, I suspect." Katherine leaned closer and clasped her hand over mine, then leaned back and finished her cappuccino.

Katherine was good at leaving me alone with my thoughts. I'd never before met a woman who could second guess all my moves, love me to death, and give me plenty of rope to hang myself.

Mrs. Hunnicut and I met later the following day for tea at The Far East Cafe. To ensure our privacy, I had asked Mr. Lee to direct us to a curtained booth, the only one in the restaurant. The greasy spoon was a favorite of mine. Mrs. Hunnicut had never before set foot inside. Once settled, I began to interrogate her.

"Why didn't Roger just ask you for a divorce?"

Mrs. Hunnicut smiled. "Roger had signed a prenuptial agreement that stated he wouldn't be entitled to a dime if he filed for a divorce.

With my death, he'd stand to inherit a million dollars, plus my Bel Air estate."

"And what if you filed for divorce?" I cracked open a fortune cookie and watched Mrs. Hunnicut sip her tea. She was wearing a creamy beige suede suit and her lips were pale tangerine. There was something different about her, a sense of determination in the way she stretched her jaw, in the way her eyes cross-fired every time she spoke. She appeared to be a woman driven by more than a desire to seek justice. I wondered what Mrs. Hunnicut was like in bed.

"If I filed, which I never thought I would, I had agreed to pay Roger eighty thousand a year for three years."

Eighty thousand sounded like a lot of money to me. I looked down at the slip of paper I'd just removed from my fortune cookie. Fool's gold tarnishes. Was there a moral to this scribble? Why did Hunnicut's yarn fascinate me? Was I attracted to the money or the power? Maybe a little bit of both. Was this some voyeuristic quest to go poking through the dirty lingerie of her marriage? To pick apart the ragged emotions and make sense of it all? Something wasn't adding up, though. Roger didn't have such a bad deal, but it was hardly a million bucks. And if Roger was capable of murder, had he ever attempted anything like that before? "Could there have been any other reason Roger may have wanted you . . . dead?"

Mrs. Hunnicut looked rather distressed. Had I hit a nerve?

"I've been a good wife to Roger."

"I'm sure you have, Mrs. Hunnicut. But could something have happened to trigger this diabolical scheme of his?"

"I'm not sure I know what you're getting at." Mrs. Hunnicut sipped her tea thoughtfully.

"Let's move on. Tell me, how do you manage to dress so well if you haven't gone home in several days?"

Mrs. Hunnicut paused before responding. "What are you insinuating?"

I watched her finger her fortune cookie. Her nails looked as if they'd just been done. They were the same color as her lips, only shinier. "I'm not insinuating anything, Mrs. Hunnicut. You're my client and I simply have the prerequisite questions to ask. It's the fiber of my profession."

"Of course. I'm rather edgy today," she replied, apologetically. "As for my wardrobe, I have a special account. It isn't difficult to withdraw money without my husband knowing about it. Anyway, I have no idea whether or not Roger has reported me missing. As far as anyone knows, I'm still visiting with a friend. I'm not due back until tonight."

"Is it possible your friend . . . in Laguna . . ."

"Mary?"

"Yes, Mary, could have phoned the house to see what happened to you?"

"It might be possible. However, she was getting ready to go off on a ski trip. If she *did* call, I suppose Roger would have to alert the police and report me missing."

As I watched Mrs. Hunnicut carefully, my thoughts drifted back to events that had preceded this meeting. I felt as if I'd been watching her all night long in my sleep. That beautiful face of hers had haunted me in more ways than one. The obvious I'll leave out. But then there had been the nightmare. I'd seen her face and body—actually it was the naked body of Roger's squeeze—all green and bloated, floating in the sea. I was helpless, unable to rescue her from a school of sharks that swam around and around in some sort of cultish circle. I screamed. A shark lunged for her, gripping the lifeless body in its huge jaws. The water turned vermilion. I screamed again, only that time Katherine was holding me in her arms. After that, I couldn't go back to sleep.

I'd driven around the city for half an hour before the world claimed the sidewalks. And at nine o'clock sharp I found myself at the Hall of Records. With the help of a double espresso, I was sufficiently fired up to plow through the tomes of statistics and facts, musty footprints of the past. After an hour's dig and several phone calls, I'd discovered—thanks to Stanford's yearbook—that her college sister, a Mary Wexler, did indeed live in Laguna. And I found out something else.

When I examined the one photo of Mary, with her hair pulled back in a ponytail and wearing hardly a trace of makeup, I instantly thought of the woman in the photos Mrs. Hunnicut had shown me. Of course I had only a profile to go on, but my hunch was that Mary Wexler was two-timing her old college chum. Maybe it had been the juxtaposition of Roger's paramour and Mrs. Hunnicut's face in my dream, but whatever it was—even a dose of good old-fashioned intuition—I'd had the odd sensation that Mary Wexler played a pretty important part in this mess.

I'd left the Hall of Records, hit the pavement, put on my Ray-Bans, and walked along Spring toward the Baltimore Hotel. It was close enough to lunchtime and I knew I could make a few calls from there.

The Wexler girl had made it easy for me. She was listed in the phone book—and she just happened to be at home when I called. At first she denied having seen Mrs. Hunnicut.

"I haven't seen *her*," she said, with distinct distaste, "since the wedding."

"You mean, since she married Roger?"

She hesitated. "Yes. Look, who are you and what's this all about?" she asked me again.

"My name is Angie Marino. I'm a private investigator and my client hired me to protect his interests and yours." The lie came easily enough.

There was a long pause and then a cough. "I don't know what you're talking about."

I blurted out what I could only guess was one of her favorite positions and told her that in case her memory was still vague, I could produce a few dozen photos. I guess she got the message because suddenly her memory came back.

"What is it you want?"

"Have Mr. or Mrs. Hunnicut, for that matter, called you in the last day or two?"

She hesitated again. I could practically hear the soft whir of cerebral machinery, a veritable slot machine as her thoughts ricocheted from left to right and back again.

"Mona called and said she wanted to speak to me in person. She said she had something very important to discuss with me. That it concerned Roger—" She stopped.

"Go on."

"She said she wanted to . . . work things out, That my coming would be in Roger's best interest . . . as well as my own."

"So?"

"So . . . I agreed to meet her at the Santa Monica pier this evening.

"What time?"

"Midnight." She sighed and took a deep breath. Mary sounded as if she'd been through the mill and back.

"Isn't that a rather strange place and hour for a sorority reunion?"

"Yes. I told her so myself. But she said, 'Indulge me. You owe me that much.' She also said she knew about our affair and that if I was cooperative, she would be reasonable about letting him go."

"Tell me something," I said, lighting up my first cigarette of the day. "Why'd you do it? Why'd you go sticking your pretty neck out where it didn't belong?"

"I love Roger. I've always loved Roger. *She* stole him from me and made him marry her."

"The man's a big boy," I said.

She sniveled. "Yeah. A big boy with big ideas about his future. Poor Roger's no match for Mona. She'll eat him alive."

"Lucky for him he's got you, then," I said. It seemed to make her feel a little bit better.

"I'm going to call Roger," she said suddenly.

"Look, Ms. Wexler. I'm in between a pretty nasty war of the sheets right now and from this angle, it don't look so good for you and it don't look so good for Roger."

I heard her sniffle a bit. She was crying and my heart went out to her. "Can you meet me here in L.A. . . . at my office . . . at seven o'clock tonight?"

She blew her nose. "Well, I suppose so."

"Good. Because when I tell you what I've got to tell you, I want to make sure you're sitting down." I gave her the address and told her that under no circumstances was she to call either Roger or Mona. It was a gamble, but I liked long shots and I figured fifty-to-one Mary Wexler wouldn't pick up the phone.

I forced my thoughts back to the present as the waiter brought us a fresh pot of tea, and I watched Mrs. Hunnicut examine the bottom of her cup, where fragments of tea leaves had settled.

She smiled and looked up at me. "Someone once asked me: 'If a man's worth was measured in gold, how rich would he be?' I thought of Roger and said he'd be as rich as Croesus. Funny how time and circumstances can change all that," she said.

I got the feeling that Mrs. Hunnicut might be thinking Roger wasn't worth a plugged nickel. Maybe I was wrong. She reached across the table and cupped her hand over mine. The collar of my button-down Ralph Lauren seemed to stiffen. I loosened the button.

Mrs. Hunnicut's lower lip trembled. Her fingertips felt as if they were grazing my flesh. "I'm sorry. This all seems such a mess."

I pulled my hand out from under Mrs. Hunnicut's and poured myself some more tea. My hands felt warm and safe around the ceramic cup. I thought it best to keep them there.

"You see, the day Roger and I went sailing, we actually had an awful row. I said some unforgivable things, things I just can't repeat to you . . . but I felt helpless. Roger was slipping away from me every day and . . . I didn't know what to do. You see, all my life I've been used to getting attention. Roger only gives it when he's so inclined and I just can't put up with that." She tapped her fingers on the wood surface and fidgeted under the table.

"I'm still not quite sure what you want me to do, Mrs. Hunnicut."

"I'll pay you ten thousand dollars," she said, her voice low and her green eyes peering into mine. She snapped her fortune cookie and pulled out the slip of paper.

I nearly choked on my tea. I studied her face. She was damn serious and meant every dollar's worth. "Ten thousand dollars! To do what?"

"I'd like you to help me scare my husband to death."

It was nearly midnight. Bel Air, a swanky neighborhood tucked away in the foothills of the city, was a heavily patrolled province, but tonight it didn't appear as though anyone were on the payroll.

I had no intention of pulling off Mrs. Hunnicut's ludicrous scheme and I had told her so, in no uncertain terms. Instead, I had agreed to secure certain things she couldn't get for herself. I didn't expect any trouble gaining entry into her estate. She had assured me there were no dogs, no alarms, and no bodyguards on the premises. She also assured me that Roger would be sound asleep. I knew it was some sort of setup, but I wasn't quite sure how it would all wash out. I had to wonder, though: was it the case itself or was it Mrs. Hunnicut who lured me further into this domestic coronary meltdown? Mind you, I had no intention of putting the moves on this broken-hearted creature. I valued my life too much. And in spite of her trying to pull the wool over my eyes with the yarn about Mary, I still imagined she'd gotten the raw end of the deal, married to a bad egg like Roger. Sure, we've all had people walk out on us, but how many of us can say our loved ones had murder in their heart?

I parked my Volvo in front of the gated estate, darted between two thick bushes, and found my way on the other side of the gate. A dog howled in the night. I checked my watch. It was ten minutes before twelve. I figured it would take me no longer than fifteen minutes to do what I had to. Mrs. Hunnicut had instructed me to crack open the wall safe and remove her will, along with several thousands of dollars in cash and six rolls of undeveloped film, which could be used as evidence against her husband.

The wood floorboards on the patio creaked slightly as I made my way inside the Hunnicut estate. I wasn't sure what I'd find. I believed I had sufficiently calmed Mrs. Hunnicut, convincing her that the best recourse was to get what she needed to prove her accusations and leave her husband with little or no ammunition that he could use in court. With her testimony and my confirmation, I felt confident that Roger would soon be behind bars. As far as I was concerned, that was revenge enough.

I turned on my small flashlight and followed the makeshift map Mrs. Hunnicut had given me. I stopped long enough to examine the wedding photo on a coffee table in the study. The perfect couple. How happy they looked. How time and greed had changed all that. I was just about ready to tackle the safe when I heard a blood-curdling scream come from directly above me.

I don't know how I made it up the stairs so quickly. I pulled out my .38 and with gun and flashlight in hand I stopped to listen outside the door of the master bedroom. The door was half opened.

"My God," a man's voice moaned. "Oh my God, you're not dead."

"That's right, darling. You didn't do a very good job of killing me."

"I don't understand—I thought I'd gotten rid of you for good."

I inched closer to the door. It sounded as if Roger was foaming at the mouth. From where I stood I could see Mrs. Hunnicut, dressed to kill in a silver lamé nightgown, looking as if she'd traversed a designer netherworld to give her husband a kiss of death, her face pale and determined in the shimmer of moonlight that sliced the room.

Roger must have lunged for her like a rabid wolf, half-starved and out of its mind. But she'd been out of his reach. "Oh my God," he groaned, and I caught sight of the shiny glint of a butcher's knife in her outstretched hand.

Within a split second Mrs. Hunnicut lifted her arm and threw the knife like a javelin.

"Hold it, lady," I yelled as I kicked open the door. Luckily she hadn't aimed to kill. The blade landed in the wood paneling about two feet above Roger's head.

"Angie, look what the man's reduced me to," she said without taking her eyes off Roger. "I hope you've enjoyed what little freedom you've had these last few days."

Roger, at least what I could see of him, sat up trembling, his forehead drenched with sweat, his eyes bulging as he stared over at the haunting apparition of his dearly departed wife.

Mrs. Hunnicut sneered at her husband. "Thought you'd gotten rid of me, did you? Well, your little plan didn't work and now I'm home, darling. Come here and show me how much you've missed me and maybe I'll forgive you."

I watched Roger's white face as the color slowly crept back into his cheeks. His fleecy chest seemed crushed from the clamp of wed-lock. Roger moved like a slug toward his wife.

Mrs. Hunnicut held her cheek up toward Roger. He leaned down and kissed her, then buried his face in her neck as she stood there, petting his matted hair.

They seemed to have forgotten that I was in the room, so I let out a cough to remind them. When Mrs. Hunnicut turned to me, she had an envelope in her outstretched hand.

"You've been an expert witness, Angie, but I won't be needing your services any longer. That is, unless Roger decides to be a bad little boy and misbehave again."

I gave Mrs. Hunnicut a hard look. She was smiling pretty. Her eyes appeared to relax now that she had Roger in her arms again. I finally realized that the black widow had hired me to do what Fletcher didn't have the stomach for. After all, he was a married man himself. A dick, even a shady one, has to draw the line somewhere. I decided that this was the time to throw a wrench into her plans.

"You can come in now," I called out, and Mary Wexler stepped through the open door.

Mrs. Hunnicut's face was a candy cane of emotion as she looked at Mary and then over to Roger. Poor Mary stood there, probably wondering how it had all come to this. Till death do us part, was ringing in my ears. Roger may have botched Mona Hunnicut's murder, but Mona hadn't done much better. I knew I'd never be able to prove it, but I was sure Mrs. Hunnicut had made plans to get rid of Mary. She must have thought she could rely on me as a witness, a convenient alibi, in case anyone ever made any inquiries, or Roger got out of control again and decided to blab to the police. She'd probably hired some third-rate henchman to do the job right there on the Santa Monica pier. My stomach was twisted in a knot. I suddenly had no appetite for my work. Mrs. Hunnicut slavishly urged me to take the envelope, but I walked out, empty-handed.

It was still dark when I crept into Katherine's bed. Her skin smelled of sleep and her naked body was the only antidote I knew of to kill the taste of the evening.

"Darling," she murmured, barely above a whisper. "Are you all right?"

I wasn't in the habit of showing up unannounced at my lover's doorstep at five in the morning. I had a key, but I'd never used it before tonight. Something about familiarity and the proper amount of propriety and healthy independence. I cupped Katherine's breasts in my cold hands and felt her body shiver, then cave in from the pressure of my embrace.

"Is she as beautiful by moonlight?" Katherine asked as she bit my earlobe.

I answered with a long kiss that buried the sound of Roger's scream and wiped out the scent of Ramona Millicent Hunnicut.

Katherine and I made love with such passion that even I was surprised. And as the first yellow rays of dawn streamed through the Levelors, I noticed, as if for the first time, Katherine's fine blond hair on the white lace pillowcase. She'd fallen into a light sleep in the crook of my arm. I was almost too exhausted to join her, but then the tide of her breathing lulled me. I knew that for a few hours, at least, I could leave the desperate, the lonely hearted, the emotionally indigent on those mean streets where they belonged.

★

RAKESH RATTI

~~~~~~~~~~~~~~~~~~~~~~~~~~~~~~~~~~~~~

PROMENADE

"DON'T BE SO GODDAMMED weak," he told me as he sat on the foot of my bed. "It won't kill you to touch a girl. Hell, you might even enjoy it. You know I do."

"Is that why you keep coming back to me, because you enjoy girls so much?" I countered coldly. "Almost every Sunday you drop a flower in some girl's hands and then come knock on my door when it gets dark. What the hell do you think I am, Marco, some beggar?"

A wounded look fell across his face for a moment. Then the green eyes hardened and he covered his vulnerability.

"And then you brag about what you do with them!" I continued. "Do you really think I want to know? It kills me, listening to you."

"It isn't like that," came Marco's hollow reply. He made a small movement in my direction, then seemed to think better of it. "Martin, I tell you everything so you will see that it isn't so bad." He looked to me for some response. I said nothing, and he seemed to gather strength from my silence. "Why do you do this to me? I don't care about them. Only you. But we live in this fucking village! We can't let anyone know about us."

"Nobody knows," I hissed. "And I thought we were going to leave this place, go to the city. Do you want to live here all your life?"

"No, I don't. But we're here now."

There was a short silence, as if he was regrouping, marshaling his forces. I knew what would come next.

"People are talking about you more and more, Martin. How you never look at girls, how you finish the promenade with your hand full of confetti every Sunday. The only girl you ever talk to is Lucia, and everyone knows she might as well be your sister." He scowled at the bored look on my face. "Dammit it! Martin, you don't have to screw them. Most of them wouldn't let you anyway. Just play the game. They don't say anything about me, do they?"

The look in my eyes must have been pure venom. This was a litany I had heard much too often. "Of course not. You're such a man. Well, I can't stand the thought of kissing a woman or playing your fucking game."

His eyes narrowed with anger.

"Maybe you're right. Maybe I am weak," I continued, buying his position as I always did. "But I can't help it. It makes me sick every time I see you walk off with a girl."

"You better get used to it. I'm not going to give anyone reason to talk." His voice was cold, the voice of a Marco who seemed to be drifting beyond my fingertips. The anger hardened his face well beyond his seventeen years. "And if they suspect you of anything, you won't see me again. I won't be dragged down because you don't have the guts to touch a woman."

I did not know what to say, and he did not wait for me to collect my thoughts. In one movement he rose off my bed. He passed through the low doorway without looking back. I did not move, did not try to stop him. The argument itself did not frighten me; it was an old one. But Marco's stance had never been so hard, so unbending. It left me immobilized, speechless. The night outside my window fell silent, the darkness deepened. I was still trying to stop the dizzy spinning of my mind when I surrendered to uneasy sleep.

The following morning, a Sunday, unfolded like every other day of God in the withered village I called home. Shrouded in the colors of the monotone desert it sprouted from, the hamlet of San Felipe was like a beehive, small but full of activity. The houses huddled together on the narrow, signless dirt streets, varying little from one part of the town to another. The homes were almost universally made of adobe, stifling the hamlet with unending earth tones. A handful of the more wealthy villagers had erected houses with brick walls, but with the passing of time even these were taking on a faded, arid appearance.

The one building that really stood out in San Felipe was the church. It shone like a gem in a field of common stones. Marco and I often joked about how what little wealth our village possessed seemed to find its way into the holy coffers. My neighbors and their neighbors were proud of the pale yellow concrete building and its stained glass windows. It was the center of their social life, a central facet of their identity. I could not share their sentiment. No amount of prayer had dispelled the cycle of bitterness from my life. Thanks to the deaf ear their God had turned to me, I had grown to be a most practical young man. I hated the church.

This particular morning began with the journey to the house of worship. My mother and I walked side by side through the dirt streets. It was a weekly event for me. Unwanted. Unavoidable. My mother, devout Catholic that she was, nearly lived in the church, singing the praises of a God who had long forgotten her. As usual, I left my house this morning dressed in my finest, most uncomfortable clothes. For fifteen years I had wondered what pleasure Jesus derived from the presence of the sweaty, drooping youth who could not stop twitching in his sticky abrasive suit. I thought that barefoot and cool I might have benefited from a word or two that boomed out of the pulpit, but I would never find out. The hated polyester suit could not be escaped. The wearing of it was a compromise but it no longer frustrated me. Sunday had always been full of compromises. I was afraid it always would be.

This morning I took special care to tread softly around my mother. The monthly envelope, the bane of my existence, had arrived the day before. My mother had been silent this morning, speaking only to scold me about a scuff on my shoe, a wrinkle in my jacket. Once she started she could not seem to stop. She would not reach the height of her fury for a couple of days yet, but the bitterness was beginning to creep into her face. I felt for her. I would feel for her even as I would come to hate her tomorrow or the day after. Silently I walked, resigned to the scolding, my thoughts drifting between her incessant chatter and the memory of Marco's anger.

My mother quieted only when we entered the huge wooden doors of the brick-walled house of Jesus. Her position of supplication was perfect as she knelt before the pathetic figure on the cross—limp, eyes rolling in death, graying blood staining his hands, feet, and forehead. Had he been alive, I would have ached for him. Had I felt a secure love for my mother, I might have shared some of the devotion she exhibited. When I was a child, the bleeding man with eyes turned skyward had frightened me. Little by little the personification of suffering had lost its morbidness. Faint resentment was all that it aroused in my heart now. He was my mother's deity and I had ceased to separate the two long ago. I wondered, as I knelt beside her now, if she would ever rise to her feet. Her eyes were closed, mine were fixed on the crucifix in a pretense of piety.

After the parish was seated on the wooden benches, I slipped behind my best facade of interest. I sat as still as my suit would allow, and listened to the haranguing words of the padre without objection. It was a practiced game, losing myself in immaterial flights for the length of the pious man's performance. Today I was paying closer attention than usual, conscious that my slightest infraction would nourish my mother's anger.

Four rows in front of me and to my right sat Marco, winking at me mischievously. It was a favorite game of his, this attempt to break through my holy facade. It was a private joke, an inversion of our normal roles. The ceremony mattered no more to him than it did to me. He was light of heart and found humor in it as he did in all else. He could not know that the postman had brought the envelope. Had he known, he would not have teased me this morning. I clenched my jaw, refused to be drawn into his teasing. He soon gave up and turned away, and I relaxed once again behind my pious mask.

The end of the service was merciful, if overdue. I took a deep breath as I stepped past the wooden doors and left behind the feeling of suffocation. My eyes searched the faces that were streaming out behind me, but I could not locate Marco. I turned my back upon the door and caught a glimpse of him in a throng of boys. He waved to me, motioned for me to join them, but I shook my head. I knew what he was up to, and he knew that I knew. I did not want to be cajoled, I did not want to be coerced. He shrugged his shoulders at my refusal, then turned back to his friends.

Like churches in most villages, ours faced an open plaza. The floor of the square was faded red brick, the wealth of the church having trickled into the adjoining space. In the middle of the square was a small bandstand, and on this bandstand stood a handful of sweaty, dusty men. They cradled a ragtag collection of instruments and filled the air with songs of love and sorrow. The unmarried youths of our village gathered together, walked in two circles around the bandstand. We boys circled in one direction, while the girls walked the opposite way in a smaller circle inside our own. Many of the boys were clad in suits as uncomfortable as my own, though a few seemed infinitely more at home in them. The girls sported their most colorful dresses, fluttered between us like a flock of stray butterflies.

This was the promenade, an inescapable facet of our Sundays. It was a ceremony rooted in my Catholic heritage, a tradition of my grandfathers and their grandfathers. A ritualized dating game, the promenade was eagerly anticipated by most of the young villagers. The boys now clutched handfuls of confetti. A flower was tucked into a pocket here and there. One of Marco's friends was already tossing his confetti at a girl he was fond of. It was her prerogative to accept or reject the invitation.

The sides of the plaza were lined with adults, gathered in social clusters of their own. In a casual fashion they chaperoned us, seemingly lost in their own conversation. They seemed detached, but we were well aware of how closely they watched us. Young couples, those who were paired already and thus skipped the promenade, loitered throughout the plaza, teasing those of us in the circles. Children chased one another through the square, oblivious to our ritual.

On one side of the church stood my mother, talking to her sister Rosita. When I glanced her way now and then, I could see that she was not pleased. Why are you so sullen, Martin? Why don't you walk with the more popular boys? How will you find a decent girl if you keep your eyes glued to the ground? She was constructing the chain of rebukes and accusations she would try to strangle me with later. She is hurting, I told myself. She does not mean it. In another few days the bitterness will pass.

A vivid image of the bloody cross filled my mind as I trudged along with my peers. For me it was inseparably entwined with this ritual. I did not look up often while I walked. There was no need to watch my step. Two years of practice, two years of compromise. I knew how it felt to be a captive link in a chain, a circular tie that moved without direction, without goal. I was pushed by the link behind, pulled by the one ahead, and in the end I was always left filling my own footprints. The world surrounding me would not change. It would devour me if I did not begin to mirror the thoughts of the youths around me. How fortunate they are, I thought. They laugh and tease while I brood through the length of the square. I hated them, hated this plaza, hated my mother along the sidelines.

I could have refused to take part in the promenade. But I would not. That would have multiplied my mother's bitterness. Every son in the village took part in the age-old ceremony. Even the shyest youths mustered the courage to step into the ceremony. The veneer of normality was important to my mother, she whose life was one unending void. I had neither the heart nor the strength to take the comforting facade away from her. But I hated it. No matter how much the youths around me teased me and tried to draw me into the festivity of the occasion, I remained a singularly unmovable figure.

Marco walked a few feet ahead of me with a trio of youths. They were jostling one another, making insinuating comments that elicited giggles from the passing girls.

"She's winking at you, Marco," I overheard one of them comment.

The ground felt unsteady beneath my feet. I would never grow used to it. I followed his gaze to a cluster of girls who were

approaching them. Sure enough, one of them was staring rather sugges-
tively at my Marco, a wide smile showing her abundant white teeth.

"What's happening, Rosa?" Marco grinned at the girl, winking
seductively for her.

The rat. The sinking feeling fled my body. Marco would do no
more than flirt with her. He would not waste his confetti on her, just
as he would not toss it at Rubia, the girl walking beside Rosa. Marco
did not date the girls I disliked; that was one small concession he had
made to me long ago. And I did not dislike Rubia or Rosa for anything
they had done to me. No, it was their intense, unending interest in
Marco that bothered me, that tugged at my insecurities.

My friend Marco. What a handsome boy he is, I thought. Jet
black hair and dancing green eyes. The face, with its fine lines, the
smile that had always been so contagious. At times he made me feel
so inadequate. I felt helpless in the presence of his power. How could
I not feel intimidated? If I closed my eyes I would not have stood out
in a crowd. A pair of huge, moody eyes were my one and only mark
of distinction. Marco's fine points I could not count. He had an ease
with people, an ease I would never possess, and they were drawn to
him no end. The boys of our village vied for his friendship; the girls
played coy games with him.

More than one pair of soft eyes was fixed on Marco now, and,
as always, he would have his choice. He is mine! I wanted to scream.
But I never would. I hated them, I hated the promenade. Hate can
only be measured by love, and at this moment I hated Marco most
of all.

I was walking, as was my habit, with one of the shyer youths,
the two of us seeking shelter from the teasing of the other boys. Today
it was Arturo who walked beside me, an amber-eyed boy who limped
badly from a severe childhood fall. I thought he was the luckier of us
two; his handicap was a visible one. Neither Arturo nor I could handle
competing in Marco's group. In each other's company we had nothing
to prove.

Marco looked my way periodically, his eyes sparkling with mis-
chief. How proud he would be, I thought, if I opened my hand and
freed the confetti over the head of some smiling girl. Apprehensions

relieved, doubts dispelled. I turned away from his eyes. It would never happen.

"If you don't use that confetti, we're going to make you walk in their circle, Martin," a stocky youth walking in front of me turned to say. He was nodding at the circle of girls.

"Fuck you! You couldn't make me take a step," I replied. I had become used to such remarks. It was pathetic, how they would never say anything if Marco was beside me. This youth may have been bigger than me, but I did not worry. He feared Marco more than I feared him.

There had been occasions in the past, isolated though they were, when a girl had smiled at me, misinterpreted my shy grin, and I had gifted her with my confetti. These moments had all ended in disaster, however, though they had satisfied my mother and Marco greatly. A few uncomfortable minutes of conversation after the promenade was all that I shared with the girls. Nearly always they had walked away feeling inadequate or slighted, and rarely looked me in the eye at another promenade. I had felt only relief each time the encounter ended.

I looked at the ground, looked at the buildings lining the edge of the plaza. I reasoned that if I established no eye contact with the girls, I would not need to approach any of them. Beside me Arturo chattered incessantly. I acknowledged him with some corner of my mind, but my attention was focused on Marco. Would he slip away with a girl today? The thought filled me with anger. Too often I suspected that, what to me was love, was merely one more game to Marco.

"Hey, Martin, why don't you give me your confetti?" a youth near Marco shouted loudly. "We know you don't have the balls to use it!"

There was a burst of laughter. I shouted an epithet at the boy, then searched out Marco's face. He said nothing to the boy, was not even looking at him. He was looking at me, his eyes full of scorn. My face burned with anger now. That bastard Marco! He was blaming me!

I released his gaze, resumed my walk. The insecurity that had gripped me last night terrified me, left me feeling hollow. This village was a trap for me, and Marco was my one hope of escape. I could not flee it, could not break my mother's stifling grip, on my own. But Marco's nature was carefree, so different from my own. He could partake of whatever came along in life without uttering a single protest. I kept committing myself to him, he seemed committed only to himself.

I came out of my reverie when I saw a tall girl in a green dress sashay toward Marco. It was Rubia. The baker's daughter was pretty, nicely curved, and not at all shy. Marco locked eyes with me across the twenty feet separating us, then he opened his hand, covering Rubia's blondish-brown hair with bits of white. I wanted to scream but could not in front of all these people. I wanted to flee the circle but could not risk my mother's wrath. So I walked on, sinking further into the ground with each step. So his smiles today had been just a part of some game. The anger wilted quickly; only sorrow remained. A budding awareness that maybe the life of this village and the bitterness of my mother and our monthly envelope would be all that the world would offer me. I continued walking mechanically, clutching in my hand the flower my mother insisted on, while Marco and Rubia disappeared from view.

Needless to say, I finished the promenade with only Arturo by my side. My reward was my mother's sharp tongue that did not rest on the way home.

"Why do you walk with the lame one and others like him? How will you find a nice girl that way? Why can't you be like Marco? You two spend so much time together, and he is always surrounded by girls. Why don't you walk with him?" She castigated me, her voice low enough to escape gossip.

What could I say to her? That it bothered me too much to have him slip from my side in the company of some girl? That the few times we walked together had ended in horrendous fights? I hid behind an impassive mask while she ranted at me in her controlled voice. I knew that in a few days she would regain some measure of kindness, but her words stung me now. I gave my mother my silence, but in my heart I cursed my father.

I had long ceased to hear my mother's words by the time we

reached our house. It was an average house we lived in. Four rooms with low ceilings that were supported by adobe walls. A hard dirt floor that my father had meant to cover with concrete. Until he neglected to come home fifteen years ago.

The doorway we entered led into the large front room. My mother spent much of her day in this room, and it was full of the boundaries of her life. Segments of fabric lay in stacks beside clothes waiting to be mended. A sewing machine, bought by my father long ago, and its entourage of threads and needles rested in one corner, half-finished embroidery lay in another. In this room also sat a black-and-white television set, the last present my father had delivered in person. My mother's tireless hands kept it looking shiny and new.

To the left of the front room was the small kitchen I had surrendered to my mother years ago. As a child it had been a welcome haven. Marco and I had chased one another in and out of the room daily. Back then my mother had been young, pretty, full of kindness and life. Now her dark hair was graying rapidly, her severe face was etched with lines. Now the kitchen reeked of the hostility my father had cowardly escaped. Hostility I had inherited.

As soon as we were inside the house I scurried for the sanctuary of my room. She would not follow. As a child I had shared her room with her, but a few years of her bitterness had driven me away. Why is all the hatred directed at me? the wide gaze of the child Martin had asked more than once. The unvoiced answer in her eyes never varied. You are your father's child. You have your father's name. This was the legacy my father had left me. As much as I hated her, I hated him more.

My mother and I did not live together in any familial sense of the word; we shared a space, shared a pain. Most of the time we lived with a tension-filled truce, scratching beneath the surface less and less often as the years passed. Then the envelope would come. If I reacted in any way to her bitterness, the house would be engulfed in open warfare. I was the image of my father, she would scream, and she would have been better off without me. I would cower behind the locked door while she railed at me. But I was a child of her house, and I soon became steeled by its bitterness. She was a victim, I knew that, but even as I pitied her, I yearned to escape her.

Absently I could hear the rustling in the next room. Her presence quickly vanished from my consciousness, however, as thoughts of Marco flooded over me once more. Why would he go out of his way to hurt me today? I slipped out of the polyester pants and jacket quickly and reached for the prized jeans that had arrived a few months before. They were a little large for me, but I didn't care. They were from California. The envy of all my peers. I could stop hating my father long enough to put them on.

Was Marco getting ready to walk away from me? I folded my suit neatly and laid it inside a drawer. The dresser was a luxury for most village youths. Well, I would have to stop relying on him. I would have to start thinking about myself. My eyes traveled across the walls and floor of the dark room, wondering how long I would remain its captive. My estrangement from Marco was making me realize that escape might be all but impossible. I shuddered with the thought. I wanted to cry, to let the sadness flow out of me, but I couldn't. I no longer knew how.

It was ironic, I thought. My intimacy with Marco had been made possible by my alienation from my mother. Long ago she had become habituated to Marco's presence in my room, and never had she given a hint that she knew we were lovers. At first Marco had worried that locking the door to my room would arouse her suspicion. His fear was unfounded. As long as he stayed away during her tirades, she would ask no questions.

All day long I did not venture from my room, did not face my mother. When she called me for dinner, I hurried to the front room; having to call me a second time might set her off. Throughout dinner she sat silently, radiating sorrow, her eyes hurling accusations at me. After the meal she dragged a bit of her embroidery into the cave that was her bedroom. I cleared the dishes, then quietly slipped into my own room.

I lay on my bed, my head propped against the earthen wall, unable to keep Marco and Rubia out of my mind. How could I call him mine when he was probably rolling in some dark corner with her right now? The bastard! I could picture him, his tight arms wrapped around her body, his lips brushing across her skin as they did against mine. The picture became more graphic as my mind preyed upon itself. Helplessly I felt myself sinking deeper into the despair that had tugged at me all day.

I did not hear Marco when he entered the house. The look on my face must have been pure surprise when my bedroom door swung open, and he slipped in wearing his most playful smile. Quickly he latched the door behind him, then turned on the small radio on my dresser. It was like him, to think of the precautions before they ever entered my mind.

"What the hell are you doing here?" I demanded, not moving to touch him in greeting. The sight of him warmed my being and I felt pulled to reach out and touch him. But I would not. Not tonight.

"She didn't see me come in," he answered, seating himself beside me on the bed. Immediately his arm slipped beneath my neck.

I shook my head, pulled away from him. "I don't want you here tonight."

The smile deserted his face.

"What's the matter with you?" he asked quietly.

"Nothing." The one word came out like a pregnant phrase.

He reached out to touch me again, but I drew away.

"Is it last night? Are you still mad over that?"

"You threatened to walk out on me," I responded.

He rolled his head in frustration. He shook my shoulders playfully, placed his forehead against mine.

"I always say things like that when we argue. You always laugh at me. Why are you taking it so seriously this time?"

I could not voice the intangible feeling that filled me with fear. I could only pull away. He continued to search my eyes until I felt compelled to say something, anything.

"Why don't you go spend the night with Rubia?" I nearly shouted.

He stiffened visibly at the mention of her name. Experience should have taught me that he would come out swinging.

"I would, if that was what I wanted," he answered coldly. He rose from beside me, settled on the wooden chair at the foot of the bed.

"And I'd be waiting like in this bed, like some beggar, right?" I spat my accusation. Our fury was whispered. Caution had long become a habitual companion.

His lips moved to interrupt me, but I raised my hand to stop him.

"You were right last night. I am weak. I can't play the game. But I can't go on like this, being eaten up with jealousy every time you slip away with a girl. Maybe it's time we stopped all of this."

He looked at me in disbelief. "What are you talking about? You've stopped caring for me in one night?"

"No." I shook my head. "But I'm going to. I don't want to rely on someone who may leave me anytime."

His shoulders sagged, he looked at the floor. Neither of us spoke for some time.

"Maybe you're right," he finally answered, his voice immensely sad.

I was stunned. He was supposed to disagree with me, to shout that I was talking nonsense. Once again silence rose between us. We did not look at one another. In the end it was I who broke the still.

"Strange, isn't it, Marco? Everything began in this very room."

He smiled sadly as the memory touched him.

We had been playmates from our earliest days, living as we did on the same street. The same age to the month of our birth, we had been inseparable. Throughout childhood Marco had quite often slept in my room; in a house full of fifteen kids his absence only meant a bit of extra space, and my mother had been fond of his smiling, carefree nature. Our romance started innocently enough, two thirteen year olds rubbing against one another in the safety of the night. Soon we discovered how much better it felt to be stroked by one. With each instance we had experimented further, stretched the boundaries. This new facet of our relationship had only deepened the love we had shared since childhood.

Marco shook his head now, and I was certain he was tossing away the image.

"You know what I remember most?" he asked.

I shrugged my ignorance.

"The first time that we kissed. Remember that?"

Yes, I remembered.

"We couldn't get enough of each other, could we?"

He paused for a moment, I waited passively. Finally he looked at me like the old Marco, love and concern flowing from his eyes.

"You want to toss away all of that?" he accused.

"Me?" I asked in disbelief. "You're the one who doesn't want me anymore."

"Is that what you think?" He was just as incredulous.

He walked over to me, took my hand in his.

"I'm sorry," he whispered. "I shouldn't have said that earlier about Rubia. And I shouldn't have asked her today. I don't want anything from her. But I was so mad at you. You try so damn hard to start a fight sometimes."

"I don't like this feeling of being discardable," I answered, my body tensing at his admission. "It feels like you're pulling away from me."

For a moment he said nothing. Then he rose, walked to the end of the bed. When he turned to face me, a light of understanding had spread across his eyes, a light that tugged at me.

"It's that fucking envelope, isn't it?" he whispered, anger returning in his voice.

I watched him with puzzled eyes.

"What the hell are you doing?" His voice began to rise. Automatically I reached for the radio, turned it louder. "I feel like I'm talking to your mother, not you."

"What are you babbling about?" I asked angrily, not knowing where his mind was racing.

"That woman has let bitterness ruin her life, Martin," he answered, settling down on the other end of the bed. "Is that what you want to do? She's poisoning you."

If I had made the connection, I had conveniently ignored it. Having it thrown at me now ungrounded me.

"That's not fair." I sprang to her defense, not knowing that it was myself I was shielding. "She's had so much pain in her life."

"We've all had pain, Martin. But we have to let it go, get on with our lives. So her husband went up north to find work and didn't come back. Do you think she's the only one it has happened to? And what about the others? Some of them see their men once a year—if they're lucky. Do you think they feel no pain? But your mother glorifies her grief. For three quarters of the month she's fine, and then that fucking envelope comes and she goes into her rage."

The envelope he spoke of lay on the table in the front room, unopened. What would it contain this month? One hundred and fifty, maybe two hundred American dollars? When it had first intruded into our lives, my mother's anger and sorrow had been faint, short-lived. I had expected, as had her own family, that the bitterness would fade as she came to accept the monthly stipend. We were wrong. With every month, with every year her bitterness deepened. Every woman on our block pitied my mother her loneliness, just as they envied her the envelope.

"If the money makes her so sad, why doesn't she tell the postman to stop delivering it?" Marco continued to press me.

"Because we need it," I responded. The futility of my argument, the truth of his words, were descending upon me, but I was not ready for it. "How else do you expect us to survive?"

"Us?" He spat the word at me. "Then why don't we let go of the anger and accept the money in peace?"

I could not answer the question I had pondered so often myself. I was as addicted to the money as she. I anticipated the coming of the monthly stipend with equal amounts of joy and apprehension. It made possible the radio and dresser in my room, the sewing machine and television in the front room, the new pots in my mother's kitchen. Yet all these things, even the pair of jeans that had arrived with the envelope once, leaked poison into our lives. Instead of running away from it, we learned to live with it, made it an integral part of our lives. The moment my mother's fingers clutched the white paper, her face would tighten, her shoulders would stiffen, as if she was trying to collect the pride lost long ago.

"It's up to her to change all of this, don't you see that?" Marco would not relent. "Don't become like her. It isn't fair to you," he said, his face softening. "I hate to see you go through this every month. She should have stopped this long ago, but she didn't. Now she's coloring you with her bitterness."

I watched an array of emotions sweep across his face. Just as I had sensed something new in Marco last night, so I was sensing it now. This time it did not frighten me.

"That fucking envelope!" he continued. "Has there ever been a note with it, a single word of explanation? No! Today it's set her off again. It's made you miserable. And it's eased your damned father's guilt for one more month."

He was right. I could not argue with him. It frightened me to realize that I was beginning to take on my mother's bitterness. It was the last thing in this world that I wanted to do. I crumbled against the wall now, closed my eyes. Instantly I felt Marco's arms around me. His warm breath fell on my face as he whispered my name. My body shook with uncontrollable tremors.

Marco held me quietly for a long time. Slowly I regained my composure. The doubts I had wrestled with for the last twenty-four hours began to tug at me. Where would I stand with him tomorrow? Whom would he reach for at the next promenade? My mother's cynicism had taken root deeply. I began to pull away from Marco slowly.

"You're right, you know. I can't argue with you," I whispered as he sat back and listened. "But what I said earlier about Rubia, I—"

"Don't!" He interrupted me, raising his open palm. "You seem to have your heart set on a fight with me, but I'm not going to be drawn into it. I'm not walking away from you, do you understand? I love you. Maybe I don't show it, but I do."

I listened in silence, certain there was an "if" or a "but," some condition forthcoming.

"It's silly of me to try to force you into sleeping with the girls."

He smiled at the surprise on my face. "We were wrong last night. You aren't the weak one. I am."

I did not know what to say. I could only wait, listen. He stretched his body across the bed toward me, stroking my foot gently with one hand.

"Do you know why I sleep with those girls? Because it makes life easier for me. Then I lie to you and everyone else about how wonderful it feels. I feel nothing with them, do you know that? I chose Rubia this morning to get even with you. But the thought of her body did nothing for me. I had to fantasize about you to even get hard. It seemed so pointless that I couldn't even begin the act." His eyes were sparkling now. "Don't let it swell your head, but it's always been like that. I've always had to think about you."

I smiled involuntarily at the image.

He returned my smile as if having caught my train of thought, then continued. "You're the one who is strong, Martin. You just don't realize it, and neither did I until today. You know what you feel. You don't fake anything. I take the easy way out."

The skeptical look on my face betrayed my doubts.

"You don't believe me, do you?" There was no sarcasm in his voice, only mild amusement.

"I don't know." I shrugged my shoulders. "I don't understand."

"I couldn't do it," he replied, turning his back to me as he uttered the words. "With Rubia this afternoon. You looked so fucking hurt when I walked away with her, Martin. I couldn't stop thinking about it, even when I was laying with her. I tried, and she tried, but I just couldn't get hard."

He turned around, hesitated for a moment, but I was too speechless to fill the silence.

"Then she teased me," he said, picking up the thread of his story. "I really didn't mind, until she laughed and wondered if I really liked girls. Martin, nobody has ever said that to me! She said that maybe I had been hanging around you too long and was becoming a pansy, like you!"

"That fucking bitch!" I hissed.

"I just crumbled, Martin. I just fell apart when she said that. I was terrified that someone might know me for who I am. All I could do was to try to laugh it off. She laughed too, so I guess she was just teasing. At least she didn't act strange or anything when I left her. But I kept thinking about it all afternoon."

He was looking me squarely in the eye now. "That's when I finally got it through my thick head. I fell apart when someone even teased me about it. You've had to deal with those bastards for years. They say all kinds of shit, and you throw it all back. Hell, you would have spat in Rubia's face if you had been in my place. That's why you are the stronger one, Martin. You've accepted the truth, and I've kept on trying to lie to myself. For all of your stupid hang-ups about your mother, you deal with things as they are. I try to run or hide."

I was having trouble finding words before. Now my tongue was petrified. I wanted to throw my arms around him, but I couldn't move.

"But you know what?" he continued. "Life isn't going to be easy for you and me. I better get used to that. It's time for me to learn to be strong."

My suspicion returned and I finally freed my tongue.

"What are you saying?"

"I thought you might find it hard to believe," he answered through a wide smile. "I'm saying I won't be messing around with girls anymore."

"What about your precious reputation in the village?" I would not be convinced so easily.

"The hell with that! In another six months we'll be in the city. In the meantime I'll toss my confetti at a girl now and then, but that doesn't mean I have to get into her skirt." His eyes were shining, as they always did when we shared a secret. "Who knows, maybe the old women of this town will start thinking that I'm finally becoming respectable."

A huge smile was pressing against the back of my teeth and it was all I could do to contain it.

"How do I know you aren't lying about this?" Always he had been honest with me, but still I threw out this last bit of doubt. "You spent the day with Rubia. How do I know you didn't really have sex with her?"

Marco shook his head as if to scold me. Then he reached a hand into his pocket, pulled it out full, and dropped a shower of rose petals on my smiling face.

WENDI
FRISCH

A SILENT VILLAGE

WE LIVE WHERE ICE-CREAM trucks have graffiti sides and shattered windshields and where the lovers are men robbing one another in unlit corners. But there aren't many lovers. Not many venture this far. Those who do don't bother us with questions. If they notice us at all, they see simply a man and his son. Los Angeles is an anonymous city. There are fresh vegetables and sunshine year round so that Jeremy can stay healthy and not need doctors.

A warm breeze floats in the window near where I lie on the couch reading the newspaper. My boy sits across the room from me drawing pictures. We listen to music in these late afternoons before sunset. I imagine the sound ceasing as it crosses the windowsills. It's easy to believe nothing exists outside of this room.

Jeremy holds up a drawing for me to admire. It's a lifelike rendering of a lemon and orange sitting at a table having tea. I laugh and tell him I'll call it "Still Life With Tea." He likes that and nods his head.

He draws at a table of solid oak that is the only real anchor in the improvised life we lead here. The table sits by a window so that all of its nicks and scratches, the blotches of paint and dried glue, and the coarse grain of the wood are clearly visible. I would have to completely upend it to see again where I sawed and sanded the legs so that Jeremy could reach the table's surface.

Light pours through the window during the day and streams over and around the table. When Jeremy sits drawing, another light grows out of him. It reflects around the dirty room, across the grimy walls and shabby furniture.

Jeremy draws during the day when I'm working. I come home and pages are laid out on the floor in front of him. He spends time arranging them in an order, telling stories. Jeremy and I are the only people in the drawings. Others are plants or animals: apples and pears drive down Pico Boulevard, Jeremy and I float above them on clouds. One of my favorites is a picture of Jeremy riding the back of a bird; he faces forward with the sun directly behind him, framing his head. The picture hangs on my bedroom wall so that when I wake I see him flying.

One side of the record ends and I reach to turn it over. Jeremy is starting another drawing. He has so many stories to tell. I tried to explain this to the doctors, psychiatrists mostly, but they didn't understand.

One doctor in a white tie labeled Jeremy autistic with possible catatonic tendencies. He recommended committing Jeremy for a period of observation. The doctor said that unless Jeremy began to talk again we could have no accurate measure of his emotional state. He spoke in percentages of Jeremy's chance for recovery.

Another doctor, this one in a blue tie, felt that Jeremy was intelligent, but felt he needed individualized help to process the trauma he'd suffered. His percentages for Jeremy's chance of recovery were even worse. He also spoke of a period of hospitalized observation for Jeremy.

The word *observation* came to have a particular association with doctors. It no longer described my son's gift for translating on to paper the life he saw around him. After a time I stopped taking Jeremy to doctors.

The second side of the record ends. Jeremy looks up briefly as I move to change it, but then goes back to his drawing. I return the record to its jacket and switch on the radio. I lean back with the paper again. For a moment I put my hands behind my head and relax, feeling the breeze and hearing the music. I glance at Jeremy and he's biting his lip, concentrating on his drawing. My relaxation vanishes, replaced by a gnawing anxiety. This move was meant as a new start for us. If only I could infuse him with new life. Perhaps for Jeremy there are no new starts. Ever since the accident he's been trapped within himself and now he's trapped within this apartment, by me.

But there are pictures and occasional smiles. His new start is happening every day, slowly. Jeremy holds up another picture, this one of the sun setting over some buildings I recognize from our neighborhood. I tell him it's nice and he puts it on the wall with Scotch tape. Tomorrow it will be somewhere else, rearranged among the other pictures—the orange and lemon at tea, the apples and pears driving down Pico, the boy on the bird.

At night I take him east with me to where the warehouses come closer and smaller and the city becomes like a silent village after dark. The small brick buildings comfort me. I like the peeling letters of their signs and the iron gates that conceal their entrances. I imagine lights shining out of the upper windows as if families lived there. I want to share this comfort with my son.

To the north of us, men stand on the sidewalks in the night. They can't see us as we dart across quiet streets and through the shadows cast by unused buildings. We are invisible. Blocks farther and there are no more men. We're safe and hidden in interlocking grids of one-way streets and alleys. Jeremy and I lean against a brick building. I hold him close to my side and turn his face up so that he can see the stars above the buildings. We stand this way for a long time. It's so peaceful here, I wish we could stay until morning. Jeremy leans more and more heavily against me and I realize he's sleepy.

It's past midnight, late for a little boy. I carry my son in my arms on the walk home, aware of his deepened breathing and relaxed, trusting body. A bottle shatters in the next block. The life in my arms is suddenly, inescapably fragile. I can't think of that now. I concentrate on putting one foot in front of the other in the direction of home. Stars pierce the sky and stab through me, fusing me to the earth as I move forward. The ground is a steady bridge beneath us.

Later, sirens wake me. They sound like they're in the apartment, screaming down the narrow hallway. The furniture in my room shivers against the noise and I can hear Jeremy's drawing table scraping on the floor of the front room.

The noise goes on and on as I lie in the darkness, my heart pounding in my throat, but finally it begins to subside. I notice then that I'm tensed under the sheets and that I've become so entangled in them while sleeping that I can't move my legs. As I begin to loosen the bedding, there's a movement in the corner of my room. Jeremy walks out of the shadows there and through a shaft of light cast by a street lamp.

His eyes are huge in this light and I can see him shaking. I lift him into bed beside me and begin to rub a spot on his back that sometimes soothes him. I can feel the bones of his spine through the soft fabric of his pajama top. He's grown so thin in the last year. Lying here he seems almost as delicate as the first time I held him seven years ago.

I feel Jeremy start to relax as the sirens in his head quiet, but see that he's still wide awake. I tell him I'm going to get up and turn on the light, but he knows that. We've done this many times before. He watches as I turn on the light and set up the turntable. I put the needle down on the record and the room is filled with Mozart. Jeremy's face lights up and I see him smile. This is one of his favorite records. He picks it out at the library week after week. I will make us cocoa soon and when it begins to get light, perhaps we will walk to the edge of the freeway and watch the sunrise.

In the morning Jeremy and I leave the apartment early to eat breakfast out. People push past us as we stop to look in the different store windows. I stand between Jeremy and the swarming people. My back becomes a stone wall that protects my son as he looks at some cheap toys through the glass. He taps lightly in front of a toy dog, as if the dog might respond to the noise. He looks up at me and smiles. I smile back and touch his hair.

We continue down the street together now. Jeremy pulls on my hand and bends to pick something up off the sidewalk. He straightens and holds up a little animal made of soft metal. We dust it off together and he slips it into his pocket. He'll add it to his pictures.

A woman watches us from the corner store where Jeremy and I buy groceries. The woman runs the cash register and has begun acknowledging us each week, recognizing us from visit to visit. I notice her too, find my eyes following the curves of her body as they strain against her clothing when she reaches overhead for cigarettes. I've never considered myself attractive to women, though some have found me so. I wonder if she does.

These are dangerous, reckless thoughts. The risk of letting someone into our lives is too great. Jeremy and I will not return here. We will find another market in another neighborhood. And when we are recognized there, we will find another market. Los Angeles is a big city, filled with markets. Our radius will expand larger and larger until we are no longer recognized and there will be no way of tracing us.

I guide Jeremy toward the diner on the corner. As we walk through the door, dirty yellow booths and fluorescent lights seem to rush at us. A teenage girl at the counter taps a quarter against her water glass. Jeremy and I find an empty booth and sit down.

A waitress comes up to our booth and asks to take our order. When she turns away from us, she begins to cough. It's a hollow, wracking cough that starts deep within her chest and shakes her thin torso and shoulders.

I am remembering another cough. I am remembering my mother's cough that shook the voiceless nights. I would wake, sweating, to that eternal, beckoning sound. She would prowl the hallway outside my bedroom as she dragged her nails softly against the walls. There would be the scuff of her bedroom slippers across the hardwood floor and the creak of her weight on a loose floorboard every fifth or sixth step, until another cough would bring her to a deathly, shuddering stop.

I would hear the whisper of my father as he urged her futilely, back to bed. "Once more; just once more," she would say over and over in a voice that dissolved almost before I could hear it, so different from the sharp, exacting voice she used in the daytime.

In the mornings my mother swallowed many pills with her black coffee, slapping my hands away if I tried to help her when she dropped them before they reached her mouth. My father said she had thin blood and that's why she needed so many pills.

My mother didn't eat often, usually she leaned against the door-jamb watching my father and me, smoking cigarettes that she tapped over old egg cartons. Dirty ashtrays were "common." Any sort of disorder was common. When I was disorderly, my mother's method for assisting my memory was to lock me in the cellar.

We were not common my mother would say as she shut the heavy door to the damp, dark cellar after me and turned the key in the lock. I stood for long, aching minutes on the top stair before I could summon the courage to descend into the musty darkness gathered at the bottom of the steps. Fear and time were suspended in the living darkness there. The invisible strands that connected me to my family, to school, to the outside world did not exist. I thought of nothing, not even of the spiders and night crawlers that secretly terrified me when the lights were on. I sat breathing the quiet, watching the strip of light that showed at the bottom of the cellar door, until my father came into the cellar for a bottle of beer and released me.

When the waitress brings our meal I hope she doesn't start coughing again. My hand holding the silverware is shaking. Jeremy begins to play with his hash browns and scrambled eggs. I rest my hand by my plate and watch Jeremy eat.

Sundays we usually go to the park. Before the accident, we used to attend Mass where Jeremy was fascinated by the stained glass and religious statues. He loved the organ and would do his best to sing the hymns in his sweet voice. The words he couldn't read yet he hummed vigorously. After the accident, Jeremy would begin to tremble and cry as soon as we walked through the door. We started coming to the park instead.

We begin at the lake today. It's glassy this morning, no breeze and too early in the season for paddleboats. Jeremy rushes ahead of me, kicking at the discarded milk cartons and bottle caps in his path. He stoops once to pick up a stone. It's flat and gray, undistinguished except for the fact that it's almost as large as Jeremy's extended palm.

He draws his arm back, coiling one side of his body as he does so, then snaps his wrist and elbow forward in a smooth, reflexive motion as he hurls the stone. The stone arcs high, but then drops, leveling out as it falls, and skips one, two, three times across the lake. Jeremy's body, uncoiled and fluid now, reaches after the stone as it vaults across the water, rocking back as the stone completes its course and plunges through the surface of the lake. The water shimmers, golden, where the morning sun reflects off the tips of the small waves created by the stone. I think suddenly of the picture of Jeremy riding on the back of the bird.

I join Jeremy now and we walk along the edge of the lake, my arm around his shoulder. The lake is again as smooth as the planes of my son's face. I tighten my arm around Jeremy's shoulder.

Many families with children are at the park today. I try to remember a time when I went to a park with my parents and cannot. My mother was usually busy and my father preferred spending weekends indoors drinking beer while sitting at the living room window.

As he sat at the window, my father told me over and over the stories he remembered from his childhood. The stories were etched into my consciousness, embellished with details and scenery from my own experiences, so that my father's childhood peers became more compelling than the children I encountered daily at school.

When I was quite young I liked the stories and would laugh in anticipation of my father's jokes and wait patiently for his familiar pauses and inflections. Sitting at his feet, I had only my father's voice to guide me; before the window, his face was always in shadow. I liked that he put his hand on my shoulder, and that he ruffled my hair when I laughed.

As I grew older, the stories remained unchanged, cast into patterns as if by unspoken agreement years earlier, and I began to hate them. I realized that the people in my father's stories were at least as old as the man sitting in the chair telling his stories or, worse, dead.

It occurred to me that my father never remembered having told me any of his stories before. I began to shrink away from my father's touch, which now frightened me. I learned to avoid him when he was in storytelling moods, and to ignore the guilt I felt seeing him sitting at the window, alone except for his beer, with one hand resting on his knee.

A group of children clustered at the edge of the lake attract my attention today. Some of them run back and forth excitedly, carrying sticks. They appear to be building something. I look more closely, expecting to see boats made of milk cartons, but instead see a dead pigeon that has become target for the boys' curious prods. One of its eyes is still open and a few flies, swatted at anxiously by one of the boys, circle the area with unhurried interest. I see the fascination of the boys' faces and turn away.

It's now that I remember Jeremy at my side. His fists clench and unclench rhythmically in front of his chest.

There were pigeons in front of the church where they found Jeremy abandoned by the person or persons who had abducted him. In addition to the broken ribs, bruises, and cuts, there were signs of sexual abuse. Jeremy has not spoken since that day nearly a year ago, cannot name his attackers, may never speak of it even when his voice returns.

I think I might try to say something to him and begin, "Sometimes people, even children, can be cruel—" but am stopped by his eyes. He gazes up at me with an expression in his eyes that looks something like wisdom. If Jeremy could talk, I have the feeling he would explain it all to me.

When we get back to the apartment, Jeremy pushes past me at the door and goes directly to his drawing table. He's busy for some time, head bowed, right hand scribbling across the sheet that his left hand steadies. When he finishes he doesn't hold the drawing up for my viewing as he usually does. He simply sits staring out the window with both hands resting on the table. I call his name, but he doesn't respond, so I walk over to where he's sitting.

The drawing is vivid in oranges and reds, flames, and there are two figures visible in the midst of it. I have nothing to say, so kneel beside his chair and put my arms around him. We stay this way for a long time, looking out the window, waiting for the sun to go down over the buildings on our block.

In the night we take two buses and disembark near the Santa Monica freeway. We walk through a neighborhood nearly silent at this hour, choosing back streets where no porch lights will illuminate us.

A wall borders much of the freeway here. Bridges cross the freeway every few blocks and intermittent doors for workmen interrupt the wall. It is these doors that interest us. Jeremy follows me closely, his hand gripping my belt, as I move to one of the doors. I pick the lock and we're through the door on to the other side. I slip the padlock into my jacket and close the door behind us.

The land falls away steeply on this side of the wall. Jeremy walks on the narrow path at the edge of the wall and I find footholds in the hill so that I can walk beside him. Soon we stop and sit leaning against the wall. I've brought sandwiches and juice in my knapsack and spread them out on the path between us. The freeway stretches beneath us like a river. Even though it's well past rush hour, many cars still flow in each direction, headlights sparkling in the night.

Watching the cars, I think of the night Jeremy and I left our home. It was very late that night, much later than this evening. Jeremy slept for a few hours while I packed the van for the trip. I'd wanted to leave the van behind too, disappearing into the night with only what we could carry on our backs, but knew we would need to sell it for cash when we arrived.

After I woke Jeremy that night, we walked through the house together. I wanted him to be able to say good-bye to the life he'd had there. I couldn't look back until we were well outside the city limits. Many ties still linked me to this place and pulled me back in spite of myself. Jeremy dozed on the seat beside me and occasional passing headlights illuminated his features. I took strength looking at my son and each mile passed more easily than the last. The tires turning against the surface of the highway, the signs spattering the sides of the road, the other cars rushing past us headlong into the darkness, all melted together into one voice that urged us on, away, sealing the past behind us.

I'd tried to make peace with my past. After the accident when my parents made overtures to accept Jeremy for the first time, I opened my life to them again. My mother brought sweets for Jeremy to eat while lying in bed. My father discovered a boyhood hobby of whittling and sat with Jeremy for hours, carving figures out of wood and retelling the stories I'd tried to forget so long ago.

One still, hot afternoon when every voice seemed to travel for miles, I came home unexpectedly. As I walked through the silent house to the back porch where my father sat with Jeremy, I overheard him telling my son about the room he would have in my parents' home. My father's voice stopped when I stepped out on the porch and he sat silently whittling another figure.

I imagined my parents going back to the doctors who had seen Jeremy to talk about my unwillingness to seek treatment for him. I imagined my mother calmly explaining the environment she and my father could offer a young boy as she tapped her cigarette ashes into the doctor's ashtray.

I watched my father whittling and imagined it was my heart that he was working on, trying to make me agree with his and my mother's wishes. I knew no matter how long he worked and how hard he tried he couldn't change my mind or soften my heart, which now felt as if it were made of stone. I didn't let on that I'd heard anything, but from that moment I knew that Jeremy and I would flee.

Jeremy had finished a sandwich and I put my arm around his shoulders. I make up stories for him about where the different cars are going and the people in the cars. Sometimes he looks up and smiles, like when I'm telling him about the car of hippos trying to find the circus, but I wonder if he smiles out of amusement or because he wants to make me happy.

After a while I fall silent and we watch the river of cars flowing before us. I notice a man some distance from us crossing the freeway in one of the pedestrian bridges. He raises his arms above his head and I think he is reaching for the moon. I watch as he brings his arms down to his sides and begins to run. I imagine him racing in the moonlight against himself, free, and I can remember a feeling such as this.

There was a time when I ran at night, down deserted lanes, through underbrush where startled animals scurried out of my path. As I ran, I forgot everything, myself, my family, and became someone else. My lungs filled with the cold night air and I would feel my heart beating harder and harder against my chest. I found quiet places where I could throw myself down, exhausted. Here I knew only the pounding of my heart, the sweat trickling off my forehead and down my neck, the chill air pressing against my steaming body, the sound of the leaves rustling beneath me when I moved, and the small puffs my warm breath made.

As I grew older, I began to meet girls in these quiet places lit only by moonlight, unmarked by any paths. It was here that I met Jeremy's mother, here that our son was conceived.

She was younger than me, a pretty, complicated girl who played the piano and dreamed of leaving her hometown. Late into the night we lay wrapped in a rough wool blanket we kept hidden in the hollow of a tree and talked of running away together as soon as she graduated high school. I began to believe it would be possible to start over somewhere, fresh and unmarked, if she were with me.

We moved into a tiny apartment during her pregnancy. I worked as an apprentice to a cabinetmaker and she finished school. When I think of that time, I remember macaroni and cheese eaten almost nightly. I can see her standing at the stove, reading a book about "the real world" while stirring noodles into bubbling water each night when I came home from work. Her neck always smelled sweetly of the powder she used each morning. I didn't take her in my arms as often as I might have liked because I hated to interrupt her reading.

She ran away one night, and I so tired from the day's work didn't hear her leave. It wasn't long after that I heard she'd landed in a large city and was studying music there. She remembers Jeremy on his birthday and sent word when she married.

Jeremy pats my leg. These evenings together are important. It's the only quiet, uninterrupted time that we share. I look at the cars floating below us and begin to tell Jeremy about a father and son traveling to start a new life.

*　　*　　*

On the days that I work, at noon I take my lunch pail to the nearest pay phone. The other men invariably tease me afterward for calling my sweetheart. I don't tell them I'm calling my son.

Today Jeremy picks up the phone and I talk to him. I tell him about my day, who I'm working with, what we're doing. I tell him that it's cool outside and that I miss him. For a while I stand in the phone booth with the traffic roaring by and just listen to him breathe. Nothing is more important. I ask him not to open the front door and to eat the sandwich I've left in the refrigerator for his lunch. I tell him we'll have hot dogs tonight.

The music is on in the background, classical, and his breathing so soft. I lean my head against one of the glass walls of the booth and listen. Someone's waiting to use the phone. It's time to hang up and eat. I tell my son good-bye and to be safe and then replace the receiver.

If I believed in God, now would be the time I would pray. I do it anyway: pray that Jeremy's old enough to stay by himself in the apartment, pray that there's no fire in the building, pray that he's getting better, pray to know what to do next.

The man waiting to use the phone is someone I work with. "I hope you gave your sweetheart a big kiss for me," he says as I come out of the booth. I'm wiping my face with a cloth and pretend not to hear.

This is the man's world, men's work, day labor for those of us who have nowhere else to go, no skills beyond our physical strength left to offer. I hate it with all of its false jocularity and camaraderie. It's something my father tried to introduce me to once when I was about fourteen, in another way, by taking me to the corner bar to drink beer and join in the bar conversation.

The beer tasted bitter to me and the voices seemed unnaturally loud and colored with an inappropriate hilarity. My father sat slouching at the bar and seemed as uncomfortable as I was. He had a habit of talking with his hand in front of his mouth and muffling his voice when he was in public. I had to look away in shame when the bartender asked him to repeat himself more than once.

The jokes the men in the bar told were mostly sexual. They had an undercurrent of hostility that I didn't want to know too well. I waited for my father to join the talk even if it was just to tell one of the stories I'd come to dread hearing. But as the evening wore on, he became quieter and more withdrawn. I never went back to a bar with him.

One young man has spent much of the morning talking about how much he drank the night before. No one has responded to his talk, but that's not the point of his telling. It's not important what story he recounts, whether it's a sexual exploit or a car race on a deserted highway, it's the telling that matters. Over and over throughout the morning he's been trying to establish his identity to us, mostly older men. As little as I find of interest in his story, his yearning is touching to me. Eventually some of the other men join in, topping his tale, and I stop listening.

I remember when work was more than something to be endured. I remember making furniture with my own hands—the wood rough then eventually smooth to my touch, the smell of it sweet, sawdust curly and gritty beneath my feet and through my hair by the end of the day. It didn't matter what I made. My satisfaction was in making something that people would use.

I can't afford to look back. Those feelings are tied to a social security number I no longer own and an identity no longer mine.

Tonight we ride out to the beach and cross the dark highway together to climb fences into forbidden areas. I'm careful with Jeremy here. He's afraid of the headlights and rushing tires. The fences we climb are wire. We come here often enough so that I know the bald spots on the chain-link fences that usher our entrance.

This is a place where houses were abandoned under the noise of too low airplanes. No one comes here anymore. The houses are gone, but their outlines are still occasionally visible in the ground. Jeremy likes crawling around and finding relics of the former homeowners. I imagine who lived here and how they liked to watch the ocean at night. I'm careful with Jeremy here too. I make certain he avoids the broken glass and shattered concrete.

Mostly we come to watch the airplanes because they're so beautiful at night. Jeremy draws them as fish. He can only see them as animals. He scrutinizes each passing plane and hums under his breath. I sit next to him and think about next year and the year after. And whether he'll have another good year or six months. And how I can protect him from any more pain because he can't be hurt again. Someone will find out and make me send him to school soon, I know. Or a hospital. It would kill him. And I know it. And I know that I cannot be enough for him, always.

His head leans on my shoulder as he continues to scrutinize the sky. I stroke his hair, glad for this time. I look up and see them too. They are fish swimming above us, dragging us into the future.

★

PETER CASHORALI

THE SHELL READING

"COME ON, WE'RE GOING to be late," Ricardo says, running up the steps. They were originally a single block of concrete, but as the side of the hill settled under their weight they cracked in half. The bottom portion is firmly anchored to the sidewalk, but the upper piece has pivoted outward a few inches and the steps near the top are irregular.

Mark trips on one of these but catches himself before he falls. "Right," he says. "When it's something for you, we're going to be late. If it's for anybody else it doesn't matter what time we show up." The steps arrive at the foot of a courtyard between bungalows. The pavement of the courtyard is broken and weeds flourish in the cracks. It's not a section of the city Mark's familiar with; he had to depend on Ricardo's directions and he's in a bad mood. He wishes he'd worn a jacket.

"I'm doing this for you," Ricardo says over his shoulder, walking past the bungalows toward the two-story building at the back. The *santero*'s door is marked with a flag above it, half white satin and half burlap, the colors of this year's reigning saints. Ricardo explained it to him in the car: Usually there's only one saint per year, but Saint Lazarus, patron of diseases, has been called down to co-chair because of the AIDS epidemic.

A small gray animal runs over a doorstep to avoid them and Mark pulls back, thinking it's a rat; then he sees it's a squirrel and realizes how close to Griffith Park they are. "You're doing it for yourself," he says. "This is just a way to spy on me."

"I'm not spying on you, you said you were interested." Ricardo knocks on the door while Mark shivers and stamps his feet. "Don Pedro," Ricardo calls. "Soy yo, Ricardo."

The door opens. It's Sammy Davis, Jr. He looks older than he does on television, more leathery, as though he's been hanging in a tobacco shed. "Hola, mijo," he says, and it's not Sammy Davis, Jr.'s voice at all, it's the high sticky voice of a little boy who isn't allowed outside much. "Entren, muchachos." He gestures them inside, his eyes on Mark.

Ricardo says, "Don Pedro, estes es mi marido, Mark."

Mark offers Pedro a meeting-the-in-laws smile and holds out his hand. "How do you do," he says.

Pedro grins and offers his own. It's long and crooked, as though he's just taken it out of a badly-fitting shoe. "Aha," he says, applying his private system of weights and measures to Mark, reaching conclusions, letting go of his hand, and turning back to Ricardo. "Bueno. Cafe?"

"Si, Don Pedro, gracias. Mark, do you want coffee?"

"Please. Uh, cream and sugar, if he's got it."

"Just take it black this time. Si, Don Pedro, dos cafes, por favor."

"Bueno." Pedro walks out of the room as though his feet were once broken. Mark looks around, taking in the living room. Outside the afternoon is bright and colorless, but in here it's past sunset. Quilts cover the windows. There are candles everywhere, dozens of them, and as his eyes adjust to the light he sees the largest collection of religious statues he's ever come across. It's like his grandmother's idea of heaven: a room filled with Blessed Virgins, saints, and martyrs.

Smaller statues become perceptible between the larger ones as he looks. He glances at Ricardo, who grins at him proudly and says, "Incredible, huh?"

"Definitely."

"Look at this." Ricardo pulls him over to a corner where one of the largest figures stands on a low table of its own, bowls of fruit set before it on the floor. It's more like a waxwork than a religious statue, four-feet high, with glass eyes that seem to wake up as Mark comes close. "This is San Lazaro." And yes, Mark would've picked this one out as the Master of Diseases. Lazaro is a middle-aged man on crutches, sores picked out in loving detail on his chest and legs. He's been given a burlap cape sewn with rhinestones and sequins. A ferocious little animal, the product of a rat and dog's romance, looks out from a fold of the cape and shows its teeth.

"Jesus. I didn't know Lazarus was a leper."

"It's not Lazarus. I told you, it's an African deity using Lazarus for a disguise."

"Yes, syncretic, I know."

"No, it's real. And don't say anything sarcastic, Pedro will understand."

"What's that animal supposed to be?"

"Tomen sus cafes, niños." Pedro shuffles back in with a pair of Winchell's coffee mugs. "Los caracoles estan listos," he says to Ricardo.

"Gracias, Don Pedro. He's going to read my shells first, Mark, so you just watch TV till it's your turn. Don't touch anything."

"I wasn't planning to." They disappear into the next room. Mark sits down on the overstuffed sofa and sips his coffee. It tastes like Pedro tried to make espresso with instant, and he sets his mug down at the feet of a Virgin. She's standing on a chipped crescent moon, in front of three men in a boat; the two white men are putting their oars in the plaster water, the black man in the middle has his back to Mark as he stares up at her vast calm face. She's been given a cape also, of blue satin, and the moon and the boat and its three occupants are all inside its braid-edged teepee. A boy on a throne, with a shepherd's crook in one hand and a basket of something in the other, looks back at Mark; it would be unnerving if the boy's expression weren't so benign. Mark nods his head at him and counts statues. This is where Ricardo comes late at night, after Mark's fallen asleep. He listens to the shells being rattled and thrown, rattled and thrown in the other room and tries to remember what Ricardo told him an aluminum rooster-on-a-cup like the one over the door is for. Protection against something, perhaps.

His feet are cold and he wiggles his toes inside his sneakers. He tries to let himself be engaged by what's on the television, a deep-sea discoveries program. The water looks Caribbean, but he can't tell for certain because the sound is turned down and a radio on top of the TV is tuned to a conversation in Spanish: two men who keep interrupting and correcting one another. Mark watches two men and a woman in scuba gear sift the ocean floor around the remains of a wreck, gesture to each other, stroke the snout of an inquisitive moray eel. The discussion on the radio gives way to a salsa program, and the divers are back on deck, examining several small objects they've brought up. One of them produces a knife and demonstrates that under the barnacles and mineral deposits the objects are gold and silver coins. They fall backward into the light-covered water as a cerveza commercial begins to play. Mark drowses open-eyed on the sofa and lets the images and sound approach a common meaning and veer away from it, approach and veer away.

Finally Ricardo comes into the living room, wiping his hands with a wad of paper towels. "Come on," he says, "he's ready to read you."

"Mm. About time. What took so long?"

"Come on, he's waiting."

"This isn't going to take forever, is it?"

"No. Just get in the kitchen and don't say anything."

Mark steps through the doorway and nods at Pedro, who's seated at the end of a formica table with a small crowd of beads in front of him. "Sientate aqui," he says, pushing out the chair beside him, and to Ricardo: "Que se despeje la mente."

"He wants you to empty your head as much as possible."

"Right, I'll do my best."

Pedro hands Mark a black pebble and a lump of chalk. "Just

hold those in your hands for right now," Ricardo says. The beads are
the tiniest cowrie shells Mark's ever seen, half of them with their
backs cut off so they lie flat. Pedro scoops them up in both hands
and rubs them together, throws them down on the table, looks at
them briefly, and gathers them up again. He does this several times
before he's satisfied with what he sees. He moves one or two closer
together, picks out a dark one and sets it aside, and stares at the
pattern in front of him. Mark watches him. Finally Pedro writes something down on a pad beside him and says, "Guerra entre hermanos."

Mark turns to Ricardo for an interpretation, but Ricardo's got
his elbows on the table and his face in his hands, staring at the shells.
Mark clears his throat and says, "And he said . . . ?"

Ricardo blinks and glances at him. "War between brothers."

Pedro nudges Mark. "You unnersta', uh? Whorr." The words
melt in his mouth. He bangs his two index fingers together and makes
a pantomime of peering into Mark's eyes, trying to get a reaction from
him. "Entre hermanos."

"Ah," Mark says. "Uh-huh."

The shells are picked up and cast again. Pedro points to Mark's
hands and Ricardo says, "Rub those two stones together and put one
in each of your hands. Don't let him see them." Pedro pats the table.
Mark puts his fists on it and Pedro taps the left one, which opens to
reveal the piece of chalk. "Blanco," Pedro says, and sounds neither
pleased nor bothered, but Ricardo sits back in his chair and when
Mark looks at him he's frowning.

Pedro has to take up and throw the shells four more times before
they make a figure he accepts. Each time he scatters them across the
table he points at Mark and Mark rubs his stones together, puts his
hands out for one to be chosen. He alternates which fist the chalk
winds up in; it's so much larger than the bit of black stone that there's
no question of chance. He wonders why Pedro doesn't use a smaller
piece, then realizes that the rubbing wears it down; he's already got
it all over his hands.

Mark wonders if Pedro has arthritis. When he picks up his pencil
and jots down what the shells tell him, it doesn't look like a task his
hands were designed for, it's like watching a cricket try to knit a

sweater. The kitchen doesn't bear much witness to Pedro's success as a *santero*. The two bags of trash by the door are mostly chili cans, and the dishes piled in the sink don't match. There's a Cute Kitty calendar on the wall above the table; the square for the seventh is filled in with microscopic writing. Mark holds his hands out and Pedro taps the one that holds the black chip.

The vague expectations Mark came here with are slowly gaining clarity by not being met. It's not that he wants to see light shining over the fortune teller's shoulder, although he wouldn't mind; he likes special effects and thinks a miracle would at least be proof that something was happening here. What he'd really like would be to discover a light in himself, even though he would have trouble saying what he means by "light." And he's not sure why Ricardo is so taken with all this. Pedro doesn't seem like a fake, but he certainly doesn't seem like an artist gathered up in a dialogue with something more powerful than himself. He's a competent craftsman.

Mark remembers the time Ricardo took him to the Satanist's coven. Ricardo laughed happily all the way there, and at one point in the evening's activities everyone had to stick a pin in their thumbs and make a contribution to the offering bowl. As they were driving home, Ricardo said, "No, of course I didn't. Why? Did you?" His forays in the otherworld have always been something he's giggled about with Mark, like a particular sexual quirk that would be embarrassing if they didn't know each other so well. But now he's got both hands flat on the table and watches Pedro throw the shells again and again with no thought of how he looks to Mark.

Mark asks, "Is he stuck?"

"He's trying to find out who your father is, but Elegua won't tell him."

"Who?"

"I told you already. The one who does all the talking for the others. Now be quiet."

"I already know who my father is, pal."

"Shh."

Pedro gathers in his shells and caresses them between his hands. He says, "No estan hablando. Talvez Elegua quiere un regalo."

"Si, Don Pedro. Mark, Elegua needs a gift."

"Well, all right. How much?"

"No," Ricardo says, mortified. "He's a little boy. He wants candy. Don't you still have those mints from the restaurant?"

"Yeah."

"Those'll be perfect. Just put them on the table, no, not where he's going to throw the shells. Over in the corner."

"Bueno, niño," Pedro says, and lets the shells fly. "Ah," he says, takes them back, throws them down, and taps Mark's right hand. It's the chalk. "Aha. Dile que Obatala dice que es su hijo."

Ricardo slaps his thigh. "Ai, que bueno," he says. "This is really incredible. He says Obatala is your father."

"Obatala, Obatala . . . ?"

"The one you liked, remember? The one whose song you liked so much."

"Ah, right. Right. Huh. That's interesting." Obatala is one of the reasons he came here today. Ricardo told him one night that Obatala was the father of the *orishas*, but was worshipped as the Virgin of Reglas. Ricardo had been talking about Santeria for months, and this was the first thing Mark had heard that caught his interest. Later Ricardo had shown him a picture of the Virgin of Reglas, and it had gotten even more engaging. She was holding a Baby Jesus up to her cheek, so that the crowns they wore were both on the same level. Mark wanted to know if both of them were Obatala, or if Baby Jesus was a separate entity, an associate. Ricardo didn't know and wasn't as taken with the question as Mark was, but he began telling Mark stories about the *orishas*. Nothing else was especially interesting, but as he listened to Ricardo talk Mark heard his excitement, and it seemed like Santeria led somewhere important and should be looked into. He says, "Well, great. What does that mean, exactly?"

"It means you could become a *santero*."

Mark keeps his face empty and says, "Really." He sees himself wearing white for a year, tending the *orishas* until they sprouted and then bloomed in his mind, in the air around him, demanding their ceremonies, telling him what to do. He imagines what it would be like to receive messages all day and all night from Elegua and wants to shudder and giggle. It's as though Ricardo has just told him that with a lot of hard work and sacrifice Mark could make his way back to the Middle Ages and shiver in a stone hut for the rest of his life. But even as he pushes the idea away he's aware of an appeal it has for him: the security of being contained in a body of beliefs, the relief of letting go all other possibilities. It could be like retiring early to a small town and tending a vegetable garden. He says, "Um, I don't know if I'm ready for that right now."

"Well, he's not going to do the ceremony right here at the table," Ricardo snaps. "He's just going to tell you about it."

Mark turns back to Pedro and smiles, says, "Of course. I'd like that." He figures that even with a tiny English vocabulary Pedro can follow everything they say.

Pedro smiles back and says, "Bueno." He tears the notes for the reading off the pad and pushes them across the table to Mark. "Let me hold on to those for you," Ricardo says, and puts them away in his purse.

Pedro outlines what would be needed in each of the three investiture ceremonies, pausing regularly for Ricardo to translate. He scribbles down which animals and foods need to be offered to each *orishas*, how many *santeros* need to fly from Miami Beach to officiate, what clothes Mark would need to wear. For one of the ceremonies he'd need two complete changes, shoes included, so that one outfit can be torn off of him and thrown into the ocean. Mark's stomach turns over when he hears the costs: the cheapest ceremony is more than four hundred dollars, and the final ritual to make him a *santero* could go as high as ten thousand. Ricardo says, "He says he can perform the necklace ceremony for you himself."

"Well, tell him of course I'd have it done by him, but I just don't have that kind of money at the moment."

Before Ricardo can decide whether to translate or substitute a statement of his own, Pedro puts his hand on Mark's wrist and pats it, says, "Es okay. No now; whe' you ready." And to Ricardo: "Tu amigo quiere ver mi altar de muertos?"

"He wants to know if you'd like to see his altar to the dead."

"Yes. Very much. Can I just wash the chalk off my hands first?"

Pedro sweeps the shells into a cigar box while Mark scrubs off at the sink. "Okay. Ready."

They follow Pedro back into the living room. The salsa program is still playing but the divers and their finds have been replaced by William Buckley and a panel of experts. Buckley is making some point with the end of his pen. Pedro unlocks a closet door and pulls it open, steps back like a museum guide. Mark looks in.

The closet is occupied by a small table draped with white cloth and set with candles, glasses of water and bud vases holding white carnations. There are so many candles burning that the light from them blazes past him into the living room. He's completely taken with the idea of their burning in a locked closet where no one can see. It's like a perfectly laid table set up in a restaurant too small to hold waiters, chefs, or customers. The bright fingertips of flame, the light hovering in all the crystal, make him want to go in further, but the altar itself blocks him. A dead end. But beautiful, he thinks approvingly. He steps closer and realizes the closet is wider to the left than the width of the doorway. He peeks around the corner and sees a portable clothes rack hung with costumes of some sort. "What's all that?" he asks.

"Ah, mis ropas," Pedro says proudly, and taps Mark on the shoulder to move him aside. He slips into the crevice between the corner of the altar and the doorjamb, lifts an outfit from the rack, and displays it. It's like an Ice Capades costume, powder blue satin covered with rhinestones and sequins. Mark nods and Pedro puts it back, selects one of white satin with a complicated pattern in tiny red feathers worked across the chest. He shows Mark a black outfit with silver braid, another white one covered with gold braid and dark stains. He has a dozen of them. There are hats, too. Finally he comes back out.

"Those are incredible. What are they all for?" Mark asks.

"Esto y eso," Pedro says, smiling at him from the other side of the secret. Ricardo doesn't bother to translate. Pedro locks the door. "Bueno, muchachos, quieren otro cafe?"

"Gracias, Don Pedro, pero no, nos tenemos que ir."

"Eh, bien. Tu sabes, que los caracoles no dijeron nada acerca de el SIDA."

Mark hears the Spanish for AIDS and looks at them to see if he's being spoken about. Pedro sees he's understood and flashes him a shark's grin, says, "Si, hombre. SIDA. Una palabra que tu comprendes, ah?"

"Si, Don Pedro," Mark says, and then, groping for the phrase, he manages, "un de mis pocas palabras." Pedro laughs, his face crinkling like an old leather jacket.

"I told him how worried you are, but he says the shells don't say anything about it," Ricardo says.

"*We* are," Mark corrects him, and, gesturing rapidly back and forth between himself and Ricardo, he says to Pedro, "*we* are. Both of us. *Nosotros.*"

Pedro narrows his eyes and nods, not smiling now. "Le has pedido a San Lazaro su proteccion?" he asks, but Mark doesn't catch more than the reference to Lazarus and looks at Ricardo. "Antes que de vayas, ven aqui." Pedro gestures for Mark to follow him to the statue of Lazarus, then stands with his back to the saint and speaks in a low voice. "San Lazaro es muy fuerte. Comprendes? Verry estrong. El tiene control de todas las enfermedades, si le pides su proteccion te la dara." He looks at Ricardo and nods.

"He wants you to ask St. Lazarus for protection. He says Lazarus can keep you from getting AIDS. Ask him."

"All right."

"No, really, ask him. Ask San Lazaro to take you under his protection."

"Ricardo."

"Ask him. I'm tired of hearing how afraid you are of having it. If you're afraid then do something. Ask him to take you under his protection."

Mark doesn't want to fight in front of Pedro, but he gives Ricardo a look that lets him know they'll talk about this in the car. He stands in front of the statue, taking in its delicate face like a French marionette's, the glistening sores, and thinks about AIDS: about being covered with sores like Lazarus', about his lungs filling up with fluid until there's no room for breath, about the future collapsing in front of him like a building condemned before it was inhabited. Protect me, he thinks, and shudders. Protect Ricardo. Preserve us. Take us under your cape with your funny animal that looks like Pedro on all fours. Show me a sign of your power: keep us both alive.

He watches a moment for a sign, but nothing happens. He turns away from the statue, and Ricardo and Pedro are watching him, Ricardo with relief and satisfaction, Pedro with satisfaction and approval. Envy of them blossoms briefly in his stomach. "Well," he says, "I did it."

"Did he hear you?"

Pedro catches the question before Mark can say anything. He taps his ear and says, "San Lazaro oye, San Lazaro oye."

"Mm," Mark says, ready to leave now. He looks at Ricardo.

"Mil gracias, Don Pedro."

"Por nada. Nos vemos, mijo. Goo'bye, Marr."

"Don Pedro. I'm very pleased to have met you."

Pedro holds the door for them and closes it while they're still going down his front steps. It's twilight, gray and just starting to thicken into night. None of the bungalows has lights on. "How did you like it?" Ricardo asks.

"I don't know. It wasn't what I expected."

"Are you going to have the ceremonies performed?"

"Are you kidding? Four hundred dollars just for the beads? Maybe later. What about you, pal? Are you going to become a *santero?*"

"No, I can't, I don't have the right father. All I can be is a horse for the *orishas.*"

He sounds so resigned to his fate that Mark grins and hugs him. "Well, I think you make a great horse."

Ricardo crinkles his face the way Mark likes. "Shut up," he says. "Let go of me for a minute, I want to get some of that rue. Mark, let go."

Mark watches him squat down in front of one of the big silver-green bushes that push apart the concrete of the courtyard. The thing about the *orishas,* he thinks, jamming his hands into his pockets and hunching his shoulders against the chill, is that they're not so much a road to the other world as a really nice set of knickknacks from its outskirts. Probably everyone's life finally leads to the otherworld no matter what happens, the way separate houses could have backyards looking out on the same view: a landscape that grades away from carefully tended gardens into the endless wilderness in back of everything. Suddenly Ricardo lifts his head and says, "Oh my *God*. Mark, don't move, but look."

"What is it?"

"Those bushes next to you. It's San Lazaro's dog. He's sent it to keep an eye on us."

Mark looks and sees it. He freezes. The animal looking back at him from the rue bushes is the wrong size for anything he can think of. It's too big for a rat or a cat, not the right shape for a dog, but middle ground between all three. Its face could almost be Pedro's, bleached completely white and made smooth, and it stares at him arrogantly, measuring or taking note of him for later. He lets it look all it wants and makes himself breathe slowly, trying to prepare himself for a miracle, though his chest has gotten alarmingly tight and he's not sure that he'll be able to take one. He wonders if it will speak, and his hand comes up to the base of his throat as though to hold himself in, but the animal has seen all it needs for now. It turns its salt-and-pepper hind end to him so he can stare at its naked tail as the animal pushes its way back through the bushes under the bungalow windows. "Wait a minute," he says, astonished. "That's an opossum."

He realizes what he's just fallen for and groans, turns around, ready to accept Ricardo's amusement. But Ricardo's just standing there watching him, a big bunch of bitter-smelling rue in his hand. "That's an opossum, pal," Mark prompts him, though suddenly he's uncertain that this is a joke.

Ricardo stares at him for a moment, the amazement in his face slowly condensing into pity. "You don't know anything," he says.

★

JACQUELINE
DE ANGELIS

BABY

I TOLD HER I thought they were either psychopaths or they were telling the truth. Gloria was reading her book and didn't bother to answer. I wasn't really talking to Gloria, but I did want some attention.

Gloria knows this about me, I'm sure she knows this about me, but I was barking up the wrong tree this time. Gloria does not like stories about evil parents. I'm fascinated by them. Mother beats up daughter then takes cab. Father cuts son's tongue after golf game. I've tried to explain to Gloria that violence is inherent in the parent/child relationship, but Gloria won't hear it.

I figure a large part of it has to do with the fact that Gloria's mother split at two, came back for a week when Gloria was twelve, and now sends her a Gucci purse each Christmas. Gloria's gone through a lot around all that and, still, she's got this idea of Mother, Rocking Chair, Breast Feeding, Baby in Receiving Blanket.

I, myself, had a normal family. My parents never divorced, my mother stayed at home to take care of us, we had a house, my father had a steady job, we took family vacations. Even so, my mother's eyes often had a murder scene in them and I was the star.

211

I told Gloria my theory that most people have kids because they fear their own extinction. Why else would they? I love when people say that their children will be a comfort in old age. What a joke— no one cares for their parents anymore. Besides, my mother lives in a senior citizen mobile-home community and none of them wants anyone under sixty-five around.

The couple on the TV were from Las Vegas. That's where they lost their kid at a swap meet. They say they turned around and he was gone. He was adorable, five years old. They were a mixed-race couple with one prior charge of child abuse against them. The kid's name is Richie Walker. The Walkers were surrounded by cameras, micro-phones were shoved in their faces as reporters screamed out, "Did you kill little Richie?" All Mrs. Walker said was that so much attention would never have been placed on a white couple who lost their kid at a swap meet.

The Las Vegas press thought the Walkers were callous when they decided to move out of town and had a garage sale to raise some money. They sold Richie's bike and his puzzles. The FBI and the Las Vegas police are convinced the Walkers killed Richie even though the body has never been recovered.

I couldn't tell, since they seemed sincerely upset after three years of investigation. "How do you judge a thing like that?" I asked Gloria.

"You don't."

Gloria's a lawyer, she doesn't judge. She litigates. "There's no evidence. If there were evidence they'd bring them to trial." Gloria put down her book, smiled, and reached out for my hand.

I've seen Gloria on TV many times talking to reporters about cases she didn't believe in, sounding as if all her convictions were at stake.

Gloria and I have separate apartments. We've been together for four years, but we only lived together for about fifteen minutes once. I was at least half to blame, I just wanted everything my way. Gloria hangs her pictures too high on the wall. She's unreasonable about electricity and personally I light lights, that's what they're there for. Besides, I was always afraid of the dark and my parents never paid enough attention to that fact.

I moved out after we had this huge argument about the DWP bill. Though Gloria still maintains she's right—there had been no appreciable increase in electricity costs.

I didn't even want to run across it again, but the story of the Las Vegas parents was on the cover of *People*, and there were Gloria and I in the checkout line. She was on some rape case and just wanted to get back to her house and shower. I got that same dumb feeling I always get when Gloria's attention is on her work. I'm drawn to do something that irritates her so that she'll argue with me. When Gloria argues with me I am the judge, the jury, the electric chair.

How could I resist the missing or dead Richie? There was his angel face in the right-hand corner and his beaten back in the left. I started to tell Gloria how my uncle George used to beat my cousin Chucky. How terrified I was when Uncle George was in the room. My aunt Nora would throw herself on the floor screaming and crying. I didn't understand the tactic but I got low to the ground too. Not Chucky. Chucky would start to laugh the stupidest laugh I've ever heard. "God, Chucky, why do you do that?" I used to say afterward.

"It was hatred," Gloria said, "Chucky hated your uncle George. Why are you telling me this again?"

"Well," I said, "I was just thinking about that couple and how easy it is to beat someone to death. I mean a little kid would be a cinch. The kid could have been driving them nuts. Now, Gloria, imagine if you lived with your mother and she got some guy and he came to live with you, wouldn't you want to torture him?"

"I don't know, that's a stupid question, and besides your uncle George was a drunk, for some reason you always leave that out of the story."

I got the picture. Gloria wasn't going to fight.

I am one of three. Gloria's an only child. After her mother left, she and her dad and her grandmother moved into a suburban house. Things went well for a few years. She walked the neighborhood with her grandmother, learned to ride a bike, started to read, her hair got redder and silky, and she finally got a bedroom set of her own. Then her grandmother died when a drunk driver hit her crossing the street.

After that, Gloria's life was uneasy, her father had a hard time looking her in the eyes, and her mother came home for a week.

Gloria and I each made a list of annual goals and "baby" was number one on Gloria's. I have never wished that someone was kidding more than I did when Gloria handed me her list.

My therapist tells me that Gloria will never leave me. She's said this more than once. My therapist says my need for attention and Gloria's need for someone stable is part of our foundation. Blow off, I've wanted to say. It's a sickening thing to think that what Gloria and I have is a balance of attention and stability.

So now that Gloria is going in for insemination I'm wanting to sleep in a crib and wear pj's with feet. I have even purchased a bath toy. A blue-and-white ferryboat with miniature cars, trucks, vans, and people. It gets lost in the fog of bubble bath and then frightens me when it reappears.

I'm not being irrational, Gloria and I don't have much time together. I run my catering business and big-deal lawyers like her, they work their guts out. I need some attention after all and I hate the idea of Gloria pumping her breasts at work.

When Gloria's mother came home for that week, she helped Gloria make a Popsicle-stick birdhouse. Her mother wore Chanel #5, had on a deep blue jumpsuit, and drank liquids out of small glasses. Gloria says she can still picture her mother's exceptionally long red hair falling over the back of the green velour of her grandmother's living room couch.

Gloria thought that her mother came to get her, but she didn't. She came and made a birdhouse and filed for a divorce.

I don't know where she gets this, but Gloria thinks her mother always loved her. One Popsicle-stick house in thirty-five years seems like the kind of shabby evidence Gloria would love to present a prosecutor with.

*   *   *

I tried to give Gloria some advice. We had dinner. I took her to Mike & Jacks, we had a window seat, there was the city in the distance with its thousands upon thousands of people jammed together, people who hated their lives, their parents, the traffic. "People are eating up the earth, Gloria!" I screamed and the waiter came immediately to see if we needed anything. Gloria paid the bill while I cooled off outside. It was a cold night, the parking attendants were swaying from foot to foot in tune with some music that sounded like waves slapping on sand. "Baby, Baby," one of them kept singing. "Baby, sweet sweet baby."

I called our friend Gary. I told him I wanted him to tell Gloria that she needed a mother more than she needed to be one. "Oh, God, Molly, grow up. Gloria's wanted a baby for years. You know, Molly, you really are a handful." Gary admittedly is more Gloria's friend than mine, but I thought that this baby thing would get him on my side.

If I'm a handful, Gloria's a carload. After she realized her mother wasn't going to take her, she ripped the legs off all her dolls so they couldn't walk away.

Three months after her grandmother died, Gloria's father shipped her off to convent boarding school and then married a woman with two sons.

My therapist says I'm challenged by Gloria, that I have a deep fear I'll be ignored like I was when Timothy, my brother, was born. My bright and shining brother Timothy who, when he's in town, does his laundry at my apartment and talks passionately about the reconvergence of spiritual energy that he sees in humankind. Timothy has a doctoral thesis that's been in progress so long, flies have given up on its dead body.

"Babies, babies, I hate them!" I screamed at a chair my therapist set up in the center of the room. I beat the hell out of the chair with a bataka. The whole process exhausted me and I sat down on the couch and cried about that damn little kid Richie wandering around by himself at the swap meet. Maybe he was dead and buried or maybe he was sold to some child porno ring and taken to some foreign

country. All I could see was Richie reaching out his hand, suddenly
aware that no one who tucked him in at night was ever going to be
around again.

When I got home I opened a large can of cat food and fed the entire
thing to my Siamese, Martha. It made her happy.

I opened the evening paper and saw Gloria's picture in the Metro
section. She was standing next to the mayor again, holding yet another
plaque. They were on the sidewalk in front of the Central City Child
Relief Home on Western and Third. Gloria's hair was blown a bit to
the right and the mayor's tie wasn't straight, but otherwise they were
smiling and presentable.

The mayor had his hand on a curly-haired boy's shoulder and
some tiny girl was clutching the hem of Gloria's dress. Then I noticed
the picture was swimming with kids. All kinds of them but none taller
than Gloria's waist.

★

RAMON BUD CHAMBERS

MUSIC FROM THE RAFTERS

TODAY IS THE DAY I will show him exactly how I feel, Arnie promised himself as he rose from bed, made a pot of coffee, and straightened his small apartment. As he prepared to go to work he saw the eucalyptus trees outside his window blow silently as the early-morning light cast swaying gray shadows about the room.

His resolve mounted as he drove to his job. If only I could get him to react to what I say to him, Arnie thought. I want him to do something, think something, or just tell me something. But he deals in words, I in pictures. Arnie always remembered that he was deaf.

Someday I'll be effective and my expression will cause people's hearts to move, Chet's heart to move, he repeated to himself as he parked his car next to the others on a graded-off section of the building site and unloaded his tools from the trunk.

He passed the piles of lumber still wet from the night's dew. The two-by-fours were stacked next to the bare skeleton of a house. All that moisture will make it hard to drive nails today, he thought.

He clipped his leather nail apron around his waist and climbed the ladder to where the carpenters were sitting astride roof joists and warming their hands about plastic cups of steaming coffee from their Thermoses.

Chet already had the crew gathered about him listening to his stories; daring and unbelievable exploits with girls of the night before. As the men opened their mouths in laughter, their breaths hissed clouds of steam into the cold air. Chet stopped his storytelling long enough to wave his hand in greeting to Arnie. Arnie smiled and quickly made the sign of, I want to talk to you, to Chet. Chet nodded his head and turned to his waiting audience to finish his tale. Arnie sat down behind the storyteller and watched the reactions of the listeners as he leaned against a roof beam and lit a cigarette. He waited for the day's work to begin and for a chance to communicate privately with Chet.

Presently Arnie saw the men jump to their feet as the framing contractor arrived with blueprints rolled under his arm. He yelled to the carpenters above him, "You men step it up. We finish framing today. Roofers and siders are coming tomorrow. I'll have your final paychecks for you this evening and that's all the work I can give you till next spring."

As the carpenters began pounding nails, Arnie saw their lips move in silent swear words he knew so well. The lip movements seemed to increase as the nails they were driving bent in the wet and spongy wood.

Chet and Arnie had worked together on several building jobs and it was Chet who served as deaf Arnie's ears and mute Arnie's mouthpiece. Chet had learned a score of sign words and it was he who relayed to Arnie exactly what the contractor wanted. Not that Arnie had no way of communication with the other men, for he could, through simple sign language and a few words he was able to phonicate, get an idea across. Frequently he found himself not understood, at which time he would resort to his wide carpenter's pencil and writing his message on a piece of wood.

It was in writing such lines that Arnie began composing verse for Chet. They were small one-liners at first, but they soon developed into longer poems. Chet showed excitement when he saw Arnie on the cut-off saw making up cripples for inside the walls or cutting studs to length. Chet smiled when Arnie handed him the boards with poems on them. Chet was always careful to nail up the written boards in proper order so that the entire verse could be read. For as Arnie could write, Chet would sing. Many of the carpenters told Arnie that Chet's voice sounded like Nat King Cole's. Arnie had seen pictures of the singer but had no idea what his voice sounded like, although he was sure it was one of the most wonderful sounds in the world. Arnie frequently wished he could place his hands on Chet's neck as he sang so he could feel the vibrations.

This day was not too different from other work days. About mid-morning the sun began to warm the air and to dry out the lumber. The carpenters stopped their cursing and Arnie knew they were ready for a little music. He started a poem on a board:

Nat King Cole from the rafters . . .

And he continued on another,

Pulls out the sun, a morning flower,

and on another,

Night tree dusted at my window . . .

Thus it began. Arnie wrote, Chet sang, the men pounded and listened, and the morning passed quickly. At lunchtime all the framers gathered on a sunny spot on the sub-floor. Some opened their lunch boxes and ate sandwiches while others slept. Arnie sat down beside Chet, ate, and watched him entertain the men intermittently between bites of food.

When Arnie noticed a lull in the conversation he tugged on Chet's arm to gain his attention. The work is finished today, he said by pointing to the framed house around them and then making a slashing motion across his throat.

Chet nodded his head and then opened his palms as if to say, that is the way it is.

Arnie let Chet finish his apple, then closed his fingers together and pointed to himself, directed one finger to his eye, and then let it point to Chet. Will I see you again? he asked.

"Sure, Arnie, sure," Chet said as he turned away to arrange his lunch pail. Arnie grabbed Chet's arm again and shook his head because he had not seen Chet's answer on his lips.

Chet realized Arnie had not read his lips so he turned and spoke directly to Arnie. "I said yes, Arnie," Chet replied. "Next spring we will probably be working together again. You heard the boss, he said next spring there will be more work."

Arnie had not heard the boss and Chet tried to smooth the situation, "But anyway, next spring. Understand?"

Arnie shook his head in agreement and then reinforced himself inside for what he was about to say. I . . . he again pointed all his fingers to his chest, LOVE . . . he closed his fists tightly over his heart. But the sign of pointing his finger to the person of his emotions never came. As he was about to show YOU by pointing to Chet, the latter stood up, laughing and motioning for the attention of the others.

"Hey, guys, did you see that? Arnie says he is in love. He's in love!"

"So Arnie finally found himself a girl," said one of the men, rousing from his slumber.

"I bet that Arnie is a real lady-killer," said another.

Then Chet turned toward Arnie again and asked, "What's she like, Arnie? Is she big up here?" he asked as he made a motion of breasts across his own chest.

Arnie knew Chet had not understood what he had said and he wanted to quickly correct the situation, so he tried to speak. "Ohhh," was all his confused and silent tongue was able to utter in the place of no.

"You hear that, guys," Chet continued. "He's saying LOVE. Say it again, Arnie, say LOVE, LOVE, LOVE." All the men laughed and began patting Arnie on the back and shaking his hand.

"Good old Arnie. We knew you had it in you," they said. "Have you set the date yet? You know, THE date?"

Arnie knew he had failed in showing Chet how he felt and he saw no way to correct the situation, for he had left his pencil with his nail apron up on the roof joists and the moment was already well out of hand. Chet became engaged in a story about a girl with a great body, and it was almost time to return to work.

Arnie wrote no more on the wood in that house. As he nailed up the last two-by-four, dark rain clouds shrouded the sun. He collected his final check from the contractor and walked to his car. He stored his tools in the trunk and then sat down behind the steering wheel and turned the starter key until he felt the vibrations of the running engine. He was ready to drive off when he noticed Chet walking from the building toward him, waving his arms for him to stop.

"Hey, Arnie," his lips formed. "Now that we're laid off and got a lot of time, let's make some music. Just like we do here. You write the words and I'll write music for them.

Arnie nodded his head in agreement.

"But we got to put them on paper, Arnie, on paper—understand? It's no good to just write them on wood. They all get covered up by the siding." He waited for Arnie to reply, but he did not. He only sat and picked at the steering wheel but kept his eyes slightly toward Chet.

"I got a friend in the music publishing business," Chet said as he tried to catch Arnie's full attention. "Sometimes they buy songs— for money. What do you say?"

Arnie shrugged his shoulders then nodded his head in agreement.

"I'll drop by your place in the next few days," Chet finished.

Arnie stared straight ahead at the drops of rain starting to fall on the windshield. Chet was turning up the collar of his coat with one hand and lifting the other in a farewell.

That night the rain increased and coupled itself with sheets of bright lightning and rumbling thunder that Arnie could feel in the core of his body. He sat for a long time at his small kitchen table and watched the flashes upon the wet-slick eucalyptus leaves outside his window.

Nat King Cole from the rafters, he said to himself as he stood up and breathed a deep sigh.

He turned on a lamp in the corner of the room and returned to the table. He sat down with a pocketknife, a sharpening stone, and a can of honing oil. With trembling hands he slowly and methodically worked a razor-sharp edge onto the blade. He pulled some brown paper nail bags from a drawer, split them open with the knife, carefully cut out page-sized sheets, and neatly stacked them. He then picked up a pencil and began to write.

★

TERRY
WOLVERTON

PRETTY WOMEN

NINE HARSH WINTERS HAD eaten lacy rust holes through Detroit's best sheet metal, but the engine still had a lot of power. Kit liked this big monster that looked like a piece of shit on wheels—no one ever tried to steal her car.

She'd parked it on streets where every other vehicle had gotten their windows busted out. Not hers. The old brown Pontiac was so ugly it inspired a kind of respect.

Kit thought of herself in the same way. She was a big woman, but solid, with a face no one had ever accused of loveliness. But like her car, she had all eight cylinders, and she moved with a lumbering kind of grace.

It was always a surprise to her that pretty women wanted her. It seemed like pretty women drew themselves to her like flies to honey—though she was more like a fly and they the sweetness.

Something about her—Kit never knew exactly what—made those women with the long legs and full lips want to climb into the front seat and take a drive. Which was okay by Kit. She was pushing fifty, but she still had a full tank of gas.

So she'd take 'em for a spin. Each and every lovely one of them. But Kit didn't trust a pretty woman. Not one bit. She'd admire them. She'd sweet talk 'em. She might even take them out and spend some money on them. But no way was she going to love them. She could never love a pretty woman.

Maybe that's why she attracted them. Because she would not love them, and that's what they wanted. Maybe they were lookin' for relief from all the love that usually gets heaped on pretty women.

They'd always laugh about her car, these women. They'd tell her it was horrible, they didn't want to be seen in it. They were reluctant to set their pretty new dresses down against the old plaid blanket that covered the cracked upholstery spewing forth its beige stuffing.

But they always went wherever she took them, and they always let themselves be kissed or stroked in the roomy front seat. And they were always eager to go again and desperate when she told them, as she inevitably told them, that the ride was over. Because when it came right down to it, Kit wasn't interested in a woman she could not love.

It all started the same way when she met Lola. Lola was the prettiest of them all, with red lips like the first bite of a ripe strawberry, and cheeks that curved like smooth shells. Lola wore her shiny dark hair in a million curls that danced against her shoulders, and she had a body that was both firm and soft in all the right ways.

Lola came up to Kit one night in a dark bar on the outskirts of town. Even in the dim light Lola could tell that Kit was ugly, and Kit could see right away how pretty Lola was. Lola sat right down next to Kit and in a voice like afternoon rain asked, "What're ya drinkin'?"

Kit was drinking bourbon, and in an instant she had another shot in front of her, and Lola handing a bill to the bartender.

Now, Kit never took money from women. She always paid her own way. She started to protest, but Lola wasn't asking her permission. In that same deep, husky voice she said, "Drink up," and she raised her own drink—a daiquiri—in toast.

Kit drained the glass in a long, leisurely gulp, taking the opportunity to have another look at the beauty that stood before her. Lola wore a white blouse that bared her shoulders, and the skin that rose above the white cloth looked smooth as maple cream. A red skirt clung to her hips and then flared and swirled around handsomely shaped legs that ended in red high heels. She smelled like the sun shining on a garden. Much too pretty. Kit shook her head to clear the vision from her eyes. Then she set the glass on the bar and curtly said, "Thanks."

Lola looked amused and said, "You're welcome." She swiveled on the stool and turned away from Kit to face the crowded room.

Kit knew the next move was hers, but for once she wasn't up to it. She was tired of flirting with these women she could never love, who sought her out perhaps for that very reason. That last bourbon must have been one too many. She felt dizzy and a little sad.

Pulling a couple of singles out of her back pocket, she left them for the bartender, slowly climbed down off her stool, and lumbered out of the bar without another word to Lola.

Outside, a light snow was falling. Kit zipped her flight jacket and pulled the collar snugly around her face, then crushed a knitted hat on top of her scalp. She climbed into the Pontiac, coaxed it to start, and began to pull away from the curb.

Just then she noticed Lola standing in the doorway, snow lodging in the tangled curls and melting on her shoulders. Kit leaned over to roll down the passenger window.

"Nice car," Lola proclaimed with apparent sincerity.

"Need a ride?" Kit asked before she could help herself.

Lola's smile took a long time. It spread across her face like the unfolding of a fan. "No thanks," she said finally. "I've got my own wheels." Then she disappeared into the warmth and light and laughter behind the door.

The Pontiac gobbled up the highway, headlights barely taking in the darkened, snowy landscape of their peripheral vision. The AM radio beat out an old fifties tune, jangling into the trails of smoke from Kit's Chesterfield. For weeks Kit had been driving at night, remote suburban highways, forgotten country roads, no destination except to avoid returning to the tiny bar.

The smells and sounds of Lola had stayed in her head like images from a vivid dream. Kit didn't like it. She was too old, she had seen too much, to let a woman like Lola get under her skin.

Ever since childhood, Kit had known all about pretty girls, pretty women. Their vanity. Their treachery. Their terrible loneliness. She knew that a woman like that would fall into you like a mirror, but it was you who disappeared.

So she never took them seriously. A pretty woman had always seemed to Kit like a fine European racing car—she could admire it from a distance, but knew without even considering it that the cost of upkeep would be too high.

One night Kit walked out of the factory when her shift ended to find Lola leaning up against the bumper of her old Pontiac. A harsh wind blew Lola's curls all around her head and forced tears from the corners of her eyes. A black wool coat hid the contours of her body, and the sculpted legs were encased in tall black boots. Still, there was no mistaking she was pretty. Pretty as sin.

"Do you remember me?" Lola asked as Kit approached. Her voice shot sparks like a fireplace full of logs.

Kit nodded. "You drink daiquiris."

"I found you by your car," Lola offered an explanation that had not been requested. "I asked around."

Kit nodded again. "I guess there ain't too many like this still on the road." She patted the discolored trunk self-consciously. This was a hell of a thing, and her just standing there like she was a fool.

She noticed Lola's lips were pale and a little chapped from the cold. She said, "You hungry?"

Lola looked at Kit and nodded slowly.

"Well, there's a steakhouse just a coupla miles from here. Get in," Kit said, swinging the heavy brown door on squeaky hinges. And Lola did.

Lola never said a word about the old plaid blanket, or the stuffing spilling out of the worn cushions. She just said, "What'll she do?" and Kit pressed the accelerator to the floor to show her. Lola laughed as the pistons thundered inside the old engine, rolled down her window, and let the wind roar in.

Over dinner Lola asked a lot of questions, and it made Kit uneasy.

She was used to asking the questions, like turning a golden key in a lock and watching the pretty women open. They loved to talk about themselves, their eyes brightening, growing more animated the longer she listened. She half resented Lola for trying to turn the tables, and grunted her curt answers. In the dim bluish light of the steakhouse, Kit was surprised to notice that Lola's hair, straightened by the wind, had lost some of its luster.

Afterwards Kit sped over the icy roads back to Lola's car. Lola didn't crawl across the seat to cuddle up next to Kit's bulk, like the other pretty women always had. She stayed relaxed over on her own side of the plaid blanket, lounging comfortably against the passenger door, hair flying out the open window like a banner in the night sky.

Kit was astonished to find herself talking about her years in the Navy, about the regimen, the discipline, the hiding. Her low croak of a voice filled the Pontiac, and Lola listened to every word. When they pulled into the gravel parking lot, Kit made a move to kiss her, but Lola whispered, "No."

Winter yielded reluctantly to a drab, chill spring and Kit found herself longing for Lola. The dark-haired beauty would appear, occasionally, mysteriously, and always engagingly, but Kit had no way of finding her. No woman had ever left such an imprint on her, and Kit cursed herself for breaking this cardinal rule, letting this pretty woman get next to her this way.

One night she lay wound in a blanket on her hard bed, gritting her teeth till her jaws ached, staring into the darkness as if to catch a glimpse of the shadow of what had vanished. Outside, a dog yelped in the distance, its lonely howl adding to a chorus of laments floating up from the city.

At first Kit thought she imagined the sound: a light tapping that seemed to come from the main room of the small house. She thought it was a branch against a window, she was certain it was sleet against the roof. But the noise persisted, growing more urgent, drawing her, as if involuntarily, out of her bed and onto her feet, until she found herself at the front door. She boldly swung it open as if to convince herself no one was there.

In the sheen of midnight Lola stood shivering on her front porch. As Kit gazed awkwardly through the storm door, Lola asked, in a voice like the powdery wings of moths, "May I come in?"

Kit had a moment of panic. Her house, like her car, like herself, was serviceable but unlovely. A mismatched collection of furniture had been gathered from dumpsters or donated by friends, and piles of newspapers gathered dust in every corner. Although her buddies from work dropped by for an occasional beer, Kit had never entertained a pretty woman in her home.

Lola seemed to take her hesitation for assent. She brushed past Kit and entered the shabby, comfortable room. With her arrival, the whole house was suffused with the scent of a cold late-winter night, fresh and clear and piney. Kit opened her lungs and inhaled.

Without being asked, Lola headed for the misshapen couch and took a seat. She seemed not nervous but full of purpose, like she was on a mission only she knew the reason for. Like the front seat of the Pontiac, the couch too boasted a protective covering, a worn Indian blanket with the pattern of the sun in shades of red and brown and gray. Lola curled up and made herself right at home on top of it.

Kit raked a hand through her short, disheveled hair and wrapped the belt of an old flannel robe more tightly around her waist. She was self-conscious of her bare feet. Suspicion gnawed in her gut. What had this pretty woman come for? What was it she thought she could take away from Kit?

In this state of agitation, Kit sat on the arm of a battered chair. Her guest was silent, and had in fact leaned her head back onto the blanket's rays and closed her eyes. Kit used the opportunity to study the dark-haired woman more carefully, to read her like a book of secrets, and as she did, something strange began to happen. Before her eyes Lola's image began to swim and blur. Kit ground her fists into her eyelids and when her vision cleared, she began to notice things.

Tonight Lola's hair was pulled back very severely, annihilating her curls and making the features of her face seem sharp and not at all curvy. Deep shadows bruised her eyes, and lines pinched their way like parentheses around each corner of her mouth.

Fascinated, Kit moved closer, taking a seat on the other end of the couch. Lola did not stir. Kit had never seen before how long her nose was, nor the faint mustache like an umbra on her upper lip. She felt a stirring in her chest, like an ignition firing. Lola's nails were stubby and unkempt, and underneath her dark coat, her body appeared as limp and puffy as a rag doll's. As Kit reached to touch a sallow cheek, Lola finally opened her eyes.

"Why, you ain't pretty at all," Kit growled in an awed whisper.

Lola's smile was blinding, like hi-beam headlights. In a simple gesture Kit reached out and pulled her close.

All night they drove that hard mattress, traversing potholed thighs and stretch-marked bellies, savoring imperfect curves with a relentless grace. The surface of the road grew slick with oil, but they maneuvered expertly, as if they'd been born to ride this highway. They loved hard, soaking the sheets with gasoline, moaning together like a twin-cam engine at full speed. As they reached fifth gear, the brakes gave out, and both women leaned eagerly into the crash.

She couldn't tell if they'd slept or not, but as the sky warmed from gray to golden, Kit seemed to wake. She gingerly untangled herself from the twist of limbs melded together on the sheets. At first she lay just basking in the light that streamed through the window, humbled by the generosity of Lola's gift. Then she offered a sigh, like a silent prayer, full of a feeling she could not deny was love.

★

ERIC
GUTIERREZ

MY EYE

I WAS SEVEN WHEN I lost my eye. It was the nicest one, my father used to tell me. My other eye, the one I have left, is simply brown. I had it refracted recently and found I have 20/30 vision. I wear a contact lens anyway, for cosmetic reasons. Over the empty socket I wear a black patch.

In grade school I wore a glass eye, brown and lifeless. No matter where I looked it stared straight ahead like cold dark ash.

No one ever looks me straight in the eye. They sometimes try but end up looking for something else to focus their attention. When I look someone square in the eye, I choose the left one or the bridge of their nose.

Across the bridge of my nose runs a half-hearted eyebrow. I only have one eyebrow as well, long and straight and a little weedy in the center.

The contact lens is tinted so now my eye is green. I changed my eye color on a whim. There is much whimsy in my life.

My younger brother, who acts in commercials and belongs to a violent gang of affluent suburban punks, thinks my patch is cool and tells his fellow warlords that I lost my eye in a knife fight. He acts out the drama by pushing a chopstick through a California roll at the sushi bar in the mall. His fellow punks of privilege respond with a chorus of "rad" and pour more green tea.

The Bonsai Bar is commonly known as the fortress of the CEO's, the name adopted for publicity purposes by my brother's gang. Actually, I thought of it.

Even people who close one eye see more of the world than I do through my green contact lens. My peripheral vision is almost nonexistent. Bad heiresses and certain waiters think I'm attractive. Nonetheless, I've had only one girlfriend in my life. Sometimes I let the waiters lose the tab and I'll leave them a fake phone number, the last digit off.

Several nights I've sat in the Bonsai Bar with my brother and his friends, reinventing the details of my life. How I lost my eye, how I lost the girl, where I go late at night, are all news to me. I learn these things in conversation with handsome blondes sporting daring haircuts and scabbed knuckles.

My brother just shot his fourth 7-UP commercial, but my favorite is the one where he stares into the camera earnestly confessing what a pill-popping alcoholic family terror he had been before he met the caring counselors and pure desert air at teen rehab. His voice cracks with sincerity, and he's grinning like a motherfuck because he's as sincere as a self-inflicted stigmata.

Four of the CEO's have been to teen rehab, but not my brother. He may be the family terror, but he makes more money than any of us.

Actually, our father makes more. It just hasn't trickled down to the rest of his family. When I'm here I live in the pool house, but the gas is shut off so the kitchen is worthless. When I'm hungry I'll pick out one of the Versace suits I got for interviews two years ago and call up an heiress. If I don't feel like company, I'll drink beer from the bottle in a tony restaurant and make a show of it for the waiter. Usually I eat at home.

Lately my father has been watching me closely at dinner. I pretend not to notice, but we pass the food counterclockwise and I sit to his right. Before actually releasing the plate, while my hand is out, he will look me straight in the eye like no one else can and tell me a Helen Keller joke or that Sammy Davis is headlining at Harrah's.

"I saw you admiring the crystal dolphins yesterday," he said recently. "Don't you sometimes think about all the stuff you're going to get when we're dead? Come on, admit it. I bet you sometimes think about us dying and redecorating the house."

Each night I laugh at whatever he says, and then my mother will laugh and finally he will laugh, too. I eat quickly while they talk about their next weekend trip. They quiz me on the name of the hotel, steps to securing the house, and the name of Feldman Grey, their attorney, just in case.

My brother doubts the existence of Feldman Grey or a generous will. I, on the other hand, am counting on both.

I go away just often enough to say that I'm visiting whenever I'm home. No one asks where I've been. I just come back and suddenly there's fresh linen in the pool house and several new shirts wrapped in tissue paper piled under a note from my mother. "Welcome back, sweetheart," the notes say. "Just some things to keep the prodigal son looking handsome. Don't tell your father. Love,"

People are always complimenting me on my shirts. My mother has a taste for colorful linen with collar stays and complicated patterns in heavy cotton. They are a fashion galaxy away from the men's store pastel dress shirts that are my official gifts for Christmas and birthdays. She must be sending me a secret code through these shirts. They don't come from any of the stores where she has credit cards. Buying these shirts must take a daring and romance that are the closest thing she has to a double life. Bold prints and French cuffs are our secret.

When I'm in town I drive my brother's XL convertible. I'm not supposed to drive, but it gives him a kick to see me pop it into high gear, my one eye tearing as I weave through traffic with the top down, yelling at the top of my lungs at all the drivers I can't see. We race, me in the car, him on his bike, both of us screaming.

I'm meeting him at the Bonsai Bar for dinner. A few of the heiresses have been hard to track down lately, and I just don't think

I can laugh at my father tonight. I've chosen a full-cut white linen shirt with stainless steel buttons and the silver Versace. I might go to this place after dinner where I know the waiter.

Leaving the pool house I see my parents sitting down to dinner behind the glass walls of the dining room. It's as if they were on TV or in a terrarium. The whole place is so brightly lit and all the drapes are open so that it really is like watching TV. My parents are eating on display with all of their things. By blinking my eye I can flip the channels, first looking into the kitchen, then the dining room, the living room, and finally the master bedroom. I can see it all, redone very minimalist with indirect lighting and all original art.

★

ALEIDA RODRIGUEZ

MY FACE IN THE FACES OF OTHERS

WHEN I LIVED WITH Jane life seemed threatening. Looking back, it's difficult to believe that was me back there. That it was me dreaming of walking the skinny corridor to the bathroom in the middle of the night. Dreaming of standing in front of the medicine cabinet mirror looking at my reflection with its eyes closed. Long enough to be able to see exactly what I look like with both my eyes closed. Then a black snap and the dream ends like broken film. I felt it was significant then. I even wrote about it. In a crazy, jumbled piece, I was actually able to record something—an impressionistic rendering of what I was experiencing in my inner life. I recognized the SOS's, but couldn't come to my rescue. Not unlike my woman of the tile. The apparition in my bathroom.

I was tying my shoes while sitting on the black chair when I felt something calling me over the floor. My eyes searched for the spot across the black-and-white tiles and found her. The picture was frozen, but I could tell exactly what had just happened. She was crossing the river walking on the gnarled log she's now holding onto in the water, her hair streaked with white, her white lacy dress dragged and twisted by the current. Her tragic face is thrown back: her mouth a black rectangle melting down at the edges, eyes tiny windows searching up. The river is black and churning, the tops of the waves touched with white. The other bank, the one she crossed from, is black but for a few leaves tipped in moonlight—the kind of white light that forces one to call it silvery. The log looks slippery and the light finds a place for itself along its crooked spine. Even the air is black and thick as asphalt.

She had called and I kneeled down next to her, but I couldn't find another emotion in my chest pocket right then but curiosity. She stayed there, though, and refused to melt back into the abstract design of the floor. It was a perfect photograph preserved under the veneer of fifty years of waxing. I was never in the bathroom alone again. What I mean is that I didn't have to squint and play with the focus of my eyes to see her. She would call out to me and there she'd be, having fallen in just seconds before I'd look. Every time I'd look away, the scene wound itself back again and replayed. It wasn't until much later, as I sat in the car watching the hills around Morro Bay unroll themselves like huge bolts of green cloth, that I understood what it had been trying to tell me months before the event.

The event I'm talking about is the second-to-last day of the year: December 30, 1981. I was driving home after working the last day I'd be working for someone else for a year. I would be doing my own work now. I had gotten a grant. I was thinking about endings, the unpredictability of life; I was feeling philosophical. Who would have thought, I thought, when I took this job a year ago, that I would be quitting so soon? And yet here it was the end of the year, the two endings coinciding. But I had been given a gift, and it was just beginning: a year of belonging to no one but myself. An achy sweetness in my chest and that's when I saw her legs lit up from behind by the oncoming car on my left. She was in the crosswalk with her bag of groceries, then she turned to face the car that illuminated her before sending her into the air and continuing on its way.

It's a mannequin, I told myself; it's a dummy. They're filming a movie here—where are the long vans and the little bunches of technicians holding Styrofoam cups of coffee? But then I remembered I saw her legs move. I saw her take a few steps before she was hit. The realization froze traffic, and we waited in our humming cars for the cloud to pass over us and away before easing forward.

I jerked my car around suddenly and parked in front of the Sunset Bar where a few men, having seen the accident, were grouping and commenting. I got out and walked over to the one who was standing closest to her and looking like he's going to manage the situation. He was yelling back at the others: get a goddamn blanket or something for Christ's sake. Then I saw her body facedown in the street, her dress lifted up over her ass and no underwear. The last humiliation. I told him quickly I thought I saw what kind of car it was, it was a Honda or a Rabbit or something squatty like that. He half-listened and continued yelling. He probably saw it better from the sidewalk. I turned away from him and carried myself back to the car like a fragile, overfilled vessel. On the street were her crushed and scattered groceries, a broken blue-glass bottle of something like rose water—suddenly I heard the shattering noise—she had probably gone to the botanica across the street for it. One sandal and sunglasses near my car, I opened the door, backed up, turned around, drove the last block up the hill toward home.

At home I cried for myself in her exposed body out there on the street with the sirens approaching. I felt spilled. As though I had just opened my eyes and found myself walking a tightrope holding a plate on top of which was a glass filled with my life. And a little of it had spilled. I was the one who had hit her! No, I was in the other car watching—see, there go her legs again silhouetted in front of the light and then nothing. But I still kept putting my brakes on and then, too late, I looked in the rearview mirror and glimpsed myself facedown in the street. An image I couldn't shake while on vacation with my lover.

We left the next morning. The hills around Morro Bay and further north were insistent with their message that there are things that can be seen with the eyes that the inner one starves for: a green, tasseled blanket—here and there groups of tiny red-and-black cows pinned on just so for effect. It was so clear that at the highest points in the road through the mountains you could see over the heads of the next row of mountains to the heart of the state, cool blue and gray in the distance—at least hundreds of miles away. Below us, the green flannel hills held little triangular blue-and-silver lakes between their thighs and then her legs again and the crash and the scattered groceries and I remembered the tile in my bathroom.

But there was nothing I could have done, even if I'd understood the message earlier. Besides, the message wasn't about that poor woman on her way to the people who were waiting for her and her groceries on that second-to-last day of the year, her last. I know it means I can't afford not to recognize my face in the picture, my face in the medicine-cabinet mirror. I have to open my eyes and carry myself carefully, tenderly across the street, the river. I can't trust that anyone will stop for me. Maybe not even out of maliciousness, but once they've done it they find it hard to turn around and make it better. It wouldn't have helped in her case; she couldn't have survived that one.

When I lived with Jane, life seemed dim and threatening as a corridor in the middle of the night. It should have. When I left Cuba at nine, life became a lesson in survival too early: thrown in, I flunked my first swimming class at the YWCA but not my second. When my lover wanted to leave me, life was a log I had to cross a river on, from which I was thrown off. I've held on. The dark rectangle of my mouth has formed the words that make me buoyant. I've learned to recognize my face in the faces of others. Like the one, now, who kneels down next to the tile, reaching out to me.

★

ERIC LATZKY

STUDY FOR DARKNESS: TWO VIEWS FROM VERTICAL CLIFFS

THIS IS NOT ABOUT love.

Don't move. Let him do the wanting. Be still as the end. Feel the opening inside you become suspended outside the window, travel through the darkness, across time to the adjacent, abandoned factory building. He is there: top floor, corner window. You don't know him; you know him as well as yourself.

This is not a lie.

He is watching you.

His intention was benign: a cigarette, an open window, a handful of air. He'd have gone to bed alone and slept through the night if it weren't for you. Destroy him with your thoughts. As always, your desires are murderous. Hope he is sick, hope he is decaying visibly, lesioned, discolored, grotesque. You will love him then; you have had enough of all this. Look at him. Concentrate all your power, focus it, collect it. Take the time to do this one thing completely. Inhale to the bottom of your lungs, listen for sounds along the way, close your eyes, exhale. Now hate death, now hate life; they are both fucked.

Open your eyes but remain still. He senses you are there. Light a cigarette and with the same match light a candle on the side table above your head. The glow of the flame will give him just enough to know for sure you are not a vision.

Make a move.

Do not get up off the couch. With you here he has an unobstructed view, a straight line, an undeniable object. He could fly across the way and land inside your studio. Dangle one leg down to the floor, put an arm behind your head and arch your back, as if to stretch. With the same hand that holds the cigarette, stroke the hair on your chest, slowly, like a heavy, smoke-filled dream. Look directly through the man across the way, beyond any real progression of sight, and lose yourself in his deconstructing image. See him as the subject of an evolving abstraction, framed in a dour, urban setting of muted tones: blues, browns, steel grays, shadows, glass; obscure, unidentifiable lines. There is no true color here. There is very little light.

The winds are screaming, howling through a narrow passage between your studio and the factory.

There are six stories from his windows, from your windows, to the ground. At the pinnacle you are close enough to reach across, to take his neck or arm and pull him into your own domain, your chest, your life. You are close enough to care for him, to hold him, to hurt him. Hang on to this moment, hold it until it begins to suffocate, to wither like flowers. Pick out a memory, one that is foreign and kind. Recall love; recall knowing it existed once. Turn away from the window toward the flame of the candle. Hear the light envelop you, ease you back to the days before the silence. Be blinded, set free: Gabriel is smiling at you. You are warm, enraptured, he is back with you now, reciting as he used to, the breath of his words flowing into your ear, into your head, inside you. He is holding you, tight, safe, your shadows, together, flickering on and off the far wall. Go further back, to the beginning when you met, when you first brought him here to the studio. Go to the beginning of love; love was unknown then, intriguing, still innocent. He was terrified the first time, he was young, distinguished, trembling.

Get up from the couch.

Walk over to the window, throw it open with abandon, grand, cavalier. Tilt your head back, breathing in the black, the eternal, minuscule distance between you and the man in the window across from yours. See the literal coolness of invisible air rush in past you and extinguish the flame of the candle. Look down into the pit, it is a narrow, sheer drop. The darkness annihilates the senses: you cannot see, you don't hear, you feel nothing. At the bottom are the shattered remains of souls, dried, rotting, shot out of open windows from solitary, ravaged men.

Refocus your attention. Turn your head up, away from the down. The man is still there, across the way, watching you. You have failed to intimidate him; next time you will try harder and then if he still does not show signs of fear you will assume a role. Plan the transformation into a creature of prey, a wolf, a hawk, a virus. Be silent; this is where the quickening is created, where it will grow. It is in silence, in the dark, that the power exists, that the answer will come. It may go either way. You have no way of knowing.

Recoil from the window, from his view, be drawn back toward the couch but end up, instead, favoring an unadorned, austere patch of the rough wooden floor, admiring its uncomplicated coldness. Embark from this point. Resign yourself to accepting whichever way it goes; whatever is in you will expel itself. Say you will do whatever it is you will do.

Now black out into the solitude.

Welcome the phases, challenge the levels to come, the ones that will lead you into the silence. The shouting inside will come first. This is your friend now; this is familiar. It is common, unempowered, deteriorating with no help from you. Be alone: fear is an extinct animal, powerless, it is nothing more than theoretical. Allow the volume to increase, encourage it.

Hold yourself, you have only to make it through.

At a certain level the constant pain will consume itself, execute itself like dynamite, it will explode into nonexistence. It is not an infinite entity, the pain only lives within you, independent. Allow it not to matter anymore, this is the weapon. You have obliterated the source. You have won.

Emerge into the abandoned time; recall a memory.

For several nights in a row now, Gabriel has asked you to help him die.

He goes in and out. When he is out he lies in bed viewing at once a combination of three pencil drawings you had made of him, in sequential poses, precariously hung on the far wall of the studio. They were made by the illumination of an odd number of candles, of various heights, you had placed near and far from his body. Vague, quivering light, and extreme shadows, floated over him in uncommon patterns. These images were made at the end of the evening in which you had received the gravest proclamation. They are archival; they are historical. When he is in he is in with the clarity of winter.

Tell him you will not let him die.

Restore the studio, your lives.

Light candles in each of the corners, put on a symphony or an opera and ask him to recite to you. Be still, breathless, deny the present and pretend you are both quiet and safe as you once really were. Turn the screaming inside you off like lights. It is loud, it is deaf, it is arbitrary and indiscriminate; the screaming is present and then it is gone. Tonight his words radiate a rare and pristine quality: they play off the walls. They are opaque, intangible: you hear them and they travel through you. Lead him over to the couch, lie down together, he in front of you. Wrap yourself around him, molding your bodies to a single, duplicate shape, an identical curve. Be tight, silent, rub your cheeks, your lips, effortlessly up and down along the back of his head, his neck, across the top of his back from one shoulder to the other. Adjust your position slightly, enough not to hold him tighter but more securely, to fit the curve of him more precisely. In these years you have come to know the secrets of Gabriel, you have disclosed yourselves to each other. Now kiss the violet-black lesion on the side of his neck; begin with this one. Continue on paying time and attention, devouring each of them completely.

Think: death.

Think: life.

Now try to figure the deceptive, brittle line between both of these things, between love and hate, death and love. Understand nothing. You are here tonight with Gabriel, he is alive. This is all you know. Purge the wanting in yourself, your wish to know the reason why. It is; it is unexplained. Begin to massage the brilliant patches of disease covering the body of this man who you will save, rescue, rejuvenate. Begin slowly, methodically. Be sure that you can change things, that your goal will be achieved. Concentrate.

Bring your hand up from his body and put it to his face faintly, inaudibly. The air will not sway. Move his hair in waves, mysteriously, rearrange it, replace it in an obscure sequence. Create change and observe the power inherent in displacement. He is still; still your bodies together share a single shape. Feel what he feels. Sense the tear moving from his eye, from his cheek, onto your hand. It continues further, rolls off the tip of your finger. The screaming inside you has come back.

Turn him around to face you directly. Define this action, get out only one word: no. He is not dying, he is not going to die. Tell him you will not let him. Act or react immediately; command his position. He is fragile, lost, void of decision. There is nothing left in him to resist you. Turn him onto his back, raise yourself up and ease yourself down onto him, bring your face close to his and remain there for a moment. Kiss him once, then discard gentleness and let the power come from within you. Go back for more: kiss him again, each time prowling deeper and deeper into his throat, transferring the liquids within him into your mouth, into your body. Release him. Rise high enough to pull his shirt over his head. Inspire trust, cooperation. Continue savagely until no more clothing separates you, then resume. Find another opening, kiss him there and place your mouth over him. He is already aroused, desire is the one thing that has never died. Fall together off the couch, onto the floor, never letting go.

The music is playing. A candle in one of the corners has flared up, gone out. Scour every area of him with your hands, your tongue. Turn him onto his stomach, spread his legs far apart, until at last you are inside him. Move in a motion that corresponds to violins, oboes, brasses, drums. You are loving Gabriel; it is orchestral. Stop for a moment, somewhere close to the point of climax. Without withdrawing, turn him over so he is once again on his back. Place his legs over your shoulders and take hold of him, stroking, synchronizing this movement with your own motion inside him, with the music. Arrive at a single, duplicate climax, lower your head to his chest, his stomach and drink the liquids that have come from him. Leave nothing. Consume it, swallow it, ingest it. You have accomplished what you have set out to do; you have taken the virus from his body. Now he will live. Now he will not die.

Collapse onto him.

Remain this way for a period of time.

Opposite the triptych studies of the poet on the far wall is a corresponding unfinished painting: no head, roughly penciled limbs protruding from a darkly flesh-toned oil torso. What is complete is the then sole purple spot on the side of his neck. It was the first bit of color you had applied to an empty, unprimed canvas. The small remainder of the finished image reverberated outward from this profound, eloquent center.

The man in the factory window is smoking.

He is still with you, lit from behind from the depths of his space with a single, weak bulb. It is little more than a glow; from here there is the radiant illusion of beauty. This once was intoxicating to you. Submit at last to your inability to frighten him away. He may indeed be stronger than you. Admit defeat; now become the spoils. He is victorious; he shall have you.

Observe his current position. He has opened the window so as to reveal himself completely. He is in the window, his arms stretched upward, each hand to a corner. His legs are spread, his back is arched, the man across the way is waiting, wearing nothing, exposed and framed. Get up from the floor, from the hiding, the screaming and inward travels. Disappear from the light long enough to remove your clothes, then take a position in your window, open it and face him equally.

★　　★　　★

Feel your whole body wretch with pain as Gabriel pushes you off him, as he shoves you away across the floor. Perceive the subtle, gentle sound of a small patch of flesh on your thigh ripping open as it catches on an imperfection, a rough gouge in the wood. The spectacular volume of emotion in his rejection creates an instantaneous contrast, rendering the pain of the physical wound unnoticeable. Realize only from the sight of blood streaming from you that you have been hurt.

Reach for him intending to comfort but before you are close enough to touch him feel the back of his hand travel across your cheek, your face at an incomprehensible speed. Be presently aware of the involuntary reaction of your head as it follows the curve of the strike. Feel nothing; reach for Gabriel. As his hand travels toward you again, catch it, stop it before it reaches your face. With leverage pull yourself to him, your arms surround him effortlessly, naturally, the way they have for years, since the beginning, in the time of love. Receive him, accept his tears, hold him. Offer him all the strength you have left. One last time say you will not let him die.

Your destruction comes finally as he speaks softly in a whisper. Hear him at last; his words now are not fantastic. They are simple, unadorned. Be still, speechless when he releases himself from you, stands naked, walks toward the door to the studio and goes through it. Remain empty; go to the window and survey a city, then a factory and a canyon below. Listen to a path of footsteps, to creaking on the tar roof on top of your ceiling. When the sounds stop, directly above you, recognize this as silence, an eternal moment marking the end, the beginning of an endless void. Witness the vision of Gabriel's body flying downward past you, past the window, into darkness, into the magnificent pleasure of peace at last.

To this day, from the night of his death, the combination of the three studies on the far wall of the studio, opposing the abandoned canvas, remain as they were. They are an enshrinement, they are intact; you have laid down no more color, you have worked no further. These works haunt and comfort you during the day in bleached, unintriguing sunlight, at night by the quiet illumination of candles, revealing different perceptions of the same man at various times of the days and years.

Together the four images live the posthumous existence of ghosts. The subject is present still.

The man in the factory is neither more nor less beautiful than you had imagined from the obscuring effect of distance and night. Realize that objectivity, the ability to judge, left you long ago. The man across the way is erotic or uninspiring, hideous or stunning, dead or alive; you have lost the ability to distinguish, to have options. Peel off the few pieces of clothing, mechanically, you had dressed yourself in to take the short walk around the corner. Focus for a moment on his lesions: the color of them is less brilliant, duller than what is familiar. Look at his unclothed body, eager, erect. Do not touch him yet.

Walk past him into the center of a tall, enormous space. Scan its minimal contents: a bed, a sofa, a table next to it with a lamp containing the distant, passive light. Towering, empty, soiled walls lead up to an overhead network of pipes and exposed, raw electrical tubing. The violence of it is settling. Look toward the open window offering a familiar view from an unfamiliar angle.

Say only this: you do not want to speak.

Don't move. Let him do the wanting. Hold your ground when he takes a first step. Recall for a second the time of love, allow it to pass through you and float away, out the window, dissipating like fog or smoke. Feel a trembling, powerful as the imminent danger of sex when you were young. The man is getting closer. Draw yourself toward him, involuntarily, naturally. Your thoughts are finished, suspended. Spontaneously abandon any remaining obstacle. Kiss him.

Push him back toward the sofa violently, entangled, oblivious; push him down onto it so that he is sitting. Return his glance directly and freeze together, horrified then unmoved. There are two items on the table: latex and grease. Go for one while he goes for the other, lubricate yourself and go down. Feel him rise higher and higher inside you; listen to unintelligible, internal echoes, yours and his. These are not real words. Listen to indistinguishable breathing increase in volume and intensity. Then, without warning, lift yourself up, breaking the bond. Pull the latex from him, hold it tight in a fist and go down once more. Swing your arms around his head, knocking the lamp onto the floor. Take no notice as the bulb explodes and the bit of light is extinguished, destroyed. Pull him into your chest and inspire trust: imperfect, fallible, erroneous, honest. The time of safety is over, the reign of nature, of desire is present. As you approach the end feel the opening inside you and know finally for yourself what it is now that is guiding you. From this moment on you will decide what is right for you. This is not a lie. At the point of climax open your fist and send the latex into the air. This is not about love. Visualize a piece of ephemeral, obsolete armor lob back into time and float down, through the darkness, between two vertical cliffs.

Get an idea in your mind and after some moments when you have become conscious again betray your own condition: speak. Ask this man if he will be still, if he will pose and let you draw him. When he agrees, speak further only the words to express one final thought. You do not want to know his name; tell him he should never say his name.

★

AYOFEMI
FOLAYAN

NOW, I HAVE TO
TELL THIS STORY:
TRIAL BY FIRE

IT WAS A DRY, smoggy September day, delivered courtesy of the Santa Ana winds. I had fallen asleep on the couch; it was simply too hot to do anything else. Although the windows were open, there was no sign of a breeze. My skin was covered with a thin sheen of perspiration.

In my dream, I was lost in the Painted Desert of Arizona. The splendid rock formations all began to look the same as I passed them for the third or fourth time. Large birds that I guessed to be buzzards circled overhead. The air hummed with oppressive heat. The powerful smell of kerosene made me wrinkle my nose and blink my eyes. I realized that the odor was in my apartment, not my dream.

Rising through the fog of sleep to a semi-alert state, I was overwhelmed by the odor of kerosene mixed with perspiration. I couldn't figure out where it was coming from. I rolled into a standing position and saw the man's face before I registered the short black gun in his left hand.

He was wearing oily blue coveralls, a Dodgers baseball cap, and thick military-issue black work boots. His skin was a sickly olive color and his dark hair glistened with beads of perspiration. "Take it easy," he said, "and you won't get hurt." He walked past me to the front door, swiveling his body so that his face was always toward me. He turned the key in the deadbolt and pulled the door open in a sweeping gesture that almost seemed comical. On the front porch of my little guest cottage stood two other men, dressed in similar coverall outfits and work boots. One had a cap that said, "Golden Bear Brew" and the other was hatless. The two men entered the room and gently closed the door behind them.

The hatless man was so tall he had to duck to enter the room. He was a light-skinned black man with very pale gray eyes and a bushy mustache. I was still standing in front of the couch. He came toward me and smiled, a menacing grimace that revealed badly rotting teeth. "What have we got here?" he asked, appraising me with his eyes as he approached. He snapped his fingers and the other two men disappeared into the kitchen.

Within seconds the Dodger fan came back. "Stanley," he said, "there's lots of good stuff here. Should we start loading it up?"

Stanley seemed annoyed by the interruption. "Where are your car keys?" he demanded. I pointed to a ring of keys hanging from the lock. Laughing in a high-pitched cackle, he said, "This is like taking candy from a baby!" He yanked the keys out of the door and tossed them to the Dodger fan. "Where's the car?" he asked me, and I pointed again, this time to the little gray Chevette in the driveway outside the window. I remembered that the gas tank was almost empty. I had meant to stop and fill it up, but the line at the gas station had been too long.

"Okay, guys, get busy and load it up." I could hear the third one grunting in the kitchen from the effort of moving my brand new microwave over to the kitchen door. The Dodger fan left me and Stanley in the living room.

"This is your lucky day," Stanley said with a smirk. "I bet it's been a long time since you had some good stuff like I'm gonna give you." As he unbuttoned his coveralls, the oily chemical smell filled the room. I wondered where these guys had been that they all stank of it. He came up beside me and pulled my face close to his by grabbing my hair. I held my face away from him. This enraged him. "Think you're too good for me, do you?" His voice was sharp and loud, pounding into my ears like a drill.

"I've always wanted to teach an uppity bitch like you a thing or two."

In some corner of my mind, I heard the kitchen door slam as he roughly forced my lips apart with his tongue. "You're gonna love this," he said, reaching inside my tank top and squeezing my breast. He pulled a gun from his pocket and asked quietly, "Aren't you?"

"Please, don't do this," I pleaded. "You can have the car, anything, just please don't hurt me."

"Are you going to beg?" he asked, kicking me so hard in the abdomen that I fell to the floor. "Go ahead, beg!" he snarled, grabbing me by my hair and pulling me up to a kneeling position. "What's the matter? I can't hear you!" he taunted me. He rammed the pistol into my groin. "Maybe you'd rather I shot it off, you stupid little bitch."

He half dragged, half pushed me into the bedroom. "Take off your fucking clothes," he commanded.

I sat on the end of my bed and kicked off my sandals. As I went to pull the tank top over my head, he grabbed it and twisted it around my throat, choking off my breath. "You are going to do exactly what I tell you to do. Do you understand me?" As I nodded, he released the shirt, then slapped me hard across the left side of my face. "Now hurry up and get out of those fucking clothes." Quickly, I pulled off my shorts and underpants and sat with my arms crossed over my breasts.

I tried to think of some reason for this to happen, as he pulled his erect penis out of the coveralls and pushed it into me, knocking me back onto the bed in the same motion. He just kept banging into me, his anger driving each thrust. I was too scared to cry or scream. I just prayed it would be over soon. I heard the other two men enter the room, but I was in too much agony to even care.

"Hey, Stanley, no fair, man. We should get a turn, too," the Dodger fan said.

"Wait . . . just . . . a goddamn . . . minute," Stanley gasped as he concentrated on reaching his climax. I felt the warm liquid surging into me, and wanted to vomit. He stood up, pushed his limp penis back inside his coveralls, and said, "Who wants seconds?"

I thought I was going to pass out, but some cruel joke of nature kept me conscious as the Dodger fan climbed onto me and began ramming into me. He kept saying things like, "Don't you love it, baby?" and "This is better than that guy can do, now isn't it?" but there was a huge roaring in my ears that slowly drowned out his voice.

Something snapped. I went out of my body. I was in a huge field, with the sun gently warming the skin on my back as I slept. The air was heavy with the smell of jasmine and roses. I felt so light I thought I would fly away any second. Instead, I was jerked back to the reality of the Dodger fan releasing a hot stream of semen into my body. "Your turn, Geronimo," he said to the guy in the Golden Bear cap.

"I don't want your seconds, man," Geronimo said. His coveralls pulled tight across his bulging pectoral and biceps muscles. His skin was a deep rust color, and his hair hung down thick and black from under his cap.

"Thank God," I said to myself, "maybe he'll leave me alone." As I opened my eyes, I saw his throbbing red penis in front of my face. "Suck on it, bitch!" he ordered. "And make it good."

"Hurry up, Geronimo, we ain't got all day, man," Stanley said from the doorway. He was eating a sandwich and bits of meat were caught in his mustache. I gagged as Geronimo came in my mouth. I thought to myself, now at least they'll leave me alone.

"Get the rope, Chico," Stanley said to the Dodger fan. He pulled me up and pushed me into the dining room. My legs felt like heavy foreign objects dangling from my bruised torso. Chico wound the rope tightly around my arms and legs, securing me to the chair. He grabbed a dish towel from the hook near the kitchen door and used it as a gag. I heard the sound of liquid splashing on the bathroom floor. That pig, I thought, is pissing on my bathroom floor. Then I saw the red gasoline can in his hand, as he trailed the liquid in a line from the bathroom toward the front door.

My eyes were stretched totally open. I struggled to make some noise, some contact with these beasts. Stanley just smiled that same menacing smile and said, "We can't leave any witnesses, you know.

Thanks for everything," he added sarcastically. Chico and Geronimo were already in the driveway, as he struck the match, set it in the trail of gasoline, and shut the door.

My mind raced as quickly as the stream of flame approaching me. I heard the Chevette's engine cough and sputter into motion. With all the force I could muster I strained to get free of the rope, to no avail. Thick, choking smoke scraped at my lungs. My eyes leaked tears and my nose flowed with mucus.

I must have passed out, because the next thing I realized, the paramedics had me on a stretcher and were running it down the driveway toward the ambulance. I didn't have the energy to even open my eyes. My first thought was, I can't believe I didn't die! I survived! I'm really breathing in air! A temporary sense of euphoria competed with the oxygen to rush into my body.

It didn't last. In the ambulance, the pain started to flood in. The nerve endings in my legs registered the burned flesh. My lungs felt as though a giant bear had clawed them with his paw. I sank back into unconsciousness, although I could hear the paramedic calling to me, "Honey, hang on, we're going to get you to the hospital as fast as we can." His voice sounded as though it was coming from the end of a long tunnel. There was a roaring in my ears, like the winds that bring tornadoes.

It was a rainy day in November. One where the sky gets all dark and then just spits out enough rain to raise the oil slick out of the cement sponge of the streets. One where drivers urge their cars to go just a little faster than is safe.

I stood in the cramped bathroom at the clinic and tried to stop the flow of tears. It was there on the paper I gripped so tightly in my left hand: I was pregnant. Expected due date: July 14. Bastille Day. Just the thought that those sperm had somehow managed to stay alive in my body long enough to fertilize one of my eggs made me want to attack my body for its betrayal. I wasn't sure if it was the smell of kerosene that seemed instantly to pervade the room or morning sickness that fueled my wave of nausea. I felt trapped in my body, held prisoner in its cell.

I walked out of the clinic and waited for the bus to take me home. I was twenty-two years old. I was sleeping on the fold-out couch in a friend's living room. Everything in my little cottage had been destroyed, either by the fire or the water or the smoke. When my roommate in college had an abortion, it cost her five hundred dollars. My friends had given me clothes and money, but not enough for that. My friends knew that I had been robbed. They even knew that the robbers had set my house on fire. But no one knew about the rape. There was no rape hotline. There was no one to tell why I was too afraid to even step out of the apartment into the fenced courtyard alone.

I couldn't imagine walking out of that courtyard to go to work. I tried to imagine myself sitting at my desk in the middle of an office full of other co-workers—my desk in the middle of the room with the philodendron plants on it and the big gray blotter and desk set they had given me for my five-year anniversary. I thought about Reynold bringing me a bear claw on Friday mornings or Addie bringing homemade fried chicken to share for lunch. One of them would see me and know what those men had done to me. I couldn't go back. I lost my job.

All that was left intact was my anger, but I kept that hidden away, because I was so scared those men would know and come back to find me. So I willed that baby to die. I didn't eat. I didn't sleep. I took quinine. And I didn't do anything else all day long but think about the horrible thing inside me shriveling up and dying. When I miscarried, it was the Monday after Thanksgiving. I sat in the hospital emergency room and I gave thanks through my tears and the pain for being free.

It's another hot smoggy day in Los Angeles, another Santa Ana condition. I still can't sleep with the windows open. I still can't smell kerosene without remembering. I go out on the porch to get the morning paper. I come back into my apartment and toss the rubber band into the trash. As I pour myself a cup of coffee, I read that George Bush has just vetoed federal funds for abortions, even in the case of rape or incest. And I carry my coffee over to the computer and begin to write this story.

★

RICK
SANDFORD

FÖRSTER AND
ROSENTHAL
REEVALUATED:
AN INVESTIGATIVE
REPORT

FOR AARON COHEN (1954-1988)
AND MICHAEL RUPERT

ON FRIDAY, JUNE 23, 1944, Richard Förster, *SS-Haupsturm-führer* (Captain), was allegedly shot and killed by Aaron Rosenthal, the former owner of a spice factory in Berlin, at a small railway station in Ryczków, 21 kilometers southwest of the concentration camp at Auschwitz. This is an investigation into those circumstances and how they came about, with especial regard to the relationship that existed between Richard Förster and Aaron Rosenthal over a period of nearly twenty years.

Richard Förster was born into a Catholic family on April 15, 1912, in Peine in Lower Saxony. His father was killed during the Great War and afterward his mother moved with him and his older sister to Berlin in order to marry a restaurateur, Walter Mann. During the Depression in the twenties Richard's stepfather lost two of the three restaurants he owned, but the family managed to get by with everyone helping out in one capacity or another. In school Richard displayed a propensity for writing, and on his thirteenth birthday he began a journal that he kept up with only one major interruption until his "death" in 1944. Richard met Aaron Rosenthal in the autumn of

1924, and by the time of the journal's first entry they had become friends: ". . . I had a party in the afternoon. Most of the kids from school were there. Aaron was there, too . . ."[1]

Aaron Rosenthal was born in Freiberg on March 10, 1913, and from the earliest age he attended Jewish schools. When the bank where his father worked closed down in 1924, one of Aaron's uncles, who owned a spice factory in Berlin, offered his father a job, and the family moved there that summer. They settled in a house in the Bulowstrasse across the street from the Manns'. Aaron had his bar mitzvah in March of 1926 and invited Förster to attend, but Richard's parents wouldn't allow it. Förster notes: ". . . I went to my room and wouldn't come down for supper. I snuck out later and met Aaron and gave him one of the diaries Papa gave me last year."[2] The leather-bound book Förster gave Rosenthal was inscribed "For Aaron, My Very Best Friend. With Honor, Richard."[3] Years later, after Rosenthal had married Rachel Becker, he explained to his wife that he and Richard had vowed never to believe in love—only honor.[4]

At the time Richard inscribed the diary to Aaron he seems to have been responding less to Rosenthal than reacting against his parents' wishes; Aaron is afforded no more attention in his journals than many of his other friends, and it is not until the end of the following

1. The early journals of Richard Förster have never been published before. They are in the possession of his sister, Hannah Förster Krug, who has been so kind as to allow me to translate and publish the excerpts used here. The journals Förster kept when he was at Auschwitz are in the archives there, and when I have quoted from them it has been with the permission of *Panstwowe w Oswiecimiu* (State Museum at Auschwitz). Although the Auschwitz journals have been previously published, I have not used that version for my translations but have in every instance consulted the original manuscripts. I have dated all the entries, however, so that interested readers may make a comparison if they like. The previous version is *Auschwitz: Die Tagesbucher vom Förster* by Richard Förster, edited by Dr. Arnold Kopstein, Stuttgart: Pabst and Brooks, 1957; *Auschwitz: The Diary of a Commandant*, translated by Jeremy A. Finch, New York: Foiles and Company, Ltd., 1959.
2. Early Förster journals, March 13, 1926.
3. Previously unpublished document: Rosenthal diary, 1925–1930. Excerpts printed and translated with the kind permission and assistance of Rachel Becker Rosenthal Thalberg.
4. Unpublished verbal statement: Rachel Thalberg, June 23, 1977.

summer that Aaron becomes the focus of attention that might more properly bespeak a "very best friend."

At the end of August, after much cajoling of their parents, Richard and Aaron obtained permission to go on a week-long bicycle trip together. Traveling south through the Spreewald they went as far as Dresden and then headed west toward Thuringia and the forest there, going as far as Eisenach and cycling back toward Berlin by way of Magdeburg. Once home Richard elaborated on the details of the trip in his journal, recounting their time together with a fastidiousness he would retain for the rest of his life whenever writing about Aaron. One of the more memorable images in this recounting occurred on August 26, after they had left their bikes behind and gone hiking into the Thüringer Wald: ". . . It was very quiet, and the further we hiked the closer I felt we were getting to the heart of some kind of secret. I felt like we could disappear into the forest and the trees would be our friends. In a little glade we stopped to rest. I lay back on the grass and closed my eyes. The sun was on my face and even though my eyes were closed everything was red. That's the blood in my eyelids. It was so nice and warm and I could feel the grass on the back of my legs and arms and on my neck. I felt like I could start dreaming without going to sleep.

"I don't know how long I was there, but after a while I heard Aaron getting up. I sat up and everything was blue. It was like in the movies. After the sun through my eyelids there were no other colors but blue. Aaron was standing across from me and he had his penis out. He started to pee and then he started to turn around. It went all over in a circle and the sun made it sparkle. It was funny, but it was pretty, too."[5]

There is no mention of this incident in Rosenthal's diary, and in fact their entire trip is merely indicated by an itinerary penciled in afterward. It is not until the early months of 1927 that Rosenthal starts to make particular note of his relationship with Förster: "Richard

5. Early Förster journals, September 1, 1926. Förster's mention of "movies" is in reference to the popular practice of tinting early black-and-white films, usually a single color for a single sequence.

and I have pledged to become scientists together. Richard said he wanted to win the Nobel Prize, but I told him that wasn't proper. Scientists must work for the betterment of humanity. Of course, I want to be famous too, but it isn't right to think like that."[6]

Scientific investigation received a new impetus on Aaron's fourteenth birthday. The next day, March 11, 1927, Richard wrote in his journal: "Aaron came over after school today with his new microscope and he said we were going to do some important research. We're going to see what the difference is between the Jews and everybody else by examining semen samples. I got a little nervous but Aaron said it was for science, so I said all right. Aaron said he would go first. He took off all his clothes and lay on my bed. Aaron's penis is circumcised and it is very large—I think it might even be bigger than Papa's. When he started masturbating he laughed at me because I turned so red, but I couldn't help it. Aaron ejaculated on to his stomach but part of it hit the bedboard. I told him he would have to clean it up. He put some of the semen on a slide and cleaned up the rest with his handkerchief. When he cleaned up the semen on the bedboard, he chased me around the room with it and then said he was only kidding. We looked at the slide and saw hundreds of tadpoles moving around. Aaron started making notes and then he told me I had to do it. I did, but I did it privately in the bathroom. Aaron thinks I'm silly. We put my slide in and looked, and there weren't half as many tadpoles in mine. Aaron started making fun of me but I told him he was probably a freak. He pinned me down and made me take it back."[7]

With some variation these experiments occupied Förster and Rosenthal's late afternoons for the rest of the school year. Aaron made copious notes, some of which still survive, and occasionally some of the boys from the Gymnasium where Förster attended school, or from Rosenthal's Lyceum, would stop by to participate in this scientific study. Richard relates these incidents in his journal with an increasing sense of guilt, while the entries in Rosenthal's diary seem to indicate an almost fervent desire to prove himself better than Förster.

6. Rosenthal diary, February 28, 1927.
7. At some later date Förster had penciled in under this entry, "I'm the freak."

Rosenthal, May 18, 1927: "Richard and I had an experiment today to see who could ejaculate the most number of times in one hour. I ejaculated seven times to Richard's four, and my seventh ejaculation was of a stronger consistency than his fourth . . ."

Förster, May 20, 1927: "I think Aaron is doing these experiments for fun. I don't think science has very much to do with it."

Rosenthal, June 10, 1927: ". . . Richard said he thought I was a homosexual today. You can bet I laid him out for that. He cried and begged my forgiveness, but he said he didn't think our experiments were honorable, that they didn't prove anything. They prove something."

Förster, June 10, 1927: "I told Aaron that if his experiments were of any real value he'd take them to school or show somebody. He hit me. I cried, but it wasn't because it hurt. It was because I don't know what we're doing."[8]

Rosenthal spent the summer of 1927 in Freiberg with his maternal grandparents. When he returned to Berlin in the autumn, his friendship with Förster was resumed but with a certain cool formality. Their "experiments" were not continued, and the social life of their respective schools kept them farther apart than the year before. When the summer of 1928 came around, both boys began working full time: Aaron got a job with his family's spice factory and Richard began working as a waiter in his stepfather's restaurant. This influx of money was concurrent with their interest in girls, which they wrote about with increasing frequency until they lost their virginity in January of 1929.

8. Although he didn't participate in them, Förster was present at some of the medical experiments conducted at Auschwitz under the direction of *Hauptsturmführer* Dr. Josef Mengele. He witnessed several operations involving the sterilization of males and makes reference to these three times in his Auschwitz journals: December 21, 1943, January 5, 1944, and January 22, 1944. This latter entry is of particular note: ". . . Mengele had just put the man's testes in a jar when I suddenly thought about Aaron, when we were boys, and his sperm—all those 'tadpoles'—and how easy it would be now, if he were here, to eradicate them, completely and forever. To look him in the eye, without his balls, and dare him to proclaim his ascendancy over me . . ."

Rosenthal, January 12, 1929: "Yesterday after school Richard and I were walking down the Nollendorfplatz when we saw Frl. Kost. I had told Richard I would buy him a whore one day, and I asked him if he wanted to. I don't think he did really but I convinced him. Frl. Kost is old but pretty. I told her I wanted to buy a fine time for my friend, and me, too. She took us up to a little room in a large flat. She wanted twenty marks but I told her we only had seventeen (I was lying) and she said all right. Richard was shy and acting depressed, so I told him I would show him how it was done. And it was just like I'd done it all my life. It felt good but she smelled rather funny. When Richard's turn came he was nervous but he finally got it in. But then he started to get sick. He held off till he got to the end of the corridor though. We sat in the park afterwards. I didn't know what to say so I put my arm around him. He tried to shake it off at first but then he just sat still and we were quiet. It started to snow, and when we got home it was dark."

Förster, January 11, 1929: "Aaron and I lost our virginity today. It was disgusting. I got sick. Aaron stayed with me afterwards and although we didn't say anything it was one of the first times I felt we weren't competing. Because he won. And I lost. And now I hope it doesn't matter anymore. I don't think it will. I mean I don't think he will want to be my friend anymore. I've thought for a while that the only reason he stays my friend is because I'm not Jewish."[9]

Förster and Rosenthal saw less of each other the rest of the school year, and one can't help but think that this break is more an instigation of Richard's than Aaron's. During the summer of 1929, Rosenthal met Rachel Becker, and a tentative courtship began that would culminate in marriage in December 1931. But in the autumn of 1929, as Richard and Aaron were nearing the end of their secondary schooling, they once more drew close, though the tone of their relationship changed once again.

9. There is nothing in Förster's journals to indicate that he ever had sex with a woman again. Of the people I've interviewed and spoken to, no one has been able to confirm Förster having had any kind of intimate sexual life from January 1929, until his encounter with Marcello Gattegno at Birkenau in January of 1944.

Förster, November 9, 1929: ". . . Aaron was in the window seat reading Hölderlin and the afternoon light enveloped him and, sitting there, absolutely secure in his sense of himself, he was beautiful. But it's more than that value judgment—the curls around his forehead, the dip at the end of his nose: his whole person is such an overwhelming matter of fact. Nothing can touch him. While I was looking at him it suddenly amazed me that we can even communicate. He looked up once and our eyes caught, and it was like a lamp lighting up the room: his amazing cognizance of—me. Why does it seem to be the most incredible thing I have ever seen?"

Rosenthal, January 5, 1930: "The Nazis rioted again last night. Richard and I took a walk after school and talked about it. He says he thinks they're stupid, but sometimes I catch him looking at me, like he's wondering what's wrong with me."

On Förster's eighteenth birthday, very late on the evening of the fifteenth of April 1930, a confrontation occurred between Förster and Rosenthal that permanently disrupted their relationship.

Förster, April 16, 1930: ". . . everybody was pretty drunk by the time the party ended. Mama and Papa stayed out at the Krugs', so I didn't have to worry about them. Aaron saw Rachel home and then came back for another couple of drinks. We came upstairs and poured some whiskey, and then we pretended we won the Nobel Prize and we gave acceptance speeches—for our semen samples— and then I remember Aaron was smiling at me. He put his arm around me—no, I did that."[10]

Rosenthal, April 16, 1930: "Richard is lost. I saw it last night. I was looking right in his eyes when it happened. He said he loved me and tried to kiss me. And suddenly it was over, gone. It was pathetic, and I told him so. I stood up and he grabbed my leg saying that he really loved me. I kicked him away from me and got

---

10. Förster's diary entry for April 16, 1930, stops abruptly, and this page and the two following are blotted with what appear to have been his tears.

to the door. When I looked back at him it was like all his thoughts and ideas, even his self-respect, had vanished. It was disgusting."

Förster, April 17, 1930: "Aaron hates me. I was drunk. When Aaron smiles everything seems all right, and I thought it would be all right, too. It felt like we had already said we loved each other. I didn't think. Stupid. Stupid. I wonder if he tells Rachel that he loves her. I know he thinks it's stupid. Pathetic. I feel sick."

Rosenthal, April 25, 1930: "This journal is meaningless. At best, as in Richard's case, it serves as a justification of failure."

The April 25, 1930, entry in Rosenthal's journal is his last. After his marriage his wife came across the volume and at one point they read it together. "His relationship with Richard embarrassed him a little, and after we went through it I think he wanted to throw it away, but the beginning of our relationship had been recorded there also, and that was what was important to me."[11]

Years later, at Auschwitz, when Förster was doing an inordinate amount of writing, as well as indulging in an occasional use of alcohol and drugs, he re-created his confrontation with Aaron on his eighteenth birthday in fantastical terms:

". . . We started toasting everything. We remembered our 'experiments' and laughed about them, and then I was presenting the Nobel Award to Aaron Rosenthal for his prodigious efforts on behalf of seminal investigation. I grabbed Aaron by both arms and kissed his cheeks, and then I suddenly didn't know what I was doing. I wasn't *doing* anything: I was just standing there looking at him. I couldn't move though. And I couldn't stop looking into his eyes, those eyes that met my look with a kind of questioning and were, yet, irrefutably bound to me. But their questioning must have found some kind of answer for I suddenly felt he was evaporating beneath my grasp. My grip on his arms tightened and I had to hold onto him: only he, his

11. Unpublished verbal statement: Rachel Thalberg, June 22, 1977. It is only by a stroke of fate that the journal survived the war. It was found in 1948 in the cellar of a bombed-out building, where Rosenthal had lived with his family.

presence, clasped in my hands, could make sense of the evolving anarchy of my life. And yet the more I held onto him, the farther away he seemed, until I could sense in him an edge of desperation. It was strange: we were, with hardly a movement, straining against one another. And what was he straining against? *Me*—that I miserably knew—but there was something else, as if he wanted to break through, as well as away from, something *in* me.

"He threw me up against the wall and my head resounded with the impact. He grabbed my wrists, pinning my arms above my head, and came down on my face with his mouth. Held motionless by this wet and palpable force I hardly dared to breathe. He moved his hands from my wrists to the back of my head, pressing his fingers through my hair, and pushing our faces together with his fists. His saliva smeared across my face as he moved his lips from mine and bit gently on the end of my nose. His sudden aggression was turning into something quieter, an omniscient and cruel insinuation.

"With my head gripped in his hands he beat out a rhythm with his knuckles against the wall, and his words, guttural when they came, were hot on his breath: 'Say it.' He was asking for sanction, acquiescence to my impending annihilation, and I gave it to him, my eyes filling with the tears of its truth: 'I love you.'

"The tension was expelled from his throat, almost like a sigh. His fingers tensed, the nails dug deep into my scalp, and my head was rocked forward and once more pounded into the wall, as his face mashed itself into mine, his teeth finding my tongue, and his knee, propelled upward by unutterable contempt, crushed my sex into my pelvis. And then—

"Nothing mattered.

"I started to fall forward in his arms. He slammed me back against the wall and then forced me to the floor with all the might of incensed brutality, the pressure and heat of our bodies purging our clothes of their material form and into the vapor of sizzling perspiration; his arms—locked around me, pressing my thighs back into my chest and grating my spine across splintering wood—vanquished my very existence into the vise he had become.

"Coherence spun out of me with the last of my breath, his mouth on mine relegated all volitional response to mere fevered receptivity and when he exploded my bowels burned in their desecration, the ridges of my backbone were scraped clean of their skin, his teeth cut through my lower lip and, as his weight deadened on top of me, I heard the crack of a rib. Blood filled my mouth and ran down my neck.

"Life, without compassion, ripped into my beautiful expiration: Aaron, as if impelled by the demons of hell, with new waves of strength and revulsion, tore himself out of me, veritably eradicating my entrails with his malevolent evulsion, and disappeared into the ether beyond my senses. I could hear his breathing as my own suddenly returned in gurgling gasps, and I could feel the droplets of his sweat, nearly frozen by their fall from grace.

" 'You'—a voice trying to modulate its timber—'have'—but hopelessly a human utterance—'no'—though colored now with an insidious and final morality—'honor'—echoed metallically against the interior of my skull. I could feel warmth in my veins and whatever I was, beyond this decimated flesh, I wanted to rise up and weave myself around this voice ('You have no honor'), to placate with an understanding that might mean equality: 'And you do?' To bring back into myself the verification that this terrible desolation that is my life is not the truth. And he said—I remember the sound of the words and their shape in a light that blinds—'IT DOESN'T MEAN ANYTHING TO ME.'

"And—I—breathe—"[12]

Förster and Rosenthal saw little of each other the rest of that school year, and even less of one another as they worked through the summer, Förster in his stepfather's restaurant and Rosenthal at his uncle's spice factory. Förster's journals refer to Aaron with a pronounced melan-

12. Previously unpublished document: Förster manuscripts. Printed with the permission of *Panstwowe w Oswiecimiu*. Translation is by the author. This is not officially from the journals, although the papers of which it is a part were found with them when the journals were discovered in a hiding place in one of the rooms of the main administration building at Birkenau in 1951. Information about the physical aspect of the diaries themselves and their discovery may be found in the introduction by Dr. Arnold Kopstein to the published version of the journals. See notation 1.

choly and a few undistinguished verses are tucked into the pages of the diary.

Förster began studying law at Berlin University in the autumn, and his turn away from science seems as much a reaction to Rosenthal as anything else. Concurrent with Förster's first year at the University, Rosenthal finished his last year of secondary schooling.

In the summer of 1931, Rosenthal announced his engagement to Rachel Becker, and their marriage was planned for December. Both Förster and Rosenthal now held managerial positions in their respective summer jobs, only for Förster his work in the restaurant did not end with the summer. His stepfather had suffered a stroke, and he worked with his mother through the winter while continuing school.

Rosenthal had begun attending the University in Freiberg with his courses predominantly preparatory to becoming a doctor. He returned to Berlin in December to marry Rachel. Förster notes in his journal, December 21, 1931: "I saw Aaron today. He was walking down the street. The sun was bright but it was cold and he had his scarf on. He was with Rachel and they were laughing about something. It's not that there is an aura about him—it's more like the world has been imposed around him as a background, and I am such a negligible part of that background. When I turned back to the house, and became aware of my books, and the sun, and the air in my lungs, it all seemed as if it was some lonely and monstrous irrelevance."

Rachel returned to Freiberg with Rosenthal and he continued his studies, at which he excelled and was a prize student. For his part, Förster was only doing moderately well in school, his discontent with life prompting thoughts of suicide. On March 9, 1932, Föster heard Hitler speak for the first time: "I was rather amazed. I felt like something was being asked of me—that I must call upon resources I haven't even touched. And I feel like I can be a part of something, something important. I didn't—I *don't*—feel depressed, all that seems like such an indulgence, and when I think of Aaron it suddenly doesn't matter anymore. It seems silly, and as I sit here I feel relieved somehow."

Förster continued working in his family's restaurant and when he finished his second year at the University with poor marks, he decided he would not be going back. He started attending Nationalist

Socialist meetings and began devoting more of his time to the organization. When Hitler was named chancellor of Germany in January of 1933, he participated in the torchlight parade that streamed down the streets of Berlin. In April, after Hitler had also become president, his participation in the Jewish boycott was particularly noted by Rosenthal's mother who wrote Aaron in a letter: "There was some rioting and your uncle received some more threats in the mail, but the most disturbing thing that happened was when someone threw a stone through the window. I looked out and saw the Förster boy running away. I'd heard he'd become a Nazi but I didn't believe it. Your father thinks I was seeing things but I know it was him."[13]

Rosenthal stayed on in Freiberg through the summer of 1932, continuing with his studies and working in a hospital. With the implementation of more and more anti-Jewish legislation he soon realized he would not be able to afford to go back to the University in the autumn of 1933, and that summer he and Rachel returned to Berlin and moved in with his family. He once more started working in the spice factory, and it was at this time he began to be involved with the *Centralverein Deutscher Staatsburger Judischen Glaubens* (Central Association of German Citizens of Jewish Faith). Förster, meanwhile, had officially joined the National Socialist Party, and in November of 1933 he was accepted as an applicant for joining the SS. A year later, in 1934, he had become a full-fledged member of the *Schutzstaffel*, Hitler's elite secret service.

The SS had adopted the slogan, "The aristocracy keeps its mouth shut," and Förster seems to have taken this to heart. His "journals" for the next ten years are little more than infrequent notations until he was sent to Auschwitz as the commandant at Birkenau, but on being accepted to the SS, and after concluding a series of educational seminars, he submitted an essay to his superiors that suggests, more than anything else, his willingness to adopt the party line: "The most important function of any member of the SS is the example he gives to our people. Of course, our immediate purpose is to preserve the

13. Previously unpublished document: Lillian Rosenthal, letter to Aaron Rosenthal, April 3, 1933. Translation is by the author.

internal security of our country, but there is a wider sphere for our political achievements which we must never lose sight of, a more profound ideal. Our Nordic heritage, which has come to be synonymous with the highest attainments of civilization itself, is now under siege as never before by foreign elements whose sole purpose is to tear down that which they could never build and which must serve as a constant reminder of their own diseased existence. In particular we must scourge our nation of the vicious contamination of Jewish blood, which not only seeks to undermine that which it can never be itself, but wishes to have mirrored in the world its own spiritual and physical ugliness, and nowhere is this more evident than in the duplicity whereby they have engendered their guilt in the killing of Christ, whereas the true insidiousness of their design lies in the fact that they have managed to inveigle the whole of Europe into actually *worshipping* this Jew. These parasites, with their doctrine of world communism, must be eradicated once and for all. This is the essence of National Socialism: the distillation and preservation of blood purity and with it the culture of our fatherland so that we may serve as the light, not only for our own people, but for the world."[14]

Meanwhile, Rosenthal was contributing articles to a paper, the *C-V Zeitung*,[15] and it is believed that these stories were responsible for his two arrests during the next several years. On both occasions his family managed to bribe the officials involved in order to obtain his

14. Berlin Document Center Personnel File (*SS* Service Files), Berlin. Richard Förster Personnel File, Microfilm 43. Translation is by the author. This contrasts interestingly with something he wrote at Auschwitz, when he was the commandant of Birkenau: "Hitler was wrong, I can feel it, and each new trainload of Jews here makes it even clearer: it's *not* the blood—in the end, what are we but just some pathetic mass of indeterminate protoplasm? There is no 'God,' there are no 'chosen people': all that is arrogance. *That's* why we should have killed them, not for what they are, but for what they. *believe.* Unless we kill every single one of them—and how can we?—this is going to destroy us. *Mein Führer* was wrong, and what is so painful is that when we lose this war we will only have contributed to their religion, that insupportable worship of martyrdom and self-righteous self-pity." (February 14, 1944)

15. Rosenthal, Aaron: "Judishe Erwachsenebildung" in *C-V Zeitung*, March 16, 1935; "Die inneren Voraussertzungen fur Hilfe and Aufbau in deutschen Judentum" in *C-V Zeitung*, May 31, 1935; "Er Weg der deutschen Juden" in *C-V Zeitung*, November 23, 1935.

release. On June 20, 1936, during his first imprisonment, Rosenthal's only child, David Gottfried, was born. During his second incarceration in December of 1937, he was beaten very badly and retained several scars on his face for the rest of his life. In January of 1938, Rosenthal's uncle killed himself and Rosenthal, with his father, took full control of the factory's management and ownership.

Förster and Rosenthal's paths had not notably crossed since 1931, and when they crossed again on Sunday, March 17, 1938, *Heldengedenktag* (Heroes Memorial Day), Förster was not aware of it. After participating in the invasion of the Rhineland in March of 1936, he had been promoted to the rank of *SS-Scharführer* (Staff Sergeant). Two years later, less than a week after Austria had been "annexed" to Germany and festivities were in progress to celebrate the establishment of universal military service and the end of the Versailles military restrictions, Rosenthal wrote to a friend: "There was pandemonium in the streets, and as I watched the men marching by I suddenly saw a friend of my childhood, Richard Förster. Do you remember him? He used to live across the street from us. He was marching in formation, the sun was brilliant, their power and precision were dazzling, and Richard was— this is difficult to say—he was beautiful. And I was suddenly frightened. More than anything else that has happened to us these last five years the sight of this boyhood friend of mine, straight and tall, in his black uniform, terrified me. I felt as if a chasm into hell had just opened at my feet."[16]

On November 10, 1938, *Kristallnacht*, Rosenthal was arrested again and the factory where he worked and which he now owned was burned to the ground. His wife recalls: "When they had arrested Aaron before it had been at the factory when he was working but that night they came right to the house. We already knew about the riots that were going on in some parts of the city but we didn't know it would be so extensive. I had gone to sleep, and it was after midnight when there was a pounding at the door and we heard our windows being broken. Aaron went to the door and I gathered up David. In a

16. Previously unpublished document: Aaron Rosenthal, letter to Samuel Meier, March 18, 1938. Translation is by the author with the kind permission of Norma Meier.

moment police, the *Gestapo*, were all over the house. They told us to dress quickly and we were all pushed into the street. Aaron had gone through this before and he was doing his best to reassure us. I thought we were all going to be arrested but as soon as they had Aaron and his father in their truck they left.... When we went to the *Gestapo* headquarters the next day we were told that the only way to get him out was to show proof that we were emigrating. We went through a terrible time trying to get visas for the family, going from one consulate to another, but eventually we learned that you could go to Shanghai— it was an open city and you didn't need a visa to go there, all you needed was to get a transit visa through Italy.... When Aaron found out that his release was conditioned on his leaving the country I don't think he really believed it. We were supposed to leave on December 16th, and then we would catch the ship to Shanghai in Genoa on the 20th.... On the day before we were supposed to leave, Aaron said he was going to stay—we had some property, and there was the insurance for the factory, money matters: there just wasn't enough time. I asked him to come with us, to forget about all that, but I didn't beg him, I didn't cry—I didn't get down on my knees and hold him: I didn't know.... When the train pulled out of the station I remember him standing there on the platform, I remember him saying, *'Alles ist in ordnung, alles ist in ordnung'*—'It's all right.' I never saw him again."[17]

Early in 1939, Förster became part of one of the units of *Waffen-SS*, the *SS-Totenkopfverbande* (*SSTV*; Death's Head Formations), which was in charge of the concentration camps. After the war started in September, Förster was promoted to *SS-Untersturmführer* (2nd Lieutenant). The recommendation given him at the time is fairly typical of his service record: "Förster is a serious and quiet man who has the respect, if not the affection, of the men he works with. His thinking is very ordered, and his organizational capabilities are very strong. He has a soldierly appearance and fits into the *SS* well. He obeys the orders of

17. Unpublished verbal statement: Rachel Thalberg, June 23, 1977.

his superiors diligently and displays a readiness to deal with practical undertakings. He could be an excellent officer."[18]

He was transferred to *Tiergartenstrasse* 4 (T4) in Berlin and became involved with the *Gemeinnutzige Krankentransportgesellschaft* (Public-Benefit Patient Transportation Society) where he helped and sometimes supervised the transfer of patients in the Euthanasia Program from observation institutions to euthanasia installations. Jozef Purke, who worked with Förster at this time, testified: "We had been assured that the deaths we were privy to were legal as well as humane, but starting with the experimental gassings in the vans we couldn't help questioning what we were doing. We didn't verbalize these doubts though. It would have been almost traitorous. Förster himself was inscrutable. You couldn't tell what he was thinking, and you wouldn't dare have asked, even if you'd wanted to, and I didn't."[19]

Förster was transferred to Auschwitz in the summer of 1941. Birkenau, a new camp that was just becoming operational immediately adjacent but subordinate to the jurisdiction of Auschwitz, became part of Förster's responsibility, and he helped supervise much of its building, its operation, and, through the winter, the construction of the gas chambers that would soon promote Birkenau to *Vernichtungslayer* (Death Camp), one of five such places in Hitler's Third Reich.

On May 12, 1942, the gas chambers at Birkenau were used for the first time, and Förster recorded the experience: "There were nearly a thousand women from Slovokia. It was an amazing sight—a thousand women, naked, their heads shaved, almost imbecilic-looking, standing in the yard there, crying, wretched, helpless. There was something contemptible about them. I have thought about this and dreamt about it: this capacity for killing hundreds of people, and always at the back of my mind I have thought of the people as myself, and it has shaken

18. Berlin Document Center Personnel File (*SS* Service Files), Berlin. Richard Förster Personnel File, Microfilm 43. Translation is by the author.

19. Statement by Jozef Purke, October 21, 1946, in the official record of Case IV, Cracow Trials (Reference: *Biuletyn Glowna Komisja Badania Zbrodni Hitlerowskich* [Central Commission for the Investigation of Nazi Crimes], Warsaw: 1948; Vol. III, p. 596). The translations of the material relating to the Cracow trials are by the author, with particular thanks to "F. D." for his assistance.

me at times, but today, walking through this mass of women about to die I wondered what I had been thinking. They were not even like me, much less of me, and far from being a threat they were almost completely without importance. Their will to live was pathetic to see, and when I saw the bodies later, dead, it seemed incredible that that was all they were afraid of. It was nothing."[20]

The crematoria that were built at Birkenau were not operational until late in the summer of 1942, when the burials in nearby meadows proved too laborious and time-consuming, but with their completion Förster was transferred to the Eastern front where he was to help with the liquidation of Soviet Jewry. If Förster kept any kind of personal account of his actions during this time it has not survived, but official records note his promotion to *SS-Haupsturmführer* shortly before being wounded near Minsk in March 1943. The bones in his right thigh had been shattered and he was sent back to Germany to convalesce. In the autumn of 1943, after a series of operations on his leg, he was deemed unfit for front-line service; he would walk with a limp for the rest of his life. In October he was transferred back to Auschwitz where on November 22, in a restructuring of the administration, he was made commandant of Birkenau, the camp he had helped to build. He was thirty-one years old.[21]

On January 14, 1944, a trainload of Jews from Italy arrived. Förster was at the depot during the separation of the prisoners. One of the men who was spared his life to work in the camp was named Marcello Gattegno. Förster was struck by the sight of this young man and after he had been shaved, showered, tattooed, and billeted, Förster sent for him. "I hadn't eaten in nearly a week and I was very hungry. When I entered Förster's office there was a plate of food on the desk

20. This page is not officially a part of Förster's Auschwitz journals. It was found by his sister, Hannah Förster Krug, among his surviving papers in Berlin and is published here with her permission. Translation is by the author. It was not included in *Auschwitz: Die Tagesbucher vom Förster*. See notation 1.

21. Förster's duties as the commandant of Birkenau were primarily administrative. He was responsible for the financial operation of the camp and the documents, memoranda, letters, and reports that entailed. He was not immediately in charge of the prisoners or the crematoria, and all major decisions were made in conjunction with the commandant of the main Auschwitz camp.

which he invited me to eat. When I finished I saw that he was looking at me. He motioned me around the desk to him. He stood up and looked at me some more and then he stroked my cheek with the back of his fingers. And then he kissed me. I kissed him back. Our sex was tentative and had a sadness about it. Afterwards he rocked me in his arms and cried. He called me his 'little Aaron.' "[22]

In Förster's surviving papers there is no mention of Rosenthal between 1934, when Richard joined the SS, and 1944, but the incident with Gattegno instigated a series of writings, apart from his journals, about his childhood friend that revealed a growing obsession with a relationship that he clearly regarded as the central event in his life. Friedrich Lang, *Rapportführer*, Förster's subaltern in charge of the discipline at Birkenau, testified about Förster at this time: "Sex with prisoners was absolutely forbidden, but since Höss[23] himself had a mistress what a man did—as long as he at least kept up appearances—could be overlooked. As for homosexuality, well—you know what Himmler[24] said, any SS man caught doing that would be sent to a concentration camp and shot while trying to escape—so as soon as Förster knew I was aware of what was going on he started paying me very well to keep quiet. . . . He never interfered with any of the selections on the ramp that I know of. If a boy he liked got sent to the gas I don't think he ever really got upset, after all there were plenty more. . . . We eventually got it down to a system, so that the *Blockaltester*[25] and myself were the only middlemen. . . . Yes, money passed hands, quite a bit of it actually, and food, drugs, gold—don't forget, I mean aside from everything else, Auschwitz was a commercial operation. . . . I would bring the boys to his office in the administration building late at night when no one was there and I would take them back to their barracks when he was finished with them. . . . And it was interesting,

22. Previously unpublished document: Marcello Gattegno letter to the author, July 6, 1977.

23. Rudolf Höss, commandant of Auschwitz: April 1940–November 1943, May–July 1944, September 1944–January 1945. Höss is not to be confused with Hitler's deputy and successor designate (after Hermann Goering), Rudolf Hess (1894–1987).

24. Heinrich Himmler, *Reichsführer-SS und Chef der Deutschen Polizei* (Reich SS Leader and Chief of the German Police).

25. *Blockaltester* was a male prisoner in charge of a barracks.

the more boys he had and the more drugs he took,[26] the stricter he became. He even started attending some of the shootings and gassings. After his little fling with the Italian—that was the first actually, as far as I know—he began writing a lot, and sometimes when he was alone I would hear him crying in his office. Until I read his stuff for myself I thought he was feeling bad about what he was doing in the camp— he could be a real terror if he put his mind to it—but it wasn't that at all. It all had something to do with this Jew he used to know named Aaron."[27]

On April 27, 1944, in Förster's journal only a few words were scrawled, almost indecipherable: "I killed Aaron." Lang recalls: "I'd brought the boy to the office and I left him with Förster, who was in one of his moods that night. He'd been drinking and I don't know what all. I waited in the hall and about twenty minutes later Förster suddenly started yelling my name and when I came in the room the boy was standing in front of him without any clothes on. He was shaking like a leaf and trying to cover himself. He was Greek and he didn't understand any of what Förster was going on about. I had never actually seen what Förster did with these boys but I'd heard some, and I tried to get the boy to tell him he loved him. I pointed at Förster and said the words over a couple of times, 'Ich liebe Dich, Ich liebe Dich'—'I love you.'

"It got real quiet then and I realized Förster was staring at me. He started turning red and I was about to make a run for it when the boy tried to say what I'd told him. He'd barely got out the first word when Förster pulled out his revolver and shot him. I'll never forget the look on that kid's face—he was so surprised. He looked for a moment like he might try to finish what he was saying when he fell to the ground. And then he—Förster, that is—started crying,

26. In a letter to the author, March 19, 1978, Lang elaborated: "Förster wasn't an addict, and he wasn't taking that many drugs, but he had a supply of sedatives that he got from Canada . . ." Canada was the black market at Auschwitz; it was where the belongings of the incoming prisoners were taken to be organized and shipped back to Germany.
27. Statement by Friedrich Lang, October 8, 1946, in the official record of Case IV, Cracow Trials (Reference: Biulety Glowna Komisja Badania Zbrodni Hitlerowskich, op. cit., Vol. III, pp. 346–347).

and he went over to where the boy was lying on the ground and he got down on his knees and he started babbling something about 'Aaron' and calling the boy that and begging his forgiveness, and—it was awful. It made me sick.

"The boy was still alive and then Förster started staring at the bullet hole. It was just under the rib cage where he'd shot the boy. There was a lot of blood and it was running down his side and then Förster—you have to understand that this man was a pervert and he should never even have been in the SS. . . . Anyway, he put his mouth over the wound and started sucking the blood from the boy's body. If it wasn't so sickening it would have reminded me of that statue of Christ—the one where they've taken him off the cross and he's in his mother's arms? It was sickening, and then just before the boy died he kissed him, and his mouth was all filled with blood, and it was running down their faces. The boy was reaching up to stop him when he died, and then Förster went off crying. Like he wasn't the one who had killed him in the first place."[28]

On the 6th of June 1944, Förster attended one of the train unloadings: "I was at the station when the second train of the day came in. I watched as they pulled open the doors and pushed back the sidings. These were more of the Hungarian Jews, and I was thinking that, for Jews, the boys weren't that bad looking, when my eye was caught by a man helping an older one out of one of the boxcars. He took too much time because Baretzki[29] used his whip to push the young man away. This caused the old man to fall to the ground. Baretzki was laughing and I smiled at the joke. I looked to see how the young man was responding to the old man's fall, but he wasn't watching the old man. He was looking at me—he was staring at me. And then I realized it was Aaron. *My* Aaron, my real Aaron.

28. Unpublished verbal statement: Friedrich Lang, July 2, 1977. When I first approached Lang for an interview he was typically reserved, and even rude, but when he learned I only wanted to know about Förster he opened up and became very cooperative. I think it was the first time he'd ever really talked about that time, and I felt he was actually enjoying himself as long as he wasn't the object of the questions. Translation is by the author.
29. Stefan Baretzki, *SS-Rottenführer*.

"He was thin and dirty and his clothes hung on him oppressively. There was a scar on the left side of his face. I hadn't recognized him at first, although I had noticed him because he looked so much like— he looked like Aaron. The Star of David on his coat startled me—it emphasized his nose and his hair, and I think it was the first time I've ever really comprehended that Aaron is one of *them*. I suddenly remembered one of Himmler's injunctions about sentimentality, and I realized that I now had my own 'little Jew,' my one little exception—but there can be no exceptions.

"Before I had a chance to motion to him, to acknowledge him, Baretzki had pushed him roughly toward where the men were lining up for the selection. His friend, the old man, was limping to join him in the line. His face was cut and he was bleeding. I watched him for a moment, wondering if he could be Aaron's father, but I couldn't remember. When I turned to see Aaron again he was crowded somewhere in the line.

"I started watching Mengele, he was doing the selections, and when I saw Aaron again he looked so thin and haggard I suddenly felt that Mengele might send him to the gas and in that moment I heard myself saying 'Please God.'

" *'Please God.'*

"When it was Aaron's turn and he was standing in front of Mengele it felt like there was an eternity between the seconds and I even thought I might lose consciousness—and then Mengele motioned him to the right, to work: to live. He passed me, our eyes met for a moment and then he was joining the others, and then—

"I turned to go back to my office and stretching away before me were countless cattle cars being unloaded, and a maze of people, hundreds of them, pushing and shoving, crying and talking, stumbling to where they were being directed, dogs barking and orders being yelled out. This cacophony of noise seemed to have arisen out of nothing. One of the guards violently hit a girl who was holding a boy's hand, the body of a dead man was being lifted down out of one of the boxcars, and I found myself nearly falling over a small child who was apparently lost and crying. My chest felt as if it was being contracted by some inexorable force and I couldn't breathe. I had to get out of that place, I had to get away from those people. I tried to run, but my boots kept sticking in the mud, the Auschwitz mud, and pains, shooting up my leg and sharp in my chest, kept constricting my every step. I pushed my way through them, but no matter for how brief a moment, my eyes kept catching with theirs, and the effect was like those crazy mirrors at carnivals—I kept seeing myself distorted or disfigured, or Aaron, I would see him in their eyes, reflecting back at me—accusing?—glowing: *alive.*

"I am shaking all over. I have vomited twice. I have had a couple of drinks but I can't seem to quiet myself. I'm frightened. Aaron. Aaron is here and I know he'll hate me. I feel like I was almost dead, like I'd almost disappeared, and now I'm suddenly alive again and it is terrifying. Oh, Aaron—please don't hate me. Please. God help me. Aaron."

Despite all the writing Förster did about Aaron after his arrival at Auschwitz almost none of it sheds any light on the previous five years of Rosenthal's life, and most of what we know about it is derived from the recollections of Dr. Arnold Kopstein in his book, *The Catastrophe*.[30] After seeing his family off to Italy, Rosenthal worked to settle his affairs. He had returned to Freiberg to confer with some relatives about a property settlement when he was arrested for a fourth time. This time he escaped—by jumping off a truck and running—and until he was caught in a roundup of Jews in Szentes, Hungary, five years later, he kept on running. Kopstein reports he was in Vilna in Lithuania when the war began in September, and that he remained there for nearly a year until he moved to Lwow in the Ukraine. Just before the liquidation of that ghetto in June 1941, he made his way to Bratislava in Slovakia. When the deportations began there in March 1942, he managed to get to Bansko in Bulgaria, where he stayed until the mass arrests in March 1943, forced him to escape once again—this time to Hungary and the city of Szentes, where he was finally captured and sent to Auschwitz in June of 1944.

30. Originally published as *Die Katastrophe* by Dr. Arnold Kopstein, Stuttgart: Pabst and Brooks, 1948; *The Catastrophe*, translated by Anna Bergman, London: Guinness Bros., 1949.

★　　★　　★

When the Hungarian Jews began arriving at Auschwitz the camp was already overcrowded, and many of them went to the gas, bypassing the selection process altogether. Those who weren't killed, like Rosenthal, were held in the partially completed section of the camp known as *Mexico*, where they were to await their removal to other locations.

Förster did not see Rosenthal the night he arrived, and postponed their meeting out of fear. He began drinking even more heavily than usual, and the furious lettering of his writing is almost indecipherable, but one can make out in the scrawls his great desire to somehow redeem his life through this childhood friendship. Late on the evening of Friday, June 9, 1944, he had Rosenthal sent for. On the desk in his office he had a particularly opulent meal prepared. "I had several drinks before Aaron arrived, and I tried to compose myself. I don't look well—I don't think the lines under my eyes will ever go away again. I put my dress uniform on and I tried to look distinguished. I thought that I would show Aaron how strong I had become, how far away I was from that ineffectual and pathetic child he had known and had had contempt for, but my resolve kept collapsing in on itself, and I'd feel sick and my hands would be clammy. I had just taken a sedative when Aaron was brought in.

"Lang pushed him through the door and then shut it behind him. Aaron stood across the room from me without moving. I couldn't see him—my eyes would just not focus. I think I said hello. I motioned to the desk and the food, and finally he came over to me. When he got near the light I saw him and it was horrible. His head had been shaved, of course, and it was covered with stubble; he'd gotten some new clothes, the striped prison garments, but a great change had come over him in this last week, or maybe I didn't properly see him at the depot, but his skin was yellow, and his cheeks were sunken, and he looked—well, he didn't look like Aaron.

"I asked him if he would like to eat. He fell into the chair I offered and stared at the food. I poured him a glass of Croatian slivovitz. He didn't touch it. I told him I would get him transferred out of the temporary camp, and that he would be treated much better and would get plenty to eat. I told him I would see to it in the morning. He reached out and touched the food, and finally put a bit of chicken to his mouth. I told him he could have as much as he wanted. He was about to put another bite in his mouth when he stopped and looked at me. He then took what was left of the chicken and put it in his pocket, and then some cheese and bread, all the while watching me. I told him I understood, that it was all right. After he had finished filling his pockets with food he began eating again and when he was finished he laid his head in his arms on the desk. He was very still and, as he was not looking at me, I got up my nerve and very softly I said his name, 'Aaron.' It suddenly seemed amazing to me that he could actually hear me saying that word, his name, and I asked him, I implored him, 'You don't hate me anymore, do you? Love doesn't have to be a dishonorable thing. I don't think my love for you was dishonorable. I don't think the one cancels out the other. Do you? Aaron . . . ?'

"I knew I was babbling but I couldn't help it—somehow I had to fill up his silence—and then when he finally raised his head and looked at me: his eyes were shining. And when he spoke it was with a simplicity so clear the syllable encompassed everything. He said, 'No.' "

A week later, when Rosenthal had been transferred to the *Sonderkommando*[31] in Birkenau, and was recovering from his malnutrition, he wrote the brief page that more than anything else has earned him his place in history: "Richard Förster, the best friend of my youth, is a commandant in this—hell. Can this be the price of rejection? I suddenly felt that if I apologized everything would be erased, that it would all disappear, the camps, the dying, Hitler, the war, the gas chambers, everything. This man sitting across from me seemed so terribly and horribly fragile. I moved around the desk to him very slowly, and I knelt at his feet, and it suddenly seemed possible. In a world of

31. The *Sonderkommando* (Special Command) was a group of nonpolitical, usually Jewish, prisoners who did the actual work in the crematoria; they helped allay the fears of the victims before the gassings, removed their bodies afterward, shaved their heads, pulled any gold teeth, and then burned the corpses in the furnaces. Beginning in June of 1944, they actually lived on the premises of the crematoria. They did not have to wear the striped prison garments, and because of their close proximity to *Canada* they were well fed, and even had access to books (the reading of which brought a sentence of twenty days' solitary confinement in the regular barracks).

madness it seemed as if I could eradicate all the horror there was with a simple apology. I held his hands in mine and I looked up at him and I said, 'I'm sorry,' and I repeated the only words I could think to say, 'I'm sorry, I'm sorry.' I put my arms around him and I buried my face in his lap and I cried. I hadn't done that since Rachel. I hadn't allowed the world that victory. But deliriously, for those moments with Richard, my tears seemed a mere pittance to have the world, not even as it should have been, but just as it was—when we believed in honor and were afraid to call it love. But the world as it was then would eventually have brought us here to the world as it is now, where tears are a luxury we can ill afford, and 'love' and 'honor' are meaningless words in the face of survival."[32]

32. This translation of Rosenthal's famous apology is by the author and is based on the original manuscript in the State Museum at Auschwitz. I think it might be instructive to reprint here the original in full, as it has never been previously so published in any English publication:

"Richard Förster, mein bester Freund aus meiner Jugend ist ein Kommandant in dieser—Hölle. Kann dies der Lohn sein zur Abweisung? Ich fühlte plötzlich, dass ich um Entschuldigung bitten sollte, Alles würde verschwinden, die Lager, das Sterben Hitler, der Krieg, die Gaskammern, einfach Alles. Dieser Mann, der mir gegenueber sass, schien so schrecklich zerbrechlich. Ich ging langsam um den Schreibtisch auf ihn zu und kniete vor ihm nieder. Und plötzlich schien es möglich zu sein: In einer Welt des Wahnsinns schien es mir als ob ich allen Horror mit einer einfachen Entschuldigung auslöschen könnte. Ich hielt seine Hände in den meinen, sah ihn an und murmelte: 'Es tut mir leid,' und ich wiederholte die einzigen Worte, die mir einfielen, 'es tut mir leid, es tut mir leid.' Ich legte meine Arme um ihn, und verbarg mein Gesicht in seinen Schoss und ich weinte. Das hat ich seit Rachel nicht getan. Der Welt hatte ich ein solches Zugeständnis nicht erlaubt. Aber wahnsinnigerweise, für dies Momente mit Richard, schienen meine Tränen eine Kleinigkeit zu sein: Die Welt so zu haben, nicht mal so wie sie hätte sein sollen, sondern wie sie war, als wir an Ehre glaubten, und Angst hatten es Liebe zu nennen. Aber die Welt, wie sie damals war, hätte uns eventuel zu der Welt geführt wie sie heute ist, wo Tränen ein Luxus sind, den wir uns nicht erlauben können, und 'Liebe' und 'Ehre' wertlose Worte angesichts des Ueberlebens sind."

When Dr. Kopstein brought out his book *Die Katastrophe* in 1948, he quoted this page of Rosenthal's, but he edited it, and by how much can be seen in the American translation by Anna Bergman, which follows the German version of the book very closely: "Richard Förster, the best friend of my youth, is a commandant in this—hell. I suddenly felt that if I offered an apology then this would all disappear,

After being transferred from the barracks Rosenthal recuperated under the care of Dr. Kopstein: ". . . what happened to Aaron was what happened to us all, but somehow I think it hurt him more. Maybe it's just because I never saw him develop the cynicism we all had—and which we *had* to have just to survive. . . . That he was moved from the barracks, and that he hadn't been gassed or shot, was good, but being assigned to the *Sonderkommando* was a mixed blessing: the prisoners here were the best treated in the camp but what they knew of the inner workings of the KZ[33] was too dangerous a knowledge to have and live. When Aaron arrived, there had already been ten *Sonderkommandos*. . . . I only knew Aaron Rosenthal for a week, but in that time he became like a son to me. While Aaron was recovering we had several long talks, and I told him about the camp's underground, of which I was a part. . . . He read some and wrote several pages of his impressions as a kind of testament to what was happening there. This eventually proved too upsetting and he put the writing aside. But, after

the camps, the deaths, Hitler, the war, the gas chambers, everything. In a world of madness I felt that I could eradicate the horror with a simple apology, and I cried. Madly, for a moment, my tears were a trifle: the world as it was, not even as it should be, just as it was, when we believed in honor but were afraid to call it love. But the world of that time would have eventually brought us to this world, where tears are a luxury we cannot permit, and 'love' and 'honor' are worthless words when it comes to survival."

When confronted with the disparity between the original and his edited version, Kopstein became indignant, "Förster was just a catalyst for Aaron's thoughts. Aaron was in a state of shock and those remarks about Förster were just indulgences, ultimately irrelevant specifics that distract from the larger situation he was responding to." I asked him what he thought was the meaning of one of the sentences he deleted: "Kann dies der Lohn sein zur Abweisung?" ("Can this be the price of rejection?"), and he said, "It's ambiguous, but ultimately I think it is a cry of despair. It is the cry of not just one individual man, but of a whole people. It is the cry of the rejected Jews of Europe." (Unpublished verbal statement: Arnold Kopstein, November 5, 1977.)

The exact date when Rosenthal wrote his "apology" is unknown, but it had to have been during the time when he was working with the *Sonderkommando*, between June 12 and June 23, 1944. Although the actual page that Rosenthal wrote may be viewed today at Auschwitz with special permission, it is Kopstein's edited version that is invariably quoted. As far as I know, Rosenthal's full text has only been printed once, in the Polish journal, *Biuletyn Zydowskiego Instytutu Historycznego*, Lodz: July–September 1951, p. 87.

33. *KZ* was an abbreviated designation for *Konzentration-slager* (concentration camp), pronounced "Katzet."

he was killed, when we were hiding our testaments in the brickwork of the building, I insisted we include the page Aaron had written, the 'apology.' I felt it showed a hope and strength, a kind of light on the other side of despair, that might be important for future generations to know about."[34]

On June 12, 1944, Rosenthal began working with the *Sonderkommando*; from Förster's journal: "Aaron was assigned to the showers, and I went to see him this afternoon to see if he was all right. I hadn't been by the crematoriums in a while. The Hungarian Jews are flooding the camp, and when I arrived the second group at *Krema* No. III[35] had just been exterminated. On the way I'd passed a group waiting for their turn at *Krema* No. IV. There must have been more than two thousand of them. They were waiting in the birch grove[36] across the road. In their heavy clothes they looked hot and miserable: people were sprawled on the ground, women were attending children, and other groups were surrounding the old men with the beards, the 'rabbis'—adjuring their people to bear with their suffering, no doubt. They really are contemptible and they love this: they think this is all part of some big plan, that somehow they're being ennobled. An old man tottered toward me as I passed, his hands held out beseechingly, saying 'Water'—I just wanted to grab him and shake him before he died to make him see, make him really understand: 'Being alive is just an excuse, *you* don't make any difference, *no one cares.*'

"Downstairs, at the back, they were still removing the bodies. The throb of the motors for the ventilators and the clanging of the elevator doors had created a wild dissonance. Wessel[37] was overseeing the men and seemed to be screaming just for the sport of it. About

34. Unpublished verbal statement: Arnold Kopstein, November 5, 1977.
35. In the various descriptions of the Auschwitz camp there is a discrepancy concerning the numbering of the five crematoria. For the purposes of this report I shall use Förster's own system, whereby *Krema* No. III, where Rosenthal worked, is the crematorium immediately north of the ramp and the train spur in Birkenau.
36. This birch grove was responsible for the name of the village that had been razed to build this part of the camp at Auschwitz: Birkenau (Brzezinka).
37. Karl Wessel, *SS-Unterscharführer* (Sergeant). Wessel was the *Kommandoführer* of *Krema* No. III, the SS man in charge of the prisoners. He had his own room on the main floor of the crematorium.

thirty prisoners were working and they all had gas masks on it so it was hard to distinguish Aaron at first. And then I saw him—he was hunched over, walking backwards out of the shower room dragging two bodies behind him.

"Wessel evidently didn't think he was moving fast enough and shouted at him. In an effort to get to the elevators faster he tripped, but he scurried up and in a moment was heaving the two bodies onto the pile in there. It was nearly full so he rang the bell and shut the door, and the lift went upstairs. He had turned to go back in the showers when he saw me. I couldn't really see him at that distance with his mask on. He paused for just a moment, and in that second Wessel was on him screaming some more. He hurried into the showers again, the straps in his hand,[38] and as he walked away from me I noticed his clothes were smeared with feces.

"I moved over toward the door and looked in. The bodies were piled high against the far wall, right up to the ceiling, and one of the men had a hose and was washing them down.[39] The gas smell didn't seem too bad at first. Aaron was removing an upstanding body from the pile, and as he did another body from above fell back on him, knocking him to the ground.

"The sickly-sweet gas smell seemed to have gotten worse as I stood there, and I took out my handkerchief and held it over my nose and mouth. And then Aaron was moving toward me, his back to me, dragging two more bodies. When he passed me in the doorway he glanced up for a second. His eyes were red and flushed with tears and as soon as our eyes met he looked away, pulling the bodies with him almost as if they were something I shouldn't be allowed to see.

38. Thongs were used to pull the bodies from the showers. They were made of leather and had a loop at the end.
39. When the doors were opened after the gassings the bodies of the people inside were invariably in piles—against the doors, and away from the sheet-iron pillars with the perforations where the gas escaped. The bodies of the old, the weak, and the very young were usually on the bottom, while the bodies of the strong who had fought for the clear air nearer the ceiling were on the top. The last thing the body did before dying was to defecate, so some of the men in the *Sonderkommando* would wash the bodies down with hoses before other prisoners began removing them from the showers.

"I backed away from the door and walked over to where Wessel was standing. He offered me a flask and I took a long swallow. Aaron was hefting his bodies into the elevator, and other men were passing us. 'How is the new man?' I asked.

"Wessel laughed and indicated that he'd been sick to his stomach that morning. Aaron walked back past us toward the showers without looking at me, and I could feel an emanation from him: he blames me for all this. It's just because he knows me—he knows I don't really have anything to do with any of this. If he really asked himself, what does he think I could do? I took another drink from Wessel's flask and walked over to the elevator.

"Aaron was still in the showers, and I watched him as he secured his bodies and came back toward me. In the gas mask he looked like a creature from another planet. I smiled. I wanted to share the joke with him, but when he turned to me I saw that terrible accusation there again. He pulled the bodies close to him and one at a time heaved them onto the growing pile, turned abruptly, and moved back to the showers at a trot. What does he think I could do? I looked at the bodies piled in the elevator before me. They were mostly old people and their skin was discolored. They looked awful. I wanted to ask Aaron to look at them as well and to tell me, if he could, what value their lives could possibly have had. One of the bodies was a boy, almost fourteen I'd guess. I touched his arm and tried to imagine him having sex—he probably never had. That seemed sad.

"With a brutal push that sent me back several feet Aaron shoved me away from the boy, and then deftly untied the thongs from the wrists of the two bodies he had just brought and lifted them onto the others. I had somehow dishonored the dead. Wessel hadn't seen Aaron push me, but one of the other men had and he paused to watch with curiosity my acquiescence to Aaron's gesture.

"I realized I couldn't explain anything to him there and while he was back in the showers I left. Aaron is like everybody else, he thinks death is horrible. How can it possibly be worse than life? Anybody's life. Mine, his, Hitler's, anybody's? It's so silly. How can it not be an escape and a blessing? To want to live is just some deep ingrained habit. It doesn't make any difference. People only think it's important because they don't know anything else, and as if death—nothing—is some terrible thing.

"I went outside, the incinerators were going full blast, the sky was clouded, and the day seemed murkier than usual. I felt that if only the sun had been allowed to shine through it would have been a wonderful day. Without the sun it is difficult to believe in the summer.

"I took the long way back, by *Krema* No. IV, and checked on the group there—they had just been directed down the stairs into the changing room and told to undress. A few of the people seemed panicked, and it amazed me—aren't they used to it yet?—but, of course, they've never been through all this before. It just seems like they must have: they are all the same. As I stood there watching them I noticed a boy staring at me. I can usually stare them down if they try that trick on me, but for some reason I turned away. I so wanted to go over to him and ask him what he wanted to hold onto, and why—

"I wish I could feel Aaron's outrage—it makes him beautiful, and the lack of it grays me into something dull and colorless. I just drew my razor across the end of one of my fingers and it is bleeding. I am watching the blood fill in the line of the cut, and yet I can't grasp my mortality: that I can or will STOP. Or that it will make any difference if I do."

Rosenthal did not return for work the following day. Late that afternoon he collapsed from exhaustion and a fever he'd contracted as a result of an infection from his tattoo. He was given another two days for recuperation. On June 14, Förster wrote in his journal: "I stopped by *Krema* No. III to see Aaron this afternoon. I hadn't been in the attic there since we'd made it into the living quarters for the *Sonderkommando*. I'd forgotten the hair-drying room was in No. III and how that acrid smell of singeing permeates everything; for some reason the smell from the furnaces doesn't bother me nearly so much. The day shift was at work and most of the beds were empty. I made my way through them until I found Aaron at the other end of the room, in the corner. He was sleeping. I sat on the cot across from him and I watched him. Some color had returned to his face, but his forehead was beaded with sweat. As he lay there I could see more of the Aaron I knew so long ago. I miss his hair and the stubble on his head makes me sad. I've always wanted to hold him softly, and run my fingers through it. His face, in repose, and his eyes shut, without all those awful things I see in them, was beautiful, and I wanted to kiss him— I somehow wanted to make this precious living creature before me mine, but I realized that this moment, with us together, and Aaron sleeping, was as close as I would ever get to that. It was only now, with Aaron secure in his dreams, that he could be all those things for me that I've always felt were, perhaps, the answers to my life. Because when he is awake, even when his mercy might allow forgiveness, what I see in his eyes is too much what I don't know, what can't then mean love.

"I knelt by his bed and committed his image to my heart, I regulated my breathing to correspond with his, and when, sometime later, he awoke, I lifted his hand in mine to kiss it. There, just above the wrist, on the underside of his forearm—still slightly swollen and sickly at variance with his skin tone—was the blue stenciling: A-8931. At first I'd just meant to touch his fingers to my lips but now I held his arm and gently kissed the number. When I looked up at him the things that passed through his mind, in his eyes, were too terrible to see and I got to my feet to leave, but he held my hand. 'Talk to me. Please.'

"I sat down again and when I looked at him the terrible things were gone (had I only imagined them?), so I started to try and explain everything to him but, speaking under my breath in a whisper, it became horrible and stupid. In his mind there is a clear and absolute morality that I have betrayed, and the more I said the more I found myself defending myself, and the tone that crept into my voice wouldn't go away. I finally just stopped. 'You can't do this to me,' I told him.

"He didn't say anything. He just looked at me. But it wasn't understanding that he was giving me, which I'm sure he thought it was, it was revolting self-righteous pity. I stood up, almost hitting my head on the sloping ceiling, and told him to get up and get dressed.

He looked at me and there was an insolence in his expression—it's a look that I've seen before, it's a kind of pride, an arrogance—and it is a pleasure to destroy. 'Now!' I shouted, and the men in the room turned to look at us.

"I pulled him out of his cot and as soon as he had his pants on I pushed him to the stairs, still barefoot and without a shirt, down the steps and into Wessel's room. After closing the door and locking it, I pressed him against the wall and kissed him, not softly like before on his arm, but viciously—like I'd imagined him kissing me all those years ago. He made a protest with his body but he was still weak and I could feel that, under my strength, he would give way to anything I wanted to do with him. When I looked at him again there was a disgustingly benign quality on his face. 'I love you,' I said.

"I watched him for a trace of a reaction, of revulsion perhaps, but there was nothing, and the phrase hung in the air. It was a lie and we both knew it.

"But, strangely, it filled me with relief and the action was easy. I pulled his pants off and pushed him onto a table that was in the room. His muscles flinched but he made no resistance: he just stared at me, looking up out of his nakedness. But now I could return that accusing look with a smile. 'This doesn't mean anything to you, does it?'

"He didn't say anything, and for a moment I just stood there with his body before me. It was still emaciated, but his penis, his cock, was fat and rested on his testicles—

"I leaned over and ran my tongue the length of it. I could feel my face flushing. Nothing happened then, but when I put the head of it in my mouth an instinctive spasm overcame it, and no matter what happened, no matter what he might do or say: it meant something.

"My arms stretched across him and I pressed my hands hard against his body. I filled my mouth with the whole of his cock, fleshy still and corpulent. It became harder and larger until the cavern of my mouth covered only half of it, but then, holding in my breath, I let the end of his cock slip back past the back of my mouth and down my throat where the muscles constricted against its engorged head. Aaron expelled a moan, a gasp. And suddenly the feelings that had vanished—that I might initially touch and then assault his body—

returned, warmly, in mind-wrenching waves: this was Aaron's cock, *my* Aaron, and this part of him, filling my mouth and throat until the pressure of desire inside me brought tears to my eyes, was because of me, Richard Förster, who has loved Aaron Rosenthal, always, and without honor.

"Giving himself up to me, his cries wrested out of a defenseless passion, I pushed him into me that I might even die, my hands slipping across his fevered flesh and, encompassing him in salivary ardor, his body contracted around me, his convulsions matched by the involuntary heaving of my chest, exhaustion fighting our agonized muscles and, finally sinking into inertia with spastic fits of helplessness, his taste filled my mouth with absolution.

"The tremor of a chill swept over his body and I covered him with a blanket that was in the room. As I was tucking it under him I became aware of the lightness of his body and I lifted him up into my arms, and his head rested against my shoulder, his hands curled in front of him like a baby. I felt as if I had never seen anyone, or anything, so beautiful in my life. I held him in my arms for a long time: I so wanted to carry him back to his bed, lay him down to sleep and pull the covers up under his chin. But I couldn't do that.

"When he finally recovered himself I set him down. We didn't say anything. With his back to me, he went and put his pants on and walked slowly to the door. He paused for a moment, and then turned toward me, looking at the ground and not raising his head. When I didn't any anything he turned again, unlocked the door, and left. After he was gone I stayed in the *Kommandoführer*'s room by myself for a long time. I know he meant to accuse me with his silence for his passivity, but he sanctioned me instead."[40]

Förster didn't see Rosenthal for another week. On Wednesday, June 21, he had Rosenthal brought to him: "I was looking out at the fires when Aaron arrived. As soon as Lang left us alone together Aaron

---

40. When *Auschwitz: Die Tagesbucher vom Förster* was published this was one of the passages the editor, Dr. Kopstein, deleted on the grounds of "obscenity." It has remained unpublished until now.

asked me, and his voice was clear and steady, 'What are we going to do?'

"I didn't know what to say to him. He called us *'we.'* I turned back to look out the window, and he came over and stood beside me. The Hungarian Jews are still overflooding the camp: *Krema* Nos. IV and V were going full blast, and the ditches were brilliant with fire.[41] It is so much nicer at night when the smoke doesn't make any difference. The lights on the fences are the demarcations of our place in the universe while the fires serve as the hallmarks of our power and glory.

" 'Richard,' his voice had almost softened to a whisper, 'You don't know what you're doing,' and he paused, 'do you?' I turned to look at him and there was an awful patronizing look in his eyes that almost made me laugh. I told him I knew what I was doing, that I wasn't crazy.

" 'Then how can you do it?' he asked. And then I saw it, Aaron's total egocentric inability to see anything beyond his own point of view. I told him it was my job, that I was a part of something more important than just this camp. He looked at me for a long moment. It was amazing to him, I think, that I could give myself up to be a part of something, that I could exist beyond myself. And then he asked me why, 'Why are you here?'

"Whenever anyone had asked me that question, and yet it had only been myself, I had always seen Aaron's face, and his eyes, before me, but now they really were before me, and they themselves were asking the question. I turned back to the window. The panes of glass were cold to the touch, the fires glowed in the distance, and the only sound, apart from our breathing, was a dog barking somewhere. I didn't know what to say, I couldn't tell him—I didn't know how to tell him—and yet he must know, in himself, he *must* know: I'm here because of him. And allowing that knowledge, though unspoken, I asked him what he thought I should do.

41. During the spring and summer of 1944, when the overcrowding caused by the influx of the Hungarian Jews was putting an extra strain on the operational capacities of the camp, huge ditches were built beside *Krema* No. V to help with the disposal of the bodies.

" 'Escape.'

"I laughed, and asked him where to.

" 'I don't know,' he said. 'Does it matter?'

"I turned again and looked at him. The room was in shadows but for the desk lamp and the fires outside. I smiled at him, at our being together, and he smiled back at me. It felt like when we were young and the future was in our own hands. I proffered, 'We'll win the Nobel Prize, eh?'

"Aaron nodded. I moved to touch him but he backed away. So. There would be no more accusing acquiescence. I looked down at my hands. I was suddenly tired, and all I wanted was peace. I told him, humbly, that I never meant to hurt him.

" 'You're killing me,' he said. 'Those people,' and he pressed one of his hands against his chest, 'are *me*.'

"I couldn't help but smile, and turned to look out the window again, imagining Aaron the sole cause of the flames shooting up into the night sky before me. There was a silence and I could sense a deliberation going on behind me. I suddenly wondered if he might kill me.

" 'Richard,' and he paused, almost as if he wanted me to answer. 'I've heard about the boys you bring up here.' There was another brief silence but I didn't move. 'One of the men I work with asked me if my name was really Aaron.'

"I felt like I'd been dropped down a well. I remembered the Greek boy I'd shot, and I thought, Aaron can't know about that, mustn't know about that, and I wondered, and it is terrifying: who else knows, does Höss know? Does Schurz?[42] I couldn't say anything. I could hardly breathe. And then I felt Aaron come up behind me. He put his arms around me, locking his hands over my chest, and said softly over my shoulder, 'Richard, if I'm the only thing that means anything to you, I want you to know that I am, truly, each and every person who is put to death in this camp, every woman, every child,

---

42. Hans Schurz, *SS-Untersturmführer* (Second Lieutenant), head of the Political Department of Auschwitz.

every old man——every boy you've ever whispered the name "Aaron" to.'

"I told him he was being stupid. He turned me around in his arms, his hands moving up the back of my head, through my hair, holding me, compelling me to look in his eyes. 'Richard,' he said, taking all of me in with his consideration, *'I——am——you.'*

"I didn't know what he meant, what he could mean, and I felt panicked, but he was moving his hands down and around my back, bringing himself up next to me in an embrace, and he was kissing me. I couldn't breathe, I was afraid to answer his mouth with mine, tears blurred the world, and I had to pull myself out of the kiss to just hold him, to hold him as tight as I could.

"My breathing returned in gasps, and I held him that I might somehow check what was coming out of me, but I couldn't stop it, and finally giving way I started crying into him, great long sobs, all those years, the stupidity, the regrets: the waste. Convulsively I pressed against him and into those moments, with him, holding him. And him holding me.

"When my crying had at last stopped for a moment, Aaron held me at arm's length and looked at me. I tried to wipe my face but he held my arms fast. I tried to explain, something, I don't know what, but all I could say was his name. He held me tight again and 'I love you' he said, and he said it over again, and kissed the tears from my cheeks, 'I love you I love you I . . .' once again kissing me, whispering love. He began unbuttoning my jacket and hurriedly pulling off my clothes. I couldn't move but it was all right, and then his mouth was on my chest, caressing my nipples with his teeth.

"He discarded his clothes, unbuckled my belt, and knelt before me, pulling my trousers down to my feet. He moved his hands up my legs and around my back, pressing himself against me. He held me close for a moment and then his mouth was kissing me and he rolled my cock over his face, across his eyes. Abstractedly I moved my hand out to touch him and he kissed my fingers. Once again he pressed his face into my sex and held me, his arms locked tight around my legs, his muscles trembling——

"He finally let go of me and sat back on his heels. Kneeling there in stillness, his hesitation was almost tangible. My cock, moderately tumescent, grazed his forehead. He looked up, and then gently, tentatively, pushed back the foreskin with his fingers, slowly. Our eyes met for a moment. They weren't accusing me now, they were seeking approbation, and taking all of me into him, consideration merged into lust.

"I keeled over his back, and in a moment we were mutually devouring one another, rolling over our clothes on the floor, our carnality a means of dissolution, our sweat and thrust and taste the merest outlines of function; ego, will, and ideas succumbing to sensation: this purity of action finally attaining freedom in a sudden clarity of release, our human frailty tinged with divine strength, and our separateness only perspective in which to pour love.

"Buried in the recesses of each other's bodies I wished that those moments could last forever; if we could just curl up, submerge, and disappear into that warm and filmy substance, and return, not to the womb, but that seminal existence propelled by passion. Our hearts still pounding we snuggled into each other's arms, and the unreality of the world slowly imposed itself back upon us, as we lay quiet and watched the flames flickering on the ceiling."[43]

The events of Friday evening, June 23, 1944, are shrouded in mystery. Friedrich Lang testified at Cracow in 1947 that he delivered Rosenthal to Förster's office at about ten o'clock that night. He was dismissed and ordered to come back in two hours, but a half hour later he was still in the building when he saw Rosenthal and Förster leave together. He said Rosenthal was dressed in a Nazi uniform. They got in a car, and a moment later Lang notified Höss's office that an escape was in progress.[44]

The promulgation of the story that Rosenthal shot and killed Förster is contained in Dr. Arnold Kopstein's account of the next day:

---

43. See notation 40.
44. Statement by Friedrich Lang, October 8, 1946, in the official record of Case IV, Cracow Trials (Reference: *Biuletyn Glowna Komisja Badania Zbrodni Hitlerowskich*, op cit., Vol. III, pp. 350–353). Lang was found guilty of war crimes by the Supreme National Tribunal in Cracow. He was sentenced to life imprisonment in March 1947, but had his sentence commuted in 1954. He died in Dresden in 1983.

"The day shift were just about to go to work when the crematoriums were suddenly surrounded by several truckloads of armed *SS* men. All of the men in the *Sonderkommando* were ordered into the back courtyard. This departure from routine spelled disaster. Looking at the faces around me I was overcome by the knowledge that they would be the last things I would see in this life. I prayed. An order was then suddenly called out for all the doctors to withdraw. I returned to the crematorium. Passing among the men I had come to know I felt them bequeathing me their lives, as memory. A few moments later machine-gun fire came from the courtyard. I never have, and I never will forget those men.

"Later, one of the *Kapos*[45] told me what happened: the night before a prisoner, Aaron Rosenthal, had forced *Kommandant* Förster to help him escape. They had been followed. At the train station at Ryczków there had been shooting. Rosenthal had been gunned down but before he died he had shot and killed Förster. Höss used this 'conspiracy' as his excuse to exterminate the *Sonderkommando*. Within an hour the new *Sonderkommando* was in the building, shaving the heads and extracting the gold from the teeth of their predecessors before putting them in the ovens.

"At least, I thought, Aaron hadn't died here. He had died fighting. And when the *Kapo* told me Aaron had killed Förster himself I could hardly restrain my joy. He had killed the monster."[46]

Interestingly enough, Dr. Kopstein makes no mention of Rudolf Höss's testimony during the trial of the Auschwitz garrison in 1946, which not only contradicts his own story, but sheds fascinating light on its genesis: "Rosenthal's escape on June 23 was not the only one that night. Four other prisoners escaped and also got to Ryczków. The man who came back with the story, Willi Preeze, *SS-Oberschütze* (Senior Private), said when he and Kaduk[47] arrived at the station there were eight men on the platform. Two of them were railway police and they

45. *Kapo* is the abbreviation of *Kamaradschafts Polizei*. These were generally German prisoners serving sentences for nonpolitical crimes, who were given jurisdiction over barracks and/or prisoners
46. *Die Katastrophe*, op. cit., pp. 147–8; *The Catastrophe*, pp. 213–4.
47. Ernst Kaduk, *SS-Sturmmann* (Lance-Corporal).

were searching four 'civilians.' Preeze said he and Kaduk had just approached the other two men, Förster and the man he was with, when there was a gunshot, and yelling, then shooting broke out. In the confusion Förster pulled out his revolver and started firing at them. Kaduk was killed and when it was over Preeze said the two railway police were dead, as well as three of the men who were being searched, all of whom turned out to be prisoners. We never found the fourth man, and Preeze said the last time he saw Förster and his friend they were running away across the tracks. Preeze was in my office telling me this when Eichmann,[48] who was visiting the camp at that time, suddenly stopped by. He'd heard about the escape and asked if we'd caught the Jew, meaning Rosenthal. I told him we had. When he asked about Förster, if he was all right, I told him the Jew had killed him. He was a little taken aback, but I reassured him that this subversion would be dealt with, and the entire *Sonderkommando* would be ashes by noon. This seemed to mollify him somewhat, and he witnessed the extermination himself. . . . I thought we would hear something about Förster, in which case I would just say that I had been misinformed, but we never did. Only Preeze knew about my lie[49] and I promoted him to *SS-Rottenführer*. . . . I have recently learned that Förster knew this Jew years before, and it confirms what I'd suspected for a long time: that he *helped* Rosenthal to escape, he wasn't forced.

48. Adolf Eichmann, *SS-Sturmbannführer* (Major), head of the Jewish department of *RSHA, Reichssicherheitshauptamt*, Reich Central Security Department.
49. This is not exactly true. The other prisoner who escaped, the fourth man, could have reported what happened, but a controversy about his identity has never been finally resolved (this is fully discussed in *Zycie Oswiecim* by Czeslaw Wajda, Warsaw: Sukowa, 1974, pp. 260–75). In any case, both of the men involved have died, and a resolution to the mystery does not seem likely. As for Preeze, he did not survive the war. He was overseeing the work at the incinerators in *Krema* No. IV when the *Sonderkommando* uprising in October 1944 took place. This was recounted by Hans Kohler in his deposition of December 13, 1946, in the official record of Case V, Cracow Trials (Reference: *Biuletyn Glowna Komisja Zbrodni Hitlerowskich*, op. cit., Vol. VI, p. 302): ". . . We were talking about what to do when Preeze walked in. He knew something was up, and when he started yelling at us, one of the men suddenly just went for him. We all joined him, and while Preeze was screaming we threw him headfirst into one of the furnaces. It was the wrong action at the wrong time and, ultimately, it cost us the success of our uprising, but it was a great moment . . ."

Without really knowing why at the time I think it was this feeling that prompted me to tell Eichmann that Förster had been shot by the Jew. It was to protect him from the humiliation I myself felt that I lied."[50]

Two days after Höss gave his testimony, Dr. Kopstein denounced him: "It's an outrage! Aaron Rosenthal is a hero. He committed one of the great acts of heroism to come out of this terrible war. In the face of certain death he fought back, he made an effort to stop Hitler's murdering machine, and what is his reward? To have this criminal, this mass murderer, testify that he escaped with the help of a Nazi *Kommandant*! I worked in that camp, I saw Richard Förster in his work and I tell you that he was a monster without compassion, and the idea that he would let the past play on his feelings, much less help a prisoner to escape, is preposterous. I believe in my heart that if we are to give credence to this story, or Höss himself, a psychopathic killer, a self-confessed liar and virulent anti-Semite, we are laying the first foundations in the reconstruction of Hitler's Third Reich."[51]

Dr. Kopstein's speech in Munich, the book he published two years later, and his work editing Förster's journals after the war, have done much to promote Rosenthal's "act of heroism." In numerous books and articles Höss's testimony on this point has been discredited, and Kopstein's impassioned plea not to besmirch Rosenthal's name has been heeded.[52]

Since, until now, Dr. Kopstein was one of the few people to have read Förster's complete Auschwitz journals and papers, as well as the few notes that Rosenthal himself wrote, I asked him how he

50. Statement by Rudolf Höss, November 4, 1946, in the official record of Case I, Cracow Trials (Reference: *Biuletyn Glowna Komisja Hitlerowskich*, op. cit., Vol. II, pp. 319–321). Höss was found guilty of war crimes by the Supreme National Tribunal in Cracow and was hung at Auschwitz on April 16, 1947.

51. This speech of Dr. Kopstein's was made in Munich on November 28, 1946, and was printed in *The New York Times*, February 2, 1947 in an article entitled, "Truth and Disillusion" by Mike Winocour. The rather hysterical tone of Kopstein's words is probably due to finding himself under attack at this time for participating, albeit as a prisoner, in the medical experiments of Dr. Mengele.

52. Barbara Sommer has supplied an excellent bibliography on Höss, Förster, and Rosenthal among others in Richard Ferguson's *"Arbeit Macht Frei": Work Is Freedom*, Los Angeles: Drake and Cashorali, 1958. This was updated for the book's reissue in 1984.

could honestly believe that Rosenthal would have shot Förster. "If you are referring to that filth that Förster wrote, I don't believe any of that. The man was known to be on drugs, and the things he wrote are obviously drug-induced delusions.... I knew about the escape. Aaron told me about it the day before. He told me Förster was going to help him. I asked him how such a thing could be possible, and he told me Förster was 'in love' with him. It made me sick to think about it then and it makes me sick to think about it now.... The last time I saw Aaron I warned him not to trust Förster no matter what he said, and if he had the opportunity—to kill him. Aaron said that would only bring us down to their level. I asked him to look around us—at the trains unloading just outside the windows, at the showers and ovens downstairs, and I told him he could never descend to their level no matter what he did."[53]

The last time I interviewed Dr. Kopstein he ended our encounter with a tirade: "Have you ever stopped to consider what it would mean if what Förster wrote is true? You would be saying, in fact, that Aaron Rosenthal had a sexual relationship with that—monster—to save his own life. You would be discounting, *completely*, the character of a man I knew. I *knew* Aaron Rosenthal. He was my friend and he was a good man, he was a man of decency with a spiritual morality that you would reduce to—excrement.... If you are going to publish those entries in Förster's journals as the 'truth' or as an example of a way to achieve some kind of understanding, let me tell you: it can *not* be done. Only someone as degenerate as he was could 'understand' him. '*Understand*.' Do you know what's on the other side of that understanding? Do you? I do. I know: *justification*—justification of the unjustifiable."[54]

Thus, Höss's secondhand story about what happened on the platform of a railway station outside Auschwitz has become a footnote in history, and Aaron Rosenthal is regarded as a hero in the annals of

53. Unpublished verbal statement: Arnold Kopstein, November 5, 1977.
54. Unpublished verbal statement: Arnold Kopstein, November 7, 1977. Kopstein currently lives in Tel Aviv. I have been in contact with his niece recently and she writes that her uncle has been suffering from Alzheimer's disease for the last five years and is not expected to live much longer.

Hitler's death camps. I think Aaron Rosenthal may very well be a hero but in a considerably different sense than has previously been supposed.

We will probably never know what happened to Förster and Rosenthal after they left the camp. Did they get away? Where did they go? Did they survive the war? And, most important of all, did their need for one another survive their escape?

There are no hard facts here, at best we have conjecture: the bodies of the two railway policemen killed at Ryczków remain unaccounted for and the three escaped prisoners, one of them popularly believed to have been Aaron Rosenthal at the time, were cremated; there is a record of the shooting of two unidentified Nazis by a partisan unit, *Sosienki*, fighting in the Silesian Beskids, about forty kilometers south of the camp that June[55]; stories of Aaron Rosenthal's participation in the fighting for the state of Israel in 1948 have been discounted as rumors by Rachel Thalberg[56]; and the reported sighting of Richard Förster in a Soviet labor camp by a woman named Nastasha Chernyakovsky in 1957 has not been confirmed and recent communications with Soviet authorities have elicited no records of his incarceration.[57] Therefore, after a thorough assessment of both known historical documents and those previously unpublished papers referred to and quoted above, I hereby submit the proposition that Rudolf Höss's story is true, that Richard Förster and Aaron Rosenthal *did* escape together from Auschwitz, and that Rosenthal's shooting of Förster was a fabrication concocted out of fear and "humiliation" by Höss himself, and then sustained as the truth by Dr. Kopstein out of a misguided sense of "decency."

Like so many of the histories of the people from that time the dead and lost have taken their secrets with them to the grave and beyond. In the case of Richard Förster and Aaron Rosenthal all that is left is some desperate scribbling on paper, but I believe there is more truth in that than in all of Dr. Kopstein's self-righteous indigna-

55. Wajda, Czeslaw: *Zycie Oswiecim*, op. cit., pp. 268–269.
56. Unpublished verbal statement: Rachel Thalberg, June 23, 1977.
57. See Segev, Isaac: "Unto That Good Land," *Yad Vashem Studies* 6 (1967), Jerusalem: Yad Vashem Archives, for information on the legend of Aaron Rosenthal in Israel. Correspondence with Soviet authorities is in possession of the author.

tion, and though my only proof lies in the fact of its suppression more than forty years ago, I hereby contend that that is enough.

ADDENDUM:

The last entry in Förster's journal is dated Friday, June 23, 1944. It is the recounting of a dream, or nightmare, he'd just had. It is being published here for the first time. The translation is by the author.

I just awoke.

It is still night and it is cold. I am shaking. But it is not because of the cold.

I was in my office when Lang came in to tell me that something extraordinary had happened at the showers and I must come quick. I didn't know what he was talking about but he told me Baretzki would explain everything.

I was just coming up to *Krema* No. III when I saw Baretzki approaching me. He had a young man, naked, grasped by the wrist. "One of the *Sonderkommando* volunteered to be gassed if we would save this kid."

I looked at the young man. It was the Greek boy and he looked at me in terror. I told Baretzki I would take care of him and he said he bet I would. I took the boy's hand and asked Baretzki which of the *Sonderkommando* it was.

"It was that new man, the one you transferred here. Rosenthal."

I feel my skin contract, my stomach compresses into a knot, and when I start to run I suddenly realize how impossible it is for me. I let go of the Greek boy and start toward the crematorium and as I lurch past the barracks I can sense the prisoners' eyes on me, and I feel how ridiculous I must look, and I pray I may not be too late.

When I get to the building I nearly fall going down the steps. The last of the people in the disrobing room are being led into the showers. Their heavy clothes darken the room, with the yellow stars scattered among them like flowers. Wessel is there, hurrying an old man, and smiling, "You haven't forgotten the number of your coat hook, have you?"

"Where is he?" I demand.

"Who?" Wessel asks, looking around at me for the first time.

"Rosenthal. Aaron."

Wessel takes a swig from his flask. He jerks his thumb toward the shower room, "In there," and he laughs.

At the door of the showers I look over the heads of the last of the stragglers, across a room filled with naked people, emaciated and sickly. Aaron can't be in there. I push my way past the old man in the doorway. I can't seem to focus. Aaron. I don't see him. I yell his name.

"Sir?" a voice behind me. I turn and see Wessel in consternation. I explain I have to get a man out of there. "What are you talking about?" he asks.

I turn back to the mass of bodies before me and begin to make my way into them, moving past them, turning them aside, one after another, getting them behind me: looking for him, his eyes, his recognition. They are so many. Aaron *can't* be in here. It's too preposterous. These people are going to die, they're already dead. They won't get out of my way. Impatience becomes irritation, the turning aside desperate shoving. A cry. Someone before—beneath—me, they won't let me through—

"Aaron!"

It's a swamp. I stop and try to breathe but something unclean, a festering is damp in the air, in the press, warm and pungent, of the bodies, moaning and closing upon me. Aiming for one of the pillars in the center of the room, I once more slog into the arms, chests, backs, breasts, and: skin, pushing out waves into this giving fleshy resilience, endlessly pressing back on me again. Crying somewhere, a baby: the eternal discontent echoing. Indistinct noise muttering ominous louder answering cries: Murderer! Murderer!

"Aaron!"

They seem to be rising before me. I try to get above them, to see, to somehow get free: a shoulder gives under my weight, slipping, my face mashes into sallow flesh, airless, I turn, try, around, to see, gasp and surge: we do not go down. Cries become groans, hate turning back into fear. Surfacing as if from the depths and blighting out their faces with my hands I reach toward and grasp one of the latticed pillars: there are three more to the end of the room. He can't be there, it's too far. Oh, God——

"Aaron!"

A hand clamps down on my neck: Wessel. No. He wants to get me out. Fingers entwine, hold on, finally being pulled away. No. Eyes suddenly: a face, someone, a boy—our eyes meet—not Aaron, someone, a boy.

"Aaron!"

Not him, not him. Face to face, and eyes to eyes, something, glimmers: recognition. But not him. These faces—who are they? What do they see? And these eyes—what are they saying? Accusation. *No.*

"Aaron!"

Wessel is trying to haul me out of there. One of them reaches up to me but I am mercifully yanked back, pulled away by Wessel's grasp. Sudden horrible screams of pain. Shouting. Underfoot, I feel: *them*—my feet finding ill support backwards over the bodies. They go down before Wessel and his truncheon, our boots stepping and kicking into faces and bellies, mangling and crushing. A fist pounds helplessly into my chest. Clamor echoing, murderer shouts, *my* pain ringing in my head with its name: Aaron . . .

We are nearly to the door when I suddenly understand:

It's a joke. Baretzki was lying. Aaron isn't here. I close my eyes and I know this awful stink and press and crying will be gone in a moment. I can feel myself, slack now, being pulled back over the bodies, without resisting. I open my eyes to see it once more, what a moment ago engulfed me in fear, before it is gone forever and—no——

"AARON!"

He is against the wall across from me. Not too far. I can see him clearly above the people's heads. Marshaling my strength to get free, to reach him, I lunge toward him but I am constrained still by Wessel. And now Baretzki has squeezed through to help pull me back. I heave against them. But I can't and slip, my feet kicking up into someone's body, and then I'm falling forward and down into the stench, the unwashed horror of humanity, its stink closing over me——

Can't breathe, I can't get free to see. And then they are lifting me back onto my feet. I can see—above the faces—the wall: nothing. It *wasn't* him. I was imagining things.

Someone moves and: *he*—is—clear. I can see: *we* see: each other—

"AARON!!"

I can't focus. I can't get my vision clear. Oh, God, please stop. A second.

(Let me see him: his mouth, that nose, that bump I want to kiss, his eyes. His eyes—that see what? What in me? Love?)

A little boy is suddenly lodged around my neck holding on to me. Wessel lifts his stick and beats him off. He falls back bleeding into that putrid moaning mass of *them*.

Baretzki and Wessel, with the force of their hands, catapult me back onto the cement floor, and in a thundering crashing noise the door is—

SHUT.

Aaron.

Aaron—is—in—there.

I reel to the door.

It won't—NO—open.

I smash my fists into the wood, screaming his name, pounding, again, and again, my fists, please, and again, God, and again, *no*.

Gravel: boots.

No.

Puncture: death.

NO.

"AARON—"

I hold myself to the door, my hoarseness dying out of my throat into terrible silence.

Aaron.

I slump incomprehensibly to the floor.

And then I can hear it, an answer, a pounding from the other side, and voices. I can hear them.

They're screaming.

★

CONTRIBUTORS

PETER CASHORALI ("The Shell Reading")

It's not that I don't have any background, it's that recently I saw my best friend from high school after seventeen years and, while it took him two and a half hours to tell me what had happened since we last met (and highly interesting listening it was too), it only took me about eight minutes. And yet, I don't feel like I'm wasting my life. One thing I *am* doing is trying to overcome my debilitating fear of my own mortality and that of the people whose lives are as necessary to me as my own. One of whom is certainly Caesar Bonilla, my lover of eighteen years and the man with whom I came out.

The two most influential things I've ever read in my life are *Dinner and Nightmares* by Diane di Prima and *Tiresias 1:9:B: Great Slave Lake Suite* by Leland Hickman. Di Prima's work astonished me with the news that the tiny details of life with friends were suitable material for immortalizing, and Hickman's belief that your writing isn't just your possession but has an integrity and a life of its own and merits only the best you can bring to it—as summed up in the line: "& poem, I am going to be to you what a man wd be to a man who wd love him: I swear"—is an ongoing revelation to me.

I've had poems published in *rara avis, Bachy, Mouth of the Dragon*; prose poems published in *Five Fingers Review, Santa Monica Review*, the anthology from Momentum Press, *Poetry Loves Poetry*; and a short story in *Men on Men 3*, George Stambolian, editor.

RAMON BUD CHAMBERS ("Music from the Rafters")

I was conceived in Missouri and I think I was gay in the embryo. I joined the Navy and contracted wanderlust, moved to Holland and worked in a paint factory but eventually ended up in France in the construction trades. During this period I became involved with the Mormon church and ended up helping to construct four of their buildings in France.

I later graduated from Brigham Young University with a degree in journalism. I wrote for a construction trades magazine in Denver before coming to Los Angeles to be employed as a propmaker in the movie business.

I have written all along the road of my life. I have one previous fiction publication in *Quarterly Interchange*. I am not much of a talker as I prefer to put the words on paper. However, I enjoy visiting people in the AIDS hospice and I occasionally do some repair work there. I am active in the L.A. chapter of Black and White Men Together, but mostly I enjoy growing tomatoes in my garden.

BERNARD COOPER ("Eternity")

I'm never exactly sure where a story comes from or where it is headed once I begin. I relish reading writers' accounts that hint at a similar groping approach to the creation of a story. Flannery O'Connor once confessed that, in regard to the writing of fiction, she was like "the little old lady who doesn't know what she's thinking until she says it." This "work in the dark," as Henry James described writing, is the closest I can come to a methodology. I have no theories. The writing of one story does not lessen the difficulty of the next. No rules obtain. You have entered rough terrain without a map.

I can say that, in the process of writing, when the writing is going well—as opposed to the halting, arduous setting down of words, one at a time, that writing often is—I feel wholly present, huge with perception, and yet oddly absent, exiled to oblivion. Somewhere in this paradox lies the pleasure of work.

What occurs to me regarding the meaning of a story occurs to me, generally, after the fact. As for "Eternity," it began as most of my writing begins, with some small memory that seems, suddenly, to be the kernel of an entire life. I thought about a boy I knew in elementary school who had nothing less than a genius for being a sissy and who, in his awkward oblivion to ridicule, struck me as heroic. And, like everyone, I want to live forever. How these two vastly different ideas merged, I can't remember. But the air in the story was balmy and the kisses were imminent. I wanted to be there, to see it through.

I received an MFA in visual arts from Cal Arts. My work has appeared in *Harper's, Grand Street, The Fiction Network*, and elsewhere. A story of mine appears in *Men on Men 3*, edited by George Stambolian for New American Library. My essay, "Beacons Burning Down," was chosen by Annie Dillard for inclusion in *The Best American Essays of 1988*. My book of personal essays, *Maps to Anywhere,* is published by the University of Georgia Press and includes a forward by Pulitzer Prize-winning poet Richard Howard. I am currently at work on a novel.

GILBERT DANIEL CUADROS ("Unprotected")

I was born on July 22, 1962, in Los Angeles. I've studied at East L.A. College and Pasadena Community College. My first literary influence was Genet's *Querelle* and *Our Lady of the Flowers*, which I read in high school. Later I was turned on by Tennessee Williams and William S. Burroughs. Other influences are: George Platt Lynes, MTV, MC/Visa,

Roxy Music, LSD, Nintendo, and *Drummer* magazine. I've been previously published in *The James White Review* and other small magazines.

In 1987 my lover, John Milosch, died from AIDS and the medications used to treat him. The next year I was diagnosed with AIDS-Related Complex and have been fortunate to have stayed healthy ever since. AIDS has changed my whole life. John and I were supposed to have grown old together. I was supposed to have lived to a hundred. Now I'll be lucky to reach thirty. To me AIDS is a prison term and I don't know when I'll get out. Some people say to make the best of the time that you got, you'll grow from this experience. To them I say fuck you and the hay wagon you rode in on, I don't need this kind of growth. I'm happy that I have my writing. It's the only thing that makes me feel really good now.

JACQUELINE DE ANGELIS ("Baby")

I was born and raised in Youngstown, Ohio, and have lived in California for the past twenty years. I come from a working-class Italian and Polish family. My first book, *The Main Gate*, was published by Paradise Press in 1984. I have been published in small magazines, given numerous poetry readings, and been anthologized in *Southern California Women Writers & Artists* (Books of a Feather, 1984) and *In a Different Light* (Clothespin Fever Press, 1989.) I co-founded and edited *rara avis* magazine and Books of a Feather press. In 1984 I received a writer-in-residence fellowship from Dorland Mountain Colony as well as a Vesta Award in writing from the Woman's Building. In 1991 my poem "Saucers" will be displayed on the buses in Santa Monica, California. I earn my living as Communications Manager for Kaiser Permanente Medical Care Program.

AYOFEMI FOLAYAN ("Now, I Have to Tell This Story")

What is important to me is having a planet to inhabit that has clean air and water and arable land. All the work I do emerges from that

central idea. Who I am is a complex web of feelings that is related
to my self-definition as a fat biracial lesbian with disabilities. I came
out as a lesbian in a time when homosexuality was labeled mental
illness by homophobic professionals and endured psychiatric incarceration as a result. I grew up in a biracial family in a time when we
were bombed out of our home by intolerant racists. I am a refugee,
having escaped from Boston, my birthplace, I sought sanctuary in Los
Angeles seventeen years ago. I have traveled to and lived in as many
corners of the world as possible.

My writing is the umbilical cord that attaches me to the universal
source of life. It empowers me by giving me a voice to name my
truths and share my life experiences. Without fully functional creative
energy I would not have survived. Presently my work includes regular
columns in *The Vanguard* and *Out/Week*, frequent articles and essays in
BLK and *Gay Community News*, and editing the quarterly poetry journal
Kuumba. I have recently completed the first draft of a collection of
short stories, *Sections of a Navel Orange*, and am working simultaneously
on a novel, *Onyx*, and a performance piece, "Tri-Sections."

WENDI FRISCH ("Silent Village")

I was born in Los Angeles and grew up at the beach. My early summers
were divided between swimming in the ocean and reading books that
were too old for me. I credit my early reading with inspiring my love
of language and writing.

My life as a lesbian began in the fourth grade when I married
my best friend at a slumber party. (We were subsequently divorced.)
I became interested in feminism in junior high school and was involved
in the women's movement in the late seventies and early eighties.

I've been writing short stories since the first grade where I
learned never to start a sentence with the word *and*. In high school,
I was a contributing writer to a one-edition underground paper published by the students. I studied writing formally while attending San
Francisco State University and received a B.A. in creative writing in

1984. After returning to Los Angeles I participated in the Visions and Revisions series of writing workshops led by Terry Wolverton.

I believe that most people are unaware of their true desires and I like to explore these hidden motivations in my writing. I currently live in Los Angeles and make my living as a technical writer and editor. "Silent Village" is my first published work.

ERIC GUTIERREZ ("My Eye")

Facts about me: (1) Born in the San Fernando Valley Presbyterian Hospital on July 7, 1960; (2) Raised as a Seventh Day Adventist anyway; (3) Slept with married women anyway; (4) Escaped from certain death in a barrio Del Taco to New Zealand at age sixteen, ending up in Paris as a street musician for two years; (5) First hot sex with straight fry; (6) One-year study at the Sorbonne before transferring and receiving my degree in English and American Lit. from Harvard (class of '84). Ted Koppel tells joke about Churchill's cock at Class Day celebration; (7) I can no longer deny my addiction to "Nightline"; (8) Fiction published at the *Harvard Advocate, Padam Aram Review*, journalism in various rags around the country and overseas; (9) My play, *Dead Leo*, given staged readings in L.A. and Boston. Directed as a filthy betrayal of the play's intent and my personal aesthetic; (10) I've been part of the reading series at A Different Light bookstore for the past three years, have read at the Ecce Homo/Ecce Lesbo festival and at Beyond Baroque. I've also read my trashier stuff at Bebop Records, the defunct Lhasa Club, Al's Bar, and other dives where I take off my shirt; (11) I can no longer deny my attraction to pumped studs with asymmetrical faces; (12) As a performer, I've made a living singing Dylan in the streets of Europe. At the end of 1989 I finished a run of my second original performance piece called "Mr. Llorona" at Highways in Santa Monica; (13) I took a fucking pay cut to become an editor at *High Performance* magazine—I could have been an investment banker; (14) My work is accepted into this collection of bent West Coast writers. I'm anthologized and it feels good; (15) I try to deny this but no one believes me.

JEANE JACOBS ("She Who Keeps Laughing")

I was born in Northeastern Oklahoma in 1947 to parents of mixed blood: Irish and Native American, Cherokee and Choctaw tribes. My earliest remembrance of telling stories was at the age of four. There were always lots of cats around and I carried them in a box or in the wheelbarrow. I told them stories about other animals and creatures from other worlds. Not only did I like to tell stories, I loved hearing them. My favorite line to any older person was, "Tell me about when you were a kid." I would sit for hours on the porch swing next to my aunt Delora and just listen. She told me stories about every member of our family. She'd start out naming the ancestors and where they came from and then she would remember some event in their lives. I soaked up every word.

Now I live in Los Angeles and those dusty afternoons on the porch seem so long ago and faraway, but the stories live on in my soul. My characters come from that place in me that remembers my ancestors with great respect. My love for writing grows with my age, and the need to put the words on paper increases.

My fiction and poetry have appeared in anthologies and publications, including: *And a Deer's Ear, Eagle Song, Bear's Grace* (Cleis Press), *Women For All Seasons* (the Woman's Building), *Bishnik* (Choctaw Nation), and *Blue Mesa Review* (University of New Mexico Press.)

MICHAEL LASSELL ("Skyfires")

I was born in New York City and raised on Long Island, which is where I learned about art, literature, life, and how loathsome Long Island was and still, apparently, is unless you happen to be a middle-class heterosexual white person, in which case very few places in America are loathsome, unless you happen to be introspective, which so few middle-class white heterosexuals are the point is moot. My first intimations of sexual minority rose from the dank floor of my unconscious around age ten, and had to do with Jockey shorts. By thirteen the naked body of one of the few black kids in my school confirmed what I already knew. I was for a time and might still be, if such a thing were a workable solution in Sacred-Sexless Puritan America, a bisexual, although one of my happiest affairs was with a lesbian feminist, which just goes to show you how stupid labels and limits are.

I've been the managing editor of *L.A. Style* magazine since 1985. As a journalist/critic I've written for the *L.A. Times, Mirabella*, and *Movieline*, among others. I've published poetry in numerous publications, including *Hanging Loose, Fag Rag*, and *The Literary Review*. In 1985 I won *Amelia*'s first chapbook award, resulting in the publication of my first book, *Poems for Lost and Un-Lost Boys*. I've been anthologized in *Gay and Lesbian Poetry in Our Time* (St. Martin's, 1988) and *Poets for Life: 76 Poets Respond to AIDS* (Crown, 1989).

ERIC LATZKY ("Study for Darkness: Two Views from Vertical Cliffs")

Heroin and homosexuality are the two best things that ever happened to me (I think in that order but I revere both). Heroin is the only thing I have ever truly worshipped; I worshipped one man once (maybe two), but I don't worship all men. I became gay when I was fifteen: the first time I had sex was on a bench in Central Park in New York, which is where I'm from. It was in January and it was really freezing. That summer I came out, which was more like a general press announcement, or a complete capitulation, the first of many. I found heroin when I was eighteen (I'm sure I had a biological predisposition to it, the same as to homosexuality), and then I spent the next five years being a junkie. Also during that time I was traveling and writing; I landed in Paris and it stuck for a while. That's my life: sometimes things just stick and I stay for a while, which is how I ended up in Los Angeles for four and a half years. All this (and other things) are elements of my fiction. I also write articles and essays about contemporary art, literature, and culture for *Interviews, L.A. Style, L.A. Weekly, The Advocate, Outweek*, and other publications.

BIA LOWE ("I Always Write About My Mother When I Start to Write")

One day a long time ago at the Burke School for Girls, a clique of vigilante seventh graders, posing as young ladies, scapegoated me as resident queer. Looking back, I see they were *big ones* even then, much like, I suspect, the finger-wagging homophobes of today—werewolves in nuns' clothing. This earned me a few battle scars and my first medal, a purple heart.

Of course love under siege is no simple matter, the stresses brought to bear forge something altogether uncommon, like the diamond. And someday when the wars are over and we sit at the bargaining table, this diamond will be our most coveted peace offering.

I spent much of my girlhood climbing the bay laurels and oaks of northern California. There's a kind of meditation that gets you to the next branch, not unlike the act of writing.

My work has appeared in *Caliban, The Beloit Poetry Journal*, and *The California Quarterly* among others.

SCOTT W. PETERSON ("Gods")

I am a writer and a student of history living in the Pacific Northwest. My work is anthologized in *Shadows of Love*, editor Charles Jurrist (Alyson Publications, 1989) and has appeared in the *James White Review, Seattle Gay News*, and *Wiggansnatch Literary Magazine*. I don't much like writing about myself.

ROBIN PODOLSKY ("Dignity/Uniforms/Dignity")

I write drama, poetry, fiction, and journalism, and also work in performance art. I have no plans to pick a medium and settle down. My poetry and fiction have been published in *In a Different Light* (Clothespin Fever Press, 1989) and in *Lucky* magazine, and have been accepted for publication in *Writing About Work By the People Who Do It, vol. 1*, forthcoming from Singlejack Books. My journalism has appeared in *L.A. Weekly, High Performance, The News*, and *The Lesbian News*. I also edit *Caregiver*, a publication of the AIDS Hospice Foundation. I'm currently working on an account of the years I worked as an aircraft machinist, to be published by Clothespin Fever Press.

With four others, I coauthored *Pursuit of Happiness*, a play about twenty years of lesbian and gay life in Los Angeles. With Ayofemi Folayan, I coauthored and performed *Talking About Talking: the Power to Shape the World*.

I live in Los Angeles, where I was born, and share a home with my lover Janice and her daughter Stacey, and Dinah and Sarah, the cats who have agreed to cohabit the space. I write because, like Paulo Friere, I believe that the life most conducive to ecstasy is that of persons who engage with the major themes of their time. My first childhood memory of ecstasy is sounding out words on my own, making sentences, realizing that the world of books and the experience they carried was now open to me.

LYNETTE PRUCHA ("Murder Is My Business")

I was born and raised in New York, and have been actively involved in the Los Angeles literary scene since 1985. My first novel, *Smokescreen*, was inspired by my long-standing interest in classic noir films of the 1940s. An excerpt from *Smokescreen* appears in the Clothespin Fever Press anthology, *In a Different Light*, and has also been praised and performed on the radio. The short story that appears here is also included in the third *Womansleuth Anthology*, edited by Irene Zahava for The Crossing Press. In 1990 I was a featured participant in the Lesbian Writers Series at A Different Light bookstore. I'm also a local and national member of Sisters in Crime, an organization that promotes mystery and detective fiction written by women.

I have a B.A. in literature from Queens College, and a Masters in Comparative Literature from the University of Southern California. For four years I was an instructor at USC, combining my interest in art and architecture with my ability to teach writing as it relates to film, theater, and the visual arts.

Currently I'm a senior executive with an independent film company located in Beverly Hills, where I've worked in many areas of motion picture production and distribution.

RAKESH RATTI ("Promenade")

I was born in northern India and spent my childhood in a village of about two thousand people. When I was nine years old my family immigrated to the States, settling in a small town in northern California. I've known of my gayness in one form or another since the age of twelve, but I did not come out until I was nineteen. Since that time I have been active in many gay political organizations, and I am one of the founding members of Trikone, an organization of gay and lesbian South Asians.

My basic desire in life is to develop myself in every direction open to me. When I am not writing, I paint with oils and do charcoal sketches, play tennis and volleyball, do volunteer work, and travel when possible. I am also currently a graduate student in the field of psychology. My philosophy of life is quite simple: I do everything in my power to achieve what I want, then turn it over to the universe and trust that all will be as it should be.

An autobiographical story I wrote was published in a collection of coming-out stories in 1988. I am also working on a collection of writings by gay and lesbian South Asians under contract with Alyson Publications.

ARTHUR REKER ("Do You Wanna Dance?")

I was born in Modesto, California, on September 23, 1955, and raised in Fresno. In 1972 I served as a page in the U.S. House of Representatives in Washington, D.C. Since attending Reed College in Portland, Oregon, I have been a radio station announcer, chef in a Mexican restaurant in Anchorage, Alaska, warehouseman, newspaper writer, advertising writer, and television producer. I am active in the gay political struggle and have worked with numerous AIDS education and prevention agencies.

TRUDY RILEY ("Highway Five")

I was born and raised in the Mission District of San Francisco. In 1950 I came to Los Angeles to attend summer session at UCLA and have lived here ever since.

I received a masters degree in Psychiatric Social Work in 1958. On the same day the degree was conferred I had my first child. This shocked my friends and classmates because I was unmarried at the time. A few months after that birth I did marry, had a second child a year later, and settled down to become a housewife.

During the sixties I divorced and the children and I lived a disheveled hippie life in the California desert. In the seventies I joined the radical feminist movement. I came out in 1972 in a blaze of lust and political fervor.

I have had a variety of social work jobs through the years, but in the eighties I began to take my work more seriously and was promoted to an administrative position. I view it as cosmic retribution that I, who always resented authority, have become one.

I started writing in 1985 when, on impulse, I signed up for a writing workshop given by Terry Wolverton. I have written at least four days a week ever since that time. I have not published previously. My current project is a novel that spans the lives of two women from the 1950s to the present.

ALEIDA RODRIGUEZ ("My Face in the Faces of Others")

I was born on a kitchen table in the little town of Güines, forty-eight kilometers south of Havana, Cuba, six years before the revolution. At the age of nine a very surreal thing happened: one morning I was playing with the chickens and goats in the field next to my house, and in the afternoon I was standing in a pink dress among strangers whose aluminum houses had manicured lawns, arching sprinklers, and white picket fences. And that was still in Miami! Two weeks later, when my sister and I were relocated to the home of a Presbyterian minister and his family in Springfield, Illinois, things got even weirder. They tried to poison us—or so I thought—by feeding us green grapes (I had only seen red ones) and cold milk. I have kept my eyes open ever since.

Writing has been a way of keeping my eyes open, a way of ordering the chaos, a way of reconciling the dichotomies, a way of rendering the bombardment of images.

I've been a lesbian as long as I can remember. As a tiny tot in Sunday school in Cuba I had an enormous crush on my teacher, Eva, and constantly had my arm up in the air to volunteer for saying a prayer. I stood and looked out the window while the other children bowed their heads, and described—in as much detail as I could manage—the things to thank God for: the red hibiscus bush, that incredible blue sky of Cuba, those springy white clouds like my mother's meringue. All this in order to please Eva, but pleasing me as well. The natural world still delights and nourishes me. It is often a character in my work, or a catalyst. My relationship with my cats, Foca and Franny, and my parrot, Alix, is essential to my well-being.

My prose and poetry have been published in many literary journals, including *Bachy, Calyx*, and *De Colores*, and anthologies such as *An Ear to the Ground: Contemporary American Poetry* (University of Georgia Press, 1989), *The World's Best Poetry* (a secondary school textbook; Roth Publishing, Inc., 1987), *Poetry Loves Poetry* (Momentum Press, 1985), *Cuentos: Stories by Latinas* (Kitchen Table Press, 1983), and *Lesbian Fiction* (Persephone Press, 1981). In 1990 a collection of my work, *Punto de Vista*, will be published by The Lapis Press.

RICK SANDFORD ("Förster & Rosenthal Reevaluated:
An Investigative Report")

When I started the first grade in Denver, Colorado (where I was
born), I had trouble reading. My parents sent me to a private school
with excellent credentials, called Peter Pan. They taught me how to
read, and since then I have never stopped: that pastime is the primary
component of my happiness. (But could that school also have contributed to my never having had sex with a woman, never having learned
to drive, never having had a checking account or credit card, never
having started to smoke, and so on?)

I finished high school in South Lake Tahoe, graduating in 1969.
I came to Los Angeles to see the musical *Hair* and the Russian film
version of *War and Peace*. I've been here ever since (not counting an
ill-advised hiatus in 1971–1972 as a "born-again" Christian—I've been
an atheist ever since).

The progression of my money-making activities in this city of
angels has been, roughly in this order: usher (my first job was at
Grauman's Chinese Theatre!), busboy, waiter, actor (one TV show:
"Faith for Today" and one commercial: Coca-Cola), gofer (Los Angeles
County Museum of Art and the *Hollywood Reporter*), porno star (as Ben
Barker: 13 films, including *Kip Noll and the Westside Boys, Rear Deliveries,
Skin Deep*, and *Games*), editor (three porno films and assistant on *Holly-
wood Mavericks*), extra (including *E.T./The Extra-Terrestrial* and *2010*), and
for the last several years I have worked as a stand-in for Josh Taylor
on the TV show, "The Hogan Family," and Jerry Levine on "Going
Places."

I have a "Research Assistant" credit on *David O. Selznick's Hollywood* by Ronald Haver and *50 Golden Years of Oscar* by Robert Osborne.
When I first started to put together the story in this volume, more
than ten years ago, Christopher Isherwood helped me with the German
and mentioned this story in his book, *October*. Don Bachardy, who did
the drawings in that book, featured me in his collection, *Drawings of
the Male Nude*.

I think history is an aphrodisiac.

JANE THURMOND ("Exoskeletons")

I write fiction. This story is one in a series of short stories set in my native Texas. I am also a graphic designer.

DAVID VERNON ("Negatives from Mr. Tobias's Vacation")

I was born in New York City, one of those quiet, thin, pale city children. I had my first crush at the age of eight when my family vacationed in Atlantic City. I fell in love with Mr. Peanut, a person dressed in a Mr. Peanut costume who walked along the boardwalk. Every day I would track him, watching him tip his top hat to the passersby. Before I left I found the courage to approach him and tell him that I loved him. Mr. Peanut answered that he loved me too, but in a woman's voice. It was a woman in that costume!

My family moved to Los Angeles. I studied at an all-boys Jesuit high school. In my junior year I chanced upon a creative writing class and wrote pages of tortured poems and stories full of sexual confusion. I expected to be expelled for all the stuff I was writing. The Jesuit who taught the class didn't quite get what I was writing but knew that something exciting was going on and encouraged me to keep at it.

I studied film at NYU, writing, directing, and producing several short films, then moved back to Los Angeles, where I currently reside. For the past two years I've participated in Terry Wolverton's writing workshop and have studied performance art with Tim Miller.

I've been writing seriously for the past two years and am still exploring and experimenting. I'm particularly interested in writing about a world where our perceptions have been changed forever by AIDS. I am excited and inspired by many of the gay and lesbian writers who deal unflinchingly with the effects of AIDS and homophobia on our community. We have stories that must be told.

I am currently working on several short stories, a play, and an assignment for Saturday's class. I am also, probably without knowing it, working on a novel.

DAVID WATMOUGH ("Thank You Siegfried Sassoon")

Although born in London in 1926, I grew up in the Duchy of Cornwall where my family have farmed for centuries. I attended King's College, University of London, and majored in theology. In 1949 I moved to Paris where I both published my first book and met my California-born lover who has remained my partner for the past thirty-nine years.

As I date the public affirmation of my homosexuality from my arrest and imprisonment for soliciting and importuning when aged seventeen, I have never had a closet to emerge from!

After leaving England for good, and subsequently living in France and the United States, I settled in Vancouver, Canada, in 1963. All my books have been written here over the past twenty-seven years, including *No More Into the Garden*, and *The Year of Fears*, among the seven volumes of fiction featuring my ongoing protagonist, Davey Bryant.

I have twice been awarded Canada Council Senior Literary Awards and my work has been translated into Serbo-Croation. My fiction has been frequently anthologized as well as broadcast by the Canadian Broadcasting Corporation and the BBC on both radio and TV.

Families, my latest novel, is scheduled to appear from Knight's Press, New York, in 1990.

TERRY WOLVERTON ("Pretty Women")

The influence of growing up in Detroit is all over my work—the rhythms of freeway driving, the sentiments of Motown soul music, the attitude. It was my grandmother who made me become a writer—when I was a child she'd read aloud to me until her voice was hoarse, all kinds of things, from *Alice in Wonderland* to *King Lear*.

I left Detroit when Nixon was reelected in 1972, and moved to Toronto, Canada, where I came out as a lesbian feminist. From there I moved to Vermont to participate in Sagaris, an experiment in feminist education, then to Grand Rapids, Michigan, and finally came to Los Angeles in 1976. I've been here ever since.

In a former life I was a performance artist, creating thirteen full-length performance art works that were staged in New York, San Diego, and Toronto, as well as in Los Angeles. I've also produced and exhibited audio, video, and installation artworks. I've been teaching creative writing since 1977, and have been the recipient of six artist-in-residence grants from the California Arts Council. I currently teach writing at the Gay and Lesbian Community Services Center, including workshops for people who are HIV-positive, and for health and service providers who work with people with AIDS.

I write everything: poetry, fiction, drama, journalism, art criticism. My work has appeared in numerous publications including *The Jacaranda Review, Heresies*, and *Fuse*. I've been anthologized in *Word of Mouth* (The Crossing Press, 1990), *In a Different Light* (Clothespin Fever Press, 1989), *Women For All Seasons* (the Women's Building, 1988), *Southern California Women Writers & Artists* (Books of a Feather, 1984), *Between Ourselves: Letters Between Mothers and Daughters* (Houghton Mifflin, 1983), *Learning Our Way: Essays in Feminist Education* (The Crossing Press, 1983), and *Voices In the Night* (Cleis Press, 1982.) I'm currently working on a first novel, *The Labrys Reunion*, and a screenplay, *Green*.

★